PRAISE FOR THE CONSTABLE EVANS MYSTERIES

"Few writers are capable of this deft combination of dark and light. This is a pitch-perfect book, which will charm you in one sentence, chill you in the next."

—Laura Lippman, winner of the Edgar, Shamus, Anthony, and Agatha Awards

PRAISE FOR THE ROYAL SPYNESS MYSTERIES

"Wonderful characters . . . A delight."

—Charlaine Harris

"Fans of P. G. Wodehouse looking for laughs mingled with some amateur sleuthing will be quite pleased."

—*Publishers Weekly*

"Georgie's high spirits and the author's frothy prose are utterly captivating."

—*The Denver Post*

"The perfect fix between seasons for *Downton Abbey* addicts."

—Deborah Crombie, *New York Times* bestselling author of *The Sound of Broken Glass*

"A smashing romp."

—*Booklist*

PRAISE FOR THE MOLLY
MURPHY MYSTERIES

"I devoured this flawlessly written mystery in one day, and enjoyed every word . . . The book is a wonderful read, full of interesting details that give life to the story."

—*Historical Novel Society*

"Well-written and fast-paced, with a twist that will leave readers truly surprised. This novel is not to be missed."

—*RT Book Reviews*

"A charming combination of history, mystery, and romance."

—*Kirkus Reviews*

"Perceptive and poignant writing . . . make[s] us look forward to Molly's return."

—*Chicago Tribune*

IN
FARLEIGH
FIELD

ALSO BY RHYS BOWEN

CONSTABLE EVANS MYSTERIES

Evans Above

Evan Help Us

Evanly Choirs

Evan and Elle

Evan Can Wait

Evans to Betsy

Evan Only Knows

Evan's Gate

Evan Blessed

Evanly Bodies

MOLLY MURPHY MYSTERIES

Murphy's Law

Death of Riley

For the Love of Mike

In Like Flynn

Oh Danny Boy

In Dublin's Fair City

Tell Me, Pretty Maiden

In a Gilded Cage

The Last Illusion

Bless the Bride

Hush Now, Don't You Cry

The Family Way

City of Darkness and Light

The Edge of Dreams

Away in a Manger

Time of Fog and Fire

ROYAL SPYNESS MYSTERIES

Her Royal Spyness

A Royal Pain

Royal Flush

Royal Blood

Naughty in Nice

The Twelve Clues of Christmas

Heirs and Graces

Queen of Hearts

Malice at the Palace

Crowned and Dangerous

IN
FARLEIGH
FIELD

A
NOVEL

RHYS BOWEN

LAKE UNION
PUBLISHING

Published by Lake Union Publishing, Seattle

www.apub.com

Amazon, the Amazon logo, and Lake Union Publishing are trademarks of Amazon.com, Inc., or its affiliates.

ISBN-13: 9781477818299 [HC]
ISBN-10: 1477818294 [HC]

ISBN-13: 9781503941359 [PB]
ISBN-10: 1503941353 [PB]

Cover design by Shasti O'Leary Soudant

Printed in the United States of America

First edition

This book is for Meg Ruley, who believed in it from the beginning and helped to shape it. Meg, you are my champion, and the day we met was one of the high points of my life.

September 1939

From: His Majesty's Government
To: Civilian Population of Great Britain

For the duration of the war, the following Seven Rules
are to be observed at all times.
1. Do not waste food.
2. Do not talk to strangers.
3. Keep all information to yourself.
4. Always listen to government instructions and carry them
    out.
5. Report anything suspicious to the police.
6. Do not spread rumours.
7. Lock away anything that might help the enemy if we
    are invaded.

CAST OF CHARACTERS

Roderick Sutton, Earl of Westerham, owner of Farleigh Place, a stately home in Kent

Lady Esme Sutton, Roderick's wife

Lady Olivia "Livvy" Sutton, twenty-six, the Suttons' eldest daughter, married to Viscount Carrington, mother of Charles

Lady Margaret "Margot" Sutton, twenty-three, the second daughter, now living in Paris

Lady Pamela "Pamma" Sutton, twenty-one, the third daughter, currently working for a "government department"

Lady Diana "Dido" Sutton, nineteen, the fourth daughter, a frustrated debutante

Lady Phoebe "Feebs" Sutton, twelve, the fifth daughter, too smart and observant for her own good

Servants at Farleigh (a skeleton staff)

Soames, butler

Mrs. Mortlock, cook

Elsie, parlourmaid

Jennie, housemaid

Ruby, scullery maid

Philpott, Lady Esme's maid

Nanny

Miss Gumble, governess to Lady Phoebe

Mr. Robbins, gamekeeper
Mrs. Robbins, gamekeeper's wife
Alfie, a Cockney boy, now evacuated to the country
Jackson, groom

Fairleigh Neighbours
Rev. Cresswell, vicar of All Saints Church
Ben Cresswell, the vicar's son, now working for a "government department"

At Nethercote
Sir William Prescott, city financier
Lady Prescott, Sir William's wife
Jeremy Prescott, Sir William and Lady Prescott's son, RAF flying ace

At Simla
Colonel Huntley, formerly of the British Army
Mrs. Huntley, the colonel's wife
Miss Hamilton, spinster
Dr. Sinclair, doctor
Sundry villagers, including an artist couple, a builder, and a question-
    able Austrian

Officers of the Royal West Kent Regiment
Colonel Pritchard, commanding officer
Captain Hartley, adjutant
Soldiers under command

At Dolphin Square
Maxwell Knight, spymaster
Joan Miller, Knight's secretary

At Bletchley Park
Commander Travis, deputy head of a secret government department
Trixie Radcliffe, debutante, now doing useful work
Froggy Bracewaite, code breaker

At MI5
Guy Harcourt, former playboy, now Ben Cresswell's coworker
Mike Radison, head of section

At Aerial Reconnaissance
Mavis Pugh, keen girl

In Paris
Madame Gigi Armande, famous fashion designer
Herr Dinkslager, Nazi officer and all-around dangerous man
Count Gaston de Varennes, Margot's lover

PROLOGUE

Elmsleigh, Kent
August 1939

It had been unusually hot all summer. Ben Cresswell could feel the sun scorching his thighs through his cricket whites as he sat on the clubhouse veranda, waiting for his turn at bat. Colonel Huntley sat beside him, mopping his red and sweaty face. He was wearing pads because he was next up at bat. He wasn't as good a batsman as Ben, but he was team captain, and in village cricket, seniority often took precedence over ability.

Only two overs before tea. Ben hoped that young Symmes wouldn't make one of his wild swipes and be out before the tea interval. His head was singing with heat. His mouth felt dry. He closed his eyes and listened to the satisfying thwack of bat against ball, the drone of bees on the honeysuckle behind the clubhouse, the rhythmic clatter of a lawn mower in one of the cottage gardens. The scent of new-mown grass wafted on the warm breeze, mingled with the smoke of leaves burning on a distant bonfire. *The scents and sounds of an English summer Sunday, unchanged for centuries,* Ben thought.

Polite applause directed his attention back to the match, where two white-clad figures were sprinting between wickets while a fielder ran to retrieve the ball, throwing it in too late. Another run. *Jolly good,* Ben thought. They might even win for once. Beyond the perfectly mown pitch, the spire of All Saints Church, where his father was vicar, cast a shadow over the village green. And on the far side, an old oak tree cast a similar shadow over the memorial erected to those men from the village who had died in the Great War. There were sixteen names there. Ben had counted them. Sixteen men and boys from a village of two hundred. *Senseless,* Ben muttered to himself.

"Where's young Prescott, then?" Colonel Huntley interrupted his musings. "We could have used him today. He handles a fast bowler as well as anyone I've seen."

Ben turned away from the cricket pitch to look at the colonel. He was a large, florid man, his face weathered to a perpetual beetroot colour by a long stint in India and too much Scotch. "He's taking his flying test, sir."

"His flying test? Is that what the young idiot's doing these days?"

"Yes, sir. He's been taking flying lessons. He wants to be ready, you see. When war is declared, he'll go straight into the RAF as a pilot. He didn't want to find himself up to his neck in mud in the trenches like all those poor chaps in the last war."

The colonel nodded. "That was a rum deal. Lucky for me I was on the North-West Frontier. Let's hope they don't make the same bloody mistakes this time."

"I suppose war is inevitable?" Ben asked.

"Oh yes. Absolutely. No question about it. That blighter Hitler's going to march into Poland, and we're honour-bound to declare war. In the next couple of weeks, I'd say."

He spoke with the cheerfulness of a man who knows he is too old to be called up. "We had one of those civil-defence chappies round at the house last week. They wanted me to dig up the back lawn and put in an air-raid shelter. I told him it was quite out of the question. The back lawn is where the memsahib plays her croquet. We're going to be rationed in everything else. You can't expect her to give up her croquet, too!"

Ben smiled politely. "Yes, we had a similar visit. They delivered a lot of corrugated iron and the plans. As if my father has ever built anything in his life. He's only just learned to turn on the radio!"

The colonel eyed Ben critically. "So what about you, young fellah? Are you planning on becoming a pilot as well?"

Ben gave him an apologetic smile. "I'd like to, sir, but I can't afford the flying lessons at the moment. I'll have to wait to see if the RAF will take me."

The colonel coughed, as if he'd just realised that the son of a vicar recently down from Oxford and now teaching at a very minor prep school wasn't likely to have much cash to spare. He looked around, clearly trying to think of a topic to change the subject and suddenly said in surprise, "Hello. Here's a turn-up for the books. It's Lady Pamela. I didn't know she was interested in cricket."

Ben felt a flush come over his face and was furious with himself. Pamela was walking toward him with that easy grace, looking cool and elegant in peach silk. A strand of ash-blonde hair blew across her face, and she brushed it back as she spotted Ben. The men scrambled to their feet.

"Good of you to come to cheer us on, my lady," the colonel said, offering her his place on the bench. "Sit here beside young Cresswell. I'm up next. Need to get the blood flowing into these old legs, anyway." Pamela flashed him a dazzling smile and slid onto the bench the colonel had vacated.

"Hello, Pamma," Ben said. "I didn't expect to see you here. I thought you were in Paris with your sister."

"I was. Pah ordered me to come home. Actually, he ordered me to bring Margot home with me. He's sure war is about to break out any second, and he's scared she'll be stuck on the continent. But she's refusing to budge."

"She's so keen on learning to design fashions that the threat of a war won't move her?"

Pamela's eyes held his in an amused smile. "I rather think that a certain French count is the reason she doesn't want to leave."

"Crikey," Ben said, cursing himself for sounding like a schoolboy. "Your sister has fallen in love with a Frenchman?"

"They are rather attractive, you know," Pamela said, her eyes still holding his. "So attentive. And they do things like kiss hands. Who could resist?"

"I hope you did." The words came out before he could stop them.

"I don't go for the Gallic type myself," Pamela said, then she looked around. "Is Jeremy not playing today?"

And Ben realised like a punch in the stomach that she had not come to see him after all. It was Jeremy. Of course, it was bloody Jeremy. A picture flashed unbidden into Ben's mind. He and Pamela and Jeremy on a long-ago summer afternoon like this one, climbing the big oak tree at Farleigh Place, home of Pamela's father, the Earl of Westerham. Jeremy leading as usual, with Pamela close behind him, going up and up until the branch she was perched on was swaying violently. "Don't go any higher," Ben had called. She had flashed him a challenging smile. Then the awful cracking noise. The sight of Pamela's surprised face going past them, as if in slow motion, and then the thud as she hit the ground. It had taken forever to scramble down to her. Jeremy had reached the bottom first, jumping down beside her. Ben was last, as usual. She was lying there, not moving. Suddenly she opened her eyes, looked first into Ben's worried face, then focused on Jeremy, and her eyes lit up. "I'm all right. Don't fuss," she said. She had not been all right. She'd broken an arm. But that was really the first time Ben had realised that it was Jeremy, not him, that she cared about. Also how damned much Ben cared about her.

So many memories from long-ago summers . . .

There was a yelled "Howzat?" and a groan from the crowd.

"Damned young fool," Colonel Huntley muttered. "He will swipe at it. Clean bowled again."

He got to his feet. But before he could walk out from the clubhouse to meet the dismissed batsman, there was a droning sound in the sky. Everyone looked up as a plane appeared over the hills, flying very low. The drone became a roar. The plane continued to descend.

"It can't be going to land here?" Colonel Huntley exclaimed. "What is the fool thinking?"

But the plane *was* going to land. It skimmed over the large copper beech before touching down on the field, scattering cricketers, and just missing the rolled green of the cricket pitch.

The plane was painted bright yellow and black, like an overgrown wasp. It bounced across the grass and came to a halt in front of the clubhouse. Ben heard the colonel mutter: "What the devil," but he didn't bother to answer. Before the pilot took off his goggles and helmet, Ben had known it was Jeremy. Jeremy's eyes were scanning the crowd. He spotted Ben; his face broke into the familiar grin, and he beckoned furiously.

"I've just bought her," he shouted. "Isn't she a beauty? Come on up for a spin."

Pamela stood up and ran toward the plane before Ben could react. "Can't I come up, too?"

"What ho, Pamma," Jeremy said. "Didn't expect to see you at a cricket match. I thought you were in Paris. But sorry. She's only a two-seater, and you're not exactly dressed for climbing into cockpits, however charming you look . . ." He left the rest of the sentence hanging. "I'll come over and see you later if I may," he added. "And if you like, I'll ask your pah if I may take you up in my new bird."

"Fine." Pamela turned away and walked back to the pavilion, brushing against Ben in her annoyance. "It's always a man's world in the end, isn't it?" she said. "Ask my pah, indeed. Go on, then. Go up with him. Have a good time."

"I don't want to leave you on your own. I'm sure there will be other . . ." Ben mumbled.

"Oh, for heaven's sake. I know you're dying to go up in a plane," Pamela said. "Go on. Go." And she gave him a friendly push.

Feeling very self-conscious with the eyes of the village upon him, Ben walked out to the plane. Jeremy's face was bright with pleasure. Ben had seen that look many times before—usually when Jeremy had accomplished something utterly forbidden.

"I take it you passed your test," Ben said dryly.

"With flying colours, old chap. The bloke said I was born to it. Well, I do have a falcon on my family crest, don't I? Come on, don't just stand there. Hop in."

Ben climbed into the backseat. "Don't I need a helmet or something?"

Jeremy laughed. "If we crash, a bloody helmet's not going to do you much good. Don't worry. I got the hang of it in the first five minutes. Now it's a piece of cake."

The engine revved. The plane bumped over the grass, gaining speed until it rose into the air. They circled behind the pavilion and roared over the cricket pitch again, clearing the big copper beech at the bottom of the vicarage garden with a couple of feet to spare. The village of Elmsleigh spread out below them: built around the green with the cricket pitch in the middle, the memorial to the Great War in its prominent place on one side, and St. Mary's Church with its fine perpendicular tower on the other. Below the right wing were the manicured gardens of Nethercote, Jeremy's home. The plane banked, and the town of Sevenoaks came into view, then the whole of Shoreham Valley with the line of the North Downs curving to the south. The River Medway was a bright streak to their left, the Thames an even brighter one on the distant horizon. The wind whipped through Ben's hair. He felt exhilarated.

Jeremy turned back to him. "This is the ticket all right, isn't it? I can't wait for the big show to start. This is my idea of how war should be—a gentleman's sort of war. Warrior against warrior, and the better man wins. You have to get your own licence, old chap, then we can join up together."

Ben thought there was little point in mentioning that he couldn't afford to take flying lessons. Jeremy had never understood that money might be a problem. At Oxford, he was always inviting Ben on expensive jaunts to London shows or nightclubs or even weekend trips to Paris. Jeremy would happily have paid for both of them, but Ben had too much pride to accept and had invented essays that had to be finished. Consequently, he had earned the reputation of a swot, which he wasn't. And brilliant, which he wasn't either. He had acquired a perfectly good second-class degree. Jeremy had scraped through with a third, but in his case, it didn't matter. He was an only son and would inherit the title and all that went with it someday.

"So what do you think?" Jeremy yelled.

"Absolutely smashing."

"I know. Isn't it? Let's fly to France."

"Have you got enough petrol?"

"How should I know? I just bought the thing," Jeremy said, laughing. But he banked the plane, swinging it back in a broad circle toward the village. There it was below them, the one main street of cottages leading to the green, surrounded by fields of hops and apple trees. So neat and green and typically English. Jeremy leaned over the side and pointed. "Look. There's Farleigh. Doesn't it look orderly from up here? Capability Brown did a splendid job laying out those gardens." He pushed on the joystick, and the plane dropped as Farleigh Place, Pamela's ancestral home since 1600 and something, came into view ahead of them, a vast, square grey-stone building set amid acres of parkland with a curved driveway leading past ornamental flower beds, the lake on one side, the kitchen gardens beyond.

Jeremy let out a whoop of delight. "Look, Ben, they've got guests for tea. Let's give them a surprise, shall we?"

The plane banked sharply. Ben hung on and closed his eyes as land became sky. His stomach did a bank of its own. The plane circled lower and lower until it was flying over the lake with its island folly, then over the ride lined with horse chestnut trees, from which they'd collected conkers as boys. A tennis court had been marked out on the back lawn, with tables beside it and several figures in white seated while Soames the butler was serving tea.

"I reckon there's enough room to land right beside them," Jeremy shouted. "Too bad they're not wearing the sort of hats that will sail well when they blow off."

They made their approach along the south ride, with chestnut trees on either side of the wing tips. Ben was still too exhilarated to be scared. The flying instructor was right, Ben decided. Jeremy did fly as if he were born to it. The tea guests had risen to their feet when the plane burst from the trees; they backed up in alarm as the tablecloths flapped and napkins flew. The plane was now only feet from the ground, then only inches.

Jeremy noticed the sundial at the same moment as Ben. It was standing, weathered and forgotten, in the middle of the east lawn. Ben opened his mouth to say, "Watch out, there's a s—" at the same moment as Jeremy yanked the joystick over hard to the right. The wing dipped, dug into the grass, and the plane flipped over.

PART ONE
PAMELA

CHAPTER ONE

Bletchley Park
May 1941

Lady Pamela Sutton stared at the dreary government-issued posters on the wall of her small cubicle in Hut 3. Some of them cheerful exhortations to do one's best, to soldier on with a stiff upper lip, and others dire warnings about letting the side down. Beyond the blackout curtains that covered the windows, dawn would be breaking. She could hear the chorus of birds in the woods behind the hut, still chirping madly and joyfully as they had done before the war began and would keep doing after it ended—whenever that would be. It had already gone on too long, and there was no end in sight. Pamela rubbed her eyes. It had been a long night, and her eyes were stinging with tiredness. According to civil-service regulations, women were not supposed to work on the night shift with men, in case their morals were compromised. She had found this amusing when the shortage of male translators meant that one of the girls had to do night-shift work. "Frankly, I don't think my honour is in danger from any of the chaps here," she had said. "They are more interested in maths problems than girls."

But she had come to regret her bravado many times since. Night work was brutal. Thank God her shift was soon coming to an end and she could go to bed. Not that she could ever sleep properly during the day with trains rattling past her window.

"Bloody war," she muttered and breathed onto her hands, trying to induce some warmth into her fingers. Although it was May, the huts were cold and damp overnight. The coke ration had been stopped on May first. But that wasn't entirely bad; the cast-iron stove smoked badly and spewed out noxious fumes. Everything was so horrible these days. No decent food to eat. Meals consisting of powdered eggs, canned corned beef, sausages that were more sawdust than meat. Her landlady obviously hadn't been much of a cook before the war, but what she cooked now was quite inedible. Pamela envied those on the day shift. At least they could take their main meal in the dining room, which was supposed to be quite good. She could go across and get some breakfast before she went off duty, but she was always too tired to eat by the end of a long night.

At the outbreak of the war she had been anxious to do something useful. Jeremy had joined up on the first day, welcomed into the RAF with open arms. He'd been one of the most decorated pilots at the Battle of Britain, but then in typical Jeremy fashion, he'd strayed too far into France chasing a returning German plane and been shot down. Now he was in the Stalag Luft, a camp for captured airmen, somewhere in Germany, and nobody had heard from him in months. She didn't even know whether he was alive or dead. She squeezed her eyes shut so that a tear couldn't form. *Stiff upper lip at all times,* she repeated to herself— that was what was expected these days. "We must set an example," her father had said in his normal thundering manner, pounding on the table for better effect. "Never let anyone see you are upset or afraid. People look up to us, and we have an obligation to show them how it's done."

It was for that very reason that she had been selected for this job. Her friend Trixie Radcliffe, fellow deb in the spring of 1939, had invited her for tea in London, back in the early days of the war when civilised things like tea at Brown's Hotel still existed.

"I say, Pamma, this chap I know introduced me to another chap who might want to give us a job," Trixie had said in that enthusiastic way of hers. "He's looking for girls like us. From good families. No nonsense. Nor prone to hysterics."

"Goodness. What kind of job is he offering—deportment classes for the WAACs and Wrens?"

Trixie had laughed. "Nothing like that. I gather it's something rather hush-hush. He asked me if I could be trusted to keep my mouth shut and never gossip."

"Golly." Pamela looked surprised.

Trixie leaned closer. "He seems to think that we are brought up to do the right thing. Hence, will not let the side down and give away secrets. He even asked me whether I drink a lot." She laughed. "I gather people are apt to spill too many beans when drunk."

"So what did you tell him?"

"That I'd only just come out before the war, and since rationing, I hadn't really had a chance to prove how well I hold my liquor."

Pamela laughed, too, then her face grew serious again. "I wonder what he could possibly want us for? Sending us as spies into Germany?"

"He did ask if I spoke German. Actually, he said, 'Did I have the German,' which I first took to mean a German chap. I'm afraid I broke out in a fit of giggles. I told him we'd both been to finishing school in Switzerland and that you were a whiz at languages. He seemed really interested in you, by the way. Really perked up when I said I knew you."

"Golly," Pamela said again. "I don't think I can see myself as a spy, vamping German officers. Can you?"

"No, my sweet. I can't see you vamping Germans. You always were too pure. I, on the other hand, might be quite good at it. Unfortunately, my German is spoken with a decidedly English accent. They'd detect me as a phoney in an instant. But I don't think it's spying. This chap also asked how good I was at crossword puzzles."

"What a strange thing to ask," Pamela said.

Trixie leaned even closer until she was whispering in Pamela's ear. "I rather think it may be something to do with breaking codes and things."

And so it had proved to be. The two girls had taken the train from Euston Station to Bletchley Junction, an hour north of London. It was almost dark when they arrived. The station and the town were both unprepossessing. A pall of dust from the local brickworks hung over the air. There was nobody to meet the train, and they carried their own suitcases up a long path beside the railway line until they came to a high chain-link fence topped with barbed wire.

"Crikey." This time even Trixie was alarmed. "It certainly doesn't look very inviting, does it?"

"We don't have to do this," Pamela said.

They stared at each other, each willing the other to bolt.

"We can at least find out what they want us to do and then say 'no thank you very much but I'd rather be a land girl and raise pigs.'"

This put them both in better spirits.

"Come on. Let's face the music." Trixie nudged her friend, and they walked up to the main gate. The RAF guard on duty in the concrete sentry box had their names on his clipboard, and they were directed to the main house, where they were to report to Commander Travis. Nobody offered to carry their bags, which more than anything told Pamela that they were now in a very different world from the one she was used to. The driveway passed rows of long drab-looking huts before the main house came into view. It had been built by a nouveau riche family at the height of Victorian excess and was a sprawling mixture of styles with fancy brickwork, gables and oriental pillars, and a conservatory sticking out of one end. New arrivals from lower down the social scale were often impressed, but to girls raised in stately homes, it produced the opposite effect.

"What a monstrosity!" Trixie exclaimed, laughing. "Lavatory gothic, wouldn't you say?"

"But the view's pretty," Pamela said. "Look—there's a lake, and a copse, and fields. I wonder if there are horses and one can go riding."

"It's not a house party, darling," Trixie said. "We're here to work. Come on. Let's get it over with and find out what we're in for."

They entered the main house and found themselves in the sort of impressive interior they were used to—ornately carved ceilings, panelled walls, stained-glass windows, and thick carpets. A young woman carrying a sheaf of papers came out of a side door and didn't seem surprised to see them. "Oh, I suppose you're the latest lot of debs," she said, regarding Trixie's mink collar with disdain. "Commander Travis is upstairs. Second door on the right."

"Hardly the warmest welcome," Trixie whispered as they left their suitcases and ascended a rather grand carved-oak staircase.

"Do you think we're making an awful mistake?" Pamma whispered.

"A bit late to turn back now." Trixie squeezed her hand, then stepped forward to knock on a polished oak door. Commander Travis, the deputy director, looked at them with clear scepticism.

"This is no joyride, young ladies. In fact, it's bloody hard work. But I hope you'll find it's rewarding work. You'll be doing your part to stop the enemy—just as important a job as our boys in the service are doing. And the first thing we stress here is absolute secrecy. You will be required to sign the Official Secrets Act. After that you are not permitted to discuss your work with anyone outside your unit. Not even with each other. Not even with your parents or boyfriends. Is that clear?"

The girls nodded, then Pamela got up the courage to ask, "Exactly what will our work be? We've been told nothing so far."

He held up a hand. "First things first, young lady." He produced two sheets of paper and two fountain pens. "Official Secrets Act. Read this and sign here, please." He tapped a finger on the paper.

"So you're saying that we have to promise never to divulge what goes on here before we know what goes on here?" Trixie asked.

Commander Travis laughed. "You've got spirit. I like that. But I'm afraid once you came in through that gate, you became a security risk to the country. And I assure you that your work here will be a damned sight more interesting and rewarding than other jobs you could do."

Trixie looked at Pamela, shrugged, and said, "Why not? What have we got to lose?" She took the pen and signed. Pamela followed suit. Later, when she was alone, she discovered that she was to be sent to Hut 3 to translate decoded German messages. Pamela didn't know what Trixie was doing, as they were only allowed to share information with members of their own hut, but she knew that Trixie was annoyed that she hadn't been given a more exacting and glamorous job. "Filing and typing in the index room. Can you imagine anything more boring?" she had said. "While one gathers, the men in the huts have all the fun working on strange machines. I'd never have come if I'd known I'd be doing boring, menial stuff. How about you? Is your job going to be menial, too?"

"Oh no, I'm going to be chatting daily with Herr Hitler," Pamela said, then burst out laughing at her friend's face. "A joke, darling. One has to keep up a sense of humour at all times. And yes, I'm sure my job will be utterly menial, too. After all, we're not men, are we?"

And she had never told Trixie any more than that. She was horribly conscious of the importance of her job and that a failure to translate or a mistranslation might mean hundreds of lives lost. She realised that she was usually handed the lowest-level-priority decodes and that the priority intercepts went to the men, but just occasionally, she had the satisfaction of coming up with a hidden gem.

The task had been challenging and exciting at first, but after a whole year, she had become tired and jaded. The unreality of it all, the discomforts and the constant stream of bad news from the battlefields were beginning to wear down even a cheerful person like Pamela. The huts were horribly basic, freezing in winter, sweltering in summer, always gloomy with inadequate bare lightbulbs hanging from the ceiling. And at the end of long shifts, she had to return to her billet—a dismal boarding-house room backed against the railway line. As she rode back into town on the ancient bike she had acquired, she found her thoughts turning to Farleigh in the spring—the woods a carpet of bluebells in this first week of May. Young lambs in the fields. Riding in the early morning with her sisters. And she found that she really longed to see her sisters. And she had to admit that she had never really been close to any of them, except for Margot, whom she hadn't seen in ages and missed terribly. They were all so different—Livvy, five years her senior, had been born prissy and grown-up, and was always telling the others how to behave properly.

Pamela realised with regret that she hardly knew Phoebe, the youngest daughter. She had seemed a bright little girl and had the makings of a splendid horsewoman but spent most of her life in the nursery, away from the rest of the family. And then there was the annoying Dido, two years her junior, fiercely competitive, and desperate to be grown up and out in society—to have everything Pamela had. But Dido saw her as a rival, never a partner in crime as Margot had been, and they had never shared the same intimacy.

Pamela turned back to her work when a basket of transcripts was placed in front of her. The early-morning messages were beginning to come in, which was good news. It meant that the brainy chaps in Hut 6 had got the Enigma settings right, and the resulting printouts were in real German, or at least vaguely understandable German. She picked up the first card. The Typex produced long strips of letters divided into groups of five. *X*s were periods, *Y*s were commas, and proper names were preceded by a *J*. She looked at the first one: WUBY YNULL SEQNU LLNUL LX. This was something that came through every day. *Wetterbericht.* The morning weather forecast for sector six. And *null* meant nothing important was going on. She wrote out a quick translation and dropped it into the out-basket.

The next one was equally routine. ABSTI MMSPR UCHYY RESTX OHNEX SINN. A test sending from a German command to make sure the day's codes were working. "Thank you, Hamburg, they are working very nicely," she said with a smile, as she dropped this one into the basket. The next one had come through badly corrupted. Half the letters were missing. Messages were often received like this and required the skill used to solve a crossword puzzle as well as a good knowledge of the German terminology of war. Pamela managed to deduce that the subject of the message was the twenty-first Panzer Division, part of Rommel's desert force. But the following letters— FF-I——G had her flummoxed. Was it two words or even three? If it was more than one word, then the first one might be *auf*, meaning "on." She stared harder until the letters danced in the poor light. She longed to remove the blackout curtains, but only the warden was allowed to do that at his appointed hour. Her eyes hurt. *Rest,* she thought. *I need to rest.*

Then she was alert again, a hopeful smile on her face. She tried the letters. *Auffrischung.* The twenty-first Panzer Division needed to rest and refit!

She jumped up and almost ran through to the watch room. Wilson, the older man who was watch chief, looked up with a frown. He didn't approve of women on his night shift and ignored Pamela as much as possible.

"I think I've got something interesting, sir," she said. She put the Typex in front of him with her translation underneath. He stared at it, frowning for a long time before he looked up. "Rather a stretch of the imagination, wouldn't you say, Lady Pamela?" He alone always insisted on addressing her with her title. To the rest of them she was P.

"But it could mean that the twenty-first Panzers might be withdrawn. That's important, isn't it?"

Two other men at the table leaned over to see what the fuss was about.

"She may be right, Wilson," one of them said. "*Auffrischung*. Good word." He gave Pamela an encouraging smile.

"See if you can come up with something else that makes sense, then, Wilson," the other said. "We all know her German is better than ours."

"You should pass it along to army HQ anyway, just in case," the first said. "Well done, P."

Pamela allowed herself a grin as she returned to her seat. She had just emptied her in-basket when voices at the other end of the hut signalled the arrival of the early day shift. Pamela took her coat from its peg.

"Lovely day out there," one of the young men said as he came toward her. He was tall and gangly, peering at the world through thick glasses. His name was Rodney, and he was the epitome of the studious young Oxford or Cambridge men who had been lured to work at Bletchley Park. "Lucky you get time to enjoy it. Rounders match this afternoon, I gather. If you happen to like rounders. I'm a complete duffer at it myself, I regret. And country dancing tonight, but then you'll be working, won't you." He paused and ran a nervous hand through unruly hair. "I don't suppose you care to come to the cinema with me on your night off?"

"Kind of you, Rodney," she said, "But frankly, on my night off, I'd rather catch up on sleep."

"You are looking a little hollow around the eyes," he agreed, never having shown himself to be tactful. "These night shifts do get to one after a while, don't they? Still, all in a good cause, so they say."

"So they say," she repeated. "I wish we could see that we're making progress. The country, I mean. All the news seems to be bad, doesn't it? And the poor people in London being bombed night after night. How long can we take it, do you think?"

"As long as we have to," Rodney said. "Simple as that."

Pamela looked at his retreating back with admiration. He represented the backbone of Britain at this moment. A skinny, awkward bookworm, yet determined to keep going for as long as it took to defeat Hitler. She felt ashamed of her own depression and lack of faith as she went to retrieve her bicycle and rode into town.

Her digs at Mrs. Adams's boarding-house were close to the station, and a train whistled as it approached the platform. *If my parents could see where I'm living now,* Pamela thought, with a grim smile. But then they had no idea where she was working or what she was doing. Under the Official Secrets Act, she was not allowed to divulge anything to anybody. It hadn't been easy to persuade her father to let her leave home, but she had turned twenty-one and come out into society, so he could hardly forbid her. And when she had said, "I want to do my bit, Pah. You said it's up to us to set an example, and I'm setting one,". he had reluctantly agreed.

She dismounted from her bike and wheeled it along the pavement. She felt sick with hunger and tiredness, but she sighed as she wondered what breakfast would await her today: the lumpy porridge made with water? Bread fried in the drippings from last Sunday's scrag end of mutton? Toast with a scrape of margarine and watery marmalade if they were lucky. And her mind drifted to the spread on the sideboard back at Farleigh: the kidneys and bacon and kedgeree and scrambled eggs. How long before she could go home? But if she went home, how would she force herself to come back?

There was a newsstand outside the station, and a headline read "Hero Comes Home." Pamela glanced at the front page on the pile of newspapers. Since the war began and paper was scarce, the print had become smaller and more crowded and the pictures tiny. But there, halfway down the front page of the *Daily Express*, she spotted a grainy photograph of a man in RAF uniform and recognised the jaunty grin. She fished in her pocket for tuppence and took the newspaper. "Ace pilot Flight Lieutenant Jeremy Prescott escapes against all odds from

German prisoner-of-war camp. Only survivor of a breakout." Before she could read any more, her legs buckled under her, and she sank to the ground.

Instantly there were people around her, arms lifting her up.

"Steady on, love. I've got yer," one voice said.

"Bring her over to the bench, Bert, and someone go in the station café for a cup of tea. She's as white as a sheet."

It was the kindness more than anything that produced a great heaving sob from deep within Pamela. All the tension, the long nights, the hard work, the depressing news escaped from her in that one sob, and following it, the tears started streaming down her cheeks.

She felt herself carried and placed gently on a seat. She found she was still clutching the newspaper.

"What was it, love—bad news?" the woman at the newspaper stand asked.

Pamela's body was still shaking with sobs. "No, it's good news," she managed to gasp at last. "He's alive. He's safe. He's coming home."

That afternoon she received a message to report to Commander Travis. Her heart skipped a beat. What could she have done wrong? Had someone reported the incident at the station? She was heartily ashamed and embarrassed about her complete lack of control. Pah would have been mortified, would've told her she had let the side down. And now she worried: Had she said anything she shouldn't? She had heard rumours about people who had said too much, breached security. They disappeared and were never seen again. There were nervous jokes about where they had gone, but nobody laughed too much. The jokes might have been true.

But then one was not summoned to the deputy director for everyday matters. She jumped on her bike and pedalled back to the campus.

Commander Travis looked up from his paperwork as she came in. He motioned to the chair beside his desk. She perched on the edge of it.

"I hear you had a little trouble earlier today, Lady Pamela?" he said. The formality of her title in itself was worrying.

"Trouble, sir?"

"I hear you collapsed on the street outside the station. Are you not eating enough? I know the food is not exactly always appetising."

"I'm eating enough, sir."

"The night shifts? They take their toll on the body, I know."

"But we all have to rotate and do our share. I don't enjoy them. I never seem to get enough sleep when I'm on night shift, but it must be the same for everyone else."

"You are quite well?" he asked, giving her a knowing stare. He waited a second or two before he added, "Do you have a particular attachment to one of our young men?"

She actually laughed then. "I'm not pregnant if that's what you're suggesting."

"You don't look like the fainting type to me." He leaned closer to her across his desk. "So what's up?"

"I'm sorry, sir. I feel so foolish. And you're right. I don't make a habit of doing that sort of thing."

He thumbed through her file. "How long since you've taken leave?"

"I went home for a couple of days at Christmas, sir."

"Then you're overdue."

"But we're understaffed in Hut Three. It wouldn't be right to . . ."

"Lady Pamela. I expect our people to do first-class work. I can't have them cracking up on us. Take a week off."

"But there would be nobody to take my place, and we can't have . . ."

"When does your current rotation finish?"

"At the end of the week."

"Then work your rotation and go home then."

"Oh, but sir . . ."

"That's an order, Lady Pamela. Go home. Have a good time and come back refreshed."

"Yes, sir. Thank you."

It was only when she came down the steps of the big house that the full implication of this struck her. She would be going home, and Jeremy was safely back in Britain. He might already be at Nethercote. Suddenly everything was right with the world.

CHAPTER TWO

Farleigh Place
Near Sevenoaks, Kent
May 1941

It was the gamekeeper's boy who spotted it first. He had been out at dawn checking the traps (since wartime rationing had meant that rabbit was on the menu, even at the big house). It was a chore he had taken on willingly, loving the freedom and solitude of the countryside, still in awe of the wideness and greenness of it all, of the immense arc of sky like pale-blue glass overhead. After the flat in Stepney and the alleyway with its small strip of grubby sky, Farleigh still seemed too improbable to be real.

This particular morning he was returning empty-handed. The gamekeeper suspected some village lads were helping themselves to the odd rabbit or partridge, and he talked of putting down mantraps. The thought of mantraps brought an added spice of excitement to the daily chore for the boy. He wondered how it would feel to see one of the bigger village boys caught in a trap—the boys who took delight in bullying him and pushing him around because he was a runt and an outsider. He quickened his stride for the cottage, his stomach growling for porridge and eggs, real eggs, not the powdered stuff that tasted like cardboard. It was going to be a warm and perfect early summer's day. Strands of mist lingered over the meadows, and a cuckoo was calling loudly, drowning out the dawn chorus of birds.

The boy came out of the woods and into the parkland that surrounded the big house, looking out carefully for the herd of deer because he was still rather scared of them. Smooth green grass was dotted with spreading oaks, chestnuts, and copper beeches, and beyond he caught a glimpse of the big house itself rising like a fairy-tale castle above the trees. He was about to take the path that led to the cottage when he saw something lying in the grass—something brown, and beside it, something long and light and flapping a little, like a large wounded bird. He couldn't imagine what it could be, and he went toward it cautiously, still conscious that the country was full of unexpected dangers. When he got closer, he saw that it was a man lying there. Or had been a man. He was wearing an army uniform and lying facedown, his limbs at improbable angles. From a pack on his back came strings, and the strings were attached to what looked like long strands of whitish fabric. It took him a while to realise that it was a parachute, or the remains of a parachute, because it lay there, limp and lifeless, torn and flapping pathetically in the breeze. The boy understood then that the man had literally fallen from the sky.

He stood for a moment, wondering what to do, feeling slightly sick because the corpse was horribly damaged and the grass around it stained with blood. Before he could make up his mind, he heard the thud of hoofbeats on grass and the jingle of a bridle. He looked up to see a girl on a fat white pony galloping toward him. The girl was well turned out in a velvet crash cap, jodhpurs, and hacking jacket, and as she came closer, he recognised her as Lady Phoebe, the youngest of the daughters from the big house. He realised with horror that she'd ride right into the corpse if he didn't stop her. He ran forward waving his arms.

"Stop!" he cried.

The pony skidded to a halt, whinnied, danced, and bucked nervously, but the girl kept her seat well.

"What do you think you're doing?" she demanded. "Are you mad? You could have had me off. Snowball could have trampled you."

"You mustn't go that way, miss," he said. "There's been an accident. You wouldn't want to see it."

"What kind of accident?"

He glanced back. "A man fell from the sky. He's all smashed up. It's horrible."

"Fell from the sky?" She was straining to see past him. "Like an angel, you mean?"

"A soldier," he said. "I don't think his parachute opened."

"Golly. How horrid. Let me see." She tried to urge the pony forward, but it was still snorting and dancing nervously.

The boy stepped between her and the corpse again. "Don't look, miss. You don't want to see things like that."

"Of course I do. I'm not squeamish, you know. I've watched the men butchering a hog. Now, that really was rather horrid. The way it screamed. I decided never to eat bacon again. But I happen to adore bacon, so that didn't last long."

She nudged the pony forward, making the boy step aside. The pony took a few nervous steps, then stopped, sensing that it didn't want to go any closer. Phoebe stood up in the saddle and peered.

"Crikey," she said. "We must tell somebody."

"We should tell the army blokes. He's one of them, ain't he?"

"Isn't he," she corrected. "Really, your grammar is awful."

"Bugger my grammar, miss, if you don't mind me saying so."

"I do mind. And it's not 'miss.' I'm Lady Phoebe Sutton, and you should address me as 'my lady.'"

"Sorry," he said, swallowing back the word *miss* that was about to come out.

"We must tell my father," she said firmly. "It is still his land, after all, even though the army is using it at the moment. It still belongs to Farleigh. Come on. You'd better come with me."

"To the big house, miss? I mean, my lady?"

"Of course. Pah is always up early. The rest of them will still be asleep."

He started to walk beside the pony.

"You're the boy who is staying with our gamekeeper, aren't you?" she asked.

"That's right. Alfie's me name. I came down from the Smoke last winter."

"Smoke? What sort of smoke?"

He chuckled then. "It's what us Cockneys call London."

She stared down at him critically. "I haven't seen much of you on the estate."

"I'm at school in the village all day."

"How do you like it?"

"It's all right. The village kids pick on me 'cos I'm little for my age, and I ain't got no one to stick up for me."

"That's not nice."

He looked up at her haughty little face, a face that looked so content with itself, so secure. "In case you haven't noticed, people aren't nice," he said. "There's a war on. Blokes are flying over London every night dropping bombs and not caring who they kill—women, children, old people . . . it don't matter to them. I saw a baby after a bomb had gone off. Lying there in the street, looking as if there wasn't a mark on it. And I went to pick it up, and it was stone-cold dead. And another time a woman ran down the street screaming, and all her clothes had been blown off in the blast, and do you know what she was screaming? She was screaming, 'My little boy. He's buried under all that rubble. Someone save my little boy.'"

Phoebe's expression softened. "You were sensible to come here, away from the Smoke," she said. "How old are you?"

"Eleven, almost twelve."

"I just turned twelve," she said proudly. "I was hoping they'd send me to school when I was thirteen, but I don't think it will happen now. Not with a war on. My sisters went to school, lucky ducks."

"You mean you haven't been to school yet?"

"No. I've always had a governess. It's so boring doing lessons alone. It was different for my sisters because they had each other, and they were naughty and played tricks on the governess. But I was an afterthought. Dido says I was an accident."

"Who's Dido?"

"My sister Diana. She's nineteen. She's furious about the war because she was supposed to come out last year."

"Come out of what?"

Phoebe laughed, a rather fake and superior sort of *ha-ha*. "You don't know anything, do you? Girls like us have a season and are presented at court. We go to dances and are supposed to find a husband. But Dido's been stuck here instead, dying of boredom. The older ones all had their season."

"And got married?"

"Livvy did. But she was always the good child, Dido says. She married boring Edmund Carrington and she's already produced the heir."

"Air?" Alfie asked, making her laugh again.

"Not that sort of air. I mean she's had the required son to inherit the title one day. Our parents couldn't manage a son, which means Farleigh will go to some remote cousin when Pah dies, and we'll all be turned out into the snow, Dido says. But I think she was teasing. Things like that don't happen these days, do they? Especially with a war on."

She paused while Alfie digested this information, then continued, "But the others didn't quite obey the rules, much to Pah's fury.

Margot went to France to study fashion in Paris and met a handsome Frenchman. She wouldn't leave when she had a chance, and now she's trapped in Paris, and we don't know what has happened to her. And Pamma—well, she's really nice and very clever. She wanted to go to university, but Pah said it was a waste of time educating women. I think she had someone she wanted to marry, but he went into the RAF, and he was shot down, and he's in a prison camp in Germany. So it's all rather sad, isn't it? This horrid war spoiling everybody's lives."

Alfie nodded. "My dad's with the army in North Africa," he said. "We hardly ever hear from him, and when we do, it's a tiny little bit of paper with most of the words blacked out by the censor. Mum cried the last time one came."

Alfie was getting out of breath, walking fast to keep up with the pony and talking at the same time as they crossed the soft grass of the parkland, went through a stand of trees, and came to the edge of the formal gardens. There were still perfect rows of rosebushes and herbaceous borders, but the flower beds were now overgrown, and the roses hadn't been pruned. To one side, the lawn had been dug up and turned into another kitchen garden. And beyond them, where the forecourt had once allowed carriages to draw up, there were rows of camouflaged army vehicles.

Alfie hardly ever came this close to the big house. He stared at it now in wonder. He'd been taken to Buckingham Palace once, but this was just as big and imposing. It was built of solid grey stone, was three stories high, and the roof was adorned with towers at both ends. Two wings came out from the front to create the shape of an *E* with the imposing central entry making the middle bar of the letter. The pillars at this central entrance supported a pediment adorned with classical figures engaged in a battle. The impression of grandeur was marred, however, by a group of soldiers, sauntering down the marble steps, laughing and smoking. More soldiers were standing around army vehicles of various shapes and sizes, and from the other side of the house sounded the tramp of boots and shouts of drill sergeants as the ranks were put through morning parade.

Two officers approached, walking toward them. "Hello, young lady, going out for a ride, are you?" one of them said affably.

"I've already been, thank you," Phoebe said primly. "We're just taking my pony back to the stables."

She looked down at Alfie as soon as they were past the soldiers. "Don't mention to my father that I was out riding alone. He'd be furious. I'm not supposed to go out without the groom. But that's so silly, isn't it? I'm a perfectly good rider, and the groom is getting old and doesn't like to gallop."

Alfie nodded. Now that he was close to the big house, his stomach had tied itself in knots. He remembered too clearly the day he had arrived here. When he had first come by train from the Smoke, as he called it, he had been a pathetic-looking little specimen—scrawny and small for his age, wearing short trousers one size too big, revealing skinny knees covered in scabs. His nose was running, and he wiped it with the back of his hand, leaving a trail of snot across his cheek. No wonder he had been the last of the evacuated children to find someone willing to take him in. In the end, the billeting officer, Miss Hemp-Hatchett, local justice of the peace and Girl Guide captain, had put him in the back of her Morris and driven him to Farleigh.

"You'll have to have him, Lady Westerham," she had said in the voice that made generations of Girl Guides snap to attention. "There is simply nobody else, and you do have a bigger place than the rest of us."

Then she had departed, leaving the boy standing there, staring in awe at the marble foyer with its weapons and portraits of ancestors glaring down at him with looks of distaste.

"Damned blasted cheek," Lord Westerham exploded when Lady Westerham came to report this to him. "Who does the bloody woman think she is, bossing us around? Where do these damned people think we're going to put the brat? We've already had two-thirds of our house taken from us by the army. We're reduced to one bally wing, and a damned inconvenient wing it is, too. Does she think I'm going to put a child from the London slums on a camp bed in my bedroom? Or should he bunk in with one of our daughters?"

"Don't shout, Roddy," Lady Westerham said in her calm way, after thirty years, accustomed to her husband's outbursts. "It makes your eyes bulge most unpleasantly. There is a war on. We have to do our bit, and it must seem to most people that we have more than our fair share."

"So we're supposed to have a slum child given free rein of our house? Running around pinching the silver, I shouldn't wonder. It's not on, Esme. It's simply not on. How am I to enjoy a gin and tonic in my study, never knowing whether I'm going to be interrupted by a Cockney child? Tell that Hemp-whatsit woman that we won't do it, and that's that."

"The poor little mite has to find somewhere to stay, Roddy," Lady Westerham said gently. "We can't send him back to bombed streets. His parents might even be dead. How would you feel if you were wrenched from all you knew?"

"What about the tenant farmers?"

"They've already taken in children."

"Then the outdoor staff? Aren't there any spare cottages?"

"You can't put a child in an empty cottage." She paused, a pensive look coming over her face. "I've got it. The Robbinses must have a spare bedroom since their son was called up. Robbins isn't the friendliest of individuals, I'll give you that. But Mrs. R is a good cook. The poor little mite needs fattening up."

Alfie had been overhearing this conversation as he stood alone and shivering in the foyer. They hadn't realised that his biggest fear was that he'd have to stay in a place like this, where he'd be terrified every moment of meeting a ghost or breaking something. A cottage with a good cook in it sounded like a much better idea.

"Here. Hold the bridle a moment while I dismount," Phoebe said, jerking him back into the present. Alfie realised she was used to giving orders. He did as he was told, even though he'd never touched a horse before. The pony stood, still and placid, while Phoebe kicked her feet from the stirrups and swung herself down. Then she set out for the stables, leaving Alfie to walk behind her, still leading the pony. They had just rounded the corner when a groom came running toward them, red-faced and waving his arms.

"You shouldn't have taken Snowball out alone without me, your ladyship. You know what his lordship said."

"Rubbish, Jackson. You know I ride perfectly well." Phoebe tossed her head defiantly, and it seemed that the pony mirrored her action, almost jerking the reins from Alfie's grasp.

"I know you're a splendid little rider, my lady," he said. "I think your dad is more concerned about all them soldiers hanging around here. Not safe anymore, even on our own grounds."

Phoebe's cheeks were rather pink, but she said, "You can take Snowball now. I have to tell my father something important."

The groom took the pony, and Alfie followed Phoebe, who was already striding out for the big house. He had to run to catch up with her as she headed up the front steps. For a moment he was tempted to let her go in alone—he could sneak back to the gamekeeper's cottage where he knew breakfast would be waiting. But at the last second, she turned back, holding open the door. "Come along, Alfie. Do get a move on," she said impatiently.

The entrance hall was as daunting as he remembered it; now their feet were echoing on the marble tiled floor to the painted vault of ceiling high above. A group of officers was coming down the main staircase.

"We could tell them," Alfie whispered to Phoebe.

"I told you, it's my father's land. He has to know first," Phoebe said. She passed the officers, who nodded to her as they crossed the foyer, then she turned left. The long gallery that ran the length of the building had been boarded up with plywood, with a newly erected door in it marked "Family Quarters: Private." Phoebe opened the door, and Alfie found himself in the gallery. It was lined with oak panelling. The high ceiling was carved with gilded Tudor roses, and along its length were trophy heads of animals as well as tapestries of hunting scenes. To Alfie it was quite alarming, but Phoebe strode on, not seeming to notice.

At the end of the hall, they came to another foyer with a staircase on one side, not as grand as the central one. Phoebe looked around. "I do hope he's up. I'm sure he must be up."

At the sound of her voice, a butler appeared. "You've been out riding already, my lady? A fine morning—"

"Have you seen my father, Soames?" Phoebe cut into his words. "I must find him. It's important."

"I saw him come down the stairs a few minutes ago, my lady, but I'm not sure where he went. Would you like me to locate him for you?"

"It's all right. We'll find him. Come on, Alfie," Phoebe said as she set off again down a central hallway lined with family portraits. "Pah?" she called. "Pah? Where are you?"

Lord Westerham was sitting at the breakfast table, about to attack a mound of kedgeree. *Thank God for kippers,* he was thinking. *One of the few things that are still worth eating.* Not that they appeared often at the local fishmonger's, since fishing in the North Sea had become such a dangerous occupation. But when the odd kipper was available, the fishmonger always sent a message to Farleigh and reserved a couple behind the counter. "I know how fond his lordship is of his kippers," the fishmonger's wife said. In the good old days, it would have been a pair of kippers each for breakfast. Now Mrs. Mortlock had to make the most of them by using them in a kedgeree instead of the traditional smoked haddock.

He had just taken a mouthful when he heard someone shouting. He had barely identified the voice as his youngest daughter's, as she burst into the room.

"Was that you making that unseemly row?" Lord Westerham scowled at her, waving his fork. "Does your governess not teach you the rudiments of good behaviour?"

"No, Pah, she's always telling me that a lady never raises her voice, but it's an emergency. I simply had to find you right away. We've found a body. At least Alfie found it, and he stopped me from riding over it."

"What? What's this?" Lord Westerham put down his fork and glared at Alfie, trying to remember who he was and why a strange child was in his breakfast room.

"A body, Father. In the far field. He fell out of the sky. It's rather horrible, but you have to come."

"His parachute didn't open," Alfie added, then rather wished he had stayed silent as Lord Westerham turned to glare at him. Lord Westerham's glare, under those bushy eyebrows, was quite alarming, and Alfie swallowed nervously, glancing at the door and wondering if a bolt was possible.

"What were you doing on my land? Poaching, I shouldn't wonder," Lord Westerham said.

"No, sir. I'm staying with your gamekeeper, remember?" Alfie said.

"Oh yes. So you are."

"And he sends me out to check the traps in the early morning," Alfie said. "And I saw this thing lying there, and I didn't know what it was, so I went to look, and it was this bloke, all smashed up. A right mess. And then your daughter came galloping toward him, so I stopped her, and she said we should tell you first."

"Quite right. Quite right." Lord Westerham put down his napkin and stood up. "Well, I suppose you'd better take me to see, hadn't you?" He glared in annoyance as two English setters raced toward the door, sensing that their master was about to go out. "And make sure those blasted dogs don't get out. I don't want them nosing about a corpse." He looked down at them, their feathery tales wagging excitedly, eyes fixed on him, and his tone softened in a way that he never addressed his children. "Sorry, St. John. Sorry, Missie, old girl. Can't take you this time. But we'll make up for it later." He gave them a quick pat on the head. "Now stay!" he commanded. Both dogs sat, looking worried. As their little party reached the end of the long gallery, Phoebe turned to see the dogs still sitting in a shaft of sunlight.

CHAPTER THREE

Farleigh, the kitchen
May 1941

"What was that kerfuffle all about, Mr. Soames?" Mrs. Mortlock looked up from the kitchen table, her arms elbow deep in flour as the butler was coming through the baize door. "Young Elsie said she heard shouting when she was carrying up the hot water for Miss Livvy."

"Lady Phoebe seemed most agitated about something," Mr. Soames said, in his calm and measured way. "I didn't quite hear the full story, but I caught something about a body."

"A body? Well, I never. What next?" Mrs. Mortlock brushed off her hands so that a cloud of flour rose around her. "Poor Lady Phoebe. Don't tell me she came upon a body. A shock like that could unhinge the mind of a delicate young girl like Lady Phoebe."

Mr. Soames smiled. "I rather suspect that Lady Phoebe is as tough as any of us, Mrs. Mortlock. But as you say, it is most worrying to think of a body here at Farleigh."

"Where was it found, Mr. Soames? Anyone we know?" Mrs. Mortlock asked, moving away from her mixing bowl now that she was truly interested.

"Not that I heard. Just that she had found a body. And since she had just come in wearing her riding outfit, one must assume she found it on the grounds."

"It's them soldiers," Ruby, the kitchen maid, commented from the kitchen sink. "They're all sex-starved."

There was a gasp from Mrs. Mortlock.

"Ruby, where did you hear such language?" Mr. Soames demanded. "It's not what I expect from the servants in a house like this."

"I heard it from Elsie," Ruby said. "She was telling Jenny. And she gets it from the picture papers. They're always talking about sex in Hollywood. Anyway, Elsie said them soldiers are all sex-starved. Some of them invited her to go to the pub with them when she was polishing the door knocker."

"I hope she put them in their place," Mrs. Mortlock said. "Speak to her, Mr. Soames. We can't let down standards just because there's a war on."

"I most certainly will speak to her, Mrs. Mortlock. That's what happens when there's no housekeeper and no senior servants to supervise things. The young ones get ideas."

"Did they say what kind of body it was?" Mrs. Mortlock asked.

"I bet they lured some girl from the village here and had their way with her and she died of shock," Ruby went on.

"That's enough, Ruby," Mr. Soames said firmly. "I don't wish to hear such talk again."

"And luckily, Ruby will be so fully occupied with washing up and peeling potatoes that she is not likely to encounter any of the soldiers," Mrs. Mortlock said, giving Ruby a long warning look. "And if she doesn't get a move on, we'll be behind with the luncheon. I don't know what his lordship will say when he finds out it's vegetable pie again, but we've no more meat coupons for the rest of the month."

"It don't seem fair that the family can't eat their own meat when they've got a farm and all them animals."

"Those animals, Ruby. Really your grammar leaves a lot to be desired!" Mr. Soames sighed.

"I'm not really complaining," Mrs. Mortlock said. "I know we do better than most, and it's only right that those that raise food share it with those who live in the cities. But it's certainly a challenge trying to come up with appetizing meals on the ration of a quarter pound of meat per person per week."

"And it don't seem fair that I'm stuck in a kitchen washing up when I could be making good money in a factory," Ruby muttered, half to herself.

"And what factory would take you?" Mrs. Mortlock demanded. "You have to be sharp and nimble to work in a factory. You're all thumbs. You wouldn't last a day. No, my girl. You thank your lucky stars her ladyship took you on here. Otherwise, it would have been a land girl, digging potatoes out in the freezing rain."

"I wouldn't mind. At least there would be people to talk to," Ruby said. "It's no fun now all the footmen have gone, and we're down to Elsie and Jenny and her ladyship's maid and nanny."

"It's not exactly fun for us, either, Ruby," Mr. Soames said. "I am not thrilled about waiting at table and doing footmen's work at my age and with my seniority. But I do it cheerfully, knowing that the family depends on me. Above all, we do not let the family down. We try to make it seem that this place is running as it always had. Is that clear?"

"Yes, Mr. Soames," Ruby said in a dutiful voice.

"Don't you think we should send up some hot cocoa with brandy in it to Lady Phoebe?" Mrs. Mortlock asked. "They say brandy is the thing for shock, don't they?"

"Knowing young people, I suspect that Lady Phoebe is more thrilled than shocked at finding a body, Mrs. Mortlock, and will now be tucking into a large and satisfying breakfast." Mr. Soames smiled as he walked toward the door.

Phoebe was just coming out of her bedroom when a door farther down the hall opened, and a bleary-eyed head poked out. "Was that you running up and down the hall and waking everyone at the crack of dawn?" Lady Diana Sutton asked in a petulant voice. She was wearing blue silk pyjamas, and her blonde bob was tousled.

"Dawn cracked hours ago, Dido," Phoebe said. "I've already been out riding, and you'll never guess what I found!"

"I can hardly wait. The suspense is killing me." Lady Diana came out into the hall and leaned against the doorframe, in what she hoped was a blasé and sophisticated manner. "Could it have been mushrooms? Or a fox maybe?"

"It was a body, Dido," Phoebe said.

"A body? Of a person? Dead?"

"Bodies usually are. And this one was very dead indeed. It had fallen from an aeroplane."

"How do you know that?"

"Because he was wearing the remains of a parachute that didn't open properly."

"Golly." Dido suddenly forgot her sophistication. "Have you told Pah?"

"Yes, and he's gone to talk to the army people."

"Hold on a minute," Lady Diana said. "I'll get some clothes on, and you can show me before they move it away."

"I don't think Pah would like that," Phoebe said. "Not when he's with the army people."

"Don't be such a wet blanket, Feebs," Diana said. "You know I have to make the most of the only excitement we're likely to get around here. I don't know about you, but I'm dying of boredom. It's just not fair. I should have had my season and come out by now. I might even have been engaged to a yummy French count like Margot is. Instead, there are only boring soldiers and aged farmers, and Pah won't even let me go up to London. He won't even let me be a land girl because he says the farmhands only have one thing on their minds. Doesn't he know that I'm positively drooling for that one thing?"

"What thing is that?" Phoebe asked. "A boyfriend?"

"Sex, darling. You don't understand, but you will one day." She gave Phoebe a withering look. "I hate this stupid war. And I'm going to take a look at that body whether you show me or not." She turned and went back into her bedroom, slamming the door so that the pictures on the wall shook dangerously on their hooks.

CHAPTER FOUR

A field at Farleigh
May 1941

"Well?" Lord Westerham looked up at the officer standing beside him. "One of yours, is he?" He was not at all pleased with having the Royal West Kents taking over his house, but he tolerated Colonel Pritchard, their commanding officer, reasonably well. He was a gentleman, one of the right sort, and he had gone to some trouble to make sure the army caused the least disruption possible.

Colonel Pritchard looked rather green about the gills as he stared down at the corpse. He was a small, dapper man with a neat little mustache. Out of uniform, he would not have been taken for a soldier—a city gent maybe, or a bank manager. He now moved his shoe out of the area of blood-soaked grass. "Our chaps don't go leaping out of aeroplanes," he said. "We're strictly infantry."

"But isn't he wearing your uniform?"

"Hard to tell. Looks a little like it." The colonel frowned. "But as I say, if any man under my command had been given permission to jump out of a plane, I should have been told. Besides, I also should have heard if they were not all present and accounted for."

"So what's the procedure now?" Lord Westerham demanded. "We can't have him lying here in my field, scaring my deer. Someone's going to have to remove him. Should we summon the local police and have him taken to the nearest morgue?"

"I hardly think that's appropriate," Colonel Pritchard said. "The chap is in uniform, after all. It will be an army matter. Someone will know who he is, or was, rather. Someone will have ordered a bungled parachute jump last night—although why here, I can't tell you."

"Perhaps he drifted off course in the wind."

"Hardly any breeze last night," Colonel Pritchard said. "Besides, judging by the shape that parachute is in, he didn't do much drifting. I suppose we could take a look at the poor blighter's identity discs. Then at least we'll know who he was and where he came from." He gave a shudder of supreme distaste at this thought.

Between them, they bent to turn over the body. It felt like moving a bag of odd bits and pieces, as if every bone had been smashed, and even Lord Westerham shuddered this time. The front of the corpse was a bloody mess, his face unrecognisable. The colonel turned away as he opened the top button on the uniform and hauled out the identity tags. It was hard to tell that one had been red and one green, and the cord that held them was now sticky and crusting. Flies had already located the body and were arriving in droves, their buzzing filling the quiet of the meadow. Colonel Pritchard removed a knife from his pocket and cut the cord that held the discs.

"Can't read anything at the moment. They'll have to wash away the blood." He took a starched white handkerchief from his pocket and carefully placed the tags inside it.

"There you are. He was one of yours," Lord Westerham said, pointing down at the flash on his shoulder. Through the blood and grime they could just make out the words *Royal West Kents*.

"Good God." Colonel Pritchard stared. "What did he think he was doing? Out for a joyride or some kind of prank? Had a pal in the RAF and was going to surprise us all by dropping in on morning roll call? Let's hope his fate dissuades anyone else from such foolishness."

Diana hurried down the steps and out onto the grounds. She was well aware of the surreptitious looks she was getting from the soldiers she passed and allowed herself a secret smile. She was wearing red linen trousers and a white halter top—a little too cold for the time of day, but highly fashionable. On her feet were rope-soled wedge sandals. By the time she had crossed the first lawns, the sandals were wet with dew, and she rather regretted that she had not put on a cardigan. But such thoughts vanished as she approached the group of soldiers, in the process of lifting the body onto a stretcher. It was already covered with a sheet. An ambulance stood nearby. The men looked up as Diana came toward them, and she saw the astonishment, and appreciation, in their faces.

"You don't want to come anywhere near here, miss," one of them said, coming over to intercept her. "There's been a nasty accident, I'm afraid."

"She's not 'miss.' That's his lordship's daughter," an older man, wearing sergeant's stripes, corrected him. "You have to say 'my lady.'"

"Sorry, I'm sure, my lady," the young man said.

"Don't worry about it. I really don't care about all these silly rules. My name's Diana. And I came out to see the body."

"You wouldn't want to see it, Lady Diana, trust me," the older man said. "What a mess. Poor bloke."

"Was he a spy, do you think?" Diana asked. "You hear about German spies parachuting in, don't you?"

This made them chuckle.

"If he was, he'd got hold of our army uniform," the older one said. "No, it's my guess he was on some kind of training mission that went wrong, poor bugger." Then he remembered to whom he was speaking and grimaced. "Pardon my language, your ladyship."

"They were probably trying out some new parachute prototype on him," another soldier agreed. "There's a lot they don't tell us, and they use us as guinea pigs."

His friends nodded agreement.

"He was wearing a ring, bloody poofta," the young one said with disgust.

"Well, he was married, wasn't he?"

"He was bloody stupid," the young one went on.

"Why was that?" Diana asked. "Stupid to get married?"

"No, your ladyship. Stupid because if he got his ring caught during the jump, it would have ripped his finger off."

Diana shuddered, noticing how easily they spoke of such things. But then they had already fought in France and escaped from Dunkirk. They had seen friends blown up beside them. Another failed parachute jump was nothing to them. The stretcher was loaded into the ambulance and was driven away. The men headed back to the house. Diana fell into step beside them.

"How long do you think you'll be staying here? Do you know?"

"For the duration, as far as I'm concerned," the older one said.

"Not me, Smitty. I want to see some action. I wouldn't mind heading out to North Africa tomorrow and taking on Rommel," the young soldier who had first spoken to her said.

"You've only just joined up, Tom. If you'd been with us at Dunkirk, you wouldn't feel the same way. Never more grateful in my life to get home. Those blokes in their little boats did an amazing job. I came home on someone's yacht. This posh bloke crammed about twenty of us on board. Horribly overloaded. I thought we were going to capsize, but we didn't. And when he dropped us off on the beach, he turned around and went back again. That takes guts, that does."

Diana nodded. "So what do you do all day when you're here?" she asked.

"Training. Drilling. Preparing for an invasion."

"Do you think the Germans will invade?"

"I think it's only a matter of time," one of them said. "They've got a bloody great war machine. But we'll be ready for them. They won't get past us without a fight."

"I think you all are so brave," Diana said, watching with amusement as they looked embarrassed.

"You should come down to one of the dances in the village, my lady," the bold one said. "They're good fun."

"I just might do that," Diana said. She didn't add "if my father lets me."

She was rather sorry to have reached the house, and she watched the men moving off toward their quarters.

Back at the house Phoebe went into her bedroom to change clothes. Jodhpurs were not allowed in the dining room, even with the relaxed rules of wartime. Now that she was alone, she found that she felt rather sick, but put it down to the fact that she hadn't had breakfast yet.

"Been out riding, Phoebe?" Her governess, Miss Gumble, came into the room. She was tall and thin and carried herself well. Her face was now rather gaunt, but she must have been good-looking once. In fact, she came from a good family and she might have married well, but the Great War robbed her of the chance to find a husband.

She had been hired as Phoebe's governess when Dido was sent to finishing school in Switzerland. They got along well. Phoebe was a bright little girl and a pleasure to teach, even though Miss Gumble's conscience had been nagging her to abandon her post and volunteer for war work. She had a good brain. Surely she could be useful in any number of ways.

Phoebe looked up. "Oh, hello, Gumbie. I didn't hear you come in. You'll never guess what: I found a body in the far field when I was riding this morning."

"A body? Good gracious. Did you tell your father?"

"Yes, and he and the army man went to take a look at it. It was a man whose parachute didn't open, and he must have fallen out of a plane. He was awfully smashed up."

"How horrid for you," Gumbie said.

"Yes, it was, rather," Phoebe said. "But you would have been proud of me. I didn't let anyone see I was upset. The worst thing was that I almost rode over it. Can you imagine? Luckily, the boy from London who's living with the gamekeeper ran out and stopped me. He was jolly brave, actually."

"Good for him." Gumbie came around behind Phoebe to do up the buttons on her cotton dress. Since Phoebe had now declared herself too old to have a nanny, her governess had taken over such tasks. She was smart enough to realise that a girl of twelve needed some looking after, even if she claimed she didn't. The child's mother, Lady Esme, was a nice enough person but hadn't a clue about mothering her children, essentially leaving them to fend for themselves. Miss Gumble was only surprised that they had all turned out remarkably well. She smiled at Phoebe.

"If I were you, I'd go down and have a jolly good breakfast before we start work. I always find that food is the best thing if you've had a shock. Food and hot, sweet tea. They work wonders."

Phoebe undid her pigtails and started to brush her hair. "I wonder who he was, poor man."

"I expect it was some kind of night-time training exercise that went wrong," Miss Gumble said. "You know, commando stuff."

"So many horrid things seem to be happening, don't they?" Phoebe said while she tugged at a stubborn tangle in her corn-coloured hair. "Alfie said he saw a dead baby lying in the street and a woman whose clothes had been blown off her."

"Poor Alfie," Miss Gumble said. "He was sent here to get away from the distressing sights of the war, and now the war has followed him."

She took the brush from Phoebe. "Give me your hair ribbon. You can't go downstairs looking like Alice in Wonderland."

Phoebe turned obediently and allowed her governess to tie back her hair. "Gumbie," she said. "How long do you think the war will go on? For a long time?"

"I hope so," Miss Gumble replied.

Phoebe spun around, shocked. "You want the war to go on?"

"I do. Because if it ends quickly, it will mean that the Germans have conquered."

"Conquered? You mean come into England?"

"I'm afraid so."

"Do you think that might happen?"

"I think it's all too possible, Phoebe. We'll do our best, of course. Mr. Churchill said that we would fight them on the beaches and in our back gardens, but I wonder how many people actually would when it came to it?"

"My father would," Phoebe said.

"Yes, I expect he would," Miss Gumble replied, "but there are plenty of people who wouldn't put up a fight. We've all grown tired of war already, and if it goes on much longer . . . well, we'll welcome anyone who can return life to normal."

She tied the girl's hair ribbon. "Go on. Go down before your father eats all the good stuff."

CHAPTER FIVE

Phoebe actually liked this dining room better than the cavernous oak-panelled room where they had taken their meals before the war. This had been a former music room, painted light blue with gilded trim, and tall French windows looked out over the lake. Sunlight was streaming in. It felt warm and safe because Phoebe was still cold. She had looked in vain for scrambled eggs and just served herself a plate of kedgeree when her father came in, followed by the English setters who were jumping around him excitedly.

"I hope you've left something for me, young lady," he said, striding over to the sideboard. "Would you blasted animals go away and leave me in peace? You'll not get any bacon, you know. There's a war on."

"I thought you'd had breakfast." Phoebe took a generous mouthful of rice. It was now, unfortunately, almost cold, but the bits of kipper made it taste all right.

"I was interrupted in the middle of mine, if you remember." Lord Westerham took the silver lid off the chafing dish. "Ah, good. There is still plenty. I suppose nobody else is up yet?"

"Dido is. She wanted me to show her the body."

"That young woman is going to come to a sticky end if she's not careful." He looked up as Lady Esme came in, holding an envelope in her hand. "Hear that, Esme? Your idiot daughter wanted to see the body of a man who fell into our field." He took his place at the head of the table, and the dogs sat expectantly beside him.

Lady Esme looked only vaguely surprised. "I thought I heard something of the kind when I was having my morning tea," she said. "Well, I suppose she could be curious. I suppose I was at her age. Whose body was it?"

"Some damned army chappie, although the colonel doesn't see how it can be one of his. Bit fishy if you ask me."

"Mummy, I found the body," Phoebe said.

Lady Westerham had now taken a piece of toast and sat beside her husband. "Did you, dear? That must have been exciting for you."

Phoebe glanced at her. Gumbie was perceptive enough to know that it had shocked Phoebe, but not her mother, who was now calmly opening the envelope. "Oh, it's a letter from Clemmie Churchill," she said, showing enthusiasm for the first time. "I was expecting to hear from her about the garden party at Chartwell next month."

"Garden party?" Lord Westerham bellowed. "Doesn't Clemmie Churchill know there's a war on?"

"Of course she does, but Winston misses Chartwell and needs cheering up, so she arranged this little garden party for him at the home he misses so much," she said. "Be quiet and let me read, Roddy."

Her eyes scanned the page. "Poor thing," she said.

"I hardly think that being wife of the prime minister can be described as a poor thing," Lord Westerham muttered between bites of breakfast.

"She says that Winston is horribly overworked, gets almost no sleep, and in consequence is always bad-tempered."

Lord Westerham snorted. "Winston has always been bad-tempered, ever since I've known him. The moment anything doesn't go the way he wants it to, he explodes. I should imagine losing a war would not be kind to anyone's temper."

Lady Esme was still reading. "You know how he loves Chartwell. I'd invite them to stay with us, but . . ."

"Esme, we're packed in like sardines as it is," Lord Westerham said. "You can't invite the prime minister of England to bunk up in the maid's quarters." The thought of this made him chuckle.

"Don't be silly, dear," Lady Westerham said calmly, not looking up from her letter. "Oh no," she exclaimed as she read on. "How disappointing."

Lord Westerham raised an eyebrow.

"I told you he has to come down here anyway to attend that ceremony at Biggin Hill Aerodrome next month, honouring those brave lads who were killed in the Battle of Britain. Clemmie had wanted me to help her with the garden party at Chartwell, but Winston got word of it and has put his foot down. No parties in wartime, he says. In these times of economy we have to set an example and not open up the house for one weekend. Isn't that just like him?"

"Nasty Americanism, the word 'weekend,'" Lord Westerham remarked. Although he had known Churchill for many years, he still hadn't quite forgiven him for his American mother.

"Do be quiet and stop interrupting, Roddy." Lady Westerham frowned at him across the table. "Oh, this is a splendid idea. Listen, Roddy. She wonders if they might come here for tea on the lawn after the ceremony. It would be a lovely surprise for Winston to be with the old neighbours, she says."

"The prime minister, here to tea? What do you plan to feed them? Dandelions? Are they going to bring their own ration cards?" Lord Westerham demanded.

"Don't be difficult, Roddy. You know you'd love to see the Churchills again. And we do have kitchen gardens. The strawberries should be ripe, and there would be cucumbers and cress for sandwiches. We'll manage somehow. So I'll write back, and tell her it's a splendid idea, shall I?"

Before Lord Westerham could answer, the door opened and Olivia, the eldest of the Sutton sisters, came in. Although she was only twenty-six, she was already starting to look matronly. She was wearing a navy dress with a white round collar and pin-tuck pleats at the front, which emphasised her ample bosom. And she wore her hair rolled in a coil at the back of her neck, which didn't really suit her round face.

"Charlie has a bit of a cough," she said. "I hope he's not coming down with something. Has the post arrived yet, Pah? Is there anything from Teddy?"

"Nothing but a couple of bills and a letter for your mother from Mrs. Churchill," Lord Westerham said. "Your husband is probably having far too good a time to think of writing."

"Don't say that, Pah. He's only doing his duty. He had to go where he was sent."

"And the Bahamas is not exactly a hardship posting." Lord Westerham looked at his wife, who smiled vaguely.

"How nice for him. I hear they have lovely beaches."

They all looked up as Dido came in. There were goose bumps on her bare shoulders and arms, but her face was glowing from being outside. "Golly, the whole clan is here. What are you doing up, Mummy? I thought you told me one of the few luxuries of being a married woman was breakfast in bed."

"Darling, I used to look forward to my fresh brown egg and thin soldiers of lovely fresh bread. Having toast and margarine somehow hardly makes it worthwhile staying in bed."

"I hear you went out looking for the body, Dido," her father said. He was eyeing her critically. "Don't tell me you went outside looking like that? You need your head examined—all those bloody soldiers hanging around with too much time on their hands. You'll come a cropper, my girl."

"The soldiers were very sweet to me, Pah. And besides, I was too late to see the body," Dido said, helping herself to the last of the kedgeree. "Oh goody, hooray for Mrs. Stubbins. She found kippers for us again."

"Never did I think there would come a day when we would all rejoice over kippers," Lord Westerham said. "I suppose a mere taste is better than nothing, but I really miss my pair of kippers, all to myself." He turned to wave a warning finger at his daughter. "But in future, Diana, I do not want you wandering all over the property alone, especially not dressed like that. It looks as if you're wearing your pyjamas."

"It's the height of fashion, Pah. Or at least it was when there was still *Vogue*. Not that there is any point in trying to be fashionable when one is stuck in the depth of the countryside." She put her plate down next to Phoebe's, then reached over to pat the setter's head before she picked up her napkin. "If you'd let me get a job up in London, I'd be safely out of your hair, Pah. And I wouldn't have any time on my hands, would I?" she replied bitterly. "I'm dying of boredom, you know. There's a war on. Plenty of excitement. I want to be part of it."

"We've been through this before, Dido," Lord Westerham said. "You are too young to go and work on your own in London. I don't mind you helping out with the animals on the home farm, or even helping teach the children at the village school, but that's it. And that's my final word on the subject. Don't bring it up again."

Dido sighed and took her place at the far end of the table. They all looked up at the sound of a heavy, measured tread, and Soames came in, bearing a silver salver.

"A letter for you, my lady," he said. "Hand delivered."

Lady Esme looked surprised as she took it. "Goodness. What an eventful morning. Who can be writing to me now?" The rest of the family waited as she took the envelope, noted the crest on the back, and smiled. "Oh, it's Lady Prescott. I wonder what she wants? I thought we were too impossibly dowdy and old-fashioned for them."

"Perhaps she wants to borrow a cup of sugar," Lord Westerham replied with a snort. "Times are hard for all at the moment, even the Prescotts."

"Oh, not the Prescotts, I think," Livvy said. "Every time I take Charlie out in his pram, I seem to see a delivery van pulling up at their house."

"What does it say, Mah?" Dido asked.

Lady Esme looked up, a pleased smile on her face and began to read aloud:

> Dear Lady Westerham,
> I wanted to share our good news with you before you heard it through the village grapevine. Our son Jeremy has arrived home safely against all odds. He is naturally weak, recovering from an infected gunshot wound, but we have every reason to hope he will make a full recovery.
> When he has regained his strength, we look forward to giving a little dinner party in his honour and hope that your family will be able to join us.
> Yours sincerely,
> Madeleine Prescott

She folded the letter and looked around at her family, beaming. "Isn't that wonderful? I must write to Pamela straight away. She'll be thrilled."

"Why Pamma any more than the rest of us?" Dido demanded. "Or is she the favoured child?"

"Dido, you know how sweet Pamma is on Jeremy. In fact, if there hadn't been this stupid war, I rather think there might have been an announcement by now." She gave an enigmatic smile.

"Mah, you're too keen to get your children married off, aren't you? Jeremy Prescott never struck me as the faithful type."

"I'm sure lots of young men sow their wild oats but settle down when the time comes," Lady Esme said. "Anyway, the main thing is that he's home now, and all will be well." She got up. "I must write to Pamma this very minute."

Dido watched her go. "I don't know where I'm ever supposed to find a husband," she said. "Stuck here in the country, it will have to be a pig farmer, I suppose."

This made Phoebe giggle. "He'd smell horrible," she said. "But you'd get good bacon."

"That was supposed to be sarcasm, Feebs," Dido said. "I was just reminding everyone that I didn't get my season like my sisters."

"I didn't order this blasted war," Lord Westerham said. "And you're still young. There will be plenty of chance for parties and dances when it's over."

"If you know how to do German folk dances," Phoebe said.

Lord Westerham's face turned beetroot red. "Not funny, Phoebe. Not in the least bit funny. The Germans will not win, and that's final."

He flung down his napkin and strode from the room.

Later that morning, the colonel's adjutant, Captain Hartley, sought out his commanding officer.

"We've checked the tags, sir, and they don't match anyone in the West Kents. Furthermore, all were present and correct at roll call this morning, apart from Jones, who was given two days' leave because his wife had a baby, and Patterson, who is in the hospital with appendicitis."

"So what do you think we should do now?" Colonel Pritchard scratched his head, pushing his cap askew. "Find out who this joker was and why he was wearing our uniform."

"One can't rule out the possibility, sir, that he was a spy. Wearing the uniform of the West Kents would give him a good excuse to roam around this area, wouldn't it?"

Colonel Pritchard sucked air in through his teeth. "One hears about such things, but surely they are all rumour."

"Oh, I'm pretty sure there are plenty of fifth columnists around."

"You think so?" Colonel Pritchard glared. "Englishmen deliberately wanting to work for the Hun?"

"I'm afraid so, sir. If someone needed to contact them, what better way than to parachute a man in on a dark, moonless night?"

Colonel Pritchard stared past him, out across the lawns. He found it hard to believe that this was England, Blake's green and pleasant land, and yet they were no longer safe at home. Bombs were falling indiscriminately. And now, maybe spies were working among them.

"Send the tags to army intelligence. They can come and take the body. It's out of our hands," he said, then looked up as a private approached them, walking fast. He stopped, came to attention, and saluted.

"Begging your pardon, Colonel, sir," he said, "but I was one of the men sent to get that body today. And at the time, I thought there was something that wasn't quite right. Then I realised what it was. He still had his cap tucked into his lapel, and the badge was wrong."

PART TWO:
BEN

CHAPTER SIX

Wormwood Scrubs prison
Acton, West London
May 1941

The gate to Wormwood Scrubs prison closed behind Ben Cresswell with a clang of finality. Even though he had been coming and going through this particular gate for the past three months, he still felt an odd frisson of fear when he entered and an absurd sense of relief when he was safely outside again, as if he'd got away undetected.

"Let you out early for good behaviour then, did they?" the policeman on duty asked him with a grin. The joke had now become old, but apparently the bobby still hadn't tired of it.

"Me? Absolutely not. I escaped over the wall. Didn't you notice?" Ben replied, straight-faced. "Shirking on the job?"

"Get outta here!" The policeman chuckled and gave Ben a nudge.

MI5's move to Wormwood Scrubs for security reasons was supposed to be strictly hush-hush, but everyone connected to the prison seemed to be fully aware of what the newcomers who had taken over one wing were up to. Even a bus conductor had been known to announce the stop by yelling down the bus, "All change for MI5." *So much for secrecy,* Ben thought while he crossed the street to the bus stop. As the headquarters of a secret service division, the prison had proved to be a dismal failure. The cells they had been assigned were cold and damp; some doors had actually been removed, so it was easy to overhear what was going on in the next room. Furthermore, it was more inconvenient and difficult to get to than the former headquarters on the Cromwell Road.

Recently, part of B Division, responsible for counterespionage, had been moved out to Blenheim Palace in Oxfordshire, where rumour had it that, in spite of being in a stately home, the accommodations were even more primitive than at the prison. Even so, Ben wished he'd been assigned there and was actually doing something useful for the war effort. Since he had been recruited into MI5 a year ago, his spy catching had been confined to following up on rumours and tips in the greater London area. The rumours were nearly always a waste of time. Mostly they were false alarms or a chance to even old scores. A nosy old woman had peeked out of her blackout curtain and seen a furtive man slinking past her back garden. Definitely looked like an invading Nazi. Only it turned out to be the lover of the lady next door, sneaking in while her husband was away. Or a woman suspected that her neighbours were secret German sympathisers because they always played Mozart on their radiogram. When Ben pointed out that Mozart was actually Austrian, the woman had sniffed in annoyance. *No difference really,* she'd said. *Wasn't Hitler Austrian? And besides, they were always cooking with garlic. You could smell it a mile off. And if that wasn't suspicious, what was?*

Ben turned to look back at the ornate red-and-white brick towers that housed the prison gate. Trust the Victorians to make even a prison look impressive! Then he walked down Du Cane Road to the East Acton tube station. He hoped the tube would be quicker into central London than a bus, but one never knew. One bomb on the line overnight and everything would grind to a halt. His gait was slightly uneven and jerky, thanks to the tin knee in his left leg, but he was still able to move quite fast. Just not able to play rugger nor bowl at cricket.

He was about to cross to the tube station when a man came out of the tobacconists with a paper under his arm, stared at Ben, then frowned. "Here, you, son. Why aren't you in uniform?" he demanded, waving an aggressive finger at Ben. "What are you, a bleeding conchie?"

Ben had faced similar accusations many times since the war began. "Aeroplane crash," he said. "One leg smashed up and no use to anyone."

The man's face turned red. "Sorry, mate. I didn't realise you were RAF. Shouldn't have spoken like that to one of our brave boys. God bless you."

Ben no longer tried to correct anyone. Let them think he was RAF. He would have been, if he hadn't been in that stupid plane crash at Farleigh. And if he had been? The thought danced around in his head. Shot down over Germany and now languishing in a Stalag Luft like Jeremy? What bloody use was that to the war effort? At least he was doing something vaguely useful in his current job. Or would be, if they'd give him a case he could sink his teeth into.

Ben sighed. The trouble was, the whole country was on edge, fearing the invasion at any moment. He bought his ticket and hauled himself up the steps, up to the platform, as the Underground line actually ran above ground this far out of the city. The platform was crowded, indicating that a train hadn't come for some time. He squeezed his way close to the line and waited, hoping that it would show up soon and wouldn't be too full. He had to get to central London in a hurry. For once, he had what might be an important assignment.

"You're wanted by the powers that be," his cellmate Guy Harcourt had said with relish when he returned from lunch.

"The powers that be?" Ben had asked.

"The grand pooh-bah Radison himself, no less. Most put out that you had the nerve to go off to luncheon rather than eat a cheese sandwich at your desk." He was the sort of languid and elegant young man one would expect to find at a country house party, playing croquet with Bertie Wooster. Frightfully good fun, but not too many brains. Ben thought privately that he'd make an excellent spy. Nobody would ever suspect him. They had been at Oxford together, where Harcourt never seemed to do any swotting but managed to pass his exams anyway. They had never been friends. For one thing, Harcourt was too rich, too aristocratic for Ben to be part of his circle, so Ben was surprised when Harcourt had sought him out at the start of the war and recruited him for what turned out to be MI5. They were assigned the same billet at a dreary private hotel on the Cromwell Road and got along well enough.

"I'd hardly call it luncheon," Ben said. "Do you know they are making rissoles out of horsemeat these days? I've had to have the cauliflower cheese three days in a row because the alternatives were too ghastly."

"Never eat there myself," Harcourt said. "I pop over to the Queen's Head on the corner. Beer is nourishing, isn't it? I plan to survive on it for the duration. I mean to say, horsemeat? These blighters have clearly never ridden to hounds in their lives. You wait, it will be dogs and cats next. Better lock up your Labradors."

"Did Radison say what he wanted?" Ben asked.

"My dear chap, we're supposed to be a secret service organisation, aren't we?" Harcourt asked with a grin. "He's hardly likely to come in here and tell me what he wants with another agent. There has to be some air of mystery about things."

"Did he seem annoyed with me?"

"Why, have you blotted your copybook?" Harcourt was grinning now.

"Not that I know of. I was rather short with that chap who wanted his Jewish neighbours locked up as Nazi spies."

"Better hurry up and see what he wanted, then, hadn't you? And if you don't come back, can I have your chair? It's less wobbly than mine."

"Very funny." Ben tried to sound more lighthearted than he felt. He couldn't think what he might have done, but one never knew. Departments like this were all about the old-boy network, and he didn't have connections.

Mr. Radison regarded him suspiciously after Ben knocked and entered his office.

"Been out to lunch, have we?" he asked.

"I believe I am allowed a lunch break, sir," Ben answered. "And I only went to the canteen. Horsemeat rissoles."

Radison had nodded with understanding then. "I've had a message from headquarters. You're to report to this address on Dolphin Square."

"Dolphin Square?" He had heard vague rumours about an office in Dolphin Square. Again, nobody was supposed to know that MI5 maintained an office there or whose office it was, but he was fairly sure that it was that of a nebulous character known as Captain King or Mr. K. Someone who was outside the usual hierarchy of the various divisions. Ben felt excitement tinged with apprehension. What could this person want with him? He might have a leg that didn't always work well, but none of his assignments had required cross-country sprints yet. As boring as his low-level assignments were, he'd fulfilled them perfectly. He had shown himself to be keen and willing. So perhaps this really did bode well—a promotion, a juicy assignment at last.

CHAPTER SEVEN

London
May 1941

Ben snapped out of these thoughts as the loudspeaker announced the arrival of the train, with the warning to stand clear and mind the gap. Doors opened and the crowd surged forward, bearing Ben with them. He managed to grab a pole as the doors closed and the train rattled off. He felt lucky to have something to hang on to; his balance was none too steady, and his bad leg was apt to give way at inconvenient moments. But he made it to Notting Hill Gate Station and changed to the Circle Line to Victoria. The whole journey went remarkably smooth, and he heaved a sigh of relief as he set off down Belgrave Street toward the river. It was a pleasant summery day, warm for May, and Londoners who could escape from offices for a few minutes were sitting at any little square of green they could find, soaking up the sunshine. Dolphin Square rose in front of him, a giant rectangular block of luxury flats. Ben had never seen it before and wondered now how many of those flats were still occupied by rich people who needed a London pied-à-terre. He suspected that anybody who could afford to was staying well away from the Blitz.

There were four big modern buildings around a central quadrangle; the address he had been given said 308 Hood House. He studied the bank of doorbells outside the front door and was surprised to find that 308 was listed as Miss Copplestone. Had he been given the wrong address? Was it someone's idea of a joke to send him to confront an angry spinster? It was the sort of thing that Halstead might do to liven up a boring afternoon, but the directive had come from Radison, and Radison was the epitome of a civil servant with no sense of humour. With misgivings, Ben pressed the doorbell.

"Can I help you?" said a patrician voice. Ben was tempted to walk away rapidly, but he said, "I'm not sure if I have the right address. My name is Cresswell, and I was told . . ."

"I'll let you in, Mr. Cresswell," said the efficient voice. "Take the lift. Fifth floor and turn right."

At least he was expected. A tinge of apprehension mingled with excitement as the lift rose slowly. He came out to the fifth floor. The hallway was carpeted and smelled of polish, with a lingering tinge of pipe tobacco. He found the flat and saw that Miss Copplestone was also on the doorplate. He took a deep breath before he knocked. The door was opened by an attractive young woman, her well-cut suit and patrician air betraying that in other times and circumstances she would have been a deb and then been married off to a dull young man of impeccable pedigree. For young women like her, the war had presented a great opportunity to escape, to prove that they were good at all sorts of things, not just small talk and knowing where to seat a bishop at a dinner table.

"Mr. Cresswell? Mr. Knight is expecting you. Come in," she said in a clipped upper-class voice. "I'll tell him you are here."

Ben waited, heard low voices, and was immediately ushered into a large, bright room with windows that looked down the Thames to the Houses of Parliament, barrage balloons bobbing over the buildings to prevent low-level bombing raids. The man sitting at a polished oak desk had his back to the view. He was slim and fit-looking, clearly an outdoor type, and to Ben's amazement, he was handling what Ben initially thought was a length of rope, which uncoiled and revealed itself to be a small snake.

"Ah, Cresswell. Good of you to come." He stuffed the snake back into a pocket and held out his hand to Ben. "I am Maxwell Knight. Take a seat."

Ben pulled up an upholstered leather chair.

"Cambridge man?" Knight asked.

"Oxford."

"Pity. I find that Cambridge produces men who can think creatively."

"I'm afraid I can't undo that now," Ben said. "Besides, Hertford College offered me a scholarship. Cambridge didn't."

"Scholarship boy, then?"

"Yes, sir."

"And before that?"

"Tonbridge. Also on a scholarship."

"And yet, apparently, you hobnob with the gentry. You know the Earl of Westerham."

The statement took Ben completely by surprise. "Lord Westerham?"

"Yes. I'm told you're quite pally with him. Is that correct?"

"I wouldn't say pally, sir. I wouldn't presume to claim friendship, but he knows me quite well. My father is the vicar of All Saints, Elmsleigh, the village next to Farleigh. I grew up playing with Lord Westerham's daughters."

"Playing with Lord Westerham's daughters," Max Knight repeated with the hint of a smile.

Ben's face betrayed no emotion. "May I ask what this is about, sir? Has my background anything to do with the quality of my work here?"

"Absolutely, at this moment. You see, we need insights, young man. An insider."

Ben looked up, frowning. "Insights into what?"

Max Knight's clear blue eyes still held Ben's. "Three nights ago now, a man apparently fell from a plane onto one of Lord Westerham's fields. His parachute didn't open. He was pretty much a mess, as you can imagine. Face too damaged to get an idea what he looked like. But he was wearing the uniform of the Royal West Kents."

"They've taken over most of Farleigh, haven't they?" Ben frowned. "But they're an infantry regiment. Where did the parachute come in?"

"It didn't. Their commander says that his chaps don't leap out of planes and are all present and accounted for. The identity disc belonged to a soldier who was killed at Dunkirk, *and* it turns out that the cap badge was the one the regiment wore in the Great War."

"So a possible spy, then?" Ben felt his pulse quicken.

"Quite possible. I'm also told by one of our bright young women who was going through his clothing—not an enviable task, as you can well imagine—that his socks were wrong."

"Socks? Wrong?"

"Yes, she's something of a knitter, and she says that the heel isn't turned like that in British Army regulation socks. On further investigation, she could just make out the number 42 on them."

"Forty-two?"

"Metric size."

"Oh, I see." Ben nodded now. "So the socks came from the Continent."

"I'm glad we use Oxford lads. So quick on the uptake," Max Knight said. Ben flushed.

"Therefore I suppose the question is, what was he doing in Lord Westerham's field," Max Knight continued. "Was he there on purpose or by accident?"

"Was there a high wind that night? He could have been blown off course, or the parachute malfunction might have caused him to drift."

"We've checked on that. The breeze was only two knots. Besides, you don't drift if your parachute doesn't deploy properly. You plunge straight down."

"It might just have been pure coincidence that the landing site was Lord Westerham's field," Ben said. "He was instructed to parachute down within reach of London or within reach of Biggin Hill RAF station."

"Then why not an RAF uniform instead of the West Kent Regiment?" He took a deep breath that sounded almost like a sigh. "You can see the tricky situation we find ourselves in, can't you, Cresswell? If the landing was intentional, if he was a German spy—and we have to assume that is the case—then he was sent to make contact with someone nearby, in an area where a uniform of the West Kents would not arouse suspicion."

"What about his pockets, sir?" Ben asked. "Was there nothing useful that could be retrieved from his pockets?"

"His pockets were completely empty, apart from a small snapshot in his breast pocket."

"A snapshot?" Ben asked, half-interested and half-afraid now.

"Of a landscape. Of course it was covered in blood, but the lab has been able to clean it up. We had to prise this out of the hands of army intelligence, by the way. They weren't too keen to share information. Nobody is these days." He opened a drawer and took out a slim file, which he opened and turned toward Ben. Ben stood up to look at it. It hadn't been a very good photograph to begin with. The sort of small snapshot a tourist might take on summer holiday, and now, after having been bloodied and cleaned, it was even more indistinct. From what Ben could make out, it was a general view of an English countryside with fields divided by hedges, and rising in the background, a steep-sided hill, topped with a crown of trees. Amid the trees was just the hint of a village with what looked like a square tower of a church poking above Scotch pines. Ben stared at it. "That's not anywhere I've seen, and it doesn't look like our part of Kent," he said. "It looks more bleak, and steep, and windswept. Scots pines, aren't they? More like the West Country from that square-towered church. Cornwall maybe?"

Max Knight nodded. "Could well be. So what was it doing in his pocket? Was he supposed to make his way there—in which case, why drop him in the middle of Kent? Was he supposed to hand it to someone telling the site for a rendezvous for some unknown purpose?"

"Or the name of the village is somehow significant?" Ben suggested.

Knight sighed again. "Again possibly. You'll note there were numbers written on it. Almost washed away, but the pen left an impression on the photo paper." He looked up at Ben. "It's all right to pick it up."

Ben took the photograph gingerly and held it up to the light: 1461. "Fourteen sixty-one. Any significant battles take place on that date?"

Knight looked at him long and hard. "That's for you to find out, son. I'm dumping this in your lap. Reports on you say that you are quick and you're keen, and you don't like sitting around twiddling your thumbs. Normally, I'd give something like this to a senior man, but you have what nobody else in this department has—you're one of them."

CHAPTER EIGHT

Dolphin Square, London
May 1941

Ben shifted uneasily in his seat. "Excuse me, sir, but what do you want me to do? Find out where the snapshot was taken?"

"That can wait. Right now I'd like you to go home for a few days."

"But I say, sir, isn't there an element of haste in this? The Germans wouldn't have dropped somebody into the Kent countryside unless it was for an urgent mission."

"The messenger is dead, Cresswell. And with him, presumably the message he carried. They will have to regroup and try again, likely in a different way this time, as they assume we'll be looking out for parachutists. What we have to find out is for whom the message was intended. That's where you come in. Go home. Don't make it obvious, but ask questions."

"What kind of questions?"

Maxwell Knight looked at Ben as if he were a bit dense. "I'm sure the neighbourhood will still be buzzing with news of the body. Someone will be bound to suggest that it's a German spy. Watch their reactions."

"Exactly what are you suggesting?" Ben asked cautiously.

"We must assume that the man did not parachute into that field by accident. If he was a German spy, which we have to assume is the case, why Lord Westerham's estate?"

"Maybe it was convenient open space fairly close to London."

"Then why no money in his pockets? He couldn't get far. He carried no papers, so it appears he was planning to deliver a message in person to someone nearby. Or go to a safe house nearby. And there was no sign of a radio or any way to communicate with his base. My guess is that he was planning to hand over that photograph. So the question is to whom?"

Ben gave an uneasy chuckle. "You're not suggesting that Lord Westerham or one of his neighbours is working for the Jerries?"

Max Knight gave him a long stare. "Surely you are aware that there are pro-German sentiments among certain members of the aristocracy. The Duke of Windsor is a prime example. He couldn't wait to visit Hitler in his own lair. Why else do you think he was shipped off to be governor of the Bahamas? So that the Americans can keep an eye on him and foil any plot to put him in power here as a puppet king."

"Gosh," Ben said. "But having German connections, or even German sympathies, does not mean that any Englishman would actively work to help Germany, surely? Even the Duke of Windsor would do the right thing if approached by Hitler's emissaries. He'd never agree to depose his brother . . ."

"Would he do the right thing?" Max Knight held Ben's gaze. "One hopes he would, but he has already demonstrated weakness and susceptibility to be led, has he not? He abandoned his duty for a woman—for a woman of questionable morals at that. Our present king may not have his brother's charm, but at least he has backbone. He'll see us through if anyone can."

"So you want me to go down to Farleigh and try to root out pro-German sentiments?"

"Go home and keep your eyes and ears open, that's all. Lord Westerham and his neighbours. Say you draw a five-mile radius. Who does that encompass?"

"Including the two or three villages?"

"Possibly. Although I'm sure all the villagers will tell you quickly enough about anyone who is new to the area, who behaves strangely, once went on holiday to Germany, Switzerland, or Austria, or even likes Beethoven. No, I'm interested in bigger fish, my boy. Someone who might be able to do real damage. Who exactly lives at Farleigh these days?"

Ben laughed. "An entire brigade of the Royal West Kent Regiment for one thing."

Max Knight smiled, too. "We have army intelligence working on them. So far they've come up with no leads there at all. The entire West Kent Regiment was asleep and tucked up in their beds when our man dropped in from the sky. And according to their commander, they all seemed to lead remarkably simple and boring lives before the war. Salt of the earth. Backbone of the country. The butcher, the baker, and the candlestick maker. I meant the family."

"There at the moment?" Ben paused, thinking. "Well, Lord and Lady Westerham. Their oldest daughter, Olivia, and two younger daughters, Diana and Phoebe. Olivia is married, but she returned to Farleigh with a baby while her husband is overseas in the army."

"Lord Westerham has other children?"

"Two more daughters. Margot was in Paris, last time I heard. Stuck there for the duration because she wouldn't leave a French boyfriend."

"What was she doing in Paris? Finishing school?"

"Oh no. She was already out in society. She wanted to study fashion design and apprenticed herself to Gigi Armande. Doing quite well at it, so one heard."

Max Knight scribbled something on a pad. "And the other daughter?"

"Pamela. She's doing some kind of war work in London. Secretarial stuff, I believe."

Ben was conscious that Max Knight was staring long and hard at him. The man had a powerful stare, almost as if he could read thoughts, and Ben found a flush was creeping up his cheeks. But then Max Knight looked away.

"All sounds admirable, doesn't it? The quintessential English family and their servants. No new Continental maids or Swiss butlers, I take it?"

Ben grinned. "They are down to a skeleton staff, so my father tells me. All the footmen gone off to fight. And, of course, the family has been allowed to occupy only one wing, so they don't need that many servants. The cook and Soames, the butler, have been with them for donkey's years."

"And what about the neighbours?"

"I take it you mean the upper-class neighbours, not local farmers."

Max Knight gave the ghost of a smile. "Let's say I am more interested in the upper-class neighbours."

"The closest neighbour is my father," Ben said. "His church borders the Farleigh estate. And I can assure you my father never had any interests outside of history and birds."

"Birds?"

"Passionate bird-watcher. He's a typical country vicar—dull as ditch-water, although he's a good-hearted old cove. My mother died when I was a baby. She caught the Spanish flu in 1920, and so my father's been on his own ever since."

"And other neighbours?" Max Knight had clearly dismissed Ben's father as not important.

"There are Colonel and Mrs. Huntley at the Grange. They returned from India in the mid- thirties. He's as true blue as they come. There's an elderly spinster, Miss Hamilton. And then there are the Prescotts.

Sir William and his wife. They have an estate nearby. Nethercote. He's a big noise in the city, as you probably know."

"And they have a son."

Ben nodded. "Jeremy. He and I were at Oxford together. He was RAF. Shot down over France and now in a German prisoner-of-war camp."

"Rotten luck," Max Knight said. There was something in his expression that Ben couldn't read. Almost a private joke he was enjoying. He flushed as Knight asked suddenly, "You weren't attracted to join the RAF yourself, then?"

"I would have liked to, sir. Unfortunately, I was in a plane crash before the war, and my left leg was badly damaged. Doesn't bend enough to climb in or out of planes easily."

"That's bad luck." Max Knight nodded in sympathy. "But at least you're doing useful work here, aren't you? Equally important work."

"If you say so, sir." Ben's face was blank.

"Up till now it hasn't seemed that important?" Max Knight asked, with the hint of a grin.

Ben wondered how that information got onto his files and what else they said about him. He looked up. "Will that be all, sir?"

"For the moment, yes. I'll send a memo over to Mike Radison that I'm borrowing you for a while. From now on, you report only to me. Is that clear? And I don't need to remind you that nothing said here goes any further than this room."

"Of course not, sir."

"And that it is of paramount importance that your neighbours down in Kent have no inkling of why you are there or what you do."

"I'm sure they don't, sir. They think I have a gammy leg and I'm stuck in a desk job in a ministry."

"Then let's keep them thinking that, shall we? You might even drop a hint that the work has become a bit much for you, and you've been advised to take a break."

"You want me to appear mentally unstable as well as physically incapable?" Ben's voice had a sudden sharp edge to it.

Max Knight grinned. "If it suits our purposes. You would be amazed at the cover some of those I recruit invent for themselves."

Ben remembered then that there were rumours about a certain Captain King or Mr. K., the spymaster who lived in Dolphin Square, and a thrill of excitement shot through him that he had just been recruited to be a spy, albeit on the home front.

Ben stood up. Max Knight held out his hand. "Good to meet you, Cresswell. I think you're just the man for the job."

They shook hands. Ben remembered the snake in Knight's pocket. "I say, sir. That snake. Is it some kind of pet? A good-luck charm?"

"I'm a nature lover, Cresswell. An animal lover. I found this poor blighter about to be dispatched by some village children, so I rescued him. He seems to have taken quite well to life in my office."

"Don't you ever worry that he might escape from your pocket?"

"If he does, good luck to him. But I rather think he knows on which side his bread is buttered. I suggest you do the same."

Ben hesitated. "Excuse me, sir, but how do I contact you?"

"You come here, or you send me a telegram with a number where you can be reached. We never use the telephone system, for obvious reasons."

As Ben walked to the door, Max Knight said after him, "That plane crash. Jeremy Prescott was the pilot, wasn't he? Got away without a scratch. I hope there's no bad feelings there."

Ben turned back. "I'd rather be here than in a German stalag, sir. And who knows how banged up he is, after bailing out of a plane." He paused. "It was an accident. Pure and simple. No bad feelings. We were always the best of pals."

He went then. It was only when he was in the lift going down that he realised Maxwell Knight had known all the details of his friends and neighbours before the interview started. It was he who had been investigated and put to the test.

Back at Wormwood Scrubs prison, Ben had just resumed his usual place when Harcourt breezed in. "You're back. Not dismissed on the spot with a curt 'never darken our doors again.'"

"So it would seem," Ben replied.

"Damn. So I can't take over your chair? Mine has started squeaking in a most annoying manner, as well as rocking."

"You can use it for the next week or so if you like. I've been told to take some time off."

"Time off? What for?"

"Apparently I've been overdoing it." Ben grimaced with distaste and found it hard to get the words out.

"Good God. I haven't noticed any hint of someone about to crack up," Harcourt said. He came around to perch on Ben's desk and peered down at him. "Frightfully sorry, old fellow."

"I'm not about to go loony or anything," Ben replied. He wanted to say there was nothing wrong with him. "It's just that the quack felt I should take a couple of weeks off, that's all."

"I wish my doctor would prescribe the same thing," Harcourt said. "I'm dying for strawberry and cream teas and some good village cricket."

"I don't think you'd find enough men still at home to make up a cricket team," Ben said.

"Probably not."

"I never asked," Ben said, deciding that attack was the best form of defence, "but why aren't you in uniform?"

"Strictly between ourselves, it's flat feet, old sport. Terribly embarrassing, I know. I usually tell people I have a dickey heart. Feel as fit as a fiddle, but the local doctor wouldn't sign off on me. Frankly, I'd rather be out fighting somewhere exotic and foreign. And not having to explain myself to every Tom, Dick, and Harry that I pass in the street."

"I know. It's pretty bloody, isn't it?" Ben agreed.

"At least you can lift up your trouser and show them your leg," Harcourt said. "I can tell they don't believe me about the heart, and they certainly wouldn't go along with the feet."

There was an awkward silence. "So you'll be going home for a bit?" Harcourt said.

"Just for a bit."

"Lovely. Kent in late spring. Apple blossoms. Bluebells. You lucky duck. Mind if I come down and visit? My folks are in Yorkshire. Too far away for a weekend pass."

Ben was surprised. "Of course not. You're welcome anytime. My father actually has quite a good cook. No horsemeat on the menu, I can guarantee."

"So you're off today, then?" Harcourt looked down at him again. "Going to clear out your desk?"

"It's not the end of term at school. And I'm not leaving anything confidential. Just a few pencils and the like."

"Only I heard that we might be moving down to Blenheim Palace soon to join the rest of B Division. In which case . . ."

"In which case you'll probably get a new chair," Ben said.

Harcourt stood up again with that easy grace and started to leave, but then he turned back. "So it was nothing to do with Dolphin Square, then?"

Ben turned to look at him in surprise. "Dolphin Square?"

"Yes, your little jaunt today."

"Isn't that the big ugly block of flats where rich people keep a London pied-à-terre?"

"That's right. But one also hears that"—Harcourt shrugged—"oh, never mind. I probably got the wrong end of the stick again."

"What made you think I might be going to Dolphin Square?" Ben asked.

"It's just that, well, I happened to be passing—and you know how you can hear through the bloody walls of these partitions—and I heard Radison saying, 'You want him at Dolphin Square? Now?' And then he came out into the hall and started looking for you. So naturally, being a chap who is quick on the uptake, I put two and two together."

"And made five, I'm afraid," Ben said. "So what does go on in Dolphin Square? Is it a cover for some kind of special operations?"

"How would I know?" Harcourt said. "I'm just a lowly peon like you. It's just that"—he walked over to the door and closed it—"one does hear a certain chap who goes by various names operates out of an office there. And he answers to nobody, except presumably Churchill and the king."

"Crikey," Ben said. "Is he on our side?"

"One hopes so. It seems he could do a lot of damage if he weren't."

"Then it's lucky we're stuck with good old plodding but reliable Radison, isn't it?" Ben said. He removed several pencils and a lined school notebook from his desk, along with some Rowntrees Fruit Gums, now gone hard, and a map of the Underground, and dropped them into his briefcase. "I hope to see you in a couple of weeks. Take care of yourself."

"You, too, old chap. Get well soon." And much to Ben's surprise, Harcourt shook his hand.

CHAPTER NINE

Bletchley Park
May 1941

"You're going on leave?" Trixie demanded. "When?"

Pamela had found her in their room, applying the final touches to her makeup before she headed for the late shift at 4:00 p.m. While other girls wore sensible two-piece suits or cotton frocks to work, Trixie always seemed to look as if she were about to attend a fancy luncheon. Today it was a flowery silk tea dress.

"At the end of this current rotation," Pamela said.

"But that's not fair." Trixie shook her head in annoyance so that her curls bounced. She wore her dark-brown hair tightly permed in Shirley Temple fashion, unlike Pamela's soft ash-blonde pageboy. "I applied for leave last week and was turned down. I was told that I took a whole week at Christmas, and I'd have to wait until July at the earliest before I could go again."

"Obviously, you're more valuable than I am," Pamela said.

"Is there a reason for this sudden departure?" Trixie asked. "I hope it's not bad news and compassionate leave."

"Well, it is in a way," Pamela said. "I just heard that a friend of mine has made it home to England after escaping from a German prisoner-of-war camp. We'd had no news of him for ages. We didn't know if he was alive or dead. When I found out, I was so shocked that I collapsed outside the station. I've never done anything that stupid in my life—well, only once or twice I fainted when I went to early communion service at church without any breakfast. I went through a rather religious phase in my teens."

"Golly," Trixie said, "I certainly never did. But the fainting is quite understandable. I feel awful when I'm on night shift. One never gets proper sleep. And trying to read in that poor light always gives one a headache, doesn't it?" She came over and put an arm around Pamela's shoulder. "But clever old you. You faint and make them think you're cracking up and need a break, thus achieving exactly what you wanted—to go straight home to see your chap."

"I don't know if he's exactly my chap," Pamela replied, turning pink. "We grew up together. We went dancing and things a few times, but it was never serious. He never asked me to be his girl before he went into the RAF. He hardly ever wrote. And I'm sure I wasn't the only one in his life. He's awfully good-looking and rich."

"My dear, I might just have to come down to the depths of the Kent countryside to visit you," Trixie said with a wicked grin. "Good-looking and rich. Who could resist?"

"Hands off," Pamela said, laughing. "This one is mine. At least I hope he's mine. We'll see in a few days." She put her hands up to her face. "Golly, how exciting. I can hardly wait."

"You should be prepared for a shock, old thing," Trixie said quietly. "I mean, if he crashed or bailed out of a plane, he might be quite badly wounded. Disfigured, you know."

Pamela clearly hadn't considered this. She paused, then said firmly, "He was strong enough to escape from a prison camp and make it safely home all the way across France. I think that was jolly brave of him."

"Or foolish," Trixie said. "If I were in a fairly decent prisoner-of-war camp, I think I'd stay put and sit out the war playing cards rather than being sent back to fight."

"It's different if you're a fighter pilot," Pamela said. "To them it's a huge game. Like chess in the air. Jeremy loved it."

"Jeremy? Are we talking about Jeremy Prescott?"

"Yes. Do you know him?"

Trixie's eyes lit up. "My dear, he was the talk of all the debs during our season. Eligible bachelor number one. Lucky old you if you snag him."

"I fully intend to," Pamela said. She bent to retrieve her suitcase from under the bed and opened it, ready to start packing.

The train from Bletchley seemed to take an eternity. It was shunted into sidings several times to let goods trains and troop trains pass. As the train entered London, recent bomb damage became evident. Blackened shells of buildings, a house with one wall missing revealing a complete bedroom still intact with a brass bed, a quilt with pink roses on it, and a china wash basin in the corner. On the next street a whole row had been demolished, yet one fish-and-chip shop stood unscathed in the midst of destruction with a notice tacked to the door, "Still Open for Business." Pamela shut her eyes, willing the images to go away. She was desperately tired, having come straight from work, but even the rhythmic rocking of the train couldn't lull her to sleep. She had been decidedly on edge, ever since she had overheard a conversation in her hut the night before.

The long hut in which she worked was partitioned into small rooms on either side of a central corridor. In the middle of her shift, she had needed to heed the call of nature. She had to walk the length of the hut to go to the ladies' lavatory at the far end. She had almost reached the far door when she remembered she had left her torch behind. In the blackout, she would not find the lavatories without her torch. As she returned, she heard two male voices, speaking softly.

"So are you going to tell her before she goes on leave?"

"Absolutely not. If you want to know, I still think it's a mistake. I'm going to try and talk the old man out of it."

"But she's damned good. You know that as well as I do. The right person for the job."

"Is she? She's one of them."

"She could prove to be useful in her position."

"Depends where her loyalty lies—with us or with them. I don't think we should take the risk, old chap."

Then one of them walked across and closed the door. And Pamela was absolutely sure the conversation was not meant for her ears and that they were talking about her.

So what could they possibly mean? she asked herself. Had they any reason to question her loyalty? And to whom did they think she might be loyal? Surely they couldn't suspect she was a German spy? She waited impatiently for the train to pull into Euston Station.

Charing Cross Station was in its usual state of chaos as Pamela came up from the Underground that had taken her across London from Euston: servicemen of the various branches tramping past to a new assignment or going home on leave prior to being shipped out to Africa or the Far East. Small children with labels around their necks waiting together in a group, ready to be evacuated, while mothers stood watching behind the barrier, staring with anxious eyes. The train on the adjoining platform was about to pull out. Almost every window had a serviceman leaning out, saying good-bye to his sweetheart or his mother. One girl stood on tiptoe to kiss her darling. "Take care of yourself, Joe," she said.

"Don't worry about me. I'll be just fine," he answered. "I'm like a cat with nine lives, I am."

Pamela looked at them with pity and longing. How many young men had said that same thing and never returned? And yet, she envied the way they gazed into each other's eyes, as if nobody else existed in the whole world. Her train was already standing at the platform, and she fought her way aboard with the rest of the waiting crowd. She had chosen a carriage with a corridor and squeezed past soldiers with their kit bags who had already taken up position there, chatting and smoking as if this were a Sunday jaunt.

Some of them called out harmlessly flirtatious things as she passed. "Sit here, darling." One patted a kit bag. "We'll keep you entertained during the trip. Care for a Woodbine?"

She brushed them off good-naturedly, knowing that the bravado was necessary, and a smile from a pretty girl was just what they needed right now. When she found a compartment with an empty seat, she took it, gratefully. The carriage was already occupied by a mother with a toddler, sucking a thumb contentedly on her lap, a young Wren in uniform, and two stout middle-aged ladies, complaining bitterly that the railways no longer provided ladies-only compartments. "It's a disgrace having to squeeze past those men," the chubbier one said. "Do you know that one of them said, 'Take it easy, mother. You're not exactly giving me a thrill.'"

"Shocking. The world has gone mad."

They looked at Pamela for sympathy. "I hope they didn't accost you, my dear?"

"Nothing I couldn't handle." Pamela smiled.

A whistle blew. There were running feet and slamming doors as the train lurched forward and pulled out of the station. Those newly arrived started moving past, along the corridor. Pamela turned away and stared out the window as the train crossed the railway bridge over the Thames, and a panorama of the City of London came into view, with the dome of St. Paul's rising bravely among ruins. When they pulled into Waterloo Station on the south bank, she saw that someone had come to lean against the door of her compartment—a young man in a tweed jacket. There was something definitely familiar about the way that dark hair curled around his collar. She wrenched open the compartment door, making the man step away hastily and turn around.

"Ben? Good heavens. It is you," she said, her face lighting up. "I thought I recognised the back of your head."

"Pamela?" He looked at her incredulously. "What are you doing here?"

"Same thing as you, I suppose. Going home for a few days. Come on in. There's room for one more."

"Is there? I thought it might be ladies only. If the other ladies don't mind . . ."

"Of course they don't." Pamela patted the seat across from her, and Ben put his bag up on the rack.

"What a coincidence that we're going home at the same time," she said, still smiling at him. "It is so good to see you. It's been ages."

"I got a brief glimpse of you in church last Christmas," he said. "You're looking awfully well."

"And you, too. So they're not working you too hard?"

"A lot of boring stuff. Rather repetitious, but necessary, I suppose," he replied with a self-deprecating smile.

"You're with one of the ministries, aren't you?"

"Attached to one of them. Research. Looking up lots of useless information. Aren't you doing the same sort of thing?"

"Similar. Clerical stuff. Frightfully boring filing and things. But someone has to do it."

"Are you in London itself?" he asked.

"No, my branch has been evacuated outside to Berkshire. Have to keep the records safe from bombs, you know. How about you?"

"I've been in London, but I'm not sure where I might be sent next. It seems they are sending everyone out to the country these days."

There was a silence. They exchanged a smile.

Ben cleared his throat. "Any word on Jeremy?"

Pamela's face brightened. "You haven't heard? You obviously haven't been reading the papers recently."

"Never read them. Always full of bad news."

She leaned closer to him across the aisle. "He's home, Ben. He escaped from the camp and made it all the way across France. Isn't that wonderful?"

"Amazing," Ben said. "Well, if anyone could escape from a prison camp and make it halfway across Europe without getting caught, it would be Jeremy."

"I know." She sighed. "I could hardly believe it when I read it in the newspaper, but I telephoned my family, and he's actually back at Nethercote, recuperating from his ordeal. You must come with me to see him."

"Are you sure you want me tagging along?"

"Of course. Jeremy will want to see you as much as he wants to see me. And if he is . . . you know . . . banged up or something . . . well, then, I'd rather have you there with me."

"All right," he said. "I'll come with you."

"You must come up to the house as soon as you've said hello to your father. I'm sure they'll all want to see you."

"How are they all?"

"I haven't been home since Christmas, but as far as I can tell from Mah's letters, Pah is perpetually annoyed at having to live in such cramped conditions—as if one wing of Farleigh is actually cramped." She laughed. "He's also annoyed that he's too old to do his bit, as he puts it. He's enlisted in the local home guard, but I suspect he's just a nuisance to them, wanting to give the orders. Mah just goes on in her usual sweet way, oblivious to everything. Livvy's taken over the top floor for little Charles's nursery. She's become very maternal and stodgy."

"Any news on your sister Margot?"

Pamela's face clouded. "Not for ages. It's awfully worrying. One hopes she is holed up somewhere with her French count, but one does hear terrible things about what's going on in France these days."

"And the two young ones are still at home? Or has Dido found herself a job?"

"She'd love to, but Pah says that nineteen is too young to be away from home. She's positively bursting with frustration. You know Dido—not the sort to sit at home and practise the piano. I suppose I can understand. It's very unfair on her that she won't get a season like the rest of us. No dances. No chance to meet eligible men. Last time I saw her, she was talking of running away and going to work in a factory."

"I'm sure she could find a job less dramatic than one in a factory," Ben said. "Couldn't you find someone to take her on where you work? They always seem to need extra girls for office work, don't they? She could billet with you."

"Unfortunately, I'm already sharing a room with a pal," she said. "What about your ministry? Could you do something for her? She could probably take the train up to London every day if she had a job. Pah might not object to that."

"We work shifts, that's the problem. She wouldn't be able to find a train up to London in the middle of the night, and I'm sure your father wouldn't want her walking around in the blackout. It's hard enough for me, and I simply have to get to the nearest Underground station."

Pamela made a face. "I know. I work shifts, too. It's beastly, isn't it? My body never gets used to night shifts, and I feel awful with no sleep."

"I couldn't agree more," Ben said. "Actually, that's why I was lucky enough to get some leave. They said I'd been overdoing it."

There was a snort from one of the elderly women by the window. "Overdoing it," she said, turning to glare at Ben. "You want to try being out in the desert like my grandson. Fighting Rommel, that's what he's doing. Not sitting comfortably in an office in London."

"That's enough, Tessie." The other woman reached across to rest a hand on her friend's. She looked across at Ben and Pamela. "She's had a shock. Her son's just been called up—at thirty-nine years old. She's only got the one son."

"I'm sorry," Ben said, "but . . ."

"Mr. Cresswell survived a very bad aeroplane crash," Pamela said angrily. "Show them your leg, Ben."

The first woman went bright red. "Oh, I'm sorry. I spoke out of turn. I'm upset, you see. This war's making all of us on edge, all of the time."

There was an embarrassed silence in the compartment.

"The boys where I work get the same thing," Pamela muttered to Ben. "It's so unfair. Not everybody needs to carry a gun. Wars can't be won without the right kind of support."

"Sometimes I'm tempted to go out and buy a uniform," he said. "It would certainly make things easier."

"Until they asked to see your identity discs and you weren't wearing any."

Identity discs, Ben thought. That parachutist would have been found out as soon as any military police stopped him and asked for his number. So he definitely wasn't planning to go far. Max Knight was right. His contact had to be in the immediate neighbourhood.

They changed trains in Sevenoaks and waited for the local train to go one stop to Hildenborough.

"It's a long walk from the station these days," Ben said. "It's too bad trains stopped calling at Farleigh Halt."

Pamela laughed. "We can't expect trains to stop just for us during wartime, Ben. At this moment being an aristocrat means nothing, and quite right, too. Suddenly, we're all equal."

"Is someone coming to pick you up?" Ben looked around for a waiting car.

Pamela shook her head. "I didn't tell them I was coming. I thought I'd surprise them. Everyone needs the occasional nice surprise these days, don't they?"

"I didn't tell my father I was coming, either. Are you up to a couple of miles with a suitcase? I can carry it for you if you like."

"You have your own bag," she said. "And I'm fit enough to do it. We do a lot of bike riding to get around where I work. It's a glorious day, isn't it? A walk through the countryside is just what the doctor ordered."

"It's certainly nice to breathe good fresh air again," Ben said as they set off down a lane. "The air in London is perpetually full of smoke and dust from bombs."

"I'm lucky. I'm out in the country, and I have fields and trees around me."

"Where exactly did you say you are?" he asked.

"About an hour north of London. We've taken over a big house. Definitely not as pretty as Farleigh."

"Some of our boys are being sent out to Blenheim Palace."

"Golly. That's quite a step up for most people, isn't it?"

Ben laughed. "I gather from reports that it isn't particularly comfortable. They've partitioned it into horrible plywood cubicles, and there is no heat, and bats inhabit the top floor."

"Sounds lovely." She looked up at him, and his eyes held hers for a moment. He had awfully nice eyes, she thought suddenly. That deep greeny blue, like looking into the ocean. Strange that she'd never noticed before. "I'm so glad to see you again," she said at last. "You never change. I feel as if you're dear Ben, steady as a rock. Always there for me."

"That's me. Good old Ben," he said, then regretted his sarcasm. "But yes, I am always there whenever you need me."

She reached across and slipped her hand into his. They walked side by side in silence while larks rose from new hayfields, singing overhead, and the scent of apple blossom was sweet in the air.

"Will you come and see Jeremy with me this afternoon?" she asked eventually, breaking the spell.

"I said I would. Why don't we both stop off at my father's place and have something to drink, then I'll carry your case the rest of the way to Farleigh with you."

"Lovely." She gave him that dazzling smile again.

CHAPTER TEN

All Saints vicarage, Elmsleigh, Kent
May 1941

The vicarage was a big redbrick Victorian building at the edge of the churchyard. They passed the weatherworn gravestones, and Ben let himself in at the front door. It was never locked.

"Well, I never. Mr. Ben!" Mrs. Finch threw up her hands in surprise, coming out of the kitchen at the sound of the door closing. Then the look of surprise turned to astonishment. "And Lady Pamela, too. It's good to see you, your ladyship."

"How are you, Mrs. Finch?" Pamela asked.

"Can't complain, your ladyship. We're getting along as well as can be expected. A lot better than the poor blighters in London, getting bombed every night. And we don't do too badly for food, either. I've got a good little kitchen garden going out back, and the two hens provide us with eggs when the rats or foxes don't get at them first. Added to that, everyone's fond of the vicar around here, and we often find the odd bit of meat or fish on the doorstep. I shouldn't be surprised if they are not illegal or even black market, but of course I don't tell the vicar. What he don't know can't hurt him."

And then she chuckled. "You're in luck today, as it happens. We were given a brace of pigeons yesterday, and I've made pigeon pie. I'm just about to get the vicar's dinner for him, so why don't you stay to join us, your ladyship?"

She still called it dinner, although the vicar had tried to educate her for years that the working classes had their dinner at midday, but the upper classes had luncheon.

"I really should be getting home. The family will be waiting to see me," Pamela said.

Without thinking, Ben covered her hand with his own. "Do stay," he said. "If the stuff you've been eating is anything like the stodge from our cafeteria, then I can assure you that Mrs. Finch's pigeon pie will seem like manna from heaven."

Pamela did not withdraw her hand. Instead, she smiled. "After a buildup like that, how could I resist? Thank you, Mrs. Finch." She looked around at the well-worn oak furniture, highly polished for years by Mrs. Finch and by the housekeepers who came before her. Then her gaze moved from the view out of the window across the fields to where she glimpsed the shape of Farleigh rising above the trees. And she thought, *This is where I feel safe.*

Reverend Cresswell came up the path from the church just as Mrs. Finch was laying the table. A smile crossed his tired face. "Well, this is a nice surprise, my boy. We had no idea you were coming."

"It was all very last minute," Ben said, going over to shake hands with his father. "Someone decided I was due for a few days' leave, so here I am."

"And Pamela, too." He turned to smile at her, then examined her critically. "Looking a bit peaky, my dear."

"It's night shifts. I can't seem to sleep during the daytime."

"Of course you can't. But a few days here will have you right as rain. Good food. Country air. You can put the war aside for a few days. It's just as it always was out here."

"Apart from an army regiment living in my house," Pamela reminded him.

"And that body in your field," Mrs. Finch said as she put the pie on a trivet on the dining table.

"Body? In a field?" Pamela asked.

"A parachutist whose chute didn't open," Mrs. Finch said with great relish. "They say he was an awful mess."

"How terrible for him. Who was he?"

Mrs. Finch leaned closer. "He was wearing an army uniform, but it's my belief he was one of them German spies. They say they're everywhere these days. Even dressed up as nuns, if you can believe it."

"Mrs. Finch, what have I told you about gossip?" Reverend Cresswell said. "Remember the posters: 'Careless Talk Costs Lives.' We have no reason to believe this poor man was anything more than the victim of a training exercise gone wrong. I protested when they had him taken away. I'd like to have given him a decent burial."

Leaning forward to cut into the piecrust, he was clearly dismissing the matter. The rich aroma of herbs came out, and he nodded in satisfaction. "Now that's what I call a proper meal. Give me your plate, young lady, and you'll have some real food for the first time in ages."

They ate until they were full. The flaky crust covered a succulent portion of young bird in rich herb gravy and was accompanied by cauliflower with a white sauce, then followed by stewed apples and custard.

"I really should be getting home." Pamela stood up. "But I'm dying to see Jeremy. I don't suppose the family will mind much if I go over to Nethercote first. I didn't tell them exactly when I'd be arriving. And you said you'd come with me, Ben." She looked at him appealingly.

"If you want me to." He stood up also, placing his napkin on the table. "All right with you, Father, if I walk Pamma over to Nethercote?"

"You don't have to ask my permission, my boy. You're a grown man now. If Pamela wants you with her when she goes to visit her young man, then by all means."

Ben reacted to the words *her young man* as if they were a punch in the gut. He knew they were true, of course. They had always been true. But he'd always had hope, especially when Jeremy was reported missing. And now his job was to deliver Pamela back to his rival. He wondered if she realised, if she had any inkling of what he was feeling?

They set off through the village. The one street there was almost devoid of life. A bell tinkled as a woman came out of Markham's General Store and Post Office with a basket over her arm. She greeted them with a polite nod. "Lady Pamela. Mr. Ben. Pleasant weather for the time of year, isn't it?" And went on her way, as if their sudden return was nothing out of the ordinary. London and points beyond Sevenoaks were out of her sphere of experience and thus not of interest. From the school came the sound of children's voices chanting a times table. A farm cart came toward them with a load of manure. They hadn't spoken to each other since they left the vicarage. Now Pamela turned to him.

"Nothing changes here, does it? It's just like it always was."

"Except no young men," he said.

She nodded.

They left the village behind them, and the road narrowed to a lane with a riot of flowers growing from the banks. As they came to the impressive wrought-iron gates at the entrance to the Prescotts' home, Nethercote, Pamela suddenly froze.

"I suppose it's all right to go in uninvited? Should we have telephoned first to let them know we were coming?"

"When did we ever need to wait for an invitation to Jeremy's house?" Ben had to laugh.

"But things are different now," she said, her forehead creased into a worried frown. "Jeremy's home from a prison camp. He may not want to . . . to see us."

Ben took a deep breath. "It's my belief that he's been dreaming about seeing you again since the day he took off in that plane," he said.

She flashed him a nervous smile.

"And if we are told that he's not up to visitors, then we go away."

"Ben, I'm so glad you're here," she said. "I would have flunked it and run off like a frightened rabbit."

"You're never like a frightened rabbit, Pamma. You're the strongest of any of us. Come on. Let's go and surprise Jeremy."

They passed through the gateway and walked up the broad gravel drive. The elegant Georgian house stood ahead of them, red brick with white trim, perfectly proportioned, with formal gardens on either side of the drive. The beds were a mass of tulips. Wisteria hung from trellises. The lawns were perfectly manicured. It was clear that gardeners were still at work here, war or no war.

As they approached the house, they saw an old bicycle, standing beside the front steps, looking out of place in the otherwise perfect scene. Ben was about to comment on it when the front door opened and Lady Diana Sutton came out.

"Of course I will. Thanks awfully. Bye," she called, waving to an invisible person inside as she ran down the steps.

Then she saw Pamela and Ben. "Hello, you two. What a surprise!"

"What are you doing here, Dido?" Pamela asked in a clipped voice.

"Well, that's what I call a warm welcome," Dido said. "How about 'It's lovely to see you again after so long, dear sister'?"

"Well, of course I'm pleased to see you." Pamela still sounded flustered. "It's just that . . ."

"If you must know, I've been representing the family and visiting Jeremy to cheer him up." She picked up the bicycle. "Somebody had to."

Then she rode off without another word, her tyres scrunching on the gravel.

PART THREE

MARGOT

CHAPTER ELEVEN

Paris
May 1941

She had not realised before that fear had a smell. She had always been told that dogs can smell fear, but she'd never heard it said of humans. Yet, she identified it now—sweet and palpable—as she sat on the chair in a dark room. She was not sure whether the fear was coming from her own pores or was part of the building, oozing from the walls where so many people had felt terror and desperation. She had been blindfolded in the car that brought her here, but she did not need to be told where she was. She was in Gestapo headquarters, and they were leaving her alone in the darkness to break her spirit.

Lady Margot Sutton sat on the upright wooden chair, not moving, staring out into blackness. She had no idea how long she had been sitting there or whether it was light outside yet. Clearly, the room had no window because even with blackout curtains, there were always chinks of light. They had come for her in the middle of the night—two men, who said nothing more than "You must come with us, please" in English.

Her upbringing had kicked in. "What do you mean? Why should I come with you? I'll do no such thing. It's the middle of the night, and I was asleep."

Then one of them said, "You will come with us now, Fräulein. We will give you one minute to put some clothes on." He eyed her lacy robe with distaste.

It was the word *Fräulein* that did it. They were not in uniform, but they were Germans. That could mean only one thing. Gestapo. And one did not resist the Gestapo. All the same, she was not going to let them see she was afraid. Her aristocratic English background was her one trump card at the moment. The Germans respected the English aristocracy, having given up their own.

"This is most irregular," she said, her voice becoming an imitation of Queen Victoria not amused. "On whose authority are you here? What can you possibly want with me?"

"We just obey orders, Fräulein," he said. "You will find out soon enough who wishes to speak to you."

"I am not 'Fräulein,'" she said. "I am Lady Margaret Sutton, daughter of Lord Westerham."

"We know very well who you are." The man's face was expressionless. "One minute, Lady Margaret, or we will be forced to take you wearing your nightclothes."

She fled back into her bedroom, mind racing. What should she take with her? The pistol Gaston had given her? No, her best chance was to convey innocence and indignation. *And after all, I am innocent,* she told herself. *I know nothing. I can tell them nothing.*

Thus reassured, she grabbed a black suit that had come from the House of Armande and put on a white blouse and pearls. She was not going to let those bastards see that she was in any way afraid of them. Then the thought crossed her mind: *What if Gaston comes back to the flat and I'm not here?* How could she let him know where she was?

"Lady Margaret?" a voice called outside her door.

"I'm just brushing my hair," she called back. "Do I need to take a toothbrush with me, or will I be returning home immediately?"

"I suspect that's up to you," the voice said.

As she ran lipstick over her lips, she noticed Madame Armande's card lying on her dressing table. She took the lipstick, printed "CALL HER" on the back and left it lying there. Gaston was quick on the uptake, and Armande knew everybody in Paris. She'd know how to find a missing Englishwoman. *If I'm still alive by then,* Margot thought.

It was cold and damp in that dark space where they had put her, and she felt an urgent need to pee. But she willed herself not to. Rumour had it that certain royal persons trained their bodies to go without bathrooms all day when on tours abroad. She thought she detected a shout in the distance. Or was it a cry? She couldn't tell if it came from outside the building or inside. She stiffened when she heard footsteps coming closer—heavy footsteps of booted feet. They came very close, then passed, and she let out a small sigh of relief as they receded in the distance. She turned her mind to other things: Farleigh in the summer. Tennis on the lawn. Strawberries and cream. Pah, red-faced and wearing that ridiculous white floppy hat. Mah always looking cool and composed, no matter what her brood was doing. "Farleigh," she whispered. "I want to go home."

She jumped as a door opened, letting in a beam of light. A man came in—a tall man wearing a German officer's uniform. He turned on a switch with a click, and Margot blinked in the sudden light. For the first time, she saw she was in a featureless room, about ten-by-eight feet. In the corner was a bucket she could have used, had she known it was there. The officer pulled up a second chair and sat facing her.

"Lady Margaret, I must apologise for the rough and impolite way you were brought here. I'm afraid my order to bring in someone for questioning is sometimes misinterpreted. Would you like some coffee?"

Coffee was something rarely seen now in Paris. She heard herself saying "Yes, please, that would be very nice" before she had time to consider whether she should remain aloof and defiant. *Maybe I'm reading too much into this,* she thought. *Maybe they just want to ask me some small question about why I'm still here.* Coffee was brought, with cream and sugar. It seemed she had never tasted anything so delicious. "Thank you," she said. "You're very kind."

The officer nodded. "My name is Dinkslager. Baron von Dinkslager. So you see we are social equals. We just need to ask you a few questions, then you can return home." His English was excellent, with only the slightest trace of accent. And he was extremely handsome, having an almost-matinee-idol bone structure and the arrogance of a German officer. "You are Lady Margaret Sutton, daughter of Lord Westerham, is that correct?"

"That is correct."

"And would you tell us why you are still in Paris? Why did you not go home before the occupation, when you could?"

"I was studying fashion design with Madame Armande," she said. "I suppose I was naïve, but I thought that life in Paris would be allowed to go on as usual."

"But it is," he said.

"Hardly. Nobody has enough to eat. We haven't seen coffee like this in months."

"Blame your English bombers for that. And the Resistance. If they destroy supply lines, then it is not our fault the Parisians don't have enough to eat."

He crossed his legs. He was wearing high black boots, perfectly polished. "So fashion design was the only reason you decided to stay."

"No," she admitted, seeing no reason to lie. "I fell in love with a Frenchman."

"The Count de Varennes. A fellow aristocrat," he said.

She nodded. "That's right."

"And where is the Count de Varennes now?"

"I don't know. I haven't seen him for months."

"When was the last time you saw him?"

"Just after Christmas. He told me he had to leave Paris."

"Did he say why?"

"I understood he had properties in the South of France that needed attending to. Also, his grandmother at the château was growing increasingly frail, and he wanted to see if he could do anything to help her."

"His grandmother." A smile crossed his lips. "You are either very naïve or a very good liar, Lady Margaret. His grandmother has been dead for five years."

"Then I'm obviously very naïve," she replied. "Our nanny washed out our mouths with soap if we ever told a lie. The threat of the soap has stuck."

"Did it not cross your mind that your lover might be working for the Resistance?"

"Yes, it did cross my mind," she said defiantly, "but Gaston would tell me nothing. He said it was better that way. Then, if I was ever questioned, I could truthfully say that I knew nothing."

"And you have not seen him since Christmas?"

"No."

"Would it surprise you then to know that he has been in Paris several times since then?"

Margot fought to keep her expression neutral. "Yes, it would surprise me. Perhaps he did not wish to put me at risk. He is a very considerate man."

"Or perhaps he had found a new love?" The slightest of smirks crossed Dinkslager's lips.

"Perhaps he has. He is also a very attractive man."

"And if he has found a new love?"

"Then I suppose I'd have to get on with my life, go back to my fashion design, and learn to live without him."

He chuckled now. "I admire the British, Lady Margaret. A French girl who loses her lover would weep and beat her breast."

"Then we should be glad I'm not French. So much easier to deal with."

He was still smiling. "I like you, Lady Margaret. I like your spirit. I am also from a noble family. We understand each other well."

"Then you will understand that I'm speaking the truth when I say I have nothing to tell you. I lead a simple life in Paris. I go to the workshop. I do what Madame Armande tells me. I go back to my small apartment in the Ninth. I eat a simple supper and go to bed."

"You would no doubt like to go home to England now, given the chance."

She hesitated. *Of course I'd like to go home, you idiot,* she wanted to shout. But instead she said, "I understand life in England is no more pleasant than life in Paris at present, what with constant bombings and the threat of an imminent invasion."

He uncrossed his legs, tilting the wooden chair backward as he looked at her. "You have not heard from Gaston de Varennes for months. That is correct?"

"It is."

"So it would surprise you to learn that we have him in our custody at this moment?"

This really did jar her composure. He saw it in her eyes, the sudden flicker of apprehension before she said, "Yes. It does surprise me."

"And alarm you?"

"Of course it alarms me." Her voice took on a sudden sharp edge. "Herr Baron, I love Gaston de Varennes, whether he still loves me or not."

"And you approve of his work with the Resistance?"

"As I told you, I had no idea he was with the Resistance until now. But he is a Frenchman. I can understand his desire to drive out invaders of his country. If the Germans invaded Britain, I'd expect my family to do the same."

He let the chair legs fall with a sudden clatter as he leaned closer to her. "Gaston de Varennes is proving to be very stubborn, Lady Margaret.

You can understand that his life is not worth *that*"—he snapped his fingers, and the sound echoed, surprisingly loud in the confined space—"unless he tells us what he knows."

"You want me to persuade him to talk? That is ridiculous, Baron. I am flattered that you think I have that great a hold over him, but I can assure you I don't."

"You do realise, my lady, that if I snap my fingers right now, you will be dragged down the stairs to a room much less pleasant than this one, and down there you would be made to tell us every single little detail of your life."

Again, she forced her face to remain composed. "I have heard about such things, but I really do assure you, Baron von Dinkslager, that I have nothing to tell that you would find remotely interesting."

"Trust me, Lady Margaret, if you are taken to such a room, you would wish you had something to tell. You would invent things to tell us. You would betray your lover, your mother, anything to get out of there alive."

Margot stared at him coldly. "If you are going to kill me, then please, do it now and get it over with. I see you wear a revolver. Shoot me now."

"I have no wish to shoot you. You are much more valuable to me alive than dead. But I am surprised. Would you let your lover go to his death without fighting for him? Truly the British are so cold."

"I assure you I am not cold, and I don't want Gaston to die. But I rather suspect that nothing I can say will make you change your minds." Then suddenly it dawned on her. "I understand now. You don't think I can tell you anything important. I'm the bait, aren't I? You are going to use me to make him talk."

"I suppose it depends on how precious you are to him, and whether he puts you before his country. We shall have to wait and see, shan't we?" He broke off and looked up in surprise. Outside the door came raised voices, one of them female. Dinkslager had just stood up when the door burst open and Gigi Armande stormed in. She wore a black fur draped carelessly around her shoulders, and her face was perfectly made up. Even if Margot hadn't known her, there would be no mistaking who she was.

"What is this?" the German officer demanded in French. "Who let you in here?"

"My poor petite," she said, completely ignoring him and going over to give Margot a kiss on both cheeks. "What were they thinking, bringing you to a place like this? You should be ashamed of yourself, Baron, for intimidating an innocent child like this. A young British aristocrat, no less, who leads a perfectly blameless life, slaving away for me making dresses. I am Madame Armande, in case you are the one person in Paris who does not recognise me. I assure you that the highest-ranking officers in your German army know me well and allow me to live at the Ritz."

"Madame Armande," he said, "I am well aware who you are. This innocent young lady is the mistress of a leader in the Resistance. We have taken him prisoner, but he refuses to cooperate. We are hoping this young lady can make him see sense."

"I can see her point of view," Armande said, putting a protective arm around Margot's shoulder. "If he talks, you'll kill him anyway, will you not? And if he talks and you don't kill him, his fellows in the Resistance will kill him for you."

"We could come to some sort of agreement, Madame. You see, this young lady might prove more valuable to us than a captured Resistance fighter."

"In what way?"

He turned back to Margot. "She moves in the highest circles in England. Your family knows the Churchills, I think? And the Duke of Westminster? And any number of members of the House of Lords."

"Yes, my family does. But I don't see . . ."

"I'm going to make you a proposition. I'll free the Count de Varennes if you agree to do us a small favour."

She stared at him suspiciously. "What kind of favour? And what guarantee do I have that he'll be released? That he's not already dead?"

"You have no guarantee"—he paused, spreading his hands in a gesture of futility, then added—"but you have a chance to save him. Better than knowing one hundred percent that he will die a painful death and that you might follow suit."

"Don't speak to her in that way," Madame Armande said. "I am taking her with me right now. She shall stay at the Ritz with me, under my protection, and I will go straight to your top-ranking generals to protest the way she has been treated."

Dinkslager shrugged. "You are a pragmatist, Madame. Of this we have heard. Take her with you, then. I hold you responsible for her. But make her see sense. If she agrees to do a small favour for us, I will personally guarantee that she gets home to England." He turned to Margot. "You may go, for the moment, but we will have another little chat in a day or so. Think about what I have proposed. But don't think for too long. I cannot keep Varennes alive indefinitely. Nor can I keep you at liberty. Please do not think of doing anything foolish like trying to leave Paris. You will be watched. And thank Madame for intervening on your behalf."

Stiff from sitting for so long, Margot stood up and was ushered by her employer from the room. As she reached the door, Madame Armande turned to look back at the German officer and they exchanged a smile.

CHAPTER TWELVE

Nethercote, Elmsleigh, Kent
May 1941

Jeremy was sitting on a chaise in the conservatory, propped up on pillows, a white chenille rug over his knees. The conservatory was at the back of the house, a glass-domed addition to the morning room with white wicker furniture and tropical plants. There were orchids everywhere, and the sweet scent of jasmine hung in the air. The windows looked out on the lawn with the tennis court beyond it. White clouds moved across the sky, sending shadows over the manicured grass. An arched arbour was covered in early roses, and roses also climbed the brick wall that hid the kitchen garden. Jeremy turned at the sound of footsteps. His face lit up as they came toward him.

"My God. My two favourite people. How splendid."

"You're looking wonderful, Jeremy," Pamela said. In truth he looked pale and awfully thin. He was wearing an open-necked white shirt or pyjama jacket. With his hollow cheeks and dark curls on that sea of whiteness, he looked as if he ought to be a Romantic poet—Lord Byron on his deathbed, perhaps. Pamela crossed the tiled floor to him.

"I couldn't believe it when they told me you'd come home. It's like a miracle."

"Don't go all dramatic on me, Pamma," he said. "Come and give me kiss."

Ben hung back while she leaned over Jeremy and kissed his forehead.

"I'd expect something less chaste than that," Jeremy said, laughing. "But not with Ben watching. How are you, old man? It's good to see you."

He held out his hand, and Ben shook it. Jeremy's eyes shone with genuine warmth as he grasped his friend's hand.

"Welcome home, old chap," Ben said. "And I must agree with Pamma. It's a miracle that you're here."

"Actually, it was quite miraculous, when you think of it," Jeremy said. "I certainly beat all the odds."

"Do tell us all the details," Pamma said. "I only know what I read in the newspaper."

"Not much more to tell, really." Jeremy looked a trifle embarrassed. "We planned a breakout from the damned stalag. Someone must have ratted on us because they were waiting for us in the woods at the end of the tunnel. They opened fire and mowed us all down."

"Golly!" Pamela exchanged a look with Ben. "Were you shot, too?"

"I was lucky. The shot went through my shoulder. I flung myself into the river and lay there as if I was dead. I let the current take me, then I hid under some rushes on the bank. I heard them go away, laughing. Then I swam and drifted for as long as I could. I found a piece of driftwood and let that carry me along for a while. Then my stream joined a river in an area where boats were moored. I managed to haul myself on board a low barge—one of a string of barges going upstream—in the dead of night. And can you believe my luck? It was carrying vegetables. I hid myself among the cabbages. It would have been brilliant, but the wound in my shoulder had become infected. I think I was half-delirious most of the time."

"You poor thing." Pamela touched his shoulder gently.

"It wasn't too much fun, I can tell you. We went upstream for a couple of days, then I heard someone speaking French. I decided we were either in France or Belgium. Either way, it was better than Germany. So I made my exit in the middle of the night and struck out westward. Couple of narrow escapes, but eventually my luck held. I bumped into a chap who was with the Resistance. He sent out messages, and they got me across France to a waiting boat."

Jeremy looked from Pamela's face to Ben's.

"Quite an adventure," Ben said.

"Not one I'd care to repeat," Jeremy said. "But fear is a great motivator. I knew if they caught me, they'd shoot me."

"So what will you do now? Will you go back to flying?" Ben asked.

"I'm being given a desk job until I'm deemed fit to fly again," Jeremy said. "The bullet damaged the muscles in my right arm, and I'm a bag of skin and bones. I need building up first, but that will happen rapidly here. Mother is spoiling me, as you can imagine, and Mrs. Treadwell is a wonderful cook. My God. How I dreamed of meals like this when we got our slice of black bread and watery soup."

He stared past them, out of the windows. "I suppose I can't be too impatient to get back to work. It will take a while. I can't help thinking about those other fellows. The ones who broke out of the stalag with me. All mown down in a hail of bullets. And their families, wondering how they are doing. Not knowing they are dead."

He turned back with an attempt at a bright smile. "But here I am. Exactly where I dreamed of being. And look at you, Pamma. God, you're lovelier than I remembered. More grown up."

"I am two years older," Pamma said. "And I've had my twenty-first, so I am officially an adult now."

Ben shifted uneasily at the long glance that passed between them. "I should go and leave you two in peace," he said.

"Would you, old chap?" Jeremy said. "I'm dying to kiss her, you know."

"Of course," Ben answered, trying to keep his voice light. "I'll come and visit you again soon."

"Do. That would be splendid. I'm anxious to hear what you've been doing. Anxious to get back to normality. The last year has been like a bad dream, and now I've woken up."

"I've been doing nothing thrilling, I'm afraid," Ben said. "Good to have you home again."

"Ben, you don't have to . . ." Pamela called after him, but he was already heading back into the darkness of the room beyond. He let himself out.

Jeremy looked at Pamma and eased over to make room next to himself on the chaise longue. "Come here, you delectable creature," he said.

"Which is your bad shoulder?" Pamela asked as she sat beside him. "I don't want to risk hurting you."

"All patched up and healing nicely, thank you," he said. "Here." He slipped his arm around her neck and pulled her toward him. "God, I've dreamed of this moment," he said. His kiss was hard and demanding, his lips crushing against hers so fiercely that she almost cried out in pain. His tongue thrust into her mouth, and his hand fumbled with the buttons of her blouse. One of them broke off with his persistent tugging and went bouncing across the tiled floor. His hand forced its way inside her blouse, his fingers worming inside her brassiere to cup her breast. As she felt his fingers on her warm flesh, seeking her nipple, she pulled her face away from him.

"Jeremy, not here! Anyone can see us." She laughed nervously. "I'm as anxious as you are to pick up where we left off, but . . ."

He was still looking at her hungrily. "The only people who might see are working for my father, and they are paid well to keep their mouths shut."

She sat up. "I'm sorry. It's a bit too much too soon, Jeremy. I'm so thrilled to see you again, but we had never gone this far before, had we? And it's been so long . . ."

"Dammit, Pamma," he said. "I'm only human, you know. Do you know how many times I've dreamed of doing this, while I was in that wretched hellhole?"

"I'm sorry. You caught me by surprise, that's all."

"Have to learn to control myself, won't I? Behave like the good chap again." He gave her a wicked grin. "As soon as I'm not confined to this chair, I'm going to whisk you away. We'll run off together."

"Elope, you mean? To Gretna Green?" Pamela asked, not quite sure whether to be excited or scared.

Jeremy looked amused. "My dear sweet girl, you really still are a romantic innocent, aren't you? Who can think of getting married with a war on? I want to whisk you up to a discreet hotel in London. I want to go to bed with you."

"Oh." Pamela felt her cheeks burning.

"As you just said, my darling. You are now an adult." His eyes were teasing hers. "Or is there someone else I don't know about? I'd understand if there was. I've been gone a long time, and I don't suppose you even knew whether I was alive or dead."

"There's nobody else, Jeremy," she said. "There's only you. There has only ever been you."

He looked pleased. "Well, that's all right, then."

She took a deep breath before asking, "I gather my little sister has been coming to visit."

"She has. Entertaining little kid, isn't she? Quite amusing."

Pamela felt a wave of relief.

As Ben came out of the front door, a Rolls-Royce was pulling up. The driver's door opened, and Sir William Prescott himself climbed out, brushing down his suit jacket in case it had picked up any creases during the drive. He always looked immaculate. Perfectly groomed, hair with the requisite amount of grey in it, Savile Row tailored suit. There had been a rumour at one time before the war started that he was considering running for Parliament. But the war had put a stop to such aspirations, if indeed they were any more than a rumour. He walked around the car and opened the passenger-side door.

While Ben was considering that in the days before the war a footman would have come running out to do this, Lady Prescott emerged. She was always elegant, too, but in a country sort of way. Where Sir William's image said clearly, *city, high finance, banking*, his wife's spoke more of growing prize roses for the flower show, of church bazaars and charity events. It was she who noticed Ben first. Her face broke into a beautiful smile. "Ben, how absolutely lovely to see you. We didn't know you were coming down. You've heard about Jeremy, then. Isn't it splendid? There were times when I never thought I'd see him again. And then we got the telegram. Like a miracle."

Sir William extended his hand. "Good to see you, young Cresswell. How are you? Are they keeping you busy?"

"Busy enough, sir. How are you?"

"Up to our eyes, old boy," he said. "Trying to put a deal with the Yanks in place. They might want to stay out of the war this time, but we need their help financially. Churchill's the only one who can persuade them. If we don't get their money, we're sunk."

"The Americans are going to give us money?"

Sir William gave a short, brittle laugh. "Lend, my boy. Lend. And at a pretty favourable rate to them, too. But we desperately need help. Money and equipment, all to be repaid if we ever win this damned war."

Lady Prescott was less interested in the American lease-lend deal. "You've been to see Jeremy, have you? He's so painfully thin. I can't imagine how he survived all those weeks, making his way through hostile territory. Sometimes not eating for days, he said. And with that horrible infected wound. How does he seem to you?"

"Clearly on the mend," Ben said, remembering the smouldering look he was giving Pamela. He was tempted not to mention her presence and thus let them be caught, but instead he cleared his throat. "Pamela is in with him now."

"Pamela? How lovely." Lady Prescott beamed. "I expect her mother telephoned her with the news, and she came straight down. How is she doing? We've certainly missed her."

"Doing well," Ben said. "Looks a little tired, but we're all working too many hours with night shifts and fire-watching duty."

"Doing your bit. That's what matters," Sir William said heartily.

"Are you here for long, Ben?" Lady Prescott asked.

"Not sure. A week maybe?"

"We must have you to dinner before you go back. It's been too long since we've had a dinner party. I promised Lord Westerham's lot, too. And your father, of course."

"You're very kind." Ben nodded solemnly. "I should be getting back."

"Good to see you, my boy," Sir William reiterated and took his wife's arm as they went into the house.

Ben stomped home to the vicarage, fighting back his growing anger. He should never have gone in the first place. Jeremy and Pamela obviously hadn't wanted him there, couldn't wait to get rid of him. And to see the way they looked at each other. Ben blinked to shut out the memory.

You're a fool, he said to himself. *If you'd wanted her, you should have made your move while he was missing and presumed dead. You could have comforted and reassured her, and she might have come to rely on you, and then maybe . . .*

He shut off this thought because he knew he would never have betrayed Jeremy. Pamela might have been the one he yearned for, but Jeremy was his friend. And now he supposed they'd marry and live happily ever after. He made the decision to put Pamela from his thoughts once and for all and to get on with his life.

CHAPTER THIRTEEN

All Saints vicarage, Elmsleigh
May 1941

The Reverend Cresswell was sitting in his study, staring blankly out of the window where a blackbird was singing on the wicker fence. He was roused from his trance when Ben knocked politely and came into the room.

"Sorry to disturb you, Father," he said.

"What's that, my boy? Oh, not at all. Not at all. Trying to come up with a theme for Sunday's sermon." He sighed. "So difficult these days. You can't preach hellfire anymore. They all know about hell only too well. So it has to be encouraging and uplifting. But how can you tell them that God is on our side when the Germans are told the same thing? I'm thinking Daniel in the lion's den. Trusting God against all odds. What do you think?"

Ben nodded. Since he'd gone off to Oxford, he had found it harder and harder to believe in his father's version of God. Of course, he never told the old man, but since the accident and then the outbreak of war, he had begun to wonder whether God existed at all.

"Do you still have an ordnance survey map of the area?"

"Should have, somewhere. Try the second drawer in that bureau." He watched as Ben opened the drawer and found it crammed full of papers. "Planning to do some walking along the footpaths while you're here?"

"I may." Ben dumped the tangled mess of papers on the table. "Really, Father, these need sorting out. Do you want me to do it for you while I'm home?"

"Thank you. I'd appreciate it," Reverend Cresswell said. "I never seem to have the time to get around to it. Of course, Mrs. Finch would love to get her hands on my study, but it's strictly out of bounds, except that I allow her to run the carpet sweeper over the floor. If I let her have her way, she'd have everything in the room stacked neatly and alphabetically, and I wouldn't be able to find a thing."

Ben smiled. He put aside a pamphlet on preparing for confirmation, one for last year's church fete, a programme for Gilbert and Sullivan at the D'Oyly Carte, and sundry letters, before he unearthed a map of France, one of Switzerland, and then the one he wanted. "Ah, good. Here it is," he said. "I'll start sorting this stuff for you later, but I need to borrow this now, if you don't mind."

"If you're thinking of walking, check with me first. You may find some changes. New people have bought the old oast house beyond Broadbent's farm. Arty types from London, one gathers. Needless to say, they haven't been near the church." He smiled. "But I hear that they've tried to block the footpath from going through their grounds. People have told them they can't do it. Old right-of-way from the village to Hildenborough. But I don't think it's had much effect. And in wartime, nobody is going to bother with a court case."

"I'm not worried, Father," Ben said. "Plenty of other places to walk. So have you met the new people yet?"

"Can't say I have. I gather they frequent the pub occasionally. Two men from London. One of them a well-known artist. Dr. Sinclair said he'd been for sherry with them, and the paintings were frightful. All red-and-black daubs, he said. One of them is Danish. Hansen. But he's not the famous one. Some sort of Russian name. Stravinsky? Something like that."

While his father spoke, Ben spread out the map on a table. He took a ruler and rotated it in a five-mile radius. There was a broad area of flat land toward Tonbridge. Lots of fields to land in. So if the parachutist had really chosen Lord Westerham's field, then, realistically, his contact had to be within walking distance. That meant the Farleigh estate, the village cottages, the bigger houses on the green: his father's vicarage, Dr. Sinclair, Miss Hamilton's, Colonel Huntley's. A couple of farms came within this radius: Highcroft's and Broadbent's. And then Nethercote, the Prescotts' estate, a half mile from the village. That was it.

Ben sighed. He'd known the people in the village all his life, unless there were any recent arrivals apart from the oast-house men. And the colonel and Nethercote and Farleigh. They were all as true blue and English as you come. Nobody who would want to aid the Germans. He came to the conclusion that they had got it wrong. The man who fell was not a spy trying to pass a message to a contact. He had to be an accident: a man who fell from a plane by mistake, in the wrong place.

But he'd been commissioned to investigate by a powerful and senior man. So he had to carry out the assignment and do it well. He folded up the map again. "I'll keep this for the moment, if you don't mind."

Reverend Cresswell looked up and nodded. "What? Oh no. By all means, keep it." He looked at his son. "So why are you home?"

"Why? Aren't you glad to see me?"

"Of course. But I just wondered whether that leg of yours was proving too much of a hindrance, and you weren't really able to . . ."

"You're asking whether they kicked me out? From a desk job? In wartime?" Ben's voice was sharp. "Really, Father. In spite of what anyone may think, I am not a poor cripple. I can walk perfectly well. Pamela and I walked from the station with suitcases. I just have a blasted knee that won't bend, that's all. So don't sign me up as wicketkeeper if we have a village cricket match."

His father looked shocked at the outburst. "I'm sorry, Benjamin. I really didn't mean to upset you. I just wondered when you arrived home out of the blue and one hears that nobody is getting any sort of leave these days."

Ben took a deep breath, his distaste of what he had to say already showing on his face. "As a matter of fact, I was told I had been overdoing it and needed a few days off. All those night shifts can take a toll, you know. And fire-watching duty when one isn't working."

"You're still in central London? Seen a lot of bombing?"

"Quite a bit."

"You're in one of the ministries, aren't you?"

"That's right."

"Interesting work?"

Ben smiled now. "Father, there's a war on. Even if I'm doing the most boring job in the world, I'm not allowed to tell you about it."

"I understand," his father said. "Well, it's good to have you home, my boy. Make the most of your time here. Enjoy Mrs. Finch's cooking. Get some fresh air."

"I intend to. Thanks."

As he was about to walk from the room, his father said, "And Lady Pamela, what's she doing home?"

"Same as me, I should think," he said. "Working too many long night shifts."

"They don't expect girls to work all night, do they?"

"Everybody has to work, all the time," Ben said.

"But, surely, they don't need things like filing done at night? Where did you say she works?"

"I didn't. But it's a government department, and they've been moved out of London."

"Bright girl, Lady Pamela. First-class brain," Reverend Cresswell said. "She'd have done well at Oxford. I tried to tell her father, but he wouldn't hear of it. In his mind, one marries off a daughter at the first opportunity and then is free of all obligations toward her. Positively medieval."

The word reminded Ben of his other sphere of inquiry. "That reminds me, Father. You're a history buff. Fourteen sixty-one. What happened that year? Anything significant?"

Reverend Cresswell stared past Ben out the window, where a large draught horse was pulling a cart full of manure. "Fourteen sixty-one, you say? Wars of the Roses, wasn't it?"

"Wars of the Roses?" Ben tried to remember the history lessons at Tonbridge School.

There had been endless repetitions of dates and battles that he retained in his head until the exam was passed, then he happily forgot. "The House of Lancaster versus the House of York. And York won, eventually?"

"Henry VI with his bouts of insanity was deposed by Edward IV in 1461, if I remember correctly. That's right. There were two bloody battles, one on the Welsh border at Mortimer's Cross and the other up in Yorkshire. Battle of Towton. One of the bloodiest battles ever. Scores of men killed, and Edward emerged victorious."

Ben was taking this information one step further. "And would you happen to know whether either was fought on terrain with a steep hillside behind it?"

"I have no idea." Reverend Cresswell sounded surprised. "I didn't know you were interested in battles, at least not ancient ones."

"A question I was asked at work," he said. "I get a lot of strange questions in the reference department."

"Well, the Welsh Marches are quite hilly, aren't they? And Yorkshire? You have the Dales and the Moors, but both are more gentle slopes if I recall correctly from rambling up there in my student days."

"Thank you." Ben smiled at his father. "You've been very helpful. It's good to have a father who is a fount of knowledge."

"Oh, I wouldn't say that." The vicar coughed in an embarrassed sort of way. "I've always enjoyed history, as you know. And I like to read. Not much for the wireless, and the winter evenings can seem very long and lonely. So one reads."

Ben looked at his father with compassion. All those years alone since his mother died, and yet he had happily sent his son off to boarding school, knowing it would be the right thing to do if his son wanted to get ahead.

"You don't happen to have an ordnance survey map of the whole of Britain, do you?" he asked.

"I'm afraid not. I expect they have one in the library in Sevenoaks or Tonbridge." He looked at Ben with interest. "I'm glad you're keen on taking exercise. Build up the muscles. That's the ticket."

"Actually, I was thinking more of those battles. Mortimer's Cross. Towton."

"I'm surprised that ancient battles are of interest in the middle of a modern war," Reverend Cresswell said, "but I expect you have your reasons. Good to have something to work on and keep the mind busy. And I should be getting back to my sermon."

He turned back to his open Bible.

Ben took the map and went through to the drawing room. He spread the map on a low table and looked at it again. Then he opened the little notebook he carried in his breast pocket and took out his fountain pen.

Oast-house people? He wrote. *Check village for newcomers. Then map for Mortimer's Cross and Towton.* Although how two ancient battles could possibly be connected to a modern war, he found hard to imagine. Maybe something else happened in 1461—a smaller battle, a critical turning of the tide in the Wars of the Roses. He'd need to go to the library or to his old school in Tonbridge and see if they had any books on the subject. He realised he was rather looking forward to the research aspect. Rather like a puzzle.

CHAPTER FOURTEEN

Farleigh Place, Kent
May 1941

The Rolls-Royce crunched over the gravel drive as it approached Farleigh Place. Pamela was glad she had accepted Sir William's offer to run her home. She realised she was out of practice for the long walks that country living entailed. Also, she had to admit that she was glad when Jeremy's parents came in to interrupt them. His sudden fierce passion had alarmed her. She certainly could understand it, after being locked up all that time, but she had found his advances overwhelming. She was not completely naïve. She had repelled young men's advances at debutante balls. She'd had to fight off a couple in taxis. But she had always been conscious that she was waiting for Jeremy—saving herself for him. Now his frank admission that he wanted to take her to bed had unsettled her. Of course, she wanted him to make love to her. But her fantasy had always pictured the long white dress, the flowing veil, and then the honeymoon at a lovely villa in Italy, where he'd take her into his arms and whisper, "Alone at last, my darling."

"How did you get here?" Sir William had asked when they pulled out of Nethercote's driveway onto the country lane.

"I walked with Ben," she said. "Can you believe it? We came down from London on the same train. Pure coincidence."

"Good chap, young Cresswell," Sir William said. "I can't help feeling a bit sorry for him. Stuck being a pen-pusher and missing all the fun."

"Do you really think it is fun?" Pamela asked. "For those who are actually fighting?"

"At least they know they are doing something worthwhile. Defending their country. What could be more valuable than that? A chance to prove you've got what it takes. And my son robbed him of that chance. Showing off as usual. Taking risks. It's in his nature, I'm afraid. Let's hope this latest escapade has knocked some sense into him."

They had reached the tall brick wall that enclosed the Farleigh estate; they turned in at the gateway between the stone pillars topped with lions. Pamela looked out the window at the dear, familiar surroundings. The chestnuts were in full flower with their white candles. The flower beds had been allowed to run wild, however. The lawns were certainly not as well manicured as at Nethercote. She leaned forward in her seat, anxious to get her first glimpse of the house. But as they approached, they were met by a procession of army lorries driving toward them, the convoy cutting off her view of Farleigh and reminding her abruptly that it didn't really belong to the Sutton family at the moment.

"I hope these blighters aren't messing up the place too badly," Sir William said, as the first of the lorries passed them.

"Pah hasn't complained, so I suppose it must be all right so far."

"One hears horror stories," Sir William said. "Using the ancestors' portraits for target practice, peeing on the tapestries—wanton vandalism, you know."

"Golly, I hope not," Pamma said. "Pah would kill anyone with his bare hands who damaged anything at Farleigh. But, luckily, all the good stuff was packed away when we heard that the West Kents were coming."

The forecourt was filled with lines of army vehicles, and Sir William had to manoeuvre around them. "I can't get close to the front door, I'm afraid," he said.

"Oh, please, just drop me off here. I can walk," she said.

Sir William stopped the car beside the lake. "You'll be all right, then?"

"Absolutely. Thank you for the ride. I really appreciate it. I'll have to dig out my old bicycle if I want to get around. I'm sure there's no petrol for the motorcar."

"Only for people like myself." Sir William gave a self-satisfied smile.

He got out and came around to open Pamela's door for her. "I'm glad you're here, my dear," he said. "If anyone can speed up Jeremy's road to recovery, it's you. He carried a picture of you all the time in that prison camp, you know. He was so upset when he lost it somewhere in that river during the escape."

Pamela nodded, not knowing what to say.

"Between you and me," he said in a low voice, "his mother is rather hoping that they won't let him fly again. Of course, he's dying to get back to it, but you know Jeremy. He'll be chasing Messerschmitts and Junkers into Germany the moment he's back in that bally plane."

Pamela had to smile. "I expect so. He does love it."

"He likes living on the edge. Always has." He took Pamela's hand. "Come and see us often while you're home, won't you?"

"Of course. Thank you again for the ride."

He released her hand, and she hurried up the front steps and into the house.

She heard voices from what had been the morning room but had now become the drawing room. It faced the front of the house and had a good view over the lake and the drive. She entered to find the whole family at tea. They were seated in a semicircle, and the low table now held a tea tray with a silver service on it, a plate of small sandwiches, a plate of biscuits, a hunk of fruitcake, and some other type of food hidden under a silver dome. Livvy held her baby, bouncing him on her knee while the nanny hovered nervously in the doorway. The two dogs lay sprawled at Lord Westerham's feet. Missie, always alert, pricked up her ears when she heard Pamela's footsteps, then stood up, her tail wagging.

"Pamma's here!" Phoebe noticed her first and gave her sister a beaming smile that warmed Pamela's heart.

"Hello, my dear. Welcome home." Lord Westerham also beamed at the sight of his daughter, holding out his hands to her.

Pamela went over and kissed his cheek. "Hello, Pah." She looked around the assembly. "Hello, Feebs. Mah. Livvy. I've already said hello to you, Dido."

"And greeted me so warmly, if I remember correctly," Diana said. She was wearing trousers again, royal blue this time, and a white cotton blouse knotted at the waist, looking like a rather sophisticated land girl.

"I'm sorry. It's just that I was surprised to see you at Jeremy's house. I didn't realise you even knew Jeremy."

"I was doing the charitable thing and visiting a neighbour in distress," Diana said with a smirk.

"He's very grateful. He said what a nice kid you were," Pamela said sweetly.

She went over to the low table and poured herself a cup of tea.

"Pamma, guess what, there are crumpets," Phoebe said. "Mrs. Mortlock is an absolute angel."

Pamela smiled at her sister. Phoebe had grown a lot since she'd seen her last. She was clearly at that awkward stage, poised between childhood and womanhood, but Pamela could see that she might well turn out to be a beauty. And her face was alight with refreshing enthusiasm. Pamela turned her gaze to the plate on which now only one crumpet reposed.

"It's not exactly the same with margarine on it," Lady Esme said, "but luckily, Mrs. Mortlock had the pantry stocked with a good supply of jam before sugar was rationed. If we use it sparingly, it may last us for another year, and by then let us hope that the war is over."

"Gumbie says she hopes the war won't be over soon," Phoebe chimed in.

"What?" Lord Westerham sat up in his armchair. "Don't tell me you hired a governess who is a Nazi, Esme."

"A Nazi?" Lady Westerham looked puzzled. "Oh no, dear. I'm sure she's not. She comes from Cheltenham."

"No, Pah," Phoebe said. "What she meant was that if the war ended soon, it would mean Germany had won. She said it would take a long time if we were going to beat Germany and drive them out of Europe."

"That's so true," Pamela said. "This crumpet is marvellous, isn't it? You should see the great doorstops of bread and margarine I have to face at my digs. My landlady really is the most awful cook."

"I must say our cook is managing pretty well, considering," Lord Westerham commented, helping himself to a biscuit. "Haven't had a decent joint of beef for ages, of course. But one can't expect prewar meals. So how are you, Pamela? How's the job going?"

"I'm well, thank you, Pah. The job is tiring. Long hours. Night shifts. But at least I feel that I'm doing something. And it's quite jolly on our days off—sports and concerts and various clubs."

"So what exactly are you doing, Pamma?" Diana asked. "Can't you get me a job there?"

"Just secretarial work—filing, that kind of thing. And no, I'm sure Pah wouldn't want you living in digs so far from home."

"Quite right," Lord Westerham said. "I've made it quite clear to you, Dido, that you're not old enough to move away from home."

"There are plenty of boys who join the army at eighteen," Diana said. "And plenty of eighteen-year-olds who were killed in the Great War."

"Which I think proves my point," Lord Westerham said, wagging a finger at her. "Do you think I want my young daughter going into danger? I want to protect you. I want to protect my family."

"You haven't said hello to little Charles yet," Livvy said in a peeved voice. "He can pull himself up to standing now, and I'm sure he actually said 'DaDa' the other day. You heard him, didn't you, Mah?"

"He certainly made some kind of sound," Lady Esme said. Pamela was amused to notice that she still wore what would have been a tea dress before the war, pastel chiffon with a handkerchief hemline. "Whether he knew what he was saying is another matter."

"I'm sure he did. He misses Teddy terribly. So do I. I haven't heard a thing for weeks. I do hope he's all right."

"But isn't he in the Bahamas with the Duke of Windsor?" Pamela asked.

"Yes, but there are German submarines. And plots, you know. Spies and assassins."

"Speaking of which, we had a bit of excitement here the other day," Lord Westerham said. "Damned chap fell into one of our fields."

"Fell?" Pamela asked.

"Parachute didn't open. Must have fallen from a plane."

"Golly," Pamela said. "How awful."

"And you'll never guess, Pamma," Phoebe said proudly. "I found him. Or at least the evacuated boy who lives with the gamekeeper and I found him. He was all smashed up and bloody. Quite revolting."

"How horrid, Feebs." Pamela turned back to her father. "Did you find out who he was?"

"No, but there was definitely something fishy about the chap. We thought he was one of the local West Kents, but the colonel says he wasn't. Which makes one wonder who the hell he was. Some bloody German spy, I shouldn't wonder. Still, nobody has bothered to come down here to find out."

"Don't swear in front of the children, Roddy," Lady Esme said.

"They are no longer children, and if hearing the word 'bloody' is the worst thing that happens to them, then they can bloody well consider themselves lucky."

Phoebe giggled. Pamela exchanged a grin with Livvy. But secretly she was already thinking about the German spy. She knew from conversations in her hut that Germans were sending out coded messages to Britain, presumably to sympathisers or to spies who had been planted in the communities. But it seemed almost impossible to believe that any spy would find it worthwhile to be operating in this bucolic area of north Kent, far from towns and factories and anything worth bombing.

Phoebe watched Pamela with interest. Her brain was racing, and excitement was brimming up inside her. She wriggled on her seat. She couldn't wait for tea to be over.

Lord Westerham noticed. "What's the matter with you, child?" he demanded. "Got ants in your pants?"

"No, Pah. But I've finished, and I have things I need to do."

"You don't want any cake? That's not like you," Lord Westerham said.

"I'm full of crumpet," Phoebe said, making Diana snicker. "So may I please be excused?"

"I don't see why not," Lord Westerham said. "As long as what you have planned isn't illegal, immoral, or just bloody stupid."

"Oh no, Pah," Phoebe said innocently. "I'm going out into the fresh air. It's such a lovely day, isn't it? I'll take the dogs if you like."

"Good idea, but don't let them annoy those army chappies," Lord Westerham said. "I had a complaint last week that the dogs had messed up one of their drills by running in and out when they were marching."

"I'll not go near any drills," Phoebe said.

"But no riding on your own, understand!" He wagged a finger at her. "I've heard about you sneaking Snowball out without telling anyone."

"I'm not riding, Pah." She opened the door. "Come on, dogs. Let's go. Walkies."

Both dogs needed no urging and rushed after her, their long, silky tails streaming out behind them.

Phoebe took them out through the French doors in the new dining room, rather than risk upsetting the soldiers in the main entrance hall. The dogs rushed ahead of her across the gravel, barking at a pair of ducks that had just waddled out of the lake. The ducks took off with a great flapping of wings, and the dogs waited, tongues lolling, for Phoebe to catch up with them. They skirted the lake, crossed the lawn, and entered the first stand of trees. Beyond was the far field where the body had lain. Phoebe glanced nervously, wondering if she could still see the blood on the grass. It had rained once at night, and that should have washed it nicely away.

On the other side of the trees, she picked up the bridle path that wound through the woodland. Among the trees she caught a glimpse of the fallow deer. The dogs pricked up their ears again, looking at her expectantly.

"No," she said firmly. "Your master wouldn't want you to go chasing deer."

Beyond the wood rose the wall that circled the estate, and nestled against it was a small brick cottage. Phoebe knocked at the door, and it was opened by a woman in a flowery apron. She reacted in surprise when she saw Lady Phoebe.

"Hello, Mrs. Robbins," Phoebe said brightly.

"Why, your ladyship. What a surprise. I'm afraid Mr. Robbins isn't here at the moment."

"It's not Mr. Robbins I want to see. It's your boy, Alfie. Is he at home?"

"He is, your ladyship. He's just home from school, and I've just given him his tea, as a matter of fact. If you'd care to come inside . . ." She opened the door wider.

"Sit," Phoebe said, pointing sternly at the dogs. "Stay."

She stepped into the cottage. The kitchen was off a tiny front hall. It faced the estate wall and was quite dark, but copper pots gleamed over an old-fashioned stove, and it smelled of newly baked bread. Phoebe could see the loaf in the middle of the table. Alfie was sitting there, a slice of bread, laden with jam, up at his mouth. When he saw Phoebe, he lowered the bread but traces of the jam painted a smile across his cheeks. He wiped at the jam with his finger.

"Hello, Alfie," Phoebe said.

"Hello." He looked uncomfortable.

"I came to see you," Phoebe said. "I've something I wanted to tell you."

"Would your ladyship like a cup of tea, too?" Mrs. Robbins asked. "And maybe a slice of bread? It's fresh from the oven."

In spite of the two crumpets, several sandwiches, and a cookie, Phoebe couldn't resist. "That would be lovely, thank you," she said and pulled out a chair beside Alfie.

Mrs. Robbins cut a slice, holding up the loaf and cutting toward her stomach. Phoebe half expected her to slice into her ample body, but she put an evenly cut slice on a plate and handed it to Phoebe. Then she handed Phoebe a butter dish. Phoebe tasted it and exclaimed, "This is butter."

"Well, of course it is." Mrs. Robbins laughed. "Mr. Robbins can't abide that margarine stuff, so I do a little deal with the farmer's wife at Highcroft. Only don't you go mentioning it to anyone, will you?"

"Of course not." Phoebe spread butter on the bread, then strawberry jam.

"You're very lucky to be getting such good food," she said to Alfie.

"I know. It's smashing, isn't it?" he agreed. "What did you want to see me for?"

"I'll tell you in a minute," she said, looking up as Mrs. Robbins put a big ceramic teacup beside her. She had already added the milk and sugar, and the tea looked incredibly strong.

"I'll leave you two young people to get on with it, then, shall I?" Mrs. Robbins said. "Just holler if you need anything. I'll be out back, stringing up the runner beans."

Alfie looked at Phoebe expectantly.

"I've just learned something interesting," she said, her voice just louder than a whisper, in case Mrs. Robbins was still listening.

"About our body?"

"That's right. My father says there was something wrong with his uniform. He thinks he might be a spy."

"That's what they're saying in the village," Alfie said, pleased that he had heard the information first. "Everyone's been talking about it at school. Even the big boys are jealous that I found the bloke."

"Do they have any ideas in the village what this spy might have been doing? Presumably, he was sent to make contact with someone around here, don't you think?"

Alfie shook his head. "They say Jerry is dropping parachutists all over the place."

"Well, I think he was supposed to meet somebody," Phoebe said. "So I think it's up to us. We have to find out what he was doing here."

"Blimey!" Alfie said. "You and me? Looking for possible spies?"

"Why not? Nobody would ever suspect two children, would they? What time do you get out of school?"

"Four o'clock," he said.

"Then let's meet tomorrow, and we'll make a list of possible suspects," she said.

"I'm not coming up to the big house."

"Of course not. I wouldn't want my family snooping into what I'm doing. I'll meet you in the village. By the war memorial on the green."

She grinned at him. "This is going to be fun. We'll actually be doing something useful."

They both looked up as the dogs started barking, and then they heard the pop-popping sound of an approaching motorbike.

"I wonder who that could be?" Phoebe said. She went to the window and saw a young man in uniform get off a bike and approach Mrs. Robbins while the dogs jumped up, half greeting, half warning. Phoebe went out and called them to her, reprimanding them. The motorcyclist handed Mrs. Robbins something, then rode away. Phoebe waited a long while as Mrs. Robbins stood still, staring down at the piece of paper in her hands. At last, Phoebe could stand it no longer.

"Is something wrong, Mrs. Robbins?" she asked.

The woman looked up with a stricken expression on her face. "It's our George. The telegram says his ship was torpedoed, and he's missing, presumed dead." She looked around her, bewildered. "I've got to find my husband. He'll need to know."

"I'll go and find him, Mrs. Robbins," Alfie said. "Don't you worry." And he ran off, leaving Phoebe standing beside the gamekeeper's wife.

She turned to Phoebe. "I shouldn't be surprised if this news doesn't kill him. Thought the world of that boy, he did. Thought the sun shone out of his head. Nothing was too good for our George. And he didn't want him to go and volunteer. He didn't have to. He was in a reserved occupation. But the stupid boy wanted to do his bit, said he wanted to join the navy and see something of the world." She was crying now, fat tears trickling down her cheeks. "And he were only eighteen." Then she seemed to realise she was speaking to Lady Phoebe. "I'm sorry, your ladyship. I'd no right to . . ."

"You've every right," Phoebe said.

But the woman shook her head. "I can't go making a fuss, can I? I'm no different from all the other mothers who got bad news today. We've just got to learn to get on with it. Learn to get on without him."

With that, she put a hand to her mouth and ran back into the house. Phoebe stood there, undecided about what to do next. Should she go in and try to comfort Mrs. Robbins or would the woman rather be left alone? Before she could make up her mind, Mr. Robbins came running up, red-faced and sweating, followed by Alfie.

"Where is she?" he asked.

Phoebe pointed blankly at the door. Mr. Robbins blundered in. Alfie hesitated, looking at Phoebe.

"I think I'd better go home," she said. "I'd just be in the way at the moment."

Alfie nodded.

"Tomorrow, then?" Phoebe asked.

Alfie nodded again.

Phoebe walked back to the house. She could hear the others still talking, but she crept up the stairs back to her room. Miss Gumble looked up as she came in.

"Whatever's the matter, Phoebe?" she asked.

"It's George Robbins, the gamekeeper's son. He's missing, presumed dead." She turned away. "I hate this horrid war. I hate it. Hate it. People are getting killed, and I'll never go to school now, and nothing nice will ever happen again." She picked up the stuffed rabbit that lay on her bed and flung it at the wall. Then she flung herself down on the bed, sobbing.

Miss Gumble went over to the girl, sat beside her, and put a tentative hand on her shoulder. "It's all right, darling. You have a good cry."

"Pah says we have to be strong and set a good example." Phoebe gulped, trying to control the tears.

"You're allowed to cry as much as you like with me," Miss Gumble said. "Our little secret. Here. Have a good blow." She handed Phoebe a handkerchief. Phoebe managed a watery smile.

"Do you know what, Gumbie?" she said, "I sometimes wish that we would let the Germans win the stupid war and let them come into England and stop fighting. It wouldn't be so bad, would it? Pamela went to Germany before the war, and she went skiing and had fun there. And our king had German ancestors, didn't he?"

Miss Gumble was staring at her, her face stony.

"Phoebe Sutton, don't let me hear you say that ever again," she said in a tone Phoebe had never heard her use before. "If the Germans came into England, it would be the end of life as we know it. Oh, your type of people would probably be all right, as long as your father learned to salute the Nazi flag and say 'Heil, Hitler.' But not the rest of us. Not me. My mother was Jewish. Her family fled from Germany before the last war because they didn't like the anti-Jewish sentiment. And since then, it's much worse. First it was smashing up Jewish businesses, then it was making all Jews wear a yellow star, forbidding them to go to school and university, beating up Jews in the streets. And my personal belief is that Hitler won't stop until all Jews have been exterminated."

When Phoebe had splashed cold water over her face so that nobody would know she had been crying, she went downstairs again and found the family in the drawing room. Lord Westerham looked up as she came in. "Had a good walk, then? Dogs behaved themselves?" he asked.

But Pamela noticed Phoebe's face. "What's the matter, darling?" she asked. "You look quite white."

"It's the Robbinses," Phoebe said. "They've just had a telegram to say their son's ship has been torpedoed, and he's missing, presumed dead."

"Oh, how awful for them," Lady Westerham said. "Their one son and they were so proud of him."

"We should do something, Mah," Phoebe said. "We should have a service or a memorial or something. To let them know that we care."

"He's only reported as missing at the moment," Lady Westerham said. "There may still be hope."

"Mah, if his ship was torpedoed, and he's missing in the middle of a great big ocean, there's not much chance of finding him again, even if he survived," Dido said, looking up from her magazine.

"Some chance, though. He might be in a life raft and have drifted away. Sailors have survived for remarkable periods of time before."

"But we should do something, don't you think?" Phoebe insisted.

"I'd hold off, old thing," Lord Westerham said with surprising kindness. "Let them go on hoping for as long as possible."

Pamela sat staring out of the window, fighting back the nagging worry that threatened to engulf her. Someone should have broken the U-boat code for that day. Someone should have been able to warn the convoy and send out planes to protect it. Until now, her work at Bletchley Park had seemed like an academic puzzle, unrelated to real events. But at this moment, the importance of what was being done in the huts there hit her with full force. She jumped to her feet.

"I should be getting back to work," she said. "I can't stay here drinking tea and enjoying myself when ships are being sunk and people we know are being killed."

Lady Esme stood up and put her hand on Pamela's shoulder. "You're upset, my dear. We all are. George Robbins was a decent young man. But your little job in an office is hardly going to make a difference in saving lives, is it? It's not as if you're on the front lines. So I suggest you sit down and have another cup of tea."

And, of course, Pamela could say nothing. She sat and allowed her mother to put a teacup in her hand.

CHAPTER FIFTEEN

Paris
May 1941

The occupants of the Rue des Beaux-Arts peered through their closed shutters at the big black Mercedes that had pulled up outside of number 34, early on that May morning. Strands of mist had curled in from the Seine. Those walking home with their morning baguettes crossed the street and continued on the other side, just in case. Those leaving to go to work or students on their way to an early class at the École des Beaux-Arts hurried past, eyes down. It didn't pay to look. The motorcar was too obviously German, which was confirmed when the driver got out, wearing a military uniform. They all heaved a sigh of relief when no Germans headed toward their apartments. Instead, a slim young woman emerged from the car, followed by someone who looked remarkably like Madame Armande, the fashion designer.

Gaston de Varennes had bought this apartment for Margot when they first became lovers. He himself had been living in the family mansion on the Rue Boissière in the grander sixteenth district, between the Champs-Élysées and the Seine, but in those days, he was strangely conservative in many ways. It would not have been right to bring Margot to live with him, especially when his mother sometimes arrived from the château unannounced. Marriage had been out of the question at that time. Margot was a Protestant. His grandmother detested the English, and he would not go against his family's wishes when it came to a spouse. So he had set Margot up in a small apartment on the Rue des Beaux-Arts, close to the Boulevard Saint-Germain in the sixth. If she leaned out of her window, she could glimpse the Seine and Notre Dame. It was pleasant enough and suited her well, although the lively throng of students had all but disappeared these days.

When Hitler invaded, the Germans had taken over the family mansion as well as the château in the French countryside. Gaston had joined the Resistance almost immediately and found the apartment in a quarter of bohemians and students. It suited them both. He could come and go with little risk of being noticed.

The concierge poked her head out of the cubbyhole by the front door when Margot came in.

"Bonjour, mademoiselle," she said. "It promises to be a fine day, does it not?"

"One hopes so, madame," Margot replied.

She pulled open the metal concertina door of the elevator, and Armande went to get in behind her. "Really, madame, there is no need for you to come up with me," Margot said. "All I need to do is put a few clothes and toiletries into a bag. I will only be a few minutes."

"I gave that obnoxious German my word that I would not let you out of my sight," Gigi Armande said. "And it does not do to break one's word to a German officer. Besides," she added, "I have to make sure you do not throw yourself from the window in a fit of despair."

"I promise I shall not throw myself from any window."

"Or attempt to escape across the rooftops." Armande pushed Margot into the elevator and stepped in, too. The elevator was just big enough for the two of them to squeeze inside, and Margot was conscious of the other woman's deliciously heady perfume. The cage ascended, painfully slow, creaking and groaning. Margot's brain was racing and not coming up with answers. They arrived on the third floor. She went ahead of Armande and turned the key in the lock. The apartment felt chilly and unoccupied. It was a three-room affair—a good-size living room and bedroom but a tiny kitchen, with a bathroom and lavatory off the small square of front hallway. Margot hesitated in the hallway.

"Would you mind if I made some coffee before we leave?" she asked. "I've been up most of the night, and I've a splitting headache."

"My dear, throw a few things into a bag, and we'll have breakfast at the Ritz, where I can assure you the coffee is real and not this dreadful ersatz chicory stuff." Armande went through into the living room and seated herself on the sofa, looking relaxed and beautiful.

Margot was conscious that the place wasn't particularly tidy, and the clothes she had worn the day before now lay on the floor. She picked them up, feeling embarrassed.

"Don't bother to tidy up," Armande said impatiently. She looked up at Margot. "I don't think you quite realise it yet, but you are in serious trouble, *chérie*. You are officially under arrest by the Germans. At any moment they could drag you back to that building and down to the basement where one hears about unspeakable things going on."

Her expression softened. "You have to learn to play along with them, *chérie*. I have, and I still live at the Ritz. Pretend to do what they want. Pretend to sympathise. They are far from home, and the sympathetic ear of a beautiful woman is much appreciated. If they want you to do something for them in England, then seem to be interested, seem to be considering it."

"But I couldn't," Margot said.

"Not to save your lover's life?"

Margot hesitated. "I don't see how I could put Gaston before my country. Besides, how could I have any reason to trust their word? I could carry out whatever despicable act they want me to do, and then they'd shoot Gaston anyway. They have not shown themselves to be particularly trustworthy."

"I think I could get certain powerful officers to have Gaston taken to a neutral country."

"Unless he's already dead," Margot said bitterly.

"Of course." Armande waved a gloved hand. "But one has to do what one can. You do want to save his life, don't you? He hasn't become boring to you?"

"Of course I want to save his life," Margot said hotly, "but I can't put my lover ahead of my country."

Armande sighed. "So noble, and so naïve. Learn to be a pragmatist, my dear, if you want to survive. It's always worked for me." She shifted impatiently, recrossing her legs clad in real silk stockings. "Now hurry up, do. There's a good girl."

"There are foodstuffs in the kitchen," Margot said. "What should I do with them? Vegetables, cheese. They'll spoil. One can't waste food in the current situation."

"Give them to that horrible old woman downstairs. She'll love you forever." Armande waved a hand again.

Margot went into the kitchen and was depressed by the small amount of food that was there. A quarter of a cabbage, two onions, a potato, and a square of hard cheese. Rations in Paris were now down to the bare minimum, and one snapped up whatever was going at the market. Still, the concierge would be glad of them, and she might get a chance to pass her a quick message. She put them into a string bag, then added half a bottle of cheap wine and the remains of yesterday's bread. Since she couldn't carry the rest of the milk in the jug, she picked it up and drank it, rinsing the jug out in the sink. If there was no food in the house, then Gaston or one of his friends would know she wasn't here. She was trying hard to think of a way to tell him where she was going, where someone could find her. Not that she could think of anyone who might help her at this moment. If they had Gaston, then all was lost. She hadn't allowed herself to think about it before, but now tears welled up. She blinked them back hurriedly.

She went through into the bedroom.

"My trunk is in the attic," she called to Armande.

"You're not going on a cruise, my darling," Armande said. "You need a few items. You can probably come back here if necessary at some point."

So Margot instead reached for the small suitcase on top of the wardrobe. It was the one her father had given her for her twenty-first. It still smelled of good English leather when she opened it, reminding her of saddles and the tack room at Farleigh. Into it she tossed some underwear, a cashmere cardigan, a pair of slacks, a change of stockings, another blouse, and a cotton dress. She was wearing her sensible shoes. There would be no need for heels. And she had to save enough room for toiletries.

As she approached her dressing table, she saw Armande's card with the words "CALL HER" written in lipstick. It wasn't where she had left it, and she realised that the apartment had already been searched. How lucky that the message had been so innocent. Of course, she would want friends to call her employer. She left it where it lay.

"Are you ready yet?" Armande asked.

"I need to put some toiletries together."

"My dear. Do you not think I have every kind of soap and bath salt at my place for you to use? Throw in your makeup, your toothbrush, and a face flannel, and that will be that."

"I need to spend a penny first," Margot said. "I have not been allowed to use the bathroom since I was dragged from my bed in the middle of the night."

"Very well," Armande said, "but hurry up. That German driver will find it suspicious if we are too long. Everything you do will be reported back."

Margot went into the bathroom and hurriedly stashed things into her toilet bag—her toothbrush and tooth powder, her headache powders, a clean face flannel, vanishing cream. The absurdity of this struck her—that she would want her face to look perfect if she were about to be tortured or killed. Then she relieved the call of nature. When she had finished, she turned the tap on and left it running while she tipped up the bidet and pulled back a tile beneath it. It was lucky that they had equipped her with the smaller of the two radios. This one only had a range of five hundred miles, but it was compact enough to fit into a briefcase, or under the bidet.

She stared at it, wondering what to do next. There was no better hiding place for it. If they really stripped the apartment, they would find it. And she had no way of using it with Armande in the next room. She would have to be patient. If she seemed to be compliant and willing, maybe they would let her come back here for something she had forgotten. She removed the headache powders from the toilet bag and left them on the shelf. Then she tipped the bidet back to its proper position and turned off the tap.

"*Mon Dieu*, you really did need to go," Armande commented with a chuckle.

"I really did. I thought I'd burst when I was sitting on that chair for hours, waiting for them to come and interrogate me." A thought came to her. "I don't suppose I could have a quick shower?" It was quite a loud shower, but she wasn't sure it was loud enough to drown out the noise of Morse code being sent over a radio.

"My dear, you can luxuriate in a bath at the Ritz as soon as we get there. Oodles of hot water. Divine."

Margot tried to put on a pleased and excited face. She put the sponge bag into her suitcase and closed it.

"That should be enough to keep me going for a few days," she said.

"A few days may be all you'll need," Armande said.

Margot didn't want to ask whether this meant she'd be released by that time, or she'd be in prison or dead. She picked up her suitcase and made for the half-open door.

"Ready when you are," she said.

CHAPTER SIXTEEN

Dolphin Square, London

Joan Miller, Maxwell Knight's secretary and right-hand woman, knocked and entered his inner sanctum with a grave and puzzled look on her face.

"We've just had a message, sir. From the Duke of Westminster."

"Oh yes? What did he want?"

"He has just been contacted by Madame Armande."

"The Parisian dress designer? Oh, of course, she was his mistress once, wasn't she? Many moons ago now. And many lovers ago, one understands. So what the hell does she want? To design new uniforms for our army?"

"She wanted to inform us that the Germans have got one of ours."

"Damn. Who is it?"

"Lady Margaret Sutton, daughter of the Duke of Westerham."

"Damn and blast." Even Max Knight looked uneasy at this. "The timing is interesting, to say the least. Or do you think it's coincidental?"

"I don't trust coincidences, sir." Miss Miller's face was impassive.

"Neither do I."

"Do you think she knows? Armande, I mean?"

"She has offered to help," Miss Miller said. "If we want to get her out, she'll do what she can to assist."

"Kind of her," Max Knight said. "I wonder what's in it for her?"

CHAPTER SEVENTEEN

Farleigh

Alone at last, Pamma stood in her bedroom, threw her jacket onto the bed, and heaved a sigh of relief. Seeing the family all at once, after months without them, was almost too much, coming right after her heady encounter with Jeremy. Warm afternoon sun shone in through her west-facing windows, and beyond the forecourt, a pair of mallards drifted effortlessly down onto the lake. Only the army vehicle, scrunching over the gravel, reminded her that not everything at Farleigh was as it used to be. She looked around, taking in the dear, familiar objects: the much-read books on her white bookcase, *Black Beauty* and *Anne of Green Gables*; the cowbell and dolls she had acquired when she was at finishing school in Switzerland; the framed picture of her presentation to Their Majesties. The room even smelled like home—the lingering scent of generations of furniture polish and the faint hint of winter fires.

Home, she thought. Exactly what she had dreamed of all those bleak and lonely nights in Hut 3. And yet, now that she was here, she couldn't shake off the uneasiness. A nagging thought inside her head whispered that she was needed at Bletchley. If they were one person short on her shift, maybe something critical would be missed. Would the gamekeeper's son still be alive if a submarine message had been intercepted and decoded? She was not part of the naval section, but maybe someone else's son might have survived because of a message she translated. She told herself that she was giving herself too much importance, but she also knew that every small cog in the great war machine was needed to make it run smoothly.

Her gaze fell on a small china dog on the mantelpiece. He sat up, begging, with ridiculously long ears and a sad face. Jeremy had given it to her when he went into the RAF because she had seen it in an antique shop in Tonbridge and it had made her laugh. He had told her to look at it once a day so that she remembered how to smile. Smiling had been hard when the news came that he had been shot down, and then that he was in a prisoner-of-war camp. And now, against all odds, he was safely home, half a mile away, and she should be bursting with joy. So why wasn't she?

"I am," she said out loud. "I just need a little time to get used to things."

She sank down onto her bed, her hand unconsciously going to her blouse front, feeling the place where the missing button had been. And that mixture of fear and arousal shot through her again. Of course, he had wanted to make love to her. He was, after all, a red-blooded male, deprived of female company for the longest time. He must have dreamed of this moment all those months he was shut away in a prison cell. No wonder he got carried away and couldn't control himself. *Normal behaviour, only to be expected,* she told herself. In the time he had been gone, they had both turned from adolescents to adults, and adults took sex for granted—at least her class of adult did. From what she had heard, bed-hopping was an accepted sport among her kind. Apart from her prudish parents, that is. Her mother seemed to have only the vaguest idea about the facts of life, and her father went bright red and started talking about the weather if anyone mentioned an unwanted pregnancy. But they were not the norm. Her roommate Trixie certainly wasn't a virgin and didn't mind sharing details of her many rolls in the hay. Pamela didn't think she'd be averse to it. In fact, now that she had time to examine her feelings, she was rather surprised to find that she had been excited as well as scared. But she was also uncomfortable—it was just the shock of hearing Jeremy's candid admission that he couldn't think of getting married to anyone with a war going on. Which made Pamma wonder if she was just one of many girls, if Jeremy really did care about her the way she had always loved him.

Over at the vicarage, Ben stood looking around the back garden. There was an Anderson shelter in the middle of the back lawn, and beyond it beanpoles showing the promise of a good crop of runner beans. Ben pushed the hair back from his forehead, as if this gesture would wipe away the image that still haunted him: Jeremy's face lighting up when he saw Pamma, and hers equally alight with joy. True, she had been pleased to see him when he had boarded the train, but her eyes hadn't sparkled in the way they had when she looked at Jeremy. "Damn Jeremy," he muttered out loud. Trust him to be the one to escape from a German prison camp. And he felt guilty for wishing that Jeremy hadn't come home. Jeremy was, after all, Ben's closest friend. They had shared a childhood. And it wasn't his fault that Pamela had fallen in love with him.

Ben told himself to get over it. There was a war on, and he had a job to do. He stomped down the garden path to the shed where he rescued his old bicycle from among the flowerpots and deck chairs. He sighed as he examined it in the bright sunlight. It had been far from new when it was donated to him by a parishioner, and now looked decidedly the worse for wear. Rusty in places, leather cracking on the saddle. He cleaned it up the best he could, oiled it, and took a tentative loop around the forecourt between church and rectory, wobbling a little as he got the hang of riding again. It was still operational, although he realised that riding a bike wasn't going to be easy with a knee that didn't want to bend. He felt a moment's irritation that someone like Maxwell Knight should expect him to scour the neighbourhood without giving him the means to do so. Perhaps people like Knight thought that everybody owned a motorcar. Although he realised that these days, many people might have cars but no petrol allowance to drive them.

He left the bike for longer explorations and set off on foot around the village. He didn't quite know what he was looking for. He passed Colonel Huntley's house, named "Simla," after his time in India. He paused to admire its neatly trimmed bushes and spotted the colonel's wife in the immaculate garden pruning the roses. She looked up as she heard Ben's approaching footsteps and waved to him. "Hello, Ben. Welcome home. Are you here for long? My husband would love to get a cricket team together. He complains he has nothing but schoolboys and old fogies these days."

She came toward him, wiping her hands on her gardening apron, a pair of secateurs in one hand.

"I'm afraid I'm just taking a few days' leave," he said, not about to tell her that he'd been ordered to take things easy for a while. He didn't want it all around the village that Ben Cresswell had cracked up, even though he hadn't done a day's fighting. They already looked down on him for not wearing a uniform.

Mrs. Huntley nodded and smiled. "I expect it's good to be home after London," she said. "Is it ghastly up there with all the bombing?"

"One gets used to it," he said.

"I sometimes feel that we are living in our own little world here," she said. "We have enough to eat, nobody drops bombs on us, and when we look out of our windows, we still see this—a little plot of paradise, wouldn't you say?"

Ben nodded. "Your garden is looking lovely," he said politely.

"We had some chap round the other day telling us we should turn it all over to growing cabbages or potatoes," she said. "You can imagine how my husband replied to him. Told him one of the advantages of being British as opposed to being German was that we were free to do what we wanted with our own little plots. We already had a kitchen garden that grew enough for our needs, and if his wife gained solace from growing flowers, he wasn't going to deprive her of that pleasure." She smiled now at the memory of it.

Ben looked around. "It's hard to believe that we're only an hour from London," he said. "Quite a shock to the senses to come back to a place where life is going on as it always has."

A frown crossed her face. "I suppose we can't escape completely here. We've all those soldiers at Farleigh. Dashed great lorries rumbling past at all hours and men coming out of the pub drunk and picking fights with local boys. And we've had our share of excitement recently. Have you heard that a body was found on the Farleigh estate?"

"I did hear something from Mrs. Finch," he said. "A parachutist, wasn't it? Accident with his chute not opening?"

She moved closer to him. "No accident, if you ask me. They came and took the body away in an army van. Not taken to the local morgue. You know what that means, don't you? There was something suspicious about it. My husband thinks it could be one of those German spies one hears about. Was probably sent to do some mischief at the RAF station. Sabotage the Spitfires." She paused, looking around as if afraid of being overheard. "But where are my manners? Would you like to come in for a cup of tea? I was just about to take a break."

"It's very kind of you, but I should be getting along," he said. "I haven't had a chance for much exercise, stuck in an office all day, and I'm interested to see if anything has changed in the village."

"Not much," she said. "You've heard about the strange men who have moved into the oast house? And the Baxters seem to be doing very well out of the war. Looking quite prosperous these days. Lots of work going on in their yard, but no one knows what it is."

"Sounds mysterious," Ben said. "Well, it's been good talking to you, Mrs. Huntley. Please give my best regards to the colonel."

As Ben started to walk away, she called after him, "Oh, and Dr. Sinclair has taken in a German."

"What?" Ben turned back again.

"We think he sounds like a German," she said. "Claims he's a refugee, but you never know, do you? They could easily have sent men across ahead of an invasion, ready to give directions from the spot."

"But Dr. Sinclair would never harbour . . ." Ben began.

The colonel's wife shook her head. "Too kindhearted. And lonely, since his wife died. I wonder how many of us have been hoodwinked. We're a nation of kindhearted people."

She headed back to her house, pausing to snip off a large yellow rose. Yellow petals floated down to the grass. Ben continued around the perimeter of the village green, weighing up what he had just heard. It wouldn't surprise him at all that the Baxters were making money on the side. Billy Baxter had never struck Ben as quite trustworthy, even as a boy. He remembered a purse going missing at church once, when they were both choirboys, and his father suspected that Billy Baxter had taken it. But they had never found either the purse or the truth.

At least he could eliminate Colonel and Mrs. Huntley from his list. Not that they were ever on it. But they had clearly both been interested in the mysterious parachutist, eager to talk about him. And the colonel had served his country for years in the heat and sweat of India. He looked upon his home now as a return to paradise. But the doctor had taken in a German refugee. Now that was worth following up.

He passed Miss Hamilton's solidly prosperous Victorian. Her father had made his money in manufacturing up north, then brought his family to the genteel home counties, away from the smoke and factory chimneys of the northern towns. Elderly Miss Hamilton was the sole surviving family member. Ben looked up at the big house. He wondered whether she had been forced to take in evacuees from London or whether she still lived there all alone, apart from an equally elderly servant called Ellen. He paused at the wrought-iron gate but couldn't think of a good reason to pay her a visit at that moment.

He paused at the war memorial, looking at the list of names of local lads who fell in the Great War. Sixteen from one small village. Three brothers from the same family. Would the list be longer this time? He sighed and walked on.

The Baxters' new bungalow stood beside their builder's yard. The tall gates to the yard were closed, and from inside came the sound of hammering. Ben wondered who would want building done in a time of war, then realised that there would be work repairing bomb damage in the towns. Well then, not so surprising that the Baxters were flourishing. The school day had just ended, and children were streaming out of the old school building, pushing and jostling to get through the gate. He saw a couple of big farm boys shoving a thin little kid he didn't recognise and went over to them.

"Cut that out," he said. "Save your energy for when you have to fight Germans."

The biggest boy curved his lip up in a sneer. "You're a fine one to talk. I notice you ain't fighting Germans like my brother."

"Just because I have one damaged leg doesn't mean I can't fight, Tom Haslett," he said. "For your information, I used to be junior boxing champion at Tonbridge, and I'll wager I could still knock you cold with one punch. But I don't believe in fighting someone weaker than me, and you shouldn't either. Go on. Go off home."

The boys' eyes darted nervously and they slunk away. Ben grinned at the smaller boy. "I haven't seen you around here before," he said.

"I'm Alfie. I came down from London."

"Oh, so you're the one who found the man's body," he said.

"That's right."

"It must have been quite a shock for you."

Alfie shook his head. "Nah. I saw much worse in London."

"You're a brave kid. You should stick up for yourself more. Don't let them bully you."

Alfie sighed. "They gang up, don't they? And they're bigger than me."

"I could give you a few boxing pointers while I'm home if you like."

"Would you?" Alfie looked hopeful.

"Not that I approve of fighting," he said with a wink. "As a vicar's son, you understand."

Alfie grinned.

"So what are they saying at school about this parachutist of yours?" he asked as they started to walk together.

"Nobody knows, do they? Some people reckon he was a German spy. They say the Jerries are landing parachutists all over the place so that when the invasion comes they can cut telephone wires and that sort of thing."

"People here think that the Germans will invade, do they?"

"Oh yeah," he said. "That lord bloke up at Farleigh is already having drills, teaching us how to fight with pitchforks and shovels. I don't think we'd do much good against tanks and bombers, do you?"

"Let's hope it won't come to that," Ben said, "but if it does . . ." The rest of the sentence remained unsaid.

As he left Alfie and walked on through the village, he thought about what the boy had said. That the man had been sent to sabotage ahead of the invasion. But he carried no tools on him, nothing to cut telephone wires. Which would have to mean that someone local would supply him. And house him maybe. He paused at the doctor's surgery, then shook his head. He'd known the doctor his whole life. He wasn't the sort to let the side down and house a traitor.

Ben ate a light supper of hard-boiled egg and salad with his father, then decided that he couldn't just sit around all evening, making polite conversation when he was sent there with a job to do. "I thought I'd go down to the pub, Father," he said. "See if any of my old mates are still here."

"Good idea." Reverend Cresswell nodded.

"Do you want to come with me?" Ben asked.

The older man looked amused. "Me? Oh, thank you for the invitation, but I don't think I'm the pub-going type. My one small glass of sherry wouldn't go down well among the drinking public. But you go, my boy. Go and enjoy yourself. God knows how much longer we'll have to make the most of small pleasures."

Ben nodded, went to say something positive but couldn't think of anything. There wasn't much to be optimistic about these days. Would they all be drinking German lager this time next year? Or would they all be starving, or slaves, or shut away in prison camps? It didn't bear thinking about.

Bats were swooping through a pink twilight, and rooks were cawing as they settled for the night in the big trees behind the vicarage as Ben made his way around the village green to the Three Bells. There was a pleasant hum of conversation going on as Ben pushed open the door into the pub. Several men were standing around the bar with beers in their hands, and they looked up as Ben came in.

"Evening, Mr. Cresswell," the bartender said. "Good to see you home again."

Ben went up to the bar and ordered a pint.

"You here for long, then?" one of the men asked. "Or just popped down to see your old dad?"

"I had a few days' leave coming," Ben said. "It's nice to get out of London for a break."

"Seen much bombing, then?" one of the men asked.

"We've had our share," Ben said. "But you get used to it. Nobody even looks up at work now when the air-raid sirens go off."

"What sort of job are you doing, then?" another asked.

"Working for one of the ministries," he said.

"Doing what?"

Ben grinned. "You know we're not allowed to discuss our work."

"Not allowed to discuss it," a voice behind them said, and Ben turned to see a skinny chap with bright-red hair coming toward them. Billy Baxter, the builder's son. Ben felt his hand clench into a fist. Billy had always enjoyed tormenting him when they were small boys. He was grinning. "Hush-hush work is it then, Ben?"

"He said he can't discuss it," one of the older men said.

Ben turned his gaze to the redhead. "I notice you're not in uniform either, Billy Baxter," he said.

"Ah well, I'm in a protected occupation, aren't I?" Billy said.

"Making bow windows for Britain?" Ben asked and was pleased to get a general laugh.

Billy Baxter flushed. "If your roof gets blown in during the next bombing raid, who do you think will come out and patch it before the rain gets in?"

"You seem to be doing quite well out of it," Ben said. "I noticed that new bungalow your dad has built. Looks quite fancy."

"Hard work pays off, doesn't it?" Billy said.

Ben watched Billy Baxter as he ordered a pint. He was the type who would sell his own grandmother if the price was right. But working for the Germans? Ben didn't think he'd have the temperament. At heart he was a coward, as proved that time Ben had punched him and made his nose bleed and he'd run home crying. Ben's father had lectured him on violence and restraint, but actually he had looked quite pleased.

Halfway through his pint, the pub door burst open and a group of soldiers came in, talking and laughing loudly. They barged their way up to the bar, and Ben noticed that the local men moved away. There was tension in the air. Then one of the soldiers said, "What are you drinking, miss?" and Ben noticed Lady Diana was with them. She was dressed in red trousers and her hair was tied back in a red bandanna, like a land girl's. And she was wearing bright-red lipstick.

"Don't call her 'miss.' It's 'my lady.' She's the daughter of an earl," one of the soldiers hissed at his friend.

Dido heard and laughed. "Oh, for goodness' sake. Call me Diana or Dido. I can't stand stuffiness. I'll have half a pint of shandy, please, Ronnie."

As she looked around the room, she spotted Ben at the same time and gave him a big smile. "Hello, Ben," she said. "These nice boys offered to take me with them to the pub. Wasn't that kind of them? A brief escape from captivity, you know." She laughed, but her eyes were saying "Don't tell anyone you've seen me here."

The bartender looked uncomfortable. "Pardon me, my lady, but this is the public bar. Don't you think you'd be more comfortable in the private bar next door? There are armchairs, and it's not quite as rowdy there."

"Nonsense," Dido said, giving Ben a swift glance for support. "I spend my life banished and away from people. I want to live a little. I want to hear laughter and talk to ordinary people." She looked back to the soldier who had offered her a drink. "Make that a pint, Ronnie," she said. She walked over to Ben as the pint was being drawn.

"So what are you doing these days, Dido?" Ben asked her. "Still at home?"

She gave a dramatic sigh. "Still stuck at home. Pah won't let me do anything useful. I'm dying to do my part, you know. I don't suppose you could find me a job in London, could you? At the place where you work?"

"I probably could, but I can't go against your father's wishes while you're still a minor. There must be useful things to be done in Sevenoaks or Tonbridge."

"Being a land girl and helping raise pigs? That's about it. I want to do something exciting. I'm going to ask Mr. Churchill next time we see him. Pah knows him quite well, you know. And if Mr. Churchill says he wants to employ me, then Pah certainly can't say no, can he?"

"Do you have any useful skills?" Ben asked. "Can you type and take shorthand?"

"Not really." She chewed on her lip, making him realise how young she still was.

"That's the sort of thing that women are hired to do on the whole," he said. "Office work. Clerical stuff."

"Boring, boring, boring. I'd rather drive an ambulance or learn to be a radio operator or even join the army."

"They don't let women fight. I imagine you'd still be doing clerical tasks in uniform."

"It's not fair." She pouted. "I'm just as capable as these boys. And just as brave."

"Oh no, miss," one of the soldiers said. "It was to protect ladies like you that we joined up. We have to believe that you'll be safe at home, waiting for us when we're shipped overseas."

"Will you be going overseas soon?" Ben asked.

The young soldier frowned. "We haven't heard anything. Our lot was at Dunkirk. We lost men there, but I suppose it will be our turn to ship out again soon enough. In the meantime, life in Kent isn't too bad. Especially when there are young ladies like you around." And he grinned at Dido.

Ben had just decided there was no point in staying on any longer at the pub when Dr. Sinclair came in and beside him a middle-aged man. There was something distinctly foreign in his facial features and the cut of his jacket. *The mysterious German,* Ben thought and went over to greet them. The doctor greeted Ben warmly and introduced his companion. "This is Dr. Rosenberg. He's helping me with my practice. Splendid chap."

The other man gave a correct little bow and held out his hand. "How do you do?" he said in clipped English.

"You're from Germany?" Ben asked pleasantly.

"Austria," Dr. Rosenberg said. "I was at the medical school at the University of Vienna before the war."

"One of their most distinguished professors," Dr. Sinclair added. "He managed to get out just in time."

The man looked at Ben with a bleak expression. "It never occurred to me that I was not safe, even though my grandfather was Jewish. I mean, I don't look Jewish, do I? And I was a respected man. Then the Germans marched in, and I was dismissed from my position and told I had to wear a yellow star. That was enough for me. I left everything and took the next train to Italy and then to France and then here." He paused to take the glass of beer that the doctor offered him. "I was fortunate to get out in time. I hear that my friends and relatives were not so lucky. They made my fellow professors scrub the streets while people spat on them. And others just disappeared. Nobody knew where they went, but there were rumours of camps . . ." He shook his head. "Sometimes I feel guilty that I am here, in this pleasant place, able to practise my medicine."

"You made the right decision, old chap," Dr. Sinclair said. "You acted. Others didn't. Most people don't think such things can happen to them until too late."

Ben left the Three Bells, thinking about Dr. Rosenberg. As he had said, he didn't look Jewish, with his blond hair and light greenish eyes. Ben toyed with the idea that he could have been a plant, sent over to become embedded in the community. Dr. Sinclair was a soft-hearted man, lonely, easily taken in. Perhaps the parachutist had expected to find sanctuary at the doctor's house.

CHAPTER EIGHTEEN

Farleigh again

The next morning there was great excitement in several households with the arrival of the morning post. Lady Esme looked up in surprise, waving a sheet of paper at the other occupants of the breakfast table. "Well, isn't that nice?" she said. "We're invited to a dinner party at the Prescotts to celebrate Jeremy's safe return home."

"Just you and Pah or all of us?" Dido asked.

"It says you and your family," Lady Esme said. "Not Phoebe, of course. She's too young for dinner parties."

"What?" Phoebe looked up from her porridge. "That's not fair. I'm never included in anything."

"You are not an adult, Phoebe. You haven't come out," Lady Esme said.

"Neither has Dido. Neither has anybody these days," Phoebe said.

"Don't remind me!" Dido said angrily. "If you're talking about not fair, then my missing a season is the unfairest of all. No balls. No parties. Nothing. I'll never meet a man and I'll die an old spinster."

"I don't know how they can get their hands on enough food to hold a dinner party when we are eating sawdust sausages and shepherd's pie that is ninety-percent potato." Lord Westerham interrupted this tirade. "But then that blighter Prescott always does seem to get his hands on things other people can't. He drives that Rolls of his around as if there wasn't petrol rationing."

"He's on important committees, dear," Lady Esme said. "Obviously, he has to go up to London."

"What's wrong with a train, like for the rest of us?" Lord Westerham snapped. "I am most careful about the amount of petrol I use."

"I don't believe you've taken out the motorcar once since the chauffeur was called up," Lady Esme said. "But then you've always been a hopeless driver."

"I resent that," Lord Westerham retorted. "I'm sure I could be a splendid driver if I put my mind to it. But there's always been a chauffeur, so there didn't seem much point. Besides, we are supposed to set a good example by not using any unnecessary petrol. And since I'm apparently no use to anybody in the war effort, apart from leading the local home guard, I have no justification to use petrol."

"If you'd teach me to drive, then I could chauffeur us around," Dido said. "Will you, Pah?"

"You? Drive us around? Even without the petrol coupons, the answer to that would be no, no, a thousand times no. You'd be more danger to the British populace than the Germans. You'd kill us all."

"I wouldn't," Dido said, her cheeks now bright pink. "I bet I'd be a marvellous driver. Lots of girls from good families are driving ambulances and lorries these days. Doing their bit for the war effort, unlike me, stuck here, bored to tears."

"Anyway, Roddy, you'll have to get the motorcar out to drive us to the Prescotts," Lady Esme said. "We can hardly arrive on bicycles."

"I don't know if I want to go," Lord Westerham said. "There's something about that blighter Prescott. I don't trust him. He's not one of us."

"How can you say that, Pah?" Pamma had sat quietly until now, finishing up a slice of toast and marmalade.

"Because he's not. Oh, he might have a fine house and all the airs and graces these days, but he grew up distinctly middle class."

"Well, he's one of us now," Pamma said. "He has a title, just like you."

"You either inherit a title or you buy it," Lord Westerham said dryly. "In his case, the latter. And I query how he made all that money, too. There is something too smooth about the blighter."

"You're just jealous, Pah," Dido said with a little grin. "So will you teach me to drive? I could drive us over to the Prescotts tomorrow. I can hardly hit anyone going down our driveway, can I?"

"Absolutely bloody well not," Lord Westerham stormed.

"Then what *can* I do?"

"Stay at home and help your mother until you're old enough, that's what you can do. Knit socks and helmets for soldiers."

"Knit things? You're joking. If I were a son and I was eighteen, I bet you'd be proud if I joined up."

A spasm of pain crossed his face. "But you're not, are you? I just have girls, and it's my job to protect them."

"If you're not careful, I'll run off and marry a gypsy, and then you'll be sorry." Dido stood up, dropped her napkin, and flounced out of the room.

"I'll look forward to buying clothes pegs from you," Lord Westerham called after her, chuckling.

Lady Esme looked at her husband. "You'll have to let go of her sometime, Roddy. I understand how she feels. She can't sit home doing nothing when everyone else is helping with the war effort."

"When she's twenty-one she can do as she bloody well pleases," he said. "Until then, she's under my care, and I do what I think is best for her. You know what she's like, Esme. If we let her go off to London, she'll be back with an illegitimate baby in ten minutes."

"Really, Roddy. Sometimes you go too far." Lady Esme turned pink. "I must make sure we all have something decent to wear to the Prescotts. I haven't had my good frocks out for ages, and Lady Prescott is always so chic." She looked across at Pamela, who had now risen from the table. "Did you bring an evening dress with you, darling?"

"I left most of my things here," she said. "Not much chance to wear evening dresses when I'm on night shift."

"Then pass the news on to Livvy, will you. I'm sure she'll want to come."

As Pamela left the room, she heard her father say, "I've been thinking this over, Esme, and the more I think of it, the less I want to go. Prescott will be effusive and magnanimous and handing out his single malt Scotch and getting my goat."

"But we have to go," Lady Esme lowered her voice. "For your daughter's sake."

Pamela paused in the passage outside the dining room.

"Daughter? Which daughter?"

"Pamma, of course. It's to celebrate Jeremy's safe return. Jeremy and Pamela, you know?"

"No, I didn't know. Has he asked for her hand or something?"

"No, but I'm sure he will when the time is right."

Pamma waited no longer but went on up the stairs. Her face was flushed at what she had just heard. Everyone else assumed she'd marry Jeremy, except Jeremy himself, it seemed. And now another nagging doubt had crept into her mind. Her sister Dido. She had apparently been visiting Jeremy, and then last night . . .

Dido was waiting at the top of the stairs. "Are you sure I can't come and live with you, Pamma? I'll go mad if I stay here much longer. They must be able to find me a job where you work. I'd take anything at this stage, even boring old filing."

"Dido, you can't go against Pah's wishes. You know that. Besides, I share a room with another girl in an absolutely awful boardinghouse, and we're as far out of London as we are here. Stuck in the middle of the countryside with nothing going on. You'd be just as bored as you are here."

"But you must be working with men."

"That's true. Although I wouldn't call most of them exciting, either. They're too old or they're gangly boys with pimples. Nothing exciting, I assure you." She turned to her sister. "I know. Why don't you ask Pah to see if the colonel of the West Kents could use you for office duties? That would be a start and get you some experience."

Dido's face brightened. "Yes, that would be a start, wouldn't it. Good thinking, Pamma. You're not such a bad old stick."

As she went to walk past, Pamela said in a low voice. "I know you were out last night, Dido. I heard the floorboards creaking and saw you going into your room. Where did you go?" A worrying thought had been playing in her mind that Dido had been to see Jeremy. And Dido didn't seem to have any inhibitions about sex—positively keen for it, in fact. Had she been giving Jeremy what Pamela had denied him?

Dido grinned. "To the Three Bells with some of the soldiers I met."

Pamela heard herself give a sigh of relief. "Dido, for heaven's sake, be careful. Pah would hit the roof if he found out. And soldiers? That's not exactly wise."

"It was brilliant. They were so nice to me. They treated me perfectly."

"Well, I suppose they would, given that you're the daughter of the house where they're staying. And you're a lady."

"But it wasn't like that at all. We talked. We laughed. It was so nice to be just like an ordinary person. One of the gang. Is that what it's like where you work? Do they have to call you 'my lady' and rubbish like that?"

Pamela laughed now. "Of course not. And they certainly don't treat me any differently because I'm the daughter of an earl."

"That's what I want. To be someplace where nobody cares who I am."

Pamela put a hand tentatively on her sister's arm. "Your turn will come, I promise you. And if this war goes on much longer, then I'm afraid we'll all be called upon to do our share."

"Golly, I hope so," Dido said. "Thanks, Pamma. And you won't say anything to Pah, will you?"

"I won't, but you'll be lucky if someone from the village doesn't blab. You know what gossips they all are."

"You really are a good old stick," Dido repeated.

"Thank you for the compliment." Pamma smiled as she went into her bedroom.

Phoebe stomped into her room, making her governess look up from the book she was reading.

"Why, Phoebe, whatever is the matter?" she asked.

"They've all been invited to a dinner party at the Prescotts, and I'm not included."

"Well, I wouldn't feel too badly about it," Miss Gumble said with a smile at the girl's scowling face. "I'm not invited, either."

"Well, of course you wouldn't be. You're only a governess," Phoebe said and saw a spasm of pain cross the woman's face.

"For your information, Phoebe Sutton, I grew up in a situation not unlike yours. Oh, our house wasn't quite as grand as this one, and my father didn't have a title, but it was a good-sized estate. Then my father died when I was up at Oxford, and my brother inherited everything. And his wife told me in no uncertain terms that I was no longer welcome at my old home."

"Golly, how mean," Phoebe said.

Miss Gumble nodded. "So I had no choice. With no money and nowhere to go, I had to leave university and get a job teaching other people's children because that gave me a roof over my head."

"Why didn't you get married?" Phoebe said. "You must have been quite pretty once."

"I think you mean that as a compliment." Miss Gumble gave a sad smile. "There was a young man. But he died in the trenches in the Great War, like so many others. A whole generation of young men wiped out, Phoebe. For women of my age, there were no men to marry."

"Golly," Phoebe said again. "Do you think that will happen this time? Do you think by the end of this war there will be no men left for me to marry?"

"I hope not, for your sake," Miss Gumble said. "At least when the last war ended, we were still free. And we won, however terrible the cost."

CHAPTER NINETEEN

All Saints vicarage

Over at the vicarage, Reverend Cresswell opened the morning post and looked surprised. "Well, well," he said. "We've received an invitation to a dinner party tomorrow night, at the Prescotts. That's a turn-up for the books, isn't it, Ben?"

"At the Prescotts?" Ben paused. "I suppose they've only invited us as a courtesy."

"Nonsense, my boy," the vicar said. "They've invited you, as Jeremy's oldest friend. I'm the courtesy."

"We don't have to go," Ben said.

"Not go? I personally shall look forward to a slap-up meal in these times of economy. One hears things about the Prescotts' table."

Ben wished he could come up with a good reason not to go. Lord Westerham's family would most definitely be invited, and he'd have to watch Jeremy and Pamela gazing at each other with that special look. *Get used to it,* he muttered to himself, disgusted with his own weakness. He was here to work, and the dinner party would see the leading lights in the local community assembled in one place. A perfect opportunity for observation.

"Then we can't deprive you of a good meal." Ben got up. "I'll write an RSVP note to Lady Prescott."

After breakfast he took out the bicycle. It was a brisk, windy day with the promise of rain. He went back inside again to look for his windcheater.

"I'm going for a bike ride," he said to his father.

The vicar looked at him critically. "Don't take this fitness thing too far, Benjamin. You've nothing to prove. You've made a remarkable recovery from your accident."

Ben swallowed back annoyance. "I'd hardly call pedalling around the village taking fitness too far. I thought I'd go by the old oast house and see if the artists who live there now will let me see their work."

"Good luck." The vicar smiled. "From what I've heard, I wouldn't say putting out the welcome mat was one of their virtues. In fact, they threatened to shoot someone who was using the public footpath. We had to get the local bobby to talk to them and explain about rights-of-way."

"Then it might prove to be an interesting encounter," Ben said and headed for the front door.

Half a mile out of the village, he rather regretted his bravado. The wind was coming up from the Thames Estuary, hitting him full in the side and threatening to topple him around each bend. It was fine when the lane dipped between high hedges, but when it skirted the open barley field, it was brutal. Still he was not about to get off and walk. He went first to Broadbent's farm. Old Mr. Broadbent was mucking out a pigsty when Ben cycled up, with a yapping dog on either side of him.

"Well, if it isn't young Ben," he said, wiping down his hands as he came toward the bike. He invited Ben in for a cup of tea, and they talked about the shortage of farmworkers and how the land girls had taken over from the young men.

"Good hard workers, some of them," Mr. Broadbent said. "Others are hopeless. Worry more about their hair and makeup than getting the job done. I've caught a couple going behind the haystack for a smoke. The haystack, mind you! I told them if that went up, my beasts would have no fodder for the winter, and we'd all starve." He shook his head. "Don't have much of a clue. City girls."

Ben hadn't considered that the contact for the fallen parachutist might be a woman.

"Any of them foreign?" he asked.

"There's Trudi from Austria. She's one of my good hard workers. Comes from a farm at home. I put her in charge of the hopeless ones, and she keeps 'em on their toes."

Ben brought the fallen man into the conversation, but the farmer had only vaguely heard of him and didn't seem interested. "I suppose you're bound to get some accidents in wars, aren't you?" he said and offered Ben a slice of pork pie.

On his way out, Ben stopped to chat with some of the girls and learned that Trudi was not well liked. She made the girls work too hard, and what's more, she was dating one of the soldiers stationed at Farleigh. A good-looking bloke, too. She slipped out at night to see him. They seemed delighted to tattle on her. Ben rode off again, his stomach full, and only an Austrian named Trudi to add to his list. Trudi, who was conveniently dating one of the soldiers. He went on to the infamous oast house, wondering how he could approach the two hostile owners who had shot at trespassers. They were both artists, he knew that much. It would be time to channel Guy Harcourt, who roomed next door to him. Guy was very keen on modern art and design and had tried, unsuccessfully, to convert Ben to his tastes. But today his small amount of knowledge might come in useful.

The oast house still lay between tall rows of hops, but there was now a picket fence and a gate separating the hop fields from a front garden full of roses. A rose bower curved over the front door. Ben had to admit that it created a lovely picture of rural serenity, except for the sign on the gate saying "Keep Out: No Soliciting."

Ben opened the gate cautiously and wheeled his bike up to the front door. There was a brass knocker with what looked like a demon's face on it; Ben hesitated before he knocked. The door was opened by a chubby man dressed all in black—a black fisherman's jersey, in spite of the warm weather, and baggy black trousers. He had a podgy face, a stack of straw-coloured hair, and a black cigarette hanging from one corner of his mouth. Ben took in the smell of foreign tobacco.

"Well, what do want? If you think we're donating to any metal or paper drive, you can think again." He had a slight foreign accent that Ben could not identify.

"Actually, I'm the vicar's son—" Ben said, but the man cut him off.

"And you're not getting us to church, either. We don't believe in that nonsense."

"I'm not here to convert, either," Ben said. "Someone said you were artists, and I'm an admirer of modern art myself, so I wondered . . ."

"You're an aficionado yourself? Whose work do you admire?"

Ben racked his brains for artists that Guy had talked about. He had dragged him to galleries when there were still such things. "Well, I admire Karl Schmidt-Rottluff and, of course, Paul Klee, although it's probably not permitted to admire a German artist anymore."

"Then you'd better come in," the man said. "Serge's work has been compared to Schmidt-Rottluff's." He went ahead of Ben. "Oh, Serge. Come out, wherever you are. We have a civilised visitor at last," he called in fluted tones.

Another man came out of a back room. He was tall, dark, and lean, with sharp features, and was wearing a paint-spattered smock.

"Serge, this young man is an admirer of Schmidt-Rottluff's. I told him your work has been compared to his."

"Really?" He was looking at Ben sceptically. "You admire the German expressionists?"

"Oh, definitely," Ben said, hoping the discussion did not get too deep. He looked around the room. On the walls were several awful paintings—bright daubs of primary colours and distorted figures. Ben thought that Guy might actually like them. Ben said, "Your work, Serge?"

The dark man nodded. "You approve?"

"Powerful."

The man nodded again. "You are most kind."

Ben's gaze lingered on an elongated purple woman. He was sure that he'd seen the picture before—hadn't Guy pinned up a postcard of it?

"Have you exhibited much in galleries?" he asked.

"A little." Serge shrugged.

"You are from Russia?" Ben asked. The accent was still strong.

"I am. I came here when I was no longer allowed to paint anything other than healthy peasant women operating harvesting machines. There is no art in Russia anymore."

"Did you also come here when you could no longer practise your art?" Ben asked the other man.

He smiled. "I am from Denmark, my dear, where usually anything goes. But I got out in a hurry when the Germans were about to invade. And thank my lucky stars that I did so. I would not have made a good Nazi. I don't salute well, for one thing. And I'm hopeless at taking orders." He grinned. "You are the first halfway civilised person we've met since we moved here. Most of them are philistines, aren't they, Serge?"

Serge nodded. "Philistines." He frowned at Ben. "So what are you doing in these parts?"

"My father is the local vicar. I'm here on a few days' leave."

"A soldier? A sailor?"

"Civilian, I'm afraid. I was in a plane crash."

"Don't apologise. Be grateful that you're not part of the carnage. We're certainly grateful that they are not yet calling up men over forty, aren't we, Hansi?"

The chubby man nodded. "Would you like to try our homemade parsnip wine? It packs quite a kick, I'll warn you."

Ben nodded and was handed a glass. Ben took a sip, gasped as the liquid burned his throat, then asked, "So did you come here from London?"

They both nodded. "We lived in Chelsea, naturally," the chubby Hansi said. "Then a house three doors away was bombed, and we said that's too close for comfort and fled here. We were taken with the building immediately. It has character, don't you think?"

"Definitely," Ben said, "although I still remember when the hops were hung to dry in the tower. Are you also a painter?"

"Sculptor," Hansi said. "I work with metal. Or rather I worked with metal when there was any. I used to make great outdoor pieces. Now, of course, every piece of scrap metal goes toward building another bomb or plane. So I am reluctantly switching to clay, of which there is no shortage."

Ben looked from one to the other. The saturnine Serge from Russia—Ben could picture him working with the Nazis. But the affable Hansi? And yet he worked with metal. He would have any tools that a visiting German paratrooper would need.

When he left them, half an hour later, they parted on the friendliest of terms with an open invitation for Ben to visit them whenever he was back in the area. He rode away, wobbling a little along the path, as the wind had become even stronger, and he was feeling the effects of the potent parsnip wine.

As he bicycled wearily home, he realised that he was none the wiser. The two artists seemed to have fled to England to escape from tyranny and only wanted peace and quiet to create their art. And yet, they had chosen a remote location, and Hansi wouldn't be the first German to claim he was Danish. The local farmers were solid local men he had known all his life. Their land girls beyond reproach, except for an Austrian called Trudi who was dating a soldier. But the dead man had landed in Lord Westerham's field, presumably for a good reason. Ben hoped the dinner party might give him some sort of clue.

CHAPTER TWENTY

At Nethercote
The dinner party

Ben was glad for long summer evenings as he and his father walked up the drive to Nethercote, the Prescotts' residence. He was also glad the driveway was straight. It wouldn't be so easy to walk back in the dark with just a flashlight covered in black cloth to guide their steps. No light was permitted to shine out from the windows of any house, and the whole way home would be in total darkness. Ben tried to remember if there would be a moon. He turned to ask his father.

"In its third quarter, so it won't be any use to us, unless we stay very late, which we won't," Reverend Cresswell said. "I have to admit I am looking forward to the food, but I'm beginning to find the prospect of the evening a little daunting. Still, if it's just us and the Sutton family, then it won't be too bad, will it? Just like old times."

Ben nodded. *Just like old times,* he thought. They pushed open the tall wrought-iron gates that hadn't yet been commandeered for scrap metal, and their feet crunched over the raked gravel as they walked up the path. He was marvelling at the beautifully kept state of the grounds when his father said, "I see they haven't tried to convert their lawns to potato patches. The place looks positively sinful. They must still have gardeners."

"They do," Ben said. "I saw them working when I came here with Pamela the other day."

"You came here with Pamela?"

Ben nodded. "She was worried about seeing Jeremy by herself. I think she was frightened he'd be disfigured or something. But he seemed his old self, apart from having lost a lot of weight and being rather pale."

"That young man must have been a cat in a previous existence," his father said. "He's certainly used most of nine lives."

Ben nodded again.

"And no doubt he'll be back tempting fate in a fighter plane again as soon as they'll let him."

"No doubt." Ben agreed.

They had just reached the front door when there was the sound of a motor engine behind them, and Lord Westerham's ancient Rolls came up the driveway. Lord Westerham himself, not a chauffeur, got out of the driver's seat and went around to open the passenger doors. His wife and daughters emerged one by one, smoothing out crumpled evening dresses. Ben watched Pamela step down daintily. She was wearing a pale-blue Grecian gown, the perfect shade for her ash-blonde hair and English complexion.

"Good evening, Vicar. How very nice to see you, Ben," Lady Esme called. "Lovely evening, isn't it? The weather has been so perfect lately, almost as if it's mocking us, don't you think?"

Ben's father gave a nodding bow. "Good evening, Lady Westerham. Yes, we are having a spell of glorious weather. So essential for the crops."

"Too bad we had a full motorcar, or we could have given you a lift," Lord Westerham said.

"At the speed you drive, they could have walked here faster, Pah," Dido retorted, as she emerged last from the Rolls in pale pink, making her look young and vulnerable. Ben realised that none of the girls would have had new dresses since the war started and clothing was rationed. Diana's was probably a hand-me-down from Pamela's season.

Pamela gave Ben a big smile as the girls followed their parents up the front steps. Ben and his father fell into line behind them after the door was opened by a maid, then they were ushered through to an elegant drawing room. Ben noticed that there were already several people in the room at the same time as Lord Westerham muttered to his wife, "I thought you said it was a small dinner party. This is a bloody great bean feast. I wish we'd never come."

Lady Westerham took his arm and dragged him firmly forward so that he had no chance to escape before Sir William and Lady Prescott came forward to greet them. Lady Prescott was in gold lamé, Sir William immaculate in tails.

"How good of you to come." She held out her hands to Lady Esme.

"It was good of you to invite us." Lady Esme allowed the other to hold her hands. "I can't tell you how long it's been since we've been invited out for a meal. I feel as if I'm escaping from the cage."

"We simply had to celebrate Jeremy's escape and safe arrival, didn't we? I still think it's an absolute miracle." She extended an arm to the other occupants of the room. "I'm not sure if you've met everybody," she said. "Obviously, you know Colonel and Mrs. Huntley. And Miss Hamilton. And I'm sure you must be well acquainted with Colonel Pritchard, since he now lives under your roof."

"Of course." There were polite noddings and how-do-you-dos from the newcomers to those mentioned. "But are you already acquainted with Lord and Lady Musgrove? Lord Musgrove has just inherited Highcroft Hall."

Ben took in the young, stylishly dressed couple. He tried to place Highcroft Hall.

"Is that so?" Lord Westerham, turned to his wife for confirmation. "We heard old Lord Musgrove had died some time ago, didn't we, Esme?"

"We did. We're so glad the place is to be occupied again."

The young man gave a glance at his wife before he smiled and held out his hand to Lord Westerham. "How do you do? Frederick Musgrove and my wife, Cecile. We were living in Canada, so it took some time to track us down. I can tell you it was quite a shock when a solicitor's letter arrived telling me I'd inherited Highcroft and the title. Absolutely knocked me off my feet. As a son of a younger son, I never expected to inherit anything, which is why I went to Canada. But the Great War killed off the other heirs, so here I am." He gave a boyish grin. "I've been earning my living by the sweat of my brow like everyone else."

"Hardly the sweat of your brow, Freddie," his wife said. She grinned and looked across at the company. "He's been working in a bank in Toronto."

"A bank? Really? How fascinating," Lord Westerham said and received a dig in the side from his wife.

"So let me complete the introductions," Lady Prescott went on. "These are our neighbours Lord and Lady Westerham and their daughters Olivia, Pamela, and Diana, and this is our beloved local rector, Reverend Cresswell, and his son, Ben. Ben has been our son's dearest friend since they could toddle. And speaking of our son, where can he have got to?" She looked up and a beaming smile spread across her face. "Ah, here he is, the miracle man himself."

There was a round of applause. Jeremy, looking even thinner and paler against the black of a dinner jacket, stood in the doorway and gave a sheepish grin as his mother rushed over to grab his arm and drag him toward the assembled guests. "Isn't he wonderful?" Lady Prescott said. "I can't tell you what it means to have him back with us. Against all odds."

"Mother, please." Jeremy gave an embarrassed smile.

"Dashed brave of you, young fellow," Colonel Huntley said. "Took a lot of guts to do what you did. Just shows that we British have stronger fibre than the Hun. You can't see a German doing what you did. They'd be waiting to obey orders."

"Not quite true, Colonel," Jeremy said. "There are some really terrific German fighter pilots. It's a privilege to engage in combat with them."

"Enough talk of war," Sir William interrupted. "Let's get down to more practical matters. What are we all drinking? Scotch for you, old chap?" he asked Lord Westerham. "Do you care for a single malt?"

"I wouldn't say no," Lord Westerham said. "Damned good of you, Prescott. I haven't had a decent whisky in ages."

Sir William snapped a finger to a footman standing at a drinks' table. "And you lovely ladies? A cocktail maybe? Or would you prefer a sherry?"

"Oh, I don't think I know much about cocktails," Lady Esme said, looking rather pink. "Perhaps I'd better stick to a sherry."

"Well, I'd like a sidecar, if you're offering," Dido said. "Wouldn't you, Pamma?"

Pamela hesitated, feeling Jeremy's eyes on her, and then she said, "Why not? That would be lovely."

As the footman served drinks, Jeremy came over to Pamela who was now standing with Ben.

"I see you're up and walking," she said.

"Yes, doing rather well, actually," he said. "I'm hoping the quack will certify me ready to go back to work."

"Surely not?" Pamela shot Ben an alarmed look.

"Well, they won't let me fly for a while, but at least I can be useful in a desk job like old Ben here. They've told me they can use me at the air ministry, and father says I can stay at the London flat."

"You still have a flat in London?" Ben asked.

"Yes, my father keeps a place just off Curzon Street. He used to stay up there during the week when he was working in the city more than he does now. Jolly convenient. You must all come and visit me." He looked from Ben to Dido, but his gaze lingered with Pamela. "I know. When I'm settled in, we'll have a party. How about it?"

"A party, in London?" Dido's face was alight with excitement.

"Don't get your hopes up," Pamela said in a low voice. "I'm sure Pah wouldn't let you go."

"But if I say that you and Ben will chaperone me, then Pah can't object, can he?"

"There won't be any trains back home late at night," Pamela said.

"You can all stay the night at my place. We'll make an all-nighter of it and finish up with bacon and eggs. Just like the parties in the old days during the season," Jeremy said. "Everyone's invited. You too, Livvy."

Livvy had been standing silently at the back of the group. She shook her head. "Oh, thank you, but no. It wouldn't be right with my husband away serving his country."

Jeremy laughed. "Didn't I hear that he landed a plum assignment guarding the Duke of Windsor in the Bahamas?"

"Jolly dangerous job protecting a member of the royal family," Livvy said hotly. "You know very well that the Germans would love to kidnap him and put him in the place of the king."

"Your husband is with the Duke of Windsor?" Lord Musgrove asked, coming over to join the group.

Livvy nodded. "Actually, Teddy was upset when he was removed from his regiment before they went off to Africa, but the Duke asked for him particularly. They were old polo teammates, you know."

"I must say I feel that the poor old Duke of Windsor has been rather shabbily treated." Lord Musgrove took a swig of his whisky. "Packed off into exile like Napoleon."

"For his own safety," Livvy said.

"To keep him well away from interfering in what's going on in Europe," Sir William said. "His wife has shown a great fondness for Hitler, after all."

"I still think it's a shame," Lord Musgrove said. "I've always thought he was a decent fellow. He might well have proved a useful intermediary if we ever needed to negotiate a settlement with Germany."

"Settle with Germany?" Lord Westerham turned to glare at Musgrove. "Over my dead body."

"Quite possibly." Lord Musgrove smiled.

The strong liquor stung as Pamela swallowed it. She wasn't used to drinking anything stronger than beer and cider, and before the war, the odd glass of wine. But she wasn't going to be outshone by Dido, who seemed quite at ease with cocktails. As Pamela's mother hastily led the discussion to safer waters, Jeremy moved closer to her.

"You will come to my party, won't you?" he whispered.

"I don't know if I'll be able to get time off," she said warily.

"You don't have to work in the evenings, do you?"

"I'm on night shifts at the moment, actually."

"Night shifts? What on earth are you doing, fire watching?"

"No." Pamela gave a nervous little chuckle. "But they need support staff around the clock."

"Which ministry did you say it was?"

"I didn't," she said, "but we do a bit of work for each of the services, fact-checking, looking up things."

"Jolly good for you." He rested his hand on her arm. Then he said in a quiet voice, "This party's all for you, you know. I want you to come and see the flat." His grip on her tightened, and he led her off to one side. "Look, I'm sorry we started off on the wrong foot. That was thoughtless and crass of me. I suppose I was so eager—well, you can understand, can't you? All those months of dreaming about you. Fantasising. I got a little carried away, I'm afraid. So can we pretend that never happened and start over? Take it slowly? Get to know each other again?"

He was looking earnestly into her eyes. "All right," she said.

"Jolly good." His eyes still held hers.

CHAPTER TWENTY-ONE

Still at Nethercote

The gong sounded, and they lined up to go into dinner. Ben was assigned to escort Dido at the back of the line. His father was asked to escort the elderly spinster Miss Hamilton. Naturally, Jeremy and Pamela were paired together. Ben watched the back of her head and saw her laugh as Jeremy whispered something funny to her.

"We're clearly the runts of the litter back here," Dido muttered to Ben as they started to process into the dining room. Inside, chandeliers sparkled over a long polished table. A maid and footman stood in attendance, ready to pull out chairs. Ben found himself between Colonel Huntley's wife and the commander of the Royal West Kents, whom he hadn't met before. Jeremy and Pamela sat across from him. Lady Prescott was at the foot of the table with the two lords, Westerham and Musgrove, on either side of her. Her gown and the diamonds at her throat sparkled in the light of the chandeliers, and she looked around the gathering with satisfaction.

"We should have a toast before we start eating, William," she said. "Celebrating our son's return, when we thought we'd lost him, and he made it home . . ." Her voice wavered suddenly, and she put her napkin up to her mouth to stifle the sob.

"Steady on, old thing," Sir William said. "Jeremy's home, and that's certainly worth celebrating. We'll drink a toast to him and our good friends and the fact that even in the bleakest of times, we can get together and still enjoy ourselves."

"Hear, hear." The murmur echoed around the table. Champagne corks were popped and glasses were poured.

"Where on earth did you manage to find champagne?" Lady Esme asked.

"Ah, well, that was a stroke of luck." Sir William laughed. "Little wineshop I know near Covent Garden. A bomb fell next door, and the owner panicked. I told him I'd buy the place from him, including all his stock. He was only too glad to accept my offer and flee. And I ended up with some damned fine wines—enough to last me through the war."

"If it's over in the foreseeable future," Miss Hamilton said in her clipped tones.

"It has to be," Sir William said. "We can't go on like this. If America doesn't come in, we're done for. We can't hold off the invasion forever by ourselves."

"America shows no sign of hearing the call." Colonel Huntley sniffed derisively. "Only interested in lending us some equipment at exorbitant rates. Making a profit out of our misery."

"Well, we definitely need the equipment. It has to come from some-where," the colonel of the West Kents said. "We can't fight without it. Do you know when my men were first called up, they had to drill with sticks of wood instead of rifles? That's how bad things have been. And we're losing Spitfires at an alarming rate . . ."

"Sometimes I think it would be more sensible to make a pact with Mr. Hitler," Lady Musgrove said. "I fear it will go on and on until we're on our knees and starving, and then Hitler will walk in anyway, and what will we have achieved?"

"It's that warmonger Churchill," her husband agreed. "The power has gone to his head. I think he's actually enjoying this."

"Absolutely bloody poppycock," Lord Westerham thundered. "If it weren't for Churchill, we'd all be slaves of Germany."

"Not slaves, surely. One Aryan race to another. Equals," Lord Musgrove said.

"Ask the Danes and Norwegians how well that is working," Colonel Pritchard said.

There was an uncomfortable silence.

"Let's not talk of such gloomy things tonight," Lady Prescott begged. "We're celebrating, remember? And if our son managed to escape from their beastly prison camp and came all the way across Europe to be with us, then surely that's a sign that they are not invincible. If we are brave and stand up to them, then they can't win."

"Well said, Lady Prescott," Colonel Huntley nodded approvingly. "That's the ticket. A fighting spirit. Britons never, never, never shall be slaves."

"Is that a cue for someone to break into song?" Jeremy asked with an amused look on his face. "'There'll Always Be an England'? 'Rule, Britannia'?" He winked at Pamela.

"It's a sign that we get down to some serious eating," his father said. He nodded at the servants, and soup tureens were carried around.

"Is this oyster stew?" Lord Westerham asked in amazement. "Where the devil did you manage to get oysters?"

Sir William smiled. "Usually they are found in the sea. Actually, I have a little man in Whitstable. He couldn't get me enough for a dozen each, but there was enough to make a good oyster stew."

"But the coastline is off-limits to civilians."

Sir William was still smiling. "Who said anything about being a civilian? Sorry, Colonel, or rather Colonels, but rules are made to be bent in times of need. And those oysters would die without being harvested. Such a shame."

He tucked into his bowl with relish. The others followed. Bowls were whisked away to be replaced with grilled trout. Again, Sir William smiled. "And before you ask, I stocked the lake. They are all homegrown."

After the trout there came roast pork, thin pink slices topped with crackling and a mound of sage-and-onion stuffing.

"Don't tell me you have your own pigs, too?" Colonel Huntley said.

"Actually, no. This leg of pork came from a chap who knows a chap. You can pretty much get anything, if you know where to look and are prepared to pay."

"Black market, you mean?" Lord Westerham looked as if he were about to explode again.

"You don't have to eat it, old chap," Sir William said. "In fact, it was quite legitimate. A bomb fell on a pigsty. The pigs were either killed or wounded and had to be put down anyway."

"At least that's his story and he's sticking to it," Lord Musgrove said and got a general laugh. The pork was accompanied by crispy roast potatoes and asparagus. "From our vegetable garden," Lady Prescott said proudly. "We've had a good crop this year."

Glasses of claret were poured. Ben ate as if in a dream. After the austerity of the digs he shared with Guy and the bleakness of life in London, it was almost too much for the senses to bear: to be sitting at a glittering table, eating course after course of delicious food, drinking fine wine, looking at Pamela sitting across the table from him. He expected an air-raid siren to wake him up.

"So do you have Highcroft Hall to yourselves, Lord Musgrove, or has someone been billeted on you?" Lady Esme asked.

"So far it's just us, but then the place is in bad shape and needs lots of work done. We only have a few rooms that are fit to live in.

But the fearsome old biddy in charge of requisitions did hint that we'd have to take our share of evacuees if and when they were sent from London."

"We have one at Farleigh," Lady Westerham said.

"Be honest, Mah, you palmed him off to the gamekeeper," Livvy said.

"Much kinder," Lady Esme said. "One could tell the poor little chap was terrified in a place the size of Farleigh. And I know he's well fed with the gamekeeper."

"Wasn't he the one who found that body in your field?" Ben asked innocently, seizing the chance to bring up the subject and to observe their reactions.

"Body?" Lady Prescott asked.

"That's right," Lord Westerham said. "Some poor blighter whose parachute didn't open. The gamekeeper's boy and our youngest daughter found him. Dashed brave about it, both of them, because the chap was in a nasty mess, as you can imagine."

"Were they doing training exercises?" Lady Musgrove asked.

"No idea. The body was whisked away in a hurry. He was wearing the uniform of the West Kents, but the colonel here swears he wasn't one of theirs."

"Something funny about him," the colonel said. "Not quite right, you know. His cap badge for one thing. His was the older version of Kentish horse."

"A spy! I knew it!" Miss Hamilton said with great animation. "I'll wager he was a German, dropped in to spy or to aid the invasion."

"Quite possibly," Colonel Pritchard agreed. "Much good will it do them. I don't suppose we'll ever find out now."

The roast pork was cleared away, and in its place came a dessert of chocolate profiteroles in a chocolate sauce.

"Chocolate!" Lady Musgrove exclaimed, giving a sigh of contentment. "Where did you find chocolate?"

"No doubt a bomb fell on a cocoa grove, and my father had to rescue the trees," Jeremy said, making them all laugh. The wine was having its effect. Ben looked around the table at the smiling faces, all of them relaxed and contented. How could any of them possibly be connected to an enemy agent?

They were still all in a convivial mood when the party broke up later.

"How did you get here?" Jeremy asked Ben.

"We walked."

"I'll run you home."

"Not necessary," Ben said. "It's a nice night, and it's not far."

"It's no problem. Just hang on while we get rid of the rest of them, and I'll go and get the motor." He didn't wait for an answer but went over to join his parents, saying good-bye to the other guests. Colonel and Mrs. Huntley joined Miss Hamilton in a very ancient Bentley with an equally ancient chauffeur. Lord Westerham's Rolls was not much younger. Jeremy went over to help Lady Westerham into the passenger seat, then Livvy into the back. When he came to Pamela, he put a hand under her chin, drew her to him, and kissed her. Then he smiled and Ben heard him say, "I'll come over tomorrow if my father lets me have the motor. We could go for a picnic."

Ben didn't hear Pamela's answer, but she smiled back at him. Jeremy had a rather satisfied grin on his face as he walked back over to Ben. Somewhere in the distance came the drone of approaching aircraft.

"German bombers," Jeremy said, listening intently. "God, I hope they let me fly again soon. I really miss it."

Then he turned to Ben, clearly realising that what he said was tactless. "Look, old chap," he said in a low voice. "When I start at the air ministry, I'll see whether I can find something for you."

"What do you mean?" Ben asked. "I already have a job."

"I meant something more challenging. Exciting. If you're stuck in a boring desk job . . ."

Ben was so tempted to tell him that he wasn't in a boring desk job. What he was doing was vital to national security, but of course he wasn't allowed to. "I'm being useful," he said. "I don't need excitement."

"But I'd really like to help, you know," Jeremy said. "I mean, I can't stand the thought of you stuck at some boring desk."

"Look Jeremy, I know you feel guilty about what happened, but it was an accident. I know you didn't intend to kill us both. And we both survived. Let's be glad for that. And as for my own job, I really am . . ." He broke off as the aircraft drone became a roar that drowned out his words.

"They're flying really low," Jeremy shouted. "What's the betting they are aiming for Biggin Hill Aerodrome? The Spitfires will have been given the order to scramble. God, I wish I was one of them."

The night wasn't completely dark, and Ben could make out the shapes of planes passing over, wave after wave of them. Then suddenly there were flashes and bangs. The sky lit up. The Spitfires had met the foe. There was a large explosion, and a plane went down in a spiral of fire.

"One of ours," Jeremy shouted over the roar of the planes. "Poor bugger."

The planes had passed. The noise subsided. "I'll go and get the old banger," Jeremy said.

"It really isn't necessary," Reverend Cresswell said. "We're quite capable of walking, Jeremy. We mustn't waste petrol."

"Rubbish." Jeremy laughed. "You're just an excuse, you know. I've been dying to drive a car again. It's been so long. I hope I haven't forgotten."

But as he headed toward the rear of the house, his mother called after him, "Jeremy, where are you going? You haven't said good-bye to the Musgroves." She waved to the young couple who were pulling away in a sleek and sporty new Lagonda. *They seemed to have no problem with petrol rationing,* Ben thought, while Jeremy answered, "Going to get the car to drive Ben and his father home."

Jeremy's mother grabbed his arm. "Don't be silly. You're not up to driving yet. You've already overdone it by staying up so late this evening. Don't forget you're just out of hospital. You nearly died. Daddy can drive Ben home, can't you, William?"

"Can't I what?" Sir William asked jovially. He was clearly enjoying having played host at a successful party.

"Drive the Cresswells home. I don't think Jeremy should be driving around at night yet. He's only been out of hospital for a few days and is supposed to be resting."

"Oh, but Mother . . ." Jeremy began, but his father held up a hand.

"Your mother is right, old boy. If you want to get back to flying, you need to do everything within your power to regain your old strength. You've been up later than was probably wise. We don't want a relapse, do we?"

"Really, Father, you make me sound like a bloody invalid," Jeremy said.

"Do what your mother says," Sir William said firmly, and Jeremy turned away in disgust.

"We really are quite capable of walking, Sir William," Ben said. "There is no need to drive us."

"Do you want a lift home?" Colonel Pritchard of the West Kents asked. They hadn't noticed that he was still there. "I'm afraid I can't offer a Rolls, but I can fit the two of you into the back of my humble Humber staff car."

"That would be splendid," Reverend Cresswell said, beaming. "We accept with gratitude, don't we, Ben?"

"Yes, thank you," Ben said. "We'll go driving together soon, Jeremy. I don't doubt for a moment." He smiled at his friend but was met by a surly frown. Jeremy hated not to get his own way, Ben realised. He always had as a child and apparently still did.

They clambered into the backseat of the Humber and waved as they drove away. Cool night air blew into their faces through the open driver's side window. As they reached the bottom of the drive and headed toward the village, they were aware of another smell. Acrid, burning.

Through the trees they could see an eerie glow. Flames shot into the night.

"It's Farleigh," Ben shouted. "They've dropped a bomb on Farleigh."

CHAPTER TWENTY-TWO

At Farleigh

The colonel put his foot down, and they shot forward toward the glow. As they reached the gates of Farleigh, they could see that Ben had not been wrong. Flames were rising above the trees and shooting out of the top of the west tower. It seemed to take forever to reach the house. Ben's heart was thudding, even though he knew that Pamela and her family could only just have arrived home minutes before. They wouldn't have been upstairs in their bedrooms. But a worrying thought was creeping into his head—that it might not be a complete coincidence that a man fell into Farleigh's field and right afterward the house itself was bombed. He hadn't considered before that the fallen man could possibly have anything to do with family members.

When the car finally emerged to the forecourt, they saw the house was already a hive of activity. Uniformed men were carrying sand buckets. Others were trying to hook up a hose to a pump by the lake. Ben jumped out even as the car came to a stop. As he moved toward the house, he was met by a terrified Lady Westerham, standing on the steps with the dogs barking wildly beside her.

"Charlie's up in the nursery," she shouted to Ben, grabbing at his arm. "Livvy and Pamma have gone up to fetch him. And where's Phoebe? I don't see her anywhere. Surely she can't still be asleep. And I don't know where my husband has gone. Be quiet, for goodness' sake," this latter addressed to the dogs. "Oh, Ben. Isn't it awful? Why us? Why our beautiful home?"

"Don't worry. Those army chaps will soon have everything under control," Ben said, trying to sound calmer than he felt. He covered her hand with his own, something he'd never have dared to do at any other time.

"I must go and find Phoebe," she said, but Ben put a calming hand on her shoulder. "You stay here. I'll go and find Phoebe for you. Don't worry, the flames are nowhere near the main floors yet." And he ran up the steps and into the house. The foyer was in half darkness, and he was not familiar with the way the house had been divided by the army's occupation. Men in uniform rushed past him.

"Out of the way, sir," one of them said. "You'd best get out, just in case."

"There's a baby in the nursery on the top floor, and a little girl missing," Ben shouted and pushed on past. He tried to force his stiff knee to move faster as he went up the first flight of stairs. He wasn't nearly as confident as he had sounded to Lady Westerham. How could they put it out? How could any hose reach up to the roof? He swallowed back the dread he was feeling. He reached the first landing. Still no sign of Phoebe. She must be sleeping, and he had no idea where her bedroom was—where any bedrooms were, now that the house had been divided up. He presumed that this first floor would be where the family slept, and he opened a door tentatively. Yes. Definitely a bedroom. The hallway seemed unscathed, but he ran down it anyway, hammering on doors and yelling "Fire, fire! Get out."

A door at the end opened and Phoebe stood there in a white nightdress. "Golly, Ben," she said. "What's happening?"

"I think the house got bombed," he said. "The upper floors seem to be on fire. They're putting it out, but you should go straight down to your mother outside."

"But what about Gumbie?" she demanded, her eyes wide with fear.

Ben thought she was referring to a favourite toy.

"Just leave everything," he said.

"But she sleeps on the top floor in the little turret room," Phoebe said, already trying to move past Ben. "I have to go and rescue her."

Ben realised that she was talking about a person. He grabbed her arm. "You go on down," he said. "I'll make sure Gumbie gets out safely."

"I want to come with you. Poor Gumbie. We have to rescue her." She was almost hysterical now.

Ben put a firm hand on her shoulder. "Phoebe, I promised your mother I'd get you out safely. She's terrified. You need to go straight down to her, and I promise I'll find Gumbie for you." He had to half drag Phoebe along the hall and then force her down the stairs. As he went up the second flight, he met servants, hurrying down in their nightclothes: maids clinging to each other, Mrs. Mortlock with curlers in her hair, a sobbing kitchen maid with a dirt-streaked face.

"Mr. Soames has gone with his lordship up to the roof to fight the fire," the cook shouted as she ran past. "I don't know how they are going to put it out. And Mr. Soames is no longer a young man."

"My ceiling fell in," the maid gasped between sobs. "I could have been crushed. I could have been burned alive."

"Oh, stop snivelling and get on down the stairs, Ruby," Mrs. Mortlock said, giving her a little shove. "It was only a little bit of plaster came down."

Ben went on past them. Now he could smell smoke and hear the crackle of flames. He grabbed at the banister to haul himself up; his leg was tiring and no longer wanted to obey him. Smoke curled out to meet him, and he was relieved to hear a voice saying, "Come along, Nanny. You'll be all right."

Livvy came toward him, her son in her arms—not crying but cling-ing to her, eyes wide open in terror. Behind them followed the nurse-maid, dressed in a flannel dressing gown, her hand pressed to a large breast to control her panicked gasps.

"Ben!" Livvy looked relieved to see him. "Isn't it awful?"

He nodded. "Is everybody out from up here?" he asked.

"I don't know. I saw some of the servants going down, but I don't know where Daddy went. Up to the roof to help with the firefighting, I think. I hope he doesn't do anything silly."

"Where's Pamma?" Ben asked, his heart suddenly racing. "Wasn't she with you?"

Livvy looked around. "She must have gone to make sure all the servants are out. I hope she's not trying to find Daddy on the roof. I told her not to, but she never listens to me."

"Oh, your ladyship, please don't dally. Let's get the baby to safety," the nursemaid gasped, tugging at her sleeve. "The whole place is about to go up."

"You go on down. I'll find Pamma," Ben said, urging her forward.

"Do be careful, Ben," Livvy called after him.

He hauled himself up the last steps to the corridor. The smoke was thicker now, and the crackling sound overhead had become a roar.

"Pamma?" he yelled, his voice coming out as a harsh croak. There was no answer. No sign of her. He could feel his heart thudding in his chest. He checked room after room—some doors opened, some closed—but found nobody. At last he reached the end of the hall, and through the smoke he could make out a stone spiral staircase that went up into darkness. "The turret room," he muttered. He pulled out his handkerchief and held it over his nose, not knowing how it might make a difference, then forced himself up the narrow stone steps, feeling his way along the wall. The stone felt warm to the touch. At the top of the steps, he could just make out a doorway, and a door that stood open, leading into a glow, like an entrance to hell.

He took a breath, then plunged into the smoke-filled room. Part of the ceiling had come down, and the room was lit with a red glow from above. He looked around briefly, taking in the large number of books, on shelves and stacked on a table by the window. There were also papers on that table as if someone had been working, and, to Ben's surprise, a telescope. At first he thought it was unoccupied. The bed was empty, the sheet turned back.

"Hello!" he shouted. "Anyone in here?"

When a figure rose up suddenly from behind the bed at the sound of his voice, he took an involuntary step back and almost fell down the steps. Then he identified her through the smoke.

"Pamma!" he croaked.

"Oh, Ben," Pamma said. "I'm so glad you're here. It's Miss Gumble. I can't move her."

Ben picked his way over debris and around the bed to where a woman lay half under the bed, with part of the ceiling lying across her.

"Is she dead?" he asked.

"I don't think so," Pamma replied. "But I'm not strong enough to lift her."

Ben grabbed the lump of plaster and threw it aside, then they drew her out from under the bed together. "Grab her feet," Ben said. "I'll take her shoulders."

Before they could lift Gumbie, there was a cracking sound above, and Ben was conscious of something falling. "Pamma," he shouted and flung himself at her. Together they crashed to the floor as the smouldering beam fell across the bed.

"Are you all right?" he stammered, realising that he was lying on top of her. Her face was inches from his.

"I . . . I think so," she replied.

"I'm sorry, I didn't mean to . . ."

"You saved me. That was quick thinking." She sounded equally breathless.

He got to his knees, stood up, then helped her to her feet. "Let's get her out of here," he said. Together they half dragged, half carried the unconscious woman across the room. Burning embers floated down onto them. The smoke stung Ben's eyes so badly that he could hardly see where they were going. He could no longer even make out the door.

"This way," Pamela shouted. They staggered down the steps. Miss Gumble felt surprisingly heavy for a thin and bony woman. At the bottom, they put her down for a moment, both gasping for breath.

"Thank goodness this hall isn't carpeted," Pamma said. "We can drag her down to the stairs."

"What if she's injured in some way?" Ben said. "Broken spine?"

"We have to get her out somehow, and quickly," Pamma said. "Here, take her nightdress and pull." They half ran down the hall, dragging the woman behind them. Halfway down the hall Pamma looked at Ben and grinned.

"I bet Jeremy will be furious that he isn't in on this," she said.

"He wanted to drive us home, but his parents wouldn't let him," Ben said, returning her grin. "And quite right, as it turns out. This smoke might have finished him off."

"It might finish us off if we don't get Gumbie down the stairs quickly," Pamma said. "Do you feel up to carrying her, or shall we try to bump her down?"

"I'm still worried that we might make her injuries worse. Let's try to carry her."

"What about your leg?"

"I'll be okay." He put his hands under Miss Gumble's shoulders and lifted. Pamela lifted her legs, and they proceeded one step at a time. It was slow going, and Ben wondered how long he could hold out when he heard the tramp of feet and a group of soldiers came running up, carrying sand buckets.

"Casualty, sir?" the officer in charge asked.

"We found her lying unconscious in her room," Ben said.

"Right, two of you—Ward and Simms—you leave your buckets and carry this lady down, then get back up here on the double," the officer barked. Ben and Pamela handed over Miss Gumble, and the men set off with her as if she weighed nothing at all. Ben and Pamela followed.

"It was a miracle that you showed up when you did," Pamela said. "How did you know where to find me?"

"Phoebe was worried about Miss Gumble," he replied, not wanting to admit how frantically he had looked for Pamela.

As they came out onto the front steps, Ben heard the bell of an approaching fire engine. The local fire brigade had come to help. He just hoped it wasn't too late.

Phoebe gave a cry and ran toward the two soldiers. "Oh, Gumbie, Gumbie. Is she dead?"

"I think she's going to be all right, miss," one of the soldiers said. "Smoke inhalation, probably. When she gets some fresh air . . ." And as he spoke, the woman stirred and coughed.

Phoebe grabbed his arm. "Thank you so much for saving her."

"It wasn't us, miss. The young gentleman here and the young lady rescued her. We just helped carry her down the stairs."

Phoebe turned adoring eyes on Ben. "Ben, you're wonderful. Thank you so much."

"Your sister got there first," he said. "Neither of us could have brought her out alone." He felt himself blushing and was glad it was dark.

"You are both heroes," Phoebe said, "and will earn my undying thanks."

Pamela looked at Ben and smiled. "Undying thanks. We'll remind her of that one day when she accuses me of taking the last biscuit." She paused, looking up at the burning roof. "If only we knew that Pah was safe."

"Do you want me to go up and look for him?" Ben asked.

"No, don't do that." Pamela put out a hand to restrain him. "The fire brigade is here now. And loads of soldiers."

"I wonder if it can do any good?" Ben said, but while he studied the outline of the mansion, it did seem that the flames had died down to a dull red glow. He looked around and saw his father coming toward him.

"I'm glad to see you in one piece, my boy," he said, holding out his hand to shake Ben's. "That was foolhardy of you. But well done."

Ben felt an absurd rush of pleasure that, for once, Jeremy had not been the hero. That he had been the one to rescue the damsel in distress.

Miss Gumble was now sitting up, coughing, with Phoebe beside her.

"You're the vicar's son, aren't you?" she said. "They tell me you came up to save me. My deepest thanks."

"You were jolly brave, Ben," Phoebe added.

"It was Lady Pamela who found you first," Ben said. "I helped her carry you down."

"I remember smelling smoke, trying to get up, and that's the last thing I remember," she said. She looked at Ben. "If you hadn't come in when you did . . ."

"Phoebe was worried about you," he said. "She sent me up to find you."

Suddenly she tried to stand up. "But my things. My books. My papers. I have to go and rescue them. I can't leave them to be burned."

Ben put a hand firmly on her shoulder to prevent her from moving. "You can't go up there, I'm afraid. But don't worry too much. It looks as if they are managing to put the fire out. So all may not be lost. Let's hope for the best, shall we?"

Ben watched as Phoebe squatted beside Miss Gumble and tried to comfort her, and a strange thought began to form. So many books and papers . . . and a telescope. Why did a governess need a telescope?

They waited on the forecourt, glancing upward anxiously, then focusing on the front entrance, not speaking to one another. The servants stood off in a huddle to one side. Soldiers who had been sleeping in tents on the grounds had gathered to watch. Others stood ready to move vehicles parked close to the house. But in the early hours of the morning, a group of blackened faces emerged from the front entrance with the news that the fire had been put out. What's more, the damage was not too devastating. Part of the roof and attic had been destroyed. The ceiling had come down in some of the servants' bedrooms, but the fire had not managed to reach the main floors of the house.

Among the firefighters who came down wearily was Lord Westerham, soot-covered like the rest of them.

"Damned fine group of men we've got staying here," he said as his wife rushed to his side. "We'd have lost the whole bally place without them. I consider it an act of God to have stationed the West Kents at Farleigh."

Lady Esme just smiled and wisely said nothing. Then she reverted to her role as lady of the manor. "Mrs. Mortlock, why don't you make everyone hot cocoa? I think we all need it."

"Very good, my lady," Mrs. Mortlock said. "But do you mind if the other servants go up and see what damage has been done to their rooms? They're worried that they've lost their possessions."

"Of course. By all means," Lady Westerham said. "And tell them not to worry. We'll replace what they've lost and find them somewhere else to sleep. We'll all pull through this together."

"Thank you, my lady," Mrs. Mortlock answered with a catch in her voice.

Miss Gumble was now standing. "I'd like to go up, too," she said. "Just to see what might have survived."

Ben watched her go into the house. And he found himself wondering whether the bombing of Farleigh was an accident or deliberate. He thought of those planes flying over. Why would anyone bomb a country house in the middle of nowhere?

CHAPTER TWENTY-THREE

Paris

The first thing Margot noticed as she came to consciousness from sleep was the scent. Rich, smooth, heady. Her nose wrinkled at the unfamiliar perfume. She didn't use more than a dab of eau de cologne herself, and this was a muskier, more powerful smell that hung in the air. It took her a moment to identify it. *Minuit à Paris*—Midnight in Paris, the signature perfume of Gigi Armande. And with the identification came the full memory of where she was. She opened her eyes to see the pink silk drapes, tied back with tasselled swags. Early-morning sun streamed in through tall windows. She was lying on a narrow cot, but the other occupant of the room still slept in a luxurious bed, a face mask keeping out the light. She was at the Ritz, in the room of Madame Armande.

The details of the past twenty-four hours came flooding back to her. The complete feeling of unreality that began when she was awakened in the middle of the night by a German soldier, taken to what was presumably Gestapo headquarters; then the almost miraculous intervention of her employer, Madame Armande, resulting in being whisked away and winding up here, at the Ritz, of all places. It was beyond comprehension. To have gone from pure terror to pâté de foie gras in such a brief time moved into the realm of fantasy.

The lackeys at the front entrance had opened doors for her. "Bonjour, mademoiselle," they muttered, bowing. Her small suitcase had been taken from her. They had crossed the magnificent foyer and gone up a flight of red-carpeted stairs. The only people they encountered were German officers, some with a lady at their side. Their wives, or maybe not. Then Madame Armande opened double doors and ushered Margot into her suite.

"Welcome to my humble abode," she said. "Does it remind you of your home?"

Margot took in the gilded furniture, the moulded ceiling, the heavy drapes, the soft carpet.

And flowers, flowers everywhere.

"Farleigh has a more lived-in feel to it," she said. "This is pure luxury."

"But of course." Gigi Armande looked around with satisfaction. "I know it's early, but I'll order lunch, shall I? You must be starving. What would you like?"

Margot was speechless. For too long now, food had been whatever scraps one could find at the market—vegetable soups, rough bread that tasted like sawdust, meat almost never.

"Order what you like," Gigi Armande had said. "You look as if you need fattening up."

And like magic, a rich soup, an *omelette aux fines herbes*, a thin beefsteak with *pommes frites*, and a dessert of floating island, accompanied by a bottle of crisp Alsatian wine, had been brought up to the room. She was not at all sure of Gigi Armande's part in this, whether she was a guardian angel sent from God, or a sly accomplice of the Germans, working to soften her up. But she wasn't about to turn down good food when Paris had been starving for so long.

Margot had forced back her fears, drunk wine with dinner, and been able to sleep, but now with the bright light of day came the overwhelming feeling of despair. She was now quite aware that she was in a beautiful prison and could picture no good outcome. Of course she was being softened up, made to relax so that when the strike came, she would be caught off guard. It was only a matter of time before she was returned to the Gestapo. She wasn't quite sure whether Gigi Armande was respected enough by the Germans that they accepted her guarantee to keep the prisoner safe or whether she was actively collaborating with them—part of the plot. It made little difference at this stage. All Margot knew was that she had to play along.

She felt the fear rising in her throat. She had to stay strong whatever happened, for Gaston's sake as well as her own. If there was any chance that he was still alive and that they might release him, then she had to do whatever it took. If they thought she was merely the lover of someone who happened to be in the Resistance, an innocent bystander, she might be all right. But if they went over the flat thoroughly—tore it apart—then they would certainly find the radio. She didn't think they would find the codebook. The pages were carefully inserted into a cheap novel, placed among other novels on a shelf. But the radio itself would be enough. They would take her back to Gestapo headquarters and attempt to break her. And only the fact that they wanted her alive for a particular mission would be her one trump card. She had to make them think that she would do their bidding.

There was the slightest chance that word would reach the right people about her fate. The small stamped, addressed envelope had been easy enough to slip in among the vegetables she took down to the concierge. She was sure Madame Armande hadn't noticed as she put turnips and onions into a basket with the letter already lying at the bottom of it, written in pencil, *Please mail this for me.* The old concierge hated the Germans passionately and had watched with pity as Margot was taken away, so there was a chance the letter would be mailed. There was also a chance that the address was no longer a safe house for communication. Nothing was certain these days.

Madame Armande stretched luxuriantly, removed her sleep mask, and said, *"Bonjour, ma petite,"* as if it were any normal morning. "Do you wish to bathe first while I order breakfast?"

Margot took the chance, enjoying the hot water and sweet-smelling soaps. When she came out, Gigi Armande was on the telephone. She was laughing. "You are such a naughty boy," she said. "Until later, then." And she put the phone down.

She smiled and looked up at Margot. "Breakfast will be here shortly. They make the most marvellous croissants."

Margot plucked up her courage as she went toward the balcony and stared out the windows. "Madame, I know this might seem impertinent, but why do the Germans let you stay on here in your old suite when the rest of the hotel is reserved for their officers?"

Madame Armande looked at her and laughed. "It is simple. I design lovely clothes for their wives, and I know everybody in Paris. I am useful to them. So they allow me to exist."

Margot was sure that wasn't the entire answer, but she said no more. She had just finished several croissants with real butter and real jam, not to mention real coffee, when there was a tap at the door.

Madame Armande called *"Entrez"* and in walked Herr Dinkslager, the Gestapo officer from the previous day.

"Good morning, good morning," he said heartily. "What a beautiful day, is it not? The sort of day to be out and about and go for a ride in the Bois de Boulogne. I trust you slept well, my lady?"

"I did. Thank you."

"I must apologise for the primitive nature of the bed." He pointed at the foldaway bed that had been wheeled in for Margot. "It was the best we could do at such short notice."

"There was no problem with the bed, *mein* Herr," she said politely.

"Please take a seat." He indicated the gilt-and-brocade side chair. Margot sat. The German pulled up a chair and sat looking at Margot. Madame Armande remained quietly in the background. "So the question is, what do we do with you now?" He paused. "I have colleagues who are dying to get their hands on you and make you talk, but I myself am a civilised sort of man. I believe we can communicate aristocrat to aristocrat." He gave her a friendly smile.

Margot said nothing.

"I'm sure you must hate this stupid war as much as I do," he said.

"We didn't start it," Margot replied evenly.

"Of course not. But you must realise that Hitler thinks highly of the British. We are two Aryan peoples, the cream of civilisation. We should be cooperating, not fighting. The Führer would like nothing better than to make peace with England, and I know this sentiment is shared with many of your people. If you could help to bring about this peace, wouldn't you want to do so?"

"By peace do you mean capitulation? German occupation?"

"A benevolent occupation."

"Is there such a thing?" she asked. "I heard about your benevolent occupation of Denmark and Norway."

"We must crush those who are foolish enough to resist," he replied easily. "But I'm sure you are wise enough to want to spare further English lives and cathedrals and stately homes like yours. What a terrible pity if your great heritage were to be reduced to rubble."

"What is it you want me to do?" she asked suddenly.

He stared at her long and hard. "There are those in your country who are in sympathy with our cause, who would welcome their German brothers with open arms. You would meet up with them and assist in their plans."

"Plans?"

"To remove those who stand in the way of peace, of course."

Margot stared out the window. Pigeons were sitting on the edge of the balcony. Beyond them, white clouds scudded across a blue sky.

"And Gaston de Varennes?" she asked. "Part of the bargain would be to release him? To have him safely transported to a neutral country?"

Herr Dinkslager tipped his chair back, as if contemplating. "Ah, yes. The French lover. His devoted mistress who would do anything to save him."

"I need to know if he is still alive," Margot said.

"Still alive but being most uncooperative," he replied. "We believe he can give us a great deal of information on the workings of the Resistance. But so far he has remained silent, in spite of all attempts." He looked up at her, his light-blue eyes holding hers. "You see, this puts me in a difficult position, Lady Margaret. We need this information. And trust me, we will get it somehow. My superior officers are never going to agree to release him unless he tells us what he knows. So you could help his cause . . ." He paused and rocked his chair again. Margot focused on his highly polished boots, which reflected the light from the windows.

"You don't think that I could persuade him to talk?" In spite of her fear, she laughed. "I think you underestimate Gaston de Varennes. He is a very proud man. A very independent man."

He rocked his chair forward suddenly, bringing his face close to hers. "You must see that things could not go well for you if you don't cooperate, my dear. You lived with a leading member of the Resistance movement. He must have told you things, even small hints, things that he let slip. I could have you tortured or shot with one click of my fingers right now for aiding and abetting an enemy fighter."

"But, apparently, I'm worth more to you alive than dead?" she said, sounding calmer than she felt.

The ghost of a smile crossed his face.

"You could be useful to us, that is true. But I should have no qualms in ordering your execution if you are not willing to cooperate."

"But I've told you before, he shared no information with me." Her voice had risen now, even though she fought to keep it even. "Not even that he was working with the Resistance. I have hardly seen him for months, and if we were together, then talk was the last thing on our minds."

She heard Gigi Armande give a little snorting laugh as if she appreciated this touch of wit.

"But you suspected . . ." Herr Dinkslager asked.

"Yes, I suspected. But that's all. He told me nothing. No names, no plans, nothing. He wanted to make sure I was safe, I suspect. That I could answer with absolute honesty should such a situation as this arise."

"So we reach a stalemate," Herr Dinkslager spread his hands in a gesture of futility. "I can't have him released until he gives us vital information."

"And I couldn't consider carrying out any assignment for you until I knew he was safely far away . . . in Switzerland, or Portugal, maybe."

"So you see my dilemma, Lady Margaret," he said, studying his hands now. "I am under pressure to retrieve the information that your lover holds. But I personally would like to work toward peace—to have you as my ally in working toward peace. And I'm sure you would rather go home to your family alive and in one piece?"

A picture of Farleigh sprang unbidden into her mind—horse chestnuts blooming along the drive and herself out riding with Pamma and Dido, challenging them to a race, galloping across the grass. She wrenched herself back to reality.

"Of course, I would like to go home, but I can't abandon Gaston. So you see my dilemma, Herr Dinkslager. You are asking me to betray my country to save my lover."

"I am asking you to save your country from ruin. Think of your home. Think of Westminster Abbey. Do you want them all reduced to rubble? Thousands more people killed. Thousands more homeless.

And in the end, those people will blame the ones who brought them to this misery. They will welcome the German army when it comes with rations and shelter and hope for a future."

Margot didn't want to believe this, but she had to admit that it was a possibility if the war went on long enough and the devastation continued.

"Let me see Gaston de Varennes," she said. "Take me to him. I will do what I can."

"Wise girl." He nodded. "Get your coat. We'll go now."

Margot looked across at Madame Armande. She wanted to ask if Armande could come with them, but the designer said quickly, "Off you go, then. I have a fitting with Frau von Herzhofen."

Margot allowed the German officer to escort her down the stairs and out to a waiting car. He opened the door and helped her into the backseat as if he were planning to take her to the opera. He climbed in beside her, and they drove off. Now that she was away from the safety of the Ritz, she fought back the rising panic. Was she being taken to Gaston or merely back to Gestapo headquarters where she herself would be questioned, or tortured, or killed? Had the pleasantries only been so that Madame Armande didn't realise what was about to happen?

The trees along the Champs-Élysées were in full leaf as they drove up the hill to the Arc de Triomphe. In peacetime, the cafés bordering the street would have been full with people sitting at outdoor tables, enjoying an afternoon coffee. Now, the street was almost deserted. An old woman shuffled past, head bowed as if she didn't want to be seen. Two German soldiers passed her, and she stepped aside for them. At Place de l'Étoile, that circle from which streets fanned out like the spokes of a wheel, they turned onto the wide boulevard of Avenue Foch. Before the war, this had been a good address. Tall, light stone houses with balconies and brightly painted shutters stood back from the road behind rows of trees. One would have expected to see elegant couples strolling, a little dog at their heels. Now, this street, too, was deserted, apart from German staff cars parked at the curb. When they had almost reached the end of the street at the Porte Dauphine, one of the old city gates, the car came to a halt. Margot read the house number, 84. *I must remember this,* she thought. *Just in case.* Not that she really hoped anyone would try to rescue her from what was clearly either Gestapo or similar headquarters. She clasped her hands together to stop them from shaking.

The driver came around to open the door for her, and again Herr Dinkslager escorted her inside as if he were ushering her into a good restaurant. The soldier at the door saluted. A conversation was held with a man in a black uniform. He nodded, then spoke into a telephone mouthpiece. They waited, nobody speaking. Then the telephone rang again, the man in the black uniform answered it and nodded to them. Herr Dinkslager said, "We go up now."

They stepped together into a small Parisian iron-cage elevator, and the door clanged shut with finality. Up they went, floor after floor. Margot hadn't realised the building was so tall; she had expected to be taken down to a basement or dungeon. At last the elevator wheezed and ground to a halt, and the door clanked open. She stepped out onto a landing and was motioned to go ahead of Herr Dinkslager to a door opposite. Her heels clicked loudly across the tiled floor, echoing back from the skylight above. Herr Dinkslager opened the door, took her arm, and propelled her inside. Margot's heart was thudding so loudly in her chest that she could hardly breathe, but she walked in, head held high.

Two men scrambled to their feet, one tall, blond, and erect, almost a caricature of a German soldier. The other a scrawny shadow of a man, unkempt hair, filthy clothing, with an ugly bruise on his left cheek. His left eye was swollen half-shut. Margot let out an involuntary gasp.

"Gaston!" she exclaimed.

The man looked at her with horror. "For the love of God, Margot, what are you doing here?" He turned to the Germans. "This woman knows nothing. I have told her nothing. Not one word. Let her go immediately."

"She came here of her own volition, Monsieur Le Comte. She is trying to institute your release to a neutral country, like Switzerland."

Gaston stared at Margot but said nothing. She could not interpret his gaze.

"On what terms?" he demanded.

"That you supply us with the information we want."

"I have told you before you waste your time. I will never betray my friends or my country, whatever you choose to do to me."

"I see." Dinkslager turned to Margot. "Please take a seat, your ladyship."

He pulled out a plain upright chair at a wooden table, and she sat. He pulled out the other chair and sat beside her.

"It seems we have come here for nothing, Lady Margaret. Such a pity."

"You would have me betray brave men?" Gaston asked her. He was looking at her coldly.

"No. Of course not," she said. "I wanted proof that you were still alive."

"I am alive, just. Now let her go," he said to the Germans.

Herr Dinkslager picked up Margot's hand. She flinched, but he held it tightly. "You have elegant hands, my lady," he said. "An artist's hands. And such long fingernails. Strange things, fingernails. We no longer need them now that we do not have to hunt our prey . . . in that manner."

His voice was pleasant, but Margot felt fear rising in her throat. He stroked her hand, playing with her fingers one by one.

"Since they are of no value, maybe we should just remove them?" He looked directly at Gaston. Margot wanted to snatch her hand away but couldn't. She couldn't let the German see she was afraid. He held out his hand to the young agent, who passed him something that looked like a thin piece of wood. Without saying another word he took this and placed it under the nail of Margot's forefinger. He looked up questioningly at Gaston, who remained immobile. Then he pushed down inside the nail. The pain was so red-hot and searing that tears spurted from her eyes. She clamped her lips together to prevent herself from crying out.

"Shall I go on?" He looked up at Gaston. "You wish your beloved to suffer for your stubbornness?"

Gaston remained silent.

"Shall I tear off the nails, one by one? And then there are worse things that can happen to her. This young man here, he has appetites and has been too long without a woman."

Margot watched the blood welling up onto the wood, then she looked up at Gaston's face. His expression hadn't changed. She waited for him to say something.

Then he said, in a cold voice. "She is not my beloved, and you may cut her into little pieces for all I care. But it will not make me change my mind. I will not betray my colleagues and my country, whatever you do. But I must state that I find it dishonourable that you should torture somebody else to try to extract information from me. I am sorry if this woman tried to help in a misguided sense of loyalty to me. However, if you sent me to Switzerland, I should come straight back and join the Resistance again. Why don't we stop wasting each other's time, and you kill me right now?"

Margot pulled the wedge out of her bleeding finger and stood up. "Take me away," she said. "I will do what you want."

CHAPTER TWENTY-FOUR

At Farleigh

After breakfast the next morning, Ben cycled over to Farleigh—to check on the damage, he told his father. At first glance, it appeared that nothing had changed: The horse chestnuts still bloomed. Swans were still swimming on the lake, and the great house stood, strong and defiant against a blustery sky. But the smell of burning lingered in the air, and the wind tossed down burnt fragments like a fine black shower. Then he noticed that the top-floor windows were open, and net curtains flapped out as if appealing for help. He shuddered again when he thought what might have happened to Pamela if he hadn't been there. The beam would have fallen on her. She might have been overcome by smoke inhalation, and she would only have been found much later. He remembered the feel of her body against his as he flung her forward. The way their hearts thudded in time. Then he shook his head firmly.

Get a grip, Cresswell, he said to himself.

As he dismounted and wheeled his bike up to the front steps, he encountered Phoebe coming across the forecourt with the dogs at her heels. She was dressed in riding breeches and a cotton shirt.

"Ben!" She beamed on seeing him. He was still being accorded hero status.

"Hello, Feebs. Been riding?" he asked.

"No, Pah wouldn't let me. He said things might be going on, and I'd get in the way. People looking into the bomb, you know. Actually, I've been helping Gumbie move her things. She's being put in one of the groom's flats over the stables, now we're down to one groom. She's not at all happy about it. Well, I wouldn't be, either. There's only cold water, and it does smell of horse." She kicked at the gravel, then looked up at the house. "I said she should have Margot's bedroom, since she's not likely to need it, but Pah said that standards had to be kept up, and it was not right for the staff to sleep on the same floor as the family, even if there was a war on."

Ben grinned. It was such a typical thing for someone like Lord Westerham to say. Not admitting that anything was allowed to change, even when the whole world was disintegrating around him. He stooped to pet the dogs, who were wagging tails furiously. "Apart from being moved to a stable room, how is she feeling this morning?"

Phoebe made a face. "Still a bit weepy, I'm afraid. Some of her things were damaged when water dripped down from up above. Her books and papers, you know. They were very precious to her."

"Was she writing a book?"

"Some kind of thesis or treatise or whatever you call it. She's very brainy, you know. She had to leave Oxford when her parents died and her brother turned her out with no money."

"Poor Miss Gumble."

"I know. I felt terrible when she told me."

"Is her paper to do with astronomy?" Ben asked.

"I don't know. Why?"

"Because I wondered why she had a telescope."

"Oh, I think she does bird-watching." Phoebe grinned. "The telescope's not big enough for astronomy. She managed to save that. And quite a few of her books. And we've put the rest of her books and her papers to dry out on the table in the conservatory."

"And everyone else is okay?" he asked.

"Oh yes. Mah is very cross with Pah that he took such risks up on the roof, but I think he's feeling jolly pleased with himself, especially as Farleigh was saved."

"I wonder why on earth anyone would want to drop a bomb on Farleigh," Ben said.

Phoebe looked at him, her head tilted to one side like a bird's. "Perhaps it had something to do with that German spy."

Ben looked at her with surprise. It was unsettling to have a twelve-year-old echoing his own suspicions as calmly as if she were talking about the weather. "German spy?" he asked.

"Yes, you know. The man who fell into our field. Alfie and I found him, you know. And we reckon he had to be a German spy."

"What made you think that?" Ben asked.

"Well, he was wearing the uniform of the West Kents, but they don't jump out of planes. So we thought his plan was probably to make his way to Biggin Hill Aerodrome and spy on our planes, or else go up to London and blow up Westminster Abbey or something. But now this has happened, now our house got bombed, I'm starting to wonder whether the two things might be connected. Is there someone or something at Farleigh that the Germans want destroyed?"

Before he could answer, he heard footsteps and looked up to see Pamela and Livvy coming down the steps.

"Ben, how lovely," Pamela said. "Are you recovered from last night's ordeal?"

"Except for lack of sleep," Ben said, returning her smile. "I came to see how everyone was this morning."

"We've all survived remarkably well. Pah was so cheerful at breakfast you'd have thought something good happened instead of his house nearly going up in flames."

"He's just relieved it didn't," Livvy said. "And thank God we came back when we did. If we'd dilly-dallied a little longer at the Prescotts, who would have saved little Charles? I can't bear to think of it."

"One hopes that Nanny would have," Pamela said.

Livvy shook her head angrily. "She'd have been useless. You saw her last night. A quivering jelly."

"Well, all's well now," Ben said. "And the servants? How are they taking it?"

"Ruby's still a bit weepy, and none of them like the idea of camping out in the butler's pantry and a disused storeroom, but it's better than the rain coming in onto them," Pamela said, smiling at Ben. "Actually, the army chaps have already been round this morning to survey the damage, and they say they can requisition supplies to fix the roof, which is jolly good news. And they offered to make a couple of rooms available in their part of the house for our servants." She chuckled. "Mah rejected that offer. She said she wasn't having her girls sleeping anywhere near a pack of soldiers. I think she was quite right. Our parlourmaid is not to be trusted around men, and Ruby could easily be led astray."

"I've just written to Teddy," Livvy said. "He'd want to hear that his wife and son were in danger but survived. I just wish he weren't so far away. Why couldn't they let me accompany him to the Bahamas? I wouldn't have got in the way of his duties with the duke."

"It's a war, Livvy," Pamela said. "Think of all those men being shipped around the world, leaving their wives and children behind. There would be no reason for you to get special treatment."

"We are friends of the Duke of Windsor. That should count for something," Livvy said stiffly.

"Not very much at the moment. I would say that the Duke of Windsor is more liability than asset," Pamela replied.

"I think he's been very unfairly treated," Livvy said.

"Because he took his wife to visit Hitler in his lair?" Pamela demanded. Then she looked up, and her face broke into a smile. "Look who's coming," she said. And Ben turned to see the Prescotts' sleek Rolls coming up the drive.

It came to a halt beside them, and Jeremy got out. "My God, I came as soon as I heard," he said. "We saw the fire last night, but we thought it was that plane that crashed in a field. Then this morning one of the servants came from the village and told us. How much damage was there?"

"Not too bad, really," Livvy said. "Part of the roof was destroyed. The attic was damaged. Grandmama's hideous Victorian monstrosities went up in smoke. You know stuffed birds and dried flowers and things. The ceiling came down in some of the servants' rooms. But we were extremely lucky having the whole regiment on hand. They put it out in no time at all."

"And what about all of you? Any casualties?"

He was looking at Pamela.

"No, we're all fine, thank you. At least I'm fine, thanks to Ben. I went up to rescue Phoebe's governess in the east turret. I found her passed out and lying under the bed, and I couldn't move her. The room was rapidly filling with smoke, and the ceiling was coming down. I didn't know what to do. Then Ben arrived, and we were just pulling her out when a great beam fell. He flung himself"—Ben was sure she was going to say "on top of me," but she corrected and said—"he pushed me out of the way just in time, and together we dragged Miss Gumble to safety."

Jeremy looked at Ben and grinned. "Not bad, old chap. So you're having your share of excitement after all. Maybe I shouldn't have underestimated you."

"No," Ben said calmly. "You should never do that."

"So all's well that ends well here. Jolly good," Jeremy said. "I say, Pamma. Want to come out for a drive? I've finally been allowed to get my hands on the motorcar, on the pretext of checking up on you all."

Pamela looked across at Ben.

"I have to go up to London and report in at work," he said. "I just wanted to make sure that everything was all right here."

"Can't do without you at work, eh, Ben?" Jeremy asked.

"Jeremy, don't be so horrid," Pamela said. "See how you'll feel if they don't ever let you fly again."

"I didn't mean . . ." Jeremy said.

"Yes, you did," Ben replied. "But you'll find I'm quite thick-skinned these days. Have a nice drive, you two." He went over to his bicycle, started to wheel it away, then decided to go and see Miss Gumble in her stable quarters. The room was spartan, to say the least. A single bed, a chest of drawers, and some hooks on the wall for clothes. Every surface was currently piled high with books. She was, as Phoebe had reported, a bit weepy.

"It is so good of you to come and visit me, Mr. Cresswell," she said. "I can't thank you enough for saving my life, but so many of my precious books have been destroyed. My whole life taken from me."

"I'm so sorry," he said. "Maybe more of them will be salvageable than you think."

"But my papers . . . I had hoped to finish my thesis. My former Oxford tutor said that he would petition for me to present it to the examiners. I had to leave Oxford, you know, when my father died and my brother turned me out without a penny to my name."

"Yes, Phoebe told me," he said. "I'm very sorry."

She nodded. "Life isn't always fair. Why should Farleigh be hit by a bomb?"

Ben was looking around the room, trying to bring the subject back to telescopes.

"I don't see your telescope," he said. "I hope you managed to salvage that."

"Oh yes, thank you. It's hard to destroy a telescope. It was my father's. Good solid British brass."

"Were you studying the stars?" he asked.

She laughed. "Oh, goodness gracious, no. It's just a little telescope. I indulge in a little bird-watching. I had it trained on a blackbird's nest in a big oak tree. There was a cuckoo in it. I find cuckoos fascinating, don't you? They lay their eggs in other birds' nests, and then their young one is so much bigger, and it pushes the real chicks out so that the poor blackbirds have only it to feed." She shuddered. "Life is so cruel. I shan't bother to set my telescope up here. There is no view of the woods, only the stable yard."

Ben was glad to make his escape. The telescope and the papers all sounded completely plausible. But then he had been told during his briefings that women make good spies. As he was wheeling his bicycle away, he remembered the papers that were drying in the conservatory. Miss Gumble was busy arranging things in her new quarters, so he had a good chance to take a peek at them. He made his way around the house to the conservatory on the other side. In the old days, before the war, there would have been a pack of gardeners. Now, there were only a couple of old men trying to keep things going. There was no sign of either of them as he approached the conservatory and let himself in. Inside was the sweet, moist smell of growing plants. He noticed small grapes on the grapevine in the corner and small tomato plants with yellow blooms on them. And there on the long table were the books and papers. Some of them still a soggy mess beyond hope. On others, the ink had run. He bent over them, trying to read the writing. Then he stiffened. He read the words *Wars of the Roses*. He didn't find a date, but words leaped off the page. "Struggle to replace a weak king with a more vibrant branch of the Plantagenet dynasty. Two branches of the royal line. Final battle. Outcome of the battle was defeat of the royal . . ."

Was it just coincidence that he had taken the numbers *1461* to be a date during the Wars of the Roses? Or was it possible there was some hidden message here? Two branches of the royal family. Defeat of the weaker line . . . the king who stammered? The king who was anti-Hitler? Was there possibly a plot to get rid of the king? He looked through the rest of the papers, but couldn't find anything that was obviously incriminating. Then he wondered if Miss Gumble might be working for the other side and sending and receiving messages with a hidden radio. In which case, why did they find it necessary to have someone parachute down with a photograph in his pocket?

Back at the vicarage, he changed into city clothes and then cycled to the station. By now, word had spread around the whole village, and Ben was bombarded with questions about his role in last night's drama as he came upon a group of women chatting outside the bakery.

"So it really was a bomb, was it?" one of the women called out to him. "We wondered if it was just a normal house fire."

"No, it was definitely a bomb," Ben said.

"Why would anyone want to bomb Farleigh?" a woman asked.

"Maybe because it's one of them stately homes," another woman muttered. "You know what those devils are like. They want to scare us into capitulating by bombing everything that matters to us. But they're mistaken. We can end up with rubble all around us, and we won't give in."

Ben looked at her weathered and wrinkled face. A woman whose life had been of the uttermost simplicity, who had probably never ventured past Sevenoaks or Tonbridge, and yet willing to stand up to a mighty enemy against all odds.

We might even beat them someday, Ben thought.

He was just mounting his bicycle again when a van drew up beside him. "Baxters Builders" was painted on the side. Billy Baxter wound down the window and leaned out.

"Going somewhere, Ben?"

"To the station," Ben replied. "I have to report in to work."

"Jump in. I'll give you a lift."

"It's all right, thanks," Ben replied. "I'm quite capable of riding my bike to the station."

Billy grinned. "What, that old thing? Looks like it will fall to pieces before you get round the bend."

"It's lasted at least thirty years, so I expect it will keep going a little while longer."

"Come on. Don't be standoffish. I'm heading that way myself, and what if you come back and it's pouring with rain?"

Ben hesitated. Of course, he'd rather ride in the van than pedal the ancient bike to the station, but this was Billy Baxter.

"Come to think of it, I could take you right into Sevenoaks, then you wouldn't have to change trains," Billy said.

"I'd take it, if I were you, Ben," one of the women said. "Leave your bike, and we'll see it gets back to the vicarage."

Now he had no option. "All right. Thanks," he said, nodding to the woman. He went around to the passenger side and climbed in beside Billy. They drove off.

"Where are you heading, then?" Ben asked.

"Going into the lumberyard on the other side of Sevenoaks," he said. "I reckon I'll need to stock up, after what happened at Farleigh last night. You were there, were you? Is there a lot of work to be done?"

"Quite a bit," Ben said, "but I think the army has it all in hand. Since it's now temporarily a military post, I heard they are requisitioning supplies to rebuild." It gave him the greatest pleasure to watch Billy's face.

"But they'll still need a qualified builder, won't they?" he said. "Unless they plan to make do with a few boards tacked across to keep the rain out."

Ben didn't answer this but said, "You seem to be doing quite well out of the war."

"Not too badly, old son. You've got to take your chances, haven't you? Make the most of things."

"It's a pity there aren't more houses being bombed in the Kentish countryside," Ben said.

"I have enough work to keep me going for the duration, don't you worry. And some nice little bits on the side, too."

"Bits on the side?"

"I have a petrol ration, see. I have to get around to repair bomb damage, and the nice government gives me extra coupons. So I can pick up and deliver. Tell your dad if he ever wants anything, he only has to come to me."

"Black market, you mean?" Ben asked.

Billy grinned. "Supply and demand. Doing a good service, old son. I help those who have superfluous goods load them off to someone who needs them."

"With a good markup for you in the middle."

The grin widened. "I'm not a right mug, you know."

So that ruled out Billy Baxter as a possible German contact, Ben thought. He was profiting so nicely from the war, he probably didn't want it to end. And if the Germans invaded, he'd be the sort who'd keep them supplied with necessities, too.

He was glad when they reached the station and parted cordially.

CHAPTER TWENTY-FIVE

At Dolphin Square

Ben waited in the lobby for the lift to arrive, trying to compose in his mind what he wanted to say to Maxwell Knight. Had he anything of substance to report, apart from a bomb falling on Farleigh, Miss Gumble's telescope, the two artists at the oast house . . . ? The lift came down, and the doors opened. Ben uttered a gasp at the same time as Guy Harcourt said, "My God, Cresswell. What a surprise."

"What are you doing here?" Ben demanded.

"I could ask you the same thing, old chap," Guy said. "Let's just say we're both on the same side, shall we? I never did buy that 'nervous breakdown and having to take time off' line. You're as fit as I am. So it seems we both have a standing invitation with a certain captain at Dolphin Square. Well, well."

"Good God. You too?" Ben said.

"Let's just say I'm happy to oblige as messenger boy when asked. You'll be back at our digs, will you?"

"I'm not sure," Ben said. "I, too, run errands." He grinned and stepped into the open lift.

He took a deep breath and walked down the hallway to the office. Maxwell Knight was dressed, this time, in a smart army uniform. Ben was ushered into the inner sanctum.

"Come in, Cresswell." Knight looked up from his paperwork. "Take a seat."

"I'm sorry, sir. I didn't realise you were an army officer," he said. "I should have been addressing you by your correct rank."

Knight returned his gaze. "I'm not, if you really want to know. But I felt I was doing as much as any member of the armed forces to end this war, so I decided I had as much right as any man to wear a uniform." Then he grinned, looking suddenly boyish. "I even awarded myself a couple of medals." He pointed to the strip of ribbon on his chest. "This one for rescuing badgers. This one for making a frightfully good martini." Then Knight's face became solemn again. "You have something to report, already?"

"I'm not sure, sir. Farleigh was hit by a bomb last night."

"Was it now? Much damage?"

"Luckily, not too bad. The attic caught on fire, and some of the top-floor rooms are not habitable at the moment, but no casualties, thank God. The army chaps helped put it out quickly, and, of course, the building is mainly built of stone."

"That's it?" Knight asked, his lip curling in what Ben took to be a sarcastic smile.

"I've done a recce of the neighbourhood and have a list here of possible persons of interest. Nothing too promising, I'm afraid." He handed Knight a sheet of paper. Knight studied it.

"Lord Westerham's oldest daughter, Olivia, is married to Viscount Carrington, who is chummy with the Duke of Windsor and with him in the Bahamas. She thinks the duke has been unfairly treated. But I get no hint from her that she might actively want to aid the Germans. In fact, between you and me, she has always struck me as the least bright of the girls. And easily panicked. I can't see her having the nerves to be a spy."

Knight grinned again. "Women make the best actors, you know," he said. "But you've known her all your life, so I'll take your word for it." He paused. "Who else?"

"I've put Lady Phoebe's governess on the list. She's an educated woman, good family, supposedly writing her thesis. But she did have a telescope in her window in the turret room. And she was very possessive about her papers. I wondered if perhaps she might be studying aircraft and flight paths from Biggin Hill Aerodrome and then somehow signalling them to Germany."

Knight nodded. "Interesting. Yes, she's just the sort of person they might use. Disgruntled, feels that life has cheated her. Maybe wants to get back at the British establishment."

"She seems nice and genuine enough," Ben said. "She claims to use her telescope for bird-watching."

"Does she?" Maxwell Knight smiled. "Maybe you should follow up on her. Get a look at her papers. Search her room to see if there is a hidden radio."

"I've been through her papers that were damaged in the bombing, and they all seemed to relate to a historical thesis she is writing, except for one interesting fact. They are about the Wars of the Roses. And two of the biggest battles of that war were in 1461. So I wondered if that might be a coincidence."

"Interesting." Knight nodded. "I'm not a great believer in coincidence myself. I'd follow up on her, search her room more thoroughly if I were you."

"Yes, sir." Ben thought of this assignment with distaste.

"And anyone else raised a red flag?"

Ben took a deep breath. "There are some people in the area who seem to be doing remarkably well in spite of war, but then I don't think they'd want to bring it to a speedy close. Oh, and I met a couple last night who seem to have pro-German tendencies and are also supporters of the Duke of Windsor, Lord and Lady Musgrove. They're on the list. He has just inherited a property and come from Canada. They seem to have plenty of money and enough petrol coupons to drive around. Nobody in the neighbourhood knew anything of them until recently, which made me wonder if they are who they claim to be. But they live at least five or six miles away, so why not parachute into their field?"

"Why not indeed," Knight echoed.

"Apart from those, there are two foreign artists who have recently come to live in a converted oast house. One claims to be Danish, the other Russian. They seemed to be a little too self-absorbed to be spies, but there was one thing—there was a piece of artwork on the wall that the Russian claimed as his own, but it was actually from another well-known artist."

"We'll do some checking," Knight said. "Foreigners have to register, so it should be simple to find out. Is that it?"

"Only a Jewish surgeon from Vienna, who is staying with our local GP. There are naturally rumours about him because he speaks with a German accent. But he was telling me about being persecuted in Austria. Again, he came to this country recently so should be easy to verify. Oh, and an Austrian land girl who is going out with one of the soldiers. That could be an easy way of getting information."

Knight looked up from the paper. "And what about local gossip? Anything juicy there?"

"People seem to think that the parachutist was a German spy, probably come to spy on Biggin Hill Aerodrome."

"Good work." Knight folded the sheet of paper. "So what next?"

"I take it that the place in the photograph hasn't been identified yet?" Ben asked.

"Not yet."

"Then I have a couple of suggestions," Ben said. "I mentioned that the numbers on the photograph could refer to a date in history and the Wars of the Roses. There were two major battles, one on the Welsh border and one in Yorkshire. I wondered if I should take a look at the battle sites and see if they resembled the terrain in the picture."

"By all means," Knight said. "No stone left unturned, eh?"

Ben hesitated. "Would I be entitled to travel vouchers, official reason for travel, that sort of thing?"

"Absolutely not," Knight said. "This office does not exist, Cresswell. Nothing leaves this office that can be traced back to us. Keep track of your expenses, and we'll reimburse you."

Ben stood up. Clearly, he was being dismissed. He wanted to ask about Guy Harcourt—to drop a hint that he knew Guy was also some part of Knight's stable, but he thought that protocol probably required that nobody claimed to know anyone else.

"Oh, and Cresswell," Knight said. "You don't have to stint. Stay somewhere decent. Treat yourself to a good meal for once."

Ben paused at the doorway, turning back to Knight who had swivelled his chair to face the vista along the Thames.

"Excuse me, sir," he said, "but I couldn't help wondering if the bomb had anything to do with the other incident."

Knight swivelled back. "The parachutist, you mean? What are your thoughts on that?"

"I'm not sure what to think, but when two separate enemy actions take place within a few yards of each other, one has to wonder if they have something in common. So it did occur to me to wonder if the parachutist had been sent to assassinate somebody, and having failed, the house was bombed." He paused as Knight said nothing. "I know it sounds absurdly outlandish, but . . ."

"Not at all," Knight said. "Do you think Lord Westerham or any of his daughters would be worth the risk of sending down a parachutist to kill them?"

"Frankly, no, sir."

Knight took a deep breath. "I think it's most likely that they now have the house pinpointed as an army base. Not too hard to spot the army vehicles in the front garden, even though they do have camouflage over them. So maybe this was a warning bomb that they know the West Kents are headquartered there, and they will be back."

"Yes, sir. That's the conclusion I came to."

He turned to go again.

"On the other hand," Maxwell Knight said. "There is something you should know about Lord Westerham's family. I don't think it could have any connection to our parachutist or the bomb. However . . . Lady Margot Sutton has been taken by the Gestapo in Paris."

"Crikey!" Ben blurted out before he realised how juvenile that sounded. He felt the colour drain from his face. "They've taken Margot? Because of her French lover?"

"Possibly," Maxwell Knight said. "Also, possibly because she was one of ours."

"A spy? Margot was a spy?"

"In a very minor sort of way. She went to the embassy, while it was still in operation, and asked that since she was stuck in Paris, could she be of any assistance. She was given a secret radio and passed messages along the chain. If they have found the radio, they will probably torture her and then shoot her."

"Is there to be no attempt to try and get her out?" Ben asked.

"Being arranged as we speak," Knight said.

"Sir, I'd like to volunteer to be part of that mission," Ben said.

Knight actually grinned. "I admire your pluck and your loyalty, but I suspect that if your leg was working properly, you'd be up flying a Spitfire by now. Can you really see yourself clambering over Paris rooftops, shinning down drainpipes and running from German soldiers, firing over your shoulder as you go?"

Ben opened his mouth to speak, but Knight went on, "And for that matter, can you see yourself calmly slitting the throat of a sentry on guard? It takes a particular type of chap to be able to carry out assignments like that. That's why we leave it to the commandos. They are trained."

"Does her family know any of this?"

"No, and you are not to tell them until the mission is conducted satisfactorily. If it is not, we will decide on the right time and place to inform them."

Ben nodded. "Might I ask that you let me know how the mission went?"

"Possibly. We'll have to see." He waved at Ben. "Go on. Off you go on your quest, then." As Ben left the office, he noticed that Maxwell Knight's secretary, Joan Miller, was as smartly dressed as if she were going for a meal at the Savoy. Grey silk and pearls, and a touch of makeup.

"You look very nice today, Miss Miller," he said.

She smiled. "Why, thank you, Mr. Cresswell. I have a date with some important gentlemen. One has to look one's best on such occasions."

As Ben came out into the fresh air, he shook his head. There was always an *Alice in Wonderland*–like quality about visiting Dolphin Square. He found himself wondering if either of the people there were real. He also found himself wondering if his assignment was of any value.

CHAPTER TWENTY-SIX

At Bletchley Park

On Sunday evening, Pamela caught the train back to Bletchley. Jeremy had offered to drive her.

He had just driven her home after an evening at a pub on the banks of the Medway. It was a romantic setting, but the food left much to be desired. The cod was like leather, and the cabbage boiled to a grey mass. They had laughed about it and compared it to the food at Nethercote.

"Must you go back to work?" he asked.

"Of course. It was quite out of order to allow me a week when we are so shorthanded, but I was suffering from the effects of too many night shifts and didn't really get a proper break last Christmas."

"Then we'll go together. I've got to go up to town, anyway. I have to see the quacks at Barts to make sure my gunshot wound has healed nicely and that I'm fit to report back for duty." He must have noticed the look of alarm on Pamela's face. "Oh, not back to flying, old thing. Much as I wish, I don't think I'll be allowed in an aeroplane for a few more months. But they say they'll find something for me at the air ministry. I can't say I'm looking forward to it. From what you and Ben say, they only allow you to do the routine stuff. I want to be able to plot the courses for bombing raids or interpret aerial photographs."

"You would!" Pamela laughed. "But the boring stuff has to be done, too, Jeremy. If files were not in apple-pie order, and a piece of information couldn't be found the moment it's wanted, the delay could cost lives."

"You're right." He grinned back at her. "I never was much good at doing the ordinary things, was I? I got beaten enough times at school for failing to buckle down and study. But then I aced the exams, and they had to eat their words. Most satisfying."

"You shouldn't waste petrol driving up to town when there is a perfectly good train," Pamela said.

"Oh, don't worry. My father can virtually write himself petrol coupons, you know. He has to go up to town all the time."

Pamela had a worrying vision of Jeremy insisting on driving her all the way to Bletchley. That would never do. "I'd appreciate a ride to the station," she said, "but I think I'd rather go back by train after that. I have the voucher to travel."

"Anyone would think that you were trying to avoid me."

"Not at all, Jeremy. I love being with you. You know that. We've had a splendid time today, haven't we? It's just that . . . well, I want to get my head in order before I check back to work. For all I know, I might have to go directly to another night shift."

"They've no right making women do night shifts," Jeremy said. "I think I'll come with you and tell them."

"No, you won't!" She slapped his hand.

He grabbed her hand, pulled her toward him, and kissed her with passion, gradually forcing her back onto the seat of the Rolls. She was horribly conscious of his weight on top of her, his tongue in her mouth, his knee forcing her legs apart, his hand straying downward. She sat up abruptly, pushing his hand away. "Jeremy, not here, outside my parents' house. Anyone might see."

He was looking at her, long and hard. "Pamma, I'm beginning to wonder whether you still feel anything for me. You used to love me; I know you did. My feelings for you haven't changed, you know. I can't help admitting that I want you. I want you desperately. And yet every time I get near you, you push me away."

"I don't mean to," she said. "And I do still love you. I dreamed about you every day you were away. I went to sleep with your picture under my pillow. And I do want you to make love to me. It's just . . ." She gave an embarrassed little laugh. "I'm a twenty-one-year-old virgin, and I'm hesitant to take that next step, I suppose."

He laughed now. "Then we'll have to do something about that, won't we? I won't rush you. I'll make sure the time and place are right. Our London flat is very comfortable and very private. Mayfair and all that. No family to spy on us. I'll be moving in at the end of the week. You will come and visit me, won't you?"

"I don't know when I'll get more time off," she said. "But I will come."

"We can start with my moving-in party. I thought I might hold it next Wednesday. That will give me time to get settled in. Do you have your evenings free?"

"It depends what shift I am on."

He frowned. "Surely you can swap shifts for one evening. You don't have to work seven days a week, do you?"

"No, of course not."

"And you can get into town by train?"

"Yes, easily."

He took her hand in his, playing with her fingers. "Then let's say next Wednesday. I haven't had a decent party for years. Invite your friends if you like. I bet the old man has some good booze stashed away at the flat. We'll help him drink it in case the Germans invade and confiscate it."

Pamela was sitting up very straight in the car, wanting to smooth down her skirt. "Do you think they will invade?"

"I think it's inevitable," he said. "Look how easily they walked into France and Belgium and Denmark and Norway. What have we got that those countries don't have?"

"We haven't been invaded since 1066," she said. "Napoleon walked into all those countries, but he couldn't take Britain."

He patted her knee. "That's the spirit. We'll fight them on the beaches, we'll fight them in the pubs and public loos . . ."

"Jeremy, don't make fun. It was a brilliant speech. Mr. Churchill is a brilliant orator."

"Sorry. Yes, I know he is. But with all the fighting spirit and pride in the world, we don't have the weapons to take on the Wehrmacht. If America decides to lend us some, then that may be different. But they may sit on the fence for years."

Pamela shuddered. "Let's not talk about it. You're home safe, and that's what matters."

"And you'll come to my party?"

"I'll try my best to, I promise."

Pamela went over this conversation in her head as the train bore her out from London to Bletchley. A party. That would be safe enough. Safety in numbers. Then she realised that at some time she'd have to come to terms with her relationship with Jeremy. He wanted to make love to her. She had always thought that she wanted it, too. But her vision included marriage. His didn't seem to. She'd heard too many rumours of girls who ended up in the family way. Girls who were shipped off to the country and nobody ever spoke about the baby again.

But Jeremy would marry me if that happened, she thought. *Of course he would. Besides,* she added to herself, *I have a feeling that Jeremy knows about such things.*

She was feeling better by the time she returned to Bletchley and found she was anxious to get back to work. Trixie was sitting on her bed when Pamela arrived back at their digs. She was carefully easing one leg into a silk stocking. She looked up and smiled.

"Oh, you're back. Just a minute while I try to do this without laddering my one good pair. God knows what I'll do after this. Resort to drawing a line up the back of my leg with a pencil, like everyone else, I suppose." She eased the stocking up and secured it with a suspender. "Did you have a good time?"

"Yes, thank you. Apart from our house being bombed."

"Bombed? Golly, how awful. Was it destroyed?"

"No, thank goodness. Only very minor damage. The West Kent Regiment is billeted with us, and it was a case of all hands to the rescue. They put out the fire before it could spread."

Trixie grinned. "I really must come and visit you with all those yummy soldiers on the premises. Speaking of yummy men, did you see the delicious Jeremy Prescott?"

"I did."

"And how is he? Is he—um—fully recovered?"

"Still a little pale and thin, but well on the road to recovery, thank God. He looks a little like a Romantic poet, you know, like Keats on his deathbed. But recovering rapidly." An image of Jeremy in the car, trying to pin her down, flashed across her mind. "Yes, making a remarkable recovery."

"So did you have an absolutely divine time? Confess all. Tell Auntie Trixie."

"We had family around most of the time," Pamela said. "We did go out to dinner at a pub, and then he drove me home."

"Oh God, I remember going home in a taxi with him once, after a deb's ball," Trixie said. "My dear, I had no idea you could get up to that sort of thing in the back of a taxi. Nobody had mentioned he was NSIT."

"What?" Pamela asked.

"NSIT. Not safe in taxis, darling. It was a common code among debs. Did you grow up in a nunnery?"

"No, but Farleigh was almost as bad. My parents are horribly prudish, and I knew nothing until I went away to finishing school in Switzerland."

"Where I'm sure you learned more than how to curtsey and hostess dinner parties. I know I did." She gave a knowing grin. "My dear, those ski instructors. So virile." And she pretended to fan herself.

Pamela laughed, a little nervously.

"So did Jeremy pop the question? Or did you already have an understanding, as they used to say so quaintly?"

Pamela felt herself flushing. "Jeremy thinks that one can't think of marriage until this horrid war is over."

"Quite right," Trixie said. "And who would want to get married when clothing is on ration? You won't see me getting married in a frumpy two-piece. I want the twelve-foot train, the veil, and yards of glorious silk. And a yummy trousseau, too."

"You'll be wearing white, then?" Pamela asked, raising an eyebrow and making Trixie giggle.

"My dear, if the only brides who wore white were virgins, you'd have very few white weddings," she said. As she talked, she was pulling on the second stocking. Then she stood up, studied the result in the mirror, and nodded approvingly.

"Are you going somewhere nice?" Pamela asked.

"Probably not. A chap from Hut Six I met at the concert last night invited me to the pictures. He's a bit serious and brainy for my taste, but then who isn't at this dump? Nobody exactly comes here to have fun, do they? So I thought the pictures would be better than staying in and eating Mrs. Entwhistle's cottage pie. And by the way, the food has been particularly drear this week. Boiled cabbage, mashed spuds, and a slice of Spam three nights in a row. I kept thinking of you, eating real food. Did you have some good meals?"

"I did, actually," Pamela said. "Especially one at the Prescotts'. Oysters and roast pork and chocolate mousse. And all the right wines for each course. I thought I'd die from happiness."

"Where did they get their hands on all that?"

"Black market, by the sound of it. Sir William seems to have fingers in a lot of pies."

"Then you'd better force Jeremy to marry you before some other girl snaps him up, if you want to live in luxury for the rest of your life." She applied a generous coat of lipstick. "So when will you see him again, do you think? It's rather too far to pop down to Kent on a day off, isn't it?"

"Well, he's moving to his parents' flat in London this week," Pamela said. "He starts work at the Air Ministry. Oh, and he's planning a party a week from Wednesday—a sort of flat warming. I just hope I'm not still on night duty. Maybe I can trade shifts."

"A party? How divine. Can I come?"

Pamela hesitated. Trixie would be only too anxious to get her hands on Jeremy again, she was sure. But she saw no reason to decline. "Yes, yes, of course," she said. "If we can both get a free evening. I told Jeremy I might still be working the night shift, and it might be hard to get time off."

"Maybe not," Trixie said. "I was handed a note from Commander Travis on Friday. He wants you to report straight to him as soon as you come back."

"Golly," Pamela said. "I hope it's not a reprimand."

"Why, you haven't blotted your copybook, have you?" Trixie asked. "Given away state secrets? Talked about your job here, God forbid?"

"No, of course not. Although it was rather hard at home. They all think I'm doing some boring office job in a faceless ministry, and I couldn't tell them that what we are really doing is important."

"Is it?" Trixie asked. "Sometimes I wonder. All I do is a boring office job in a faceless ministry, but I suppose your job must be more exciting than mine."

"Not exciting," Pamela said hastily, "but at least I know I'm a small cog in a long chain that does make a difference, and that's all that matters."

"Is this where I stand up, wave a flag, and sing 'Rule Britannia'?" Trixie said, laughing.

Pamela gave her a friendly shove. "Shut up and go off to your pictures. I suppose I'd better go downstairs and face Mrs. Entwhistle's Spam and spuds."

CHAPTER TWENTY-SEVEN

At Bletchley Park

At eight o'clock the next morning, Pamela parked her bike outside the big house and headed for the imposing front door. It was a glorious day. The sun sparkled from the lake where swans glided. Pigeons fluttered and wheeled in the sky. The air smelled of roses and honeysuckle. It was the sort of day to take a picnic to a riverbank. Pamela's thoughts went to lazy summer days at Farleigh before she wrenched them firmly back to the present and entered the gloom of the front hall. She couldn't think of what she might have done wrong, except for fainting. Maybe she was about to be told she wasn't up to the task here and would be sent home in disgrace. But then she wasn't the first person who had fainted or even had a nervous collapse while working here. The long hours, the dreary conditions, and the constant pressure got to other people, she knew.

The receptionist popped out of her cubby when she heard Pamela's feet on the tiled floor.

"Ah, Lady Pamela," she said. "Do go up. I'll telephone Commander Travis and tell him you are coming."

She had sounded bright and cheerful, which was encouraging, but maybe receptionists knew few details about visitors. She went up the ornate wooden staircase and tapped on the commander's door.

"Lady Pamela," he said jovially. "Do take a seat. Did you have a good week's rest at home?"

Pamela perched on an upright chair, facing the commander's mahogany desk. "I did, thank you, sir. A few nights' sleep and good food, and now I'm right as rain."

"Splendid," he said, "because I'll need you to be on your toes. I'm giving you a new assignment. It's a little out of the ordinary, even for Bletchley, and nobody else is to know about it. Do you understand? I know you are used to secrecy by now, but in this case, it is especially important."

"I see, sir," she said.

He leaned forward in his seat. "What do you know about the New British Broadcasting Corporation?"

"Isn't it a radio station broadcasting from Germany, purporting to be British and giving bogus news?"

"Precisely." He wagged a finger at her, emphasising the point. "Designed to put fear and despair into the hearts of the British people, to break down their will to fight, and to welcome the Germans when they invade."

"I don't think many Britons are taken in by it, sir," she said.

"You'd be surprised. Some people believe anything the radio tells them. They all are not as sophisticated as we are. But that's beside the point. You may also have heard that there are fifth columnists working inside Britain. Not necessarily foreigners, but English men and women who for reasons of their own are in sympathy with Germany and would like to assist Herr Hitler in any way they can."

"Surely not, sir?" Pamela asked. "I mean, one hears about fifth columnists, but one always thinks of dubious Russian émigrés and, of course, Oswald Mosley's fascists."

"You'd be surprised how many people would welcome the invasion," he said. "Even people that you and I know. In fact, we think there is some sort of plot going on at this very moment. We're not sure what it is, but we suspect it may well be to remove the royal family and bring back the Duke of Windsor in their place. We know he has strong pro-German sympathies. He has already demonstrated that."

"Gosh, that would be awful," she blurted out, realising she sounded like a schoolgirl.

"This is where you come in, Lady Pamela," Commander Travis said. "I have had good reports on you from your team leaders. You are quick and you spot things. So this is your assignment. We have a nearby radio receiving station where WRAF workers listen and transcribe all German radio broadcasts. You will receive daily transcripts from this New British Broadcasting Station, and your job will be to pick out anything that might be a message in code to sympathetic souls. It might be a repeated phrase that announces the next sentences will be a message. I can't tell you what to look for, because I don't know. But you're sharp. I think I'm right to put you up for the job."

"Will I still be working in my old hut, sir?"

"No, of course not. As I said, this is just between the two of us. Nobody else must know. It's quite possible there are sympathisers here, at Bletchley."

"Really?"

"One can't be naïve, Lady Pamela. The Abwehr is not stupid. They will attempt to infiltrate sympathisers wherever they can. So you see the need for complete secrecy."

"Of course. But what am I to say to the chaps I was working with if I meet them in the cafeteria? What about my roommate?"

"You tell them you've been seconded for a special assignment with Commander Travis because he says he likes to see a pretty face doing the filing."

She had to laugh at this. "So I'll be working here?"

"You will. I'm making a room on the top floor available. And you report to me and to me only. Do you understand?"

"Yes, sir. I hope I can live up to your expectations," she said. "I'm to be working alone, then?"

"No, you will have one colleague working with you. A very bright young man who will be checking out other German broadcasts for possible coded messages. I hope you'll help each other in discovering possibly coded messages among the harmless ones, and then being able to break those codes."

When Pamela said nothing, he added, "I have full confidence in you. I think you're the right person for this job."

"When do you want me to start?" she asked.

He smiled, making his severe face look positively human for a second. "No time like the present, Lady Pamela."

Pamela left his office and went up another flight of stairs to the designated room on the top floor. This had clearly been a servant's quarters. The hallway was not wood-panelled, and it had a disused feel to it, dusty and stuffy. She opened the door, then let out a little gasp because there was a movement to her right. A tall, gangly fellow jumped up from the table at which he was sitting.

"Golly, you made me jump," Pamela said, laughing now. "I didn't expect anyone to be here. You must be my partner in crime."

He came around the table, holding out his hand to her. "Froggy Bracewaite," he said. "And you're Lady Pamela Sutton."

"Correct," she said. "I take it your name isn't really Froggy."

"To the top brass, I have to answer to Reginald," he said. "But I was dubbed 'Froggy' at Winchester, and it has stuck. And you may not remember, but we've met before. I believe I danced with you at one of the deb balls during your season. You probably still have the bruises to prove it."

"I thought you looked familiar," she said. "And I'm sure you weren't the only partner to tread on my toes during that season. They give girls dancing lessons but never think of doing the same for their partners. Speaking of which, I'm so glad we're to be working together. This whole thing sounds horribly daunting, and I wouldn't have liked to tackle it alone."

"You must be really bright, or they'd never have asked a woman to do this," he said. "In case you haven't noticed, the men get all the plum jobs here, and the women are stuck with the clerical stuff, even though they are often better qualified."

"I was one of the lucky ones," Pamela said. "I was doing something quite interesting. But not actual code breaking. I've no idea how to even start doing that. You'll have to teach me."

He pointed to teleprinter printouts on the table. "The first batch of transcripts have been sent over from station Y," he said. "Let's have a look together, and I may be able to show you what we might be looking for."

They stood together at the table. Pamela's eyes scanned the first page.

> *Dear friends in Britain. We are sorry that your thought-less government is making you suffer needlessly. The invasion will go ahead as planned and there is nothing you can do to stop the might of the German Wehrmacht. But those who assist us, who make us welcome, will find that it will be a smooth transition and life will quickly return to normal. Lights will come on again, pubs and cinemas will reopen. There will be plenty of food again.*

"What rubbish," Pamela exclaimed, making Froggy chuckle. "Surely nobody can believe this?" she asked.

"You'd be surprised," he replied. "Especially when you hear news items like this." He pointed lower down the page.

*The Bank of England is perpetuating a giant fraud
on the people of Britain. The pound note has actually
become worthless and the government is printing . . .*

They read on. Reports on the number of British ships sunk. Cargo ships that would never reach British shores with food supplies. Britain would soon face starvation. And yet there was a secret store of food in the cellars under Whitehall so that the members of the government and those in power still eat well, while the average worker has to exist on bread made from sawdust.

After the depressing and deceptive news bulletins, there came purposed messages from British servicemen held captive in German stalags.

From Sergeant Jimmy Bolton, RAF Hornchurch, and now a prisoner at Stalag sixteen. To his wife, Minnie. "Don't worry about me, old girl. I am in good health and being fed and taken care of here. Chin up and I'll be home soon."

"I wouldn't hold my breath if I was his wife," Froggy muttered.

Pamela nodded. "All very insidious and depressing," she said, "but I don't see anything that seems like a coded message. There is nothing like 'The hedgehog comes out at midnight' that I had expected to find."

He laughed. "The Germans are quite sophisticated with their codes. Let's see if the first letters of any sentence spell any useful words."

They did that, but drew a blank. They tried similar combinations—the second sentence of every bulletin. Proper names of the purported prisoners.

"I suppose Bolton is a place," Pamela suggested.

Froggy shook his head. "But Sims and Johnson aren't, are they? I must say that nothing leaps out at me so far. No repeated words or phrases. We might have to see several days' worth of transcripts to determine if phrases are repeated at the same time each day."

By the end of the first day, Pamela felt that they had overestimated her capabilities, and she would soon be found lacking and sent back to her unit in disgrace.

When she arrived home, Trixie was waiting for her. "So what was it all about? Do tell? Did Commander Travis give you a slap on the wrist?"

"No, nothing like that," Pamela said. "It was just to move me to a new division. We were overstaffed where I was, and they needed extra help with the office work at the big house. As Commander Travis put it, he likes to see a pretty face around the place."

Trixie shook her head. "Men!" she said. "Wouldn't it be funny if a woman said 'Hire a young man, I like to see rippling muscles around the place.'"

Pamela laughed. "I'm sure some women in positions of authority do think that way. But I have to say I'm glad to be out of that hut. If the big noises work in the main house, you can bet that it will be heated properly in winter. And I'm close enough to the cafeteria to pop over during my breaks."

"But still only doing the boring stuff, like me," Trixie said. "When will they realise that we women are capable and could quite easily take on code breaking like the men?"

"Only if they ever become desperate, I suppose," Pamela said. "Actually, there are some really brainy chaps here, so I understand. Absolute maths whizzes. I wasn't bad at mathematics, but there was no way I'd ever daydream about new ways to solve algebraic problems and have numbers dancing around in my head like some of these boys."

"Some of them are half-barmy, if you ask me," Trixie said. "That chap who took me to the pictures. He made a weird sort of humming noise at the back of his throat and kept tapping his foot nervously, and he never got any farther than sliding his arm around my shoulder. We're probably the only normal people here."

Pamela was about to say that she was working with a chap she'd danced with as a deb, but then remembered that even such trivial matters had to remain secret.

A gong sounded. "I suppose we'd better go down and face the supper," she said. "I'm rather afraid I smelled fish boiling."

"Oh no, not her dreaded boiled fish," Trixie said. "At least she couldn't overcook Spam. Do you think we dare sneak out and go have a sausage roll and a pint at the pub?"

"What, and incur her wrath and be served the most gristly bits of stewed meat forever? Have you noticed that she always gives that creepy man, Mr. Campion, the best bits?"

"Of course, I have. She fancies him. But, unfortunately, he doesn't fancy her. I mean, darling, who would?" She gave a bright laugh. Then she became serious again. "There have to be better digs somewhere nearby. I'd ask my family if we have any connections around here, but I can't reveal where I am. I shall be furious if I find an aged uncle is living five miles away in a stately home and eating pheasant three times a week." She slipped her arm through Pamela's. "All right. Let's go down and face the music, or rather face the boiled cod. Then we'll go and get that pint. My treat."

CHAPTER TWENTY-EIGHT

At home and abroad with Ben

Back home after his visit to London, Ben felt uncomfortable about searching Miss Gumble's room. It wouldn't be too hard, he realised. She'd likely be with Phoebe, giving her lessons during the morning. But all the same, there was a tremendous risk: Everyone in the house knew him. If he bumped into any member of the family, he'd have to come up with a reason for being there and possibly be taken into the house for tea. If he were seen going up the steps to the flat over the stables, he'd have to explain himself. Then his father came into the room, looking up in surprise to see Ben there.

"Oh, you've come back. I thought you were off to London?"

"Just for a meeting," Ben said. "In fact, I have to go away for a few days. Up north."

"What on earth would you be doing up north?" his father asked. "I thought you worked in an office."

"Oh, I do. I do," Ben said hastily. "But I've been asked to deliver some papers personally to a research station. You can't be too careful these days. Mail could be intercepted."

"Really? Surely not. The British post office is a reliable institution."

"You never know, Dad. German sympathisers are supposed to have infiltrated all over the place."

"That's just scaremonger talk. I believe it's put out by the enemy to drive fear into our hearts. Make us suspicious of each other. Think that Germans are landing every day. You know half the village believes that the poor man whose parachute didn't open was a German spy. Utter rubbish. He was wearing an English soldier's uniform. I saw him myself. A tragic accident, that's what it was."

"Probably," Ben said. "So I'll be gone for a couple of days, then I may be coming home again, maybe not, depending on my department head."

Reverend Cresswell looked around. "Now I'm trying to remember what I came in here for. My mind is like a sieve these days. Oh, I know. Book on birds. There's an owl's nest in that big elm, and I rather think it's a screech owl. I caught a glimpse of it at twilight, but I wanted to be sure."

A brilliant idea came to Ben. Miss Gumble's telescope. He could ask to borrow it for his father. Perfect. He packed an overnight suitcase ready for his trip, then cycled over to Farleigh. As he rode up the drive, he had to pull over to the side while a convoy of army lorries drove past, and the enforced wait brought back his doubts. If he asked Miss Gumble to borrow her telescope, she'd probably go and get it for him. She wouldn't want him in her room, especially if she had something to hide. But if he went up to her room without her permission and was seen, she'd hear about it and there could be a fuss.

"Damn it," he muttered. He wasn't cut out to be a spy. He thought of those chaps who were being sent to rescue Margot Sutton from the hands of the Gestapo and how stupid he must have sounded volunteering for such a job. Margot must have nerves of steel to be receiving and delivering radio messages in occupied Paris. He remembered he'd always been a little in awe of her—she was several years older than Pamma and sophisticated and glamorous, even as a teenager. But surely it had always been Pamma who was the brave one, the one who climbed trees and accepted dares. He felt a great wave of relief that it wasn't Pamma who was in Paris now, waiting to be rescued. Because the chance of a successful rescue from German headquarters in an occupied country must be pretty slim. It was likely that they'd all end up dead. He wondered if Lord and Lady Westerham could have any idea that their child was in such danger and how difficult it was that everybody had to keep secrets.

The last lorry in the convoy passed. Ben continued his ride up to the house. He saw that panels of plywood were being unloaded and carried up the steps. Presumably repairs for the roof. The place was busy with soldiers, which enabled him to slip past unnoticed and reach the stable yard. He went up the steps and tapped on her door, just in case she wasn't at lessons with Phoebe. Then he tried the handle and pushed. The room seemed to be locked.

"Damn," he muttered and put his shoulder to the door. It swung open, and he was in Miss Gumble's room. His heart was beating fast as he looked around and saw the telescope lying on top of one of the piles. A radio. That's what he was looking for. And any incriminating papers. The room was tiny, and he went through the piles of books and her few possessions quite quickly. But no sign of a radio.

He certainly hadn't seen a radio among her things in the stable room. He wondered if he dared go up to her turret to see if there might be a radio hidden there somewhere. An excuse, that's what he needed. He remembered that he'd been wearing his dinner jacket. Yes, that would work. He went back around to the front steps, into the house and up the two flights to the top floor. Nobody stopped him until he came to the spiral stair leading to Miss Gumble's turret. Several soldiers were trying to manoeuvre a sheet of plywood up the narrow stair. One of them turned to see Ben.

"Can I help you with something, sir?" he asked. "As you can see, we're rather occupied up here now, and I'd appreciate it if you went downstairs again."

"It's just that I was the one who rescued the lady from that turret room," he said. "And I was wearing my dinner jacket, and I lost one of my gold cuff links. So I wondered if I might take a quick look. It has rather a sentimental value."

The officer nodded. "Of course, sir. Hold up, men. Let the gentleman past."

Ben hurried up the stair. The room was a sorry mess with plaster lying across the floor and blackened stains on the walls. It still smelled of smoke. Ben picked his way around, examining under the bed, the window seat, looking for any loose floorboards, but found nothing. He was forced to retreat. If she had a radio, either it was well hidden or she'd spirited it away.

There was nothing to do but to complete his assignment to the battle sites in the north of England and see if any clue became obvious when he was there. He retrieved his bike and rode home without encountering anyone he knew. Then he walked to the station and caught the train up to London.

That afternoon, right after tea, Lady Phoebe slipped out of the house and made her way down to the gamekeeper's lodge. Mrs. Robbins looked like a different person, much older, with hollow eyes and an almost dazed expression.

"He's in there, your ladyship," she said in a flat voice. "Go on through if you like."

Phoebe had forgotten for the moment that the Robbinses' son had been reported missing. She wondered if she should say something but couldn't think of the right thing, so she merely smiled and said, "Thank you, Mrs. Robbins."

She went into the kitchen and found Alfie eating a piece of bread and jam. He looked up and grinned when he saw her.

"You and I have to talk," she said. "Leave that and come where we can't be overheard."

Alfie followed her outside, and they walked some distance from the cottage before she said, "We have to get a move on with our sleuthing. There have been developments."

"There have?"

She nodded. "You must have heard our house was bombed."

"Yes. I know. Bloomin' awful."

"Well, I've started thinking—about our parachutist, you know. Why bomb Farleigh?"

"Well, there's a ruddy lot of soldiers staying there, you know." He grinned.

"All right. That would be one reason. But what if there was another?"

"Like what?"

"Someone or something at Farleigh should be destroyed. Do you know Mr. Cresswell, the vicar's son?" Alfie nodded. "He was there the night of the fire. He rescued me and my governess. Jolly brave, actually. But he was interested that Miss Gumble had a telescope. And today I was up in the schoolroom, and I happened to look out of the window and I saw him going around to the stable yard, which is where Miss Gumble is staying at the moment. So it made me wonder whether he suspects anything funny is going on. Or"—and she paused—"whether he might have something to do with that parachuting man himself."

"What do you mean?" Alfie asked.

"I mean I know he was injured in that plane crash before the war, but why isn't he in the army or something? He's the sort of person who might want the Germans to take over. He's the quiet and sneaky type, just the sort they might use. So I think you and I should get cracking. I know he went to the station, but if he comes back, we need to keep an eye on him. And I'll snoop around the house to see if there is anything suspicious there. You snoop around the village to see if you can come up with anything suspicious. All right?"

"All right," he said, "although I have been listening to people talking. Some of them think that German bloke staying with the doctor might be a spy."

"But he's Jewish and Austrian. He fled from the Nazis."

"So he says." Alfie grinned again. "But I'll do my best. I tell you who I think might be right dodgy—Baxters the builders—have you noticed the gates to their yard are always shut, and the fence is so high you can't see in?"

"Probably so no one can sneak in and steal their supplies," Phoebe said.

"Yeah, but it's more than that," Alfie said. "I watched Baxter's van drive out the other day. And someone closed the gate the moment the van went through, and young Mr. Baxter was driving and he saw me standing there and he shouted, "What are you staring at? Go on, hop it."

"So you'll do some snooping on the Baxters' yard? Excellent," Phoebe said. "We'll get to the bottom of this mystery, you'll see, Alfie. We'll surprise them all."

CHAPTER TWENTY-NINE

Paris

Margot sat in the window at the Ritz hotel and stared out at the street. Her finger still throbbed and welled blood, but it was the other hurt that was more painful. *That woman.* That is what he had called her. He had looked at her with no emotion on his face at all. She was not his beloved. He didn't care for her at all. She had risked her life by staying on in Paris when she could have been safely at home. And she had never had any chance of saving him. The Germans had been using her, pushing her into a position where she would agree to do their bidding, all for nothing.

What a fool I've been, she thought. She might be going home, but only to aid the enemy. If she didn't, then someone on the spot would surely kill either her or a member of her family. Now that she had actually seen them in action, she was sure that they would have no qualms about dispatching her. She didn't yet know what her assignment would be, but it would presumably have something to do with the fact that she was an aristocrat, that she mixed in the highest circles. She shivered and held her wounded hand up to her breast.

"I must commend you," Herr Dinkslager had said as they drove away from Gestapo headquarters on Avenue Foch. "You were very brave. Exactly what I would have expected from one of England's oldest families. I must apologise about your finger. I think you'll find there is no lasting damage. I'm sure you must realise that it was a necessity."

She had said nothing but stared out the window.

"You'll need some training first," Herr Dinkslager said. "So, for the moment, I think we'll leave you at the Ritz. Might as well make the most of the good food and wine, eh?"

He was chatting with her again as if they had been for a drive in the country—not like he had just rammed a wedge under her fingernail. He had been prepared to do the same to the rest of her fingers, and to let the young soldier rape her if he thought it might have achieved results. *What kind of man can act like that?* she wondered. To behave with a façade of civilisation, yet calmly torture and kill. Does he never think about his wife, his children, his sisters at home, and imagine such horrors happening to them?

They pulled up in front of the Ritz, and he escorted her inside. Gigi Armande's suite was unoccupied. "I'll have someone come up with a bandage for that finger," he said. "And I'll arrange for your training to begin tomorrow."

Now she sat there alone, a prisoner, waiting for doom to fall. *There must be something I can do,* she thought. A way out over the roof, through the servants' quarters. A ridiculous thought came to her: *What if I just opened the door and walked down the hall, down the stairs and to freedom?* She crossed the room and opened the door. At the sound, a German soldier standing guard by the stairs turned to stare at her. Not that way then.

She toyed with another thought. She could request something from room service. If a woman delivered it, she could overpower her, tie her up, steal her uniform, and escape that way. The idea was intriguing, but she took it one stage further. If that person struggled and fought back, could she kill her if necessary? Margot shuddered. Killing was different from tying up. But she couldn't just sit here. She picked up the telephone and found that it was dead. At that moment, Gigi Armande walked in. Margot looked up like a guilty child.

"I was trying to order a glass of wine," she said.

Armande smiled. "There is a little man at the front desk who switches on the telephone when he sees me, for security's sake. Now, what was it you wanted?"

"It doesn't matter," Margot said, moving away.

"But of course it does. I heard something about the little incident this afternoon. Did you have a cognac? So good for steadying the nerves." Margot shook her head. "But they took care of your poor hand?" She saw the bandage. "So uncivilised of them. I'll tell Spatzi—I mean Herr Dinkslager, when I talk to him next. That is not the way he behaves with my protégées, not if he wants a new frock for his wife."

She came across and picked up Margot's bandaged finger. "You must do what they say, *ma chérie*. We have to play along with them if we want to survive. I gather they want to send you home. Please don't be noble. Do what they ask, and you'll be safe and with your family."

Margot nodded. She had a horrible feeling that she might break down and cry if she opened her mouth to speak. Madame Armande being kind to her was a last straw when she had been at the breaking point for hours.

Armande picked up the phone and calmly ordered smoked salmon, a bottle of Chablis, and a large cognac. Then she replaced the receiver and smiled at Margot. "All will be well," she said.

"How can it?" Margot said bleakly.

Armande came over and put an arm around Margot's shoulder. "He is very noble, that Gaston of yours. A credit to France."

"What do you mean?" Margot looked up sharply. "He let them torture me. Do you call that noble?"

Armande smiled. "He will not betray the Resistance, whatever happens. I heard what he said about you. That you were nothing to him. I know men, *ma chérie*. I have been with a great many men. He was making sure they left you alone."

"Making sure?" Margot said angrily. "He said they could chop me into little pieces for all he cared."

"But, naturally." Armande gave that very Gallic shrug. "Don't you see? That was the only way to let you go. If he did not care one iota about you, then torturing you could have no effect on him. And it also had an added benefit in that it made you agree to do what the German schemers wanted. Now you will be their puppet."

Margot looked up at her suspiciously. "You seem to know an awful lot. You're working secretly with them, I suppose?"

"Darling, I don't work with anybody," Armande said. "But I am Spatzi's mistress, as I'm sure you've guessed by now. How else do you think I live at the Ritz and come and go as I please? And yes, I confess I was part of that little drama when you were first brought in. But only because I cared about you and wanted you to stay alive."

"Then you'll know what they want me to do in England?"

Gigi Armande shrugged. "Not exactly. I don't expect you will be told until you have contacted the right person over there."

"But they will want to use my position in society to kill somebody, don't you think? Somebody important. A member of the royal family, maybe?"

Armande shrugged again. "I tell you in all honesty that I do not know. But I do say that you must pretend to go along with them, until the very last."

"I never could have saved Gaston, could I?" Margot asked in a small voice.

"Highly unlikely, I admit," Armande answered.

Margot's suspicions were confirmed when she was taken to a shooting range the next day. She had been on pheasant shoots and was actually a good shot, but she tried to appear awkward and clumsy with a gun. Anything to give her time.

"You must do better, fräulein," the German officer in charge of her said.

"I'm afraid it still hurts me to hold a gun," she said. "You'll have to wait for my finger to heal."

"There is no time to wait," he said. "You are needed over there for an immediate assignment. Now try again. We are not leaving until you have hit the centre of the mark five times in a row."

More intense days had followed. More things to be memorised. Code words to be understood. And veiled threats made. She would be watched at all times. Her family would be watched. She had no idea how many agents were now working in Britain, but she would be doing a good thing for her countrymen. The conclusion was inevitable. The invasion would happen. But she could speed it along and save Britain from more misery.

Then, on the third day, she had just returned from her training and Gigi was still out at her salon when there was a hammering on the door. She opened it, and two strange German officers strode in.

"Fräulein, you will come with us immediately," one said in clipped English. "We have a car waiting."

"Where are we going?" she asked.

"You do not ask questions." The man shouted at her, grabbed her arm, and shoved her forward. She walked between them along the hall and down the stairs. Other German officers passed them and saluted or nodded politely. Outside was a waiting black Mercedes. One of them opened the back door for her. "Get in."

She climbed into the backseat. The two officers got into the front, and they drove off. Margot swallowed down her fear. Were they going back to Gestapo headquarters on Avenue Foch? Or had they decided she was no use to them after all, and she was being taken to be executed? She tried to stop her knees from trembling.

They were driving away from the centre of Paris. Light was fading as they passed through suburbs. So far, nobody had said a word. Then one of the men turned to the other.

"That went rather well, don't you think?" he asked in upper-class English.

The other man turned back to Margot and smiled. "It's all right. You can relax now. We've passed the first hurdle."

"You're not Germans?" she asked.

"Actually, we're special ops, sent to get you out," he said.

"But the car, the uniforms?" she asked.

"Belong to two poor chaps who had been drinking at a bar late last night."

"Where are they now?"

"Buried under a log pile."

"Dead?"

"I'm afraid so. It is war. And they wouldn't have hesitated to kill you. Now there's a dark rug in the back. If we get stopped at a checkpoint, you duck down on the floor with the rug over you, and for God's sake, don't move."

"Where are we going?"

"To the Channel, where we hope a speedboat will be waiting. Are you all right?"

"Yes. I'm all right," she said.

"I should think so, living at the Ritz," the other man said. He had a trace of northern accent, not quite as posh as the one who had first spoken to her. "Why did they take you there?"

"Gigi Armande was watching over me."

"You're damned lucky you didn't wind up at Gestapo headquarters."

"I've been there a couple of times," she said, and gave an involuntary shudder.

"And came out again. Not many people can say that. You must be worth more to them alive than dead."

"They wanted to use me to get Gaston de Varennes to talk," she said carefully.

"And did he?"

"No."

"Of course not. So it's lucky we came to get you now. Your time was distinctly limited."

They drove on.

"Might I know your names?" Margot asked.

"No names. Safer that way."

Night fell, and they drove through darkness, passing through small towns where there was little sign of life. Then after about an hour, there was the checkpoint they had feared.

"Get down," one of the men hissed. Margot curled as small as she could with the blanket over her. The car came to a halt.

"Your papers, please, Herr lieutenant," a sharp voice demanded.

Margot heard the rustle of paper. Then: "What is your mission here?"

One of the men responded in perfect German. "A message direct from Berlin to be delivered only to General von Heidenheim in Calais."

"The invasion!" the soldier exclaimed. "It must be about the invasion."

"That is not your business," the driver replied. "Now let us be on our way."

The car picked up speed again.

"You can come out now," one of them said, and they both laughed.

"How do you speak such good German?" Margot asked.

"You don't think they'd send a man on a mission like this who didn't. Actually, my mother was Austrian. I grew up speaking both languages."

"Jolly useful, as it turned out," the other said. "My German is only from a year at the Heidelberg University, but good enough in a pinch."

They drove on, pausing at a crossroads to consult a map about which route would avoid any more encounters with German forces. Once more, they were halted, but were waved through when the sentry saw their uniforms. Then at last the car bounced off the road and came to a halt among some trees.

"We have to walk from here, I'm afraid," the posh one said. "This is the dodgy part. Here, put on this black jumper. And do exactly what we tell you to. If I say run, you run like hell, got it?"

Margot nodded. The two men stripped off the German uniforms and left them in the vehicle, then put on similar black turtleneck jerseys. They pulled the turtlenecks up to hide as much of their faces as possible. Margot followed suit. One of the men produced a small flashlight, blacked out so that it only produced a glimmer. It was a cloudy night, and no lights were in evidence. Margot followed them through the woods, stumbling over tree roots and trying to keep up in her impractical shoes. They came to a cottage, but it appeared to be deserted. Nevertheless, they crept past, climbed a fence, and ran across an open field until one of the men held up his hand to halt. Margot smelled salt in the air and heard the hiss and rattle of waves on a stony beach below.

"Now let's just pray the boat has turned up and hasn't been blown out of the water. Should be all right. They are supposed to be using a low, little speedboat. Hard to detect."

The man peeled off the covering from his flashlight and sent out several bursts of light into the dark sea. After a moment they were answered with returning flickers of light.

"Good. They're there, and they've seen us. Now all we have to do is get down to the beach, cross it without stepping on mines, and climb into the boat. Piece of cake, I'd say." He laughed.

He went to the cliff edge, looked around, then motioned the others to follow him. A narrow path was cut into the chalk, leading down the cliff. They went along cautiously because the path was only a foot wide and strewn with loose rocks that had fallen. Margot kept her hand on the surface of the cliff for reassurance. Farther down the coast, a searchlight beam cut across the sky. Far above came the drone of aircraft, but they were flying high and passed over. *Another bombing raid heading for London,* Margot thought.

At the bottom of the cliff they waited. Margot was shivering, but she didn't want the men to see she was frightened. She could make out a dark shape approaching on the sea. There was no sound of a motor, and she realised it was probably being rowed. A figure jumped out and stood in the gentle surf, holding it steady.

"Go. Now!" one of the men whispered in her ear. She ran, stumbling and slithering over the stones on the beach. She reached the boat, waded into the waves, and was hauled on board. One of the men followed, then the other. They pushed off from shore and rowed out again. They were a hundred yards or so off the beach when a searchlight strafed the water, picking them up. Shots rang out. "Get down." Margot was pushed to the floor.

"Start the damned motor!" one of the men shouted.

The engine kicked, spluttered, then roared to life. The boat shot forward with incredible power as bullets sprayed into the water around them. Then they were out of range. Cautiously, they sat up again, the shoreline already well behind them.

One of her rescuers turned to the other, laughing. "No trouble at all, eh, chum? Just your average, routine rescue from the Gestapo."

And this time Margot laughed, too.

CHAPTER THIRTY

Bletchley Park

After three days of staring at sheets of printouts, Pamela and Froggy were not getting anywhere and were both frustrated.

"Maybe this is just a wild goose chase," Froggy said.

"I don't think they'd have put us to work on this unless there was some kind of suspicion that it was important, do you?"

"I don't know." He picked up a pencil and snapped it in half. "Maybe they wanted us removed from our old assignments, and this is an easy way of pushing us aside."

Pamela thought of her section leader who had been annoyed she had solved a puzzle that proved to be important. Had he asked to have her removed, and this was a way of doing it without losing face? "You know," Pamela said, "we are sure that there are fifth columnists in Britain. What easier way to contact them than through a broadcast everyone can listen to."

He nodded. "But we've tried everything, haven't we? No obvious repeated phrases, except for 'Here is the news. Now a commentary, and now here are some messages from your boys in Germany.' And we've gone through all of those messages for what might be codes. We've tried substituting letters, using every third word, every fifth word, and not come up with anything."

Pamela stared at the sheets of paper. "Maybe there's something we're missing by just seeing the words printed out. What if there is a different inflection in the voice? What if the reader coughs or clears his throat before he delivers a line of importance? What if there is a different reader for something significant?"

His face lit up. "You might be onto something there. Yes, let's ask them to send us the recordings. It will take a lot longer to listen to everything, but it may be worth it."

This request was met with complications. There was no recording equipment at the listening station, just young WAAF workers with headphones, transcribing as they listened.

"If you want to listen in real time, then I'm afraid you'll have to sit with headphones on and take notes," Commander Travis said. "And since the frequencies and hours when they broadcast are not always the same, then you'll be monitoring this between you, almost around the clock—although they haven't been broadcasting later than midnight or earlier than six or seven, so you'll get some sleep. I suggest we send you up to the radio station Y for a few days and give this a try. Boring work, I'm afraid. You sit with headphones on and listen to the radio. But the WAAFs up there are skilled at finding times and frequencies, so you won't have to do that part."

"Will we stay up there?" Pamela asked. "Is it far from here?"

"About six miles, so we could have you driven back and forth, but I suggest you camp out there for a couple of days, until we see how things are progressing. We'll have two camp beds sent up with you, so at least you won't have to bunk in with the air force ladies."

"I'd better put a ring on your finger and make an honest woman of you since we'll be spending several nights together," Froggy teased as they walked away.

Pamela grinned. "I think a room full of WAAFs might constitute enough of a chaperone. Besides, I've already been spending the night with a hut full of men, so my reputation is ruined anyway."

"It's dashed difficult not being able to tell anybody anything, isn't it?" Froggy said.

"It is." Pamela nodded. "My family thinks I'm not doing anything of importance."

"Try being a chap and not in uniform," Froggy said. "I get accosted every time I go up to London. I thought of buying one in a secondhand store. And if you tell them you failed the medical, they look at you as a weakling."

Pamela stopped and put her hand up to her mouth. "Golly, what on earth do I say to my roommate?"

"Say you can't tell her. It's confidential. That's the truth, isn't it?"

Pamela nodded. When put like that, it sounded important and exciting. *Trixie was going to be furious,* Pamela thought. She bumped into her friend that evening when she went home to pack some necessities.

"You're going away again?" Trixie asked.

"Of course not," Pamela said. "They want a couple of us to sleep on camp beds at the big house so we can be available for whenever the boffins need something."

"Lucky you," Trixie said. "At least you'll be at the big house, not in a cold draughty hut."

"But a camp bed doesn't sound too inviting, especially if I'm to be summoned at three in the morning to bring cups of tea."

"Well, you won't have the trains going past the window, or Mrs. Entwhistle's cooking," Trixie said.

"That's true." Pamela grinned. "But think—you get the room to yourself. One less for the bathroom."

"That would be ducky if I could find a way to smuggle a chap upstairs," Trixie said. "Not that I fancy anyone here. Why couldn't at least one chap have been given brains and looks, too?" She paused, then turned to Pamela. "I say, I hope you can get time off for Jeremy's party. I can't tell you how much I'm looking forward to it. It's the one bright spot in my current life of gloom."

"I hope so, too. They haven't told me about days off. We'll just have to play it by ear. But they can't expect me to work seven days a week, twenty-four hours a day. That is slave labour." She closed her suitcase. "I'll see you in a couple of days, I expect."

"You wouldn't mind if I went to Jeremy's party if you couldn't go, would you?" Trixie asked.

Pamela hesitated. Trixie had already made it clear that she was attracted to Jeremy. But it was a party, after all. A flat full of people. "Of course not," she said airily. "I'll write down the address for you. And I'll try to send a message to let you know how I'm getting along and how long I might be occupied."

Then she picked up the suitcase and left. An army staff car was waiting to take them to the radio receiving station.

"Windy Ridge. It hardly sounds inviting, does it?" Froggy said. "One step away from Wuthering Heights."

"I don't think there are too many Wuthering Heights in Buckinghamshire," Pamela replied. "We will be in a building. And it is summer."

"That's the spirit. A girl who is ready for anything," he said. "I say, I don't suppose you'd like to go out with me when we get an evening off?"

She glanced at him. Not bad-looking, especially by Bletchley standards. Good sense of humour. But then she already had Jeremy—dashing, rich, handsome Jeremy. What more could any girl want. "Thanks awfully," she said, "but I'm afraid I already have a chap. An RAF flyer."

"Just my luck," he said. "All the good ones are already taken. Ah, well, probably better if we keep on purely professional terms, what?"

The Humber drove up a hill and halted at a barbed-wire fence. Beyond it were Nissen huts and aerials. A sentry admitted them, and they were shown into a large room full of WAAFs, sitting with headphones on. "It's like a giant telephone exchange, isn't it?" Froggy whispered.

An officious female sergeant showed them where they should sit, the supply closet next to the kitchen where they could set up their camp beds. "You might as well get started right away," she said. "No time like the present."

Pamela put on the headphones. They felt heavy. She sat, doodled on her pad, and thought about things. The first broadcast came through at 7:30 p.m. A short burst of Beethoven's Fifth Symphony, then, "This is your New British Broadcasting Station, broadcasting on 5920 kilocycles, 63 metres." Pamela felt a chill run down her spine as she listened to it. *How many homes in Britain were tuned in to this*, she wondered. There was news of Allied ships sunk, then another voice, "Have you ever given any thought to the fate of your children? You realise that the government's evacuation plan, or should one say, their complete collapse, may have a profound effect on your boys and girls in years to come." It went on to say that four hundred thousand children were receiving no education because of the confusion. *Clever*, Pamela thought. *Playing on every parent's deepest fears.*

A propaganda outburst on the Jewish question followed. Then another musical interlude before messages home from boys in prison camps in Germany.

The broadcast ended. Another came later that evening, then four the next day.

"So what do you think?" Froggy asked her. "Any light dawning yet?"

Pamela shook her head. "There is nothing really. Voices rather like the real BBC announcers, lacking any sort of individuality. Interspersed with bits of stirring German music."

"Beethoven mostly," he agreed. "And Handel's *Music for the Royal Fireworks*, wasn't it?"

Pamela looked up sharply. "Could that be something? Royal fireworks? A plot to blow up the royal family?"

He stared back at her. "Now that's a thought. Communicating through music. Dashed clever. Let's make sure we listen carefully to any music tomorrow."

Pamela slept fitfully for a few hours, only to be awakened by the early shift coming in to make tea. She washed in cold water and resumed her place at the table. By the end of the day she was heartily sick of the lies and propaganda.

"What do you have?" Froggy asked her.

"Beethoven's Fifth to announce the broadcast. Different music before the news, commentary, and messages from our boys. I'm afraid I'm not well up on music. All German, I assume?"

"Yes. Luckily, I come from a musical family," he said. "I studied the cello. My family all played instruments. You might say we had music rammed down our throats. I noted two passages from Beethoven's Seventh Symphony. The messages home were mostly Bach's Brandenburg Concertos, but there were two excerpts from Wagner— 'Ride of the Valkyries' and *Götterdämmerung*."

"Impressive," Pamela said. "Now try and find a meaning to them."

"The only one that gives us anything to go on is Handel's 'Royal Fireworks,' isn't it? We should report in that one."

"But I can't see any details—no how and when. The piece that followed was about evacuating children. I've pulled that apart, and I can't find any hidden message."

"And if there was a message, it couldn't be too complicated, could it?" Pamela said. "I mean, then the average German sympathiser couldn't understand it."

"Unless they have codebooks and the word *child* means 'tomorrow' and the word *education* means 'guns.'"

"But then we'd have no chance of interpreting unless we had the codebook. Let's ask Commander Travis if any such books have been captured."

"Good idea." He got up. "Let's call it a day, shall we. My bottom is numb from sitting on a hard seat for hours."

CHAPTER THIRTY-ONE

London

It was pouring hard when Ben arrived back in London, late at night. He had endured three fruitless days of crowded trains, uncooperative people, and constant rain. He had seen no terrain that resembled the photograph, nor learned any details of the battles that might have relevance today. He stomped up the steps to his billet at the rooming house on Cromwell Road. It had been an inferior sort of hotel before the war, now requisitioned to house those working for the government. The rooms were spartan, with bed, wardrobe, table, chair, and a shelf in one corner with sink, cupboard, and gas ring. He had to drop sixpence into the meter for gas. As he put in his key, the door across the hall opened, and Guy's face peeped out. "God, you look like a drowned rat," he said. "Come on in. I'll make some tea, and I've still got a few drops of brandy to put in it."

"Kind of you, but I really don't . . ." Ben began.

"Don't be a martyr," Guy said. "We don't want you coming down with a chill and not being able to do your work, do we?"

"I'll take off my raincoat first," Ben said. He went into his own room, which felt cold, damp, and unwelcoming, hung the coat up on a peg behind the door, then went across the hall to Guy's room. In contrast, this room felt comfy and lived in. Guy had hung bright curtains at the window. Some of his favourite modern-art prints decorated the walls. A plant stood on the windowsill, and there were cushions on the chair. *Guy likes his creature comforts,* Ben thought. He sat while Guy made tea, then poured cognac into it.

"Get that down you. You'll feel better."

Ben drank, gratefully. "I've been soaked all day," he said.

"Where were you?" Guy asked.

"In Yorkshire yesterday and the Welsh border today."

"Doing what, for God's sake?"

"I don't suppose it can hurt to tell you," Ben said. "Checking the site of ancient battles."

"Are you writing a thesis, or was this something to do with actual work?"

"The latter, but I can't tell you what."

"Of course not. Did it prove fruitful?"

"Absolute bloody waste of time." Ben grinned.

"Most of the things we do are, aren't they?" Guy said. "I was sent out again today to a report of a possible German spy. And, of course, it turned out to be another Jew who has lived here since before the Great War."

Ben nodded. "But of course, the real fifth columnists must be damned clever," he said. "They wouldn't stand out in any way. I doubt if I've ever actually met one."

"No?" Guy asked. He grinned. "I'm pretty sure I have."

"Really—where?"

"At a meeting I was sent to. But I suppose I can't tell you any more. Captain King would shoot me. Or Miss Miller would. She's more formidable than Knight, isn't she?"

"Absolutely," Ben agreed. When he left Guy's room, he felt comfort, and not just from the brandy working its way through his system.

He and Guy were working for the same outfit, even if they couldn't tell each other what they were actually doing. That made it easier somehow.

The next morning Ben returned to Dolphin Square to report in and was ushered into the inner sanctum.

"Ah, Cresswell. Come in." Maxwell Knight looked up from his paperwork and held out his hand to Ben. "Successful trip? Any luck?"

"I'm afraid not, sir," Ben replied. "I visited both the battle sites, and there was nothing in the terrain that resembled the photograph. So I was wondering—isn't this something that aerial reconnaissance at the Air Ministry might be able to help us with?"

"Already sent them a copy of the photograph," Maxwell Knight replied. "No word as yet. They've got bigger fish to fry these days. But you might pop over there yourself and chivvy them up a bit."

"So you don't want me to go back down to Kent?"

"Is there anything else you might hope to accomplish there?"

"Not really, sir." As he said this, he swallowed back frustration. He had been given a plum assignment and not achieved a single bloody thing. "I suppose the question is whether that particular place was important. Whether there was a contact there who was vital to the Jerries. And if so, will they try to send another messenger or use another format to make contact?"

"Quite." Max Knight nodded. "And if the time and place weren't important, then they've already sent their message in another way—pigeon or radio."

"If it weren't important, why risk a parachutist?"

Max Knight nodded. Then he cleared his throat. "Cresswell, there is something you should know. This is strictly between ourselves, you understand. Never to leave this room."

"Yes, sir." Ben felt his pulse quicken.

"I mentioned to you before that we were only interested in the aristocrats in your part of the world. There's a reason for this. You've

281

probably heard that there are several pro-German groups working in Britain."

"Well, yes. One hears of the Anglo-German Fellowship, and of course the British fascists can't be counted out."

"Both relatively harmless. They welcome friendship with Germany in principle. I don't think either group would work actively to bring about a German takeover of Britain. However"—he paused, tipping his chair back so that it balanced precariously—"you may also have heard that there is an element of strong pro-German sentiment among the upper classes."

"You mentioned before that there are those who would like to see the Duke of Windsor on the throne," Ben said.

"And working to achieve this. We can't be sure yet whether they would go as far as actual assassination of the current royal family. But we are taking precautions. Monitoring wherever possible. You see, Cresswell, there is a small, secret group we've only just learned about. They are made up almost exclusively of aristocrats. They call themselves the Ring. Some of them have the misguided belief that they can spare Britain from total destruction by aiding the German invasion. Some believe a Hitler-style government wouldn't be so bad, that we have deep ties with Germany, including our royal family."

"Absolute fools," Ben blurted out. "Surely anyone can see that we'd be at best a puppet state with slave labour."

"You and I can see that. There are those who can't or won't. And they are dangerous, Cresswell. There are those among them who will do what it takes."

"So how do we root them out and stop them?" Ben asked.

"Good question. I have my people infiltrating their meetings whenever we get wind of them."

Ben thought for an awful moment that Knight was about to suggest he infiltrate such meetings. This was followed by the thought that he should volunteer for such an assignment. "Is there any way that I can be helpful, sir?" he asked.

"Yes. Keep your eyes and ears open, and for God's sake let's find out about that bloody photograph," Knight said. "Ask Miss Miller how you get to Aerial Reconnaissance. They are buried somewhere in the depths of the country. Top-secret hideout. I'll let them know you are coming."

As Ben went down in the elevator, he had an odd feeling. Why had Knight let him go off on a wild goose chase to Yorkshire and Herefordshire when the photograph was already being analysed by the Air Ministry? And why wait so long to tell him about the Ring? He toyed with the idea that he was being kept busy and out of the way for a reason. And he wondered whether the reason was that the dashing Max Knight was part of the secret ring himself.

As soon as Ben had left the office, Mr. Knight's secretary, Joan Miller, came in and closed the door behind her.

"You've told him about the Ring?"

"Yes. He seemed to find it hard to believe that noble Britons could possibly behave like that. He's a naïve chap, I'd say."

"Or a good actor, sir." Joan Miller held his gaze. "We can't completely discount that he's working with them. Why volunteer to rush up to Yorkshire when we know they just held a meeting up there?"

"My contacts and my gut tell me he's all right, Joan. But then I have been wrong before. You might mention his name next time you're with them. Suggest him as a possible recruit and see if you get a reaction."

"He's not of their class, sir. And not influential enough. Small-fry. They wouldn't be interested."

"If they had a particular job for him to do, they might."

Joan Miller nodded. "And you didn't tell him that we have Margot Sutton safely back in England?"

"Not yet. I'm uneasy about that one, Joan. The whole rescue was too damned easy. I think they were letting her get away. And the question is why."

Ben couldn't shake off the feeling of unease as he walked from Dolphin Square to Victoria Station. Was he being used for something? As bait, perhaps? He took the tube to Marylebone Station and then the overground train out to Buckinghamshire. He got out at Marlow, and then found he had to wait for a local bus to take him to the village of Medmenham, about three miles away. Again he experienced that feeling of unreality as he looked at the Thames, sparkling beyond Marlow's spruce little shops. There was even a rowing boat being skulled along the river. Nothing seemed to have changed here. It was amazing that somewhere so close to London could seem unaffected by war. The bus came at last, and he rode through leafy countryside where cows grazed in lush meadows. From the village he followed Joan Miller's directions to a former stately home and had to undergo three rounds of security before he was sent to the operations room. The former ballroom was now filled with tables, each one covered in maps. He was surprised to find many of the people poring over the maps were women—young women, many of them dressed in the blue uniform of the Women's Auxiliary Air Force. He waited, and a girl in civvies came over to him. "Hello," she said. "Mr. Cresswell? We were told you were on your way. It's a bit remote, but not bad digs here at all, is it?"

"Not bad at all." He returned her smile. She had a round, pleasant face and bouncy curls, a little like a grown-up Shirley Temple. Curves, but not fat, Ben noted.

"You've come about the photograph?" she asked. "Sorry. We've been overwhelmed recently, and I haven't had too much time to spend on it. It's been all about locating German factory sites and railway-goods yards. Can I get you a cup of tea?"

"Oh, no, that's not necessary—" he started, but she cut him off.

"Oh, come on. Be a sport. If we have visitors, we're allowed to open the biscuit tin!"

"All right, then. How could I refuse?" They went through to a small kitchen. She poured tea and took down the biscuit tin from the shelf. "Go on. Help yourself," she said.

"Only if you're allowed to have one, too."

"Not really, but who's counting?" She flashed a wicked grin again and picked up a Bourbon biscuit. Ben took a custard cream. "One of the perks of working here," she said. "We have to entertain visitors."

"So you haven't had time yet to work on the location of the photograph?" he asked.

"I've done some preliminary stuff. The problem is that we don't have many aerial photographs of England, especially not of the remote western bits that aren't crucial to the war effort. So it's working from an ordnance survey map, and that is more tedious going. We're looking for where the contour lines are close enough together to indicate a steep hill and which steep hill has a river about a half mile from it and a church on it. And as soon as I'm getting into it, I get called back because new photos have just come in from Germany. Is this terribly important?"

"It could be," he said. "I don't know what they told you, but a parachutist, who was almost certainly a German spy, fell to his death in a Kentish field, and the only thing he had in his pockets was this photograph. So we need to know why it mattered."

"Oh, golly. How exciting. Of course. I'll do my best. Stay late."

"Thank you. It's good of you—?" He left the query hanging.

She smiled. "It's Mavis. Mavis Pugh."

"I'm Ben," he replied. "Pleased to meet you." He wasn't sure whether he should shake her hand.

"Do you work in London?" she asked.

"Most of the time, yes. They send me out on errands like this. Are you billeted down here?"

"Not billeted. I live with my mum in Marlow, worse luck. She's a nervous sort, so it does rather cramp my style."

"Do you get up to London ever?"

"You bet," she said. "The moment we have a day off, I'm up to London on the next train. Why, were you about to ask me out?"

"I was thinking of it." Ben blushed. "I'm sorry. I'm not usually so fresh with a girl I've only just met."

"Oh, I don't mind at all," she replied. "One has to take one's chances in a war like this. We're all so horribly aware how often one of our RAF pilots doesn't come back. You can be chatting with a bloke one day, and the next you hear he's been shot down. So grab life while you can, that's become my motto."

"How about the pictures sometime, then?" he asked. "Cinema, I mean, not what you're doing here."

"I love the pictures." She flashed a smile at him. "Clark Gable. He's my favourite."

"Do you get regular days off?" he asked.

"Not really. But I get quite a few evenings free, when I'm on early shift like this. It's not that far to pop up to town, is it?" She paused, smiled at him again. "So let's make a date, shall we?"

"The only thing is I don't know if I'm supposed to be back at work in London now or still running around the countryside. I'll have to let you know."

"You're not giving me the brush-off, I hope? Is there someone else?"

"No, absolutely not. And nobody else."

"That's good, then. I must say I rather fancy going out with a chap who is not going to be shot to pieces the next day. Reassuring."

"I suppose we should get back to work and take a look at that photo," Ben said. "Do you have a telephone at home where I can ring you?"

"I'd rather you left a message for me at work," she said. "My mum is too inquisitive, and she's likely to invite you for tea, and then pepper you with embarrassing questions. She means well, I suppose. She wants to keep me safe when nobody can be kept safe."

"All right. Give me the work number."

He followed her to her table, and she wrote it down for him. A blown-up copy of his photograph was pinned next to a map. As he bent to look at it, Mavis's name was called.

"Mavis, do you have those photos ready yet? The man from the ministry is here for them," a large woman wearing sergeant's stripes called across the room, giving Ben a disapproving glance.

"All ready to go, ma'am," Mavis called back. She turned back to Ben. "Just let me hand these over to the bloke from the ministry, then I'm all yours." Her double meaning was quite clear. As she started for the door, it was pushed open and a man in an RAF uniform came in.

"I'm here to collect . . ." He began. He looked at Mavis, then at Ben.

"Good God, Ben," Jeremy said. "What on earth are you doing here?"

When Ben recovered from his shock, he realised that he should not be surprised to see Jeremy. After all, he had told Ben that he would be working at the Air Ministry until he was fit to fly again.

"Hello, Jeremy," he said.

"But what are you doing here?" Jeremy asked. "You don't work for the Air Ministry, do you?"

"No, but I was sent to pick up a photograph here for one of the bosses."

"Amazing coincidence," Jeremy said. He turned to Mavis. "This chap and I were best friends growing up. And to meet him here of all places."

"Oh, then you can tell me all the secrets of his past," Mavis said.

Jeremy raised an eyebrow. "Oh, I get it. You and she . . . you sly dog."

"We've only just met," Ben said. "But I did ask her out to the pictures."

"Tell you what," Jeremy said, "why don't you bring her to my party on Wednesday?" He turned to Mavis. "I've just moved into my parents' flat in Mayfair, and I'm going to celebrate my freedom with a flat-warming party."

"Mayfair? How grand." Mavis's eyes sparkled. "Oh, Ben. I'd love that."

"Can you get time off?"

"You bally well know I'm going to work it somehow. Even if I have to take awful shifts for a month."

"Then let me write down the address for you," Jeremy said. "We'll have fun. The old man has a good cellar, and I plan to work my way through it."

"Spiffing," Mavis said. "I'm glad you have such interesting friends, Ben."

"Interesting?" Jeremy gave a mock frown. "How about handsome, dashing, debonair?"

"Those too," she said.

"Are the Sutton girls coming?" Ben asked, trying to sound casual.

"Just Dido and Pamma. Livvy is too old and stodgy, and Feebs is too young. It was quite a job persuading Lord Westerham to let Dido come up to town. They keep her on such a tight leash."

"Probably with good reason," Ben said, and Jeremy grinned.

"There are going to be titled people there?" Mavis asked, her eyes wide now. "Crickey. You're not a lord or something, are you?" She turned to Ben.

"Just plain mister," Ben said. "Jeremy's father is a sir."

"But I'm also just plain flight lieutenant," Jeremy said. "And I haven't even told you my name yet. Jeremy Prescott. And yours is?"

"Mavis," she stammered it a little. "Mavis Pugh."

"There you are, Jeremy. You've bowled the poor girl off her feet," Ben said.

"So if you're a flight lieutenant, why aren't you flying?" she asked, sounding bolder now.

"I escaped from a stalag in Germany recently and managed to make my way back home. I was shot and in rather bad shape. I'm still supposed to be recovering, but I didn't want to sit at home doing nothing, so they're letting me work at the ministry."

"I thought your face was familiar," she said, her eyes glowing now. "I saw your picture in the papers. The girls here were talking about your escape." She looked at Ben. "Were you also a flyer once?"

"He was in a plane crash caused by my bad piloting," Jeremy said quickly. "I feel guilty about it every day of my life." He paused, then added, "And the offer still stands to get you a job at the Air Ministry, old chap. You'd have legitimate cause to visit Mavis often."

"As tempting as that sounds, I don't think you'll find it's that easy to switch around in wartime," Ben said. "And I am playing my part where I'm working right now."

"Well, I'd best be getting back to town," Jeremy said. "I'll see you two at my party, then?"

He picked up the package, gave Mavis a wink, and strode out of the room.

CHAPTER THIRTY-TWO

Bletchley Park

Pamela and Froggy Bracewaite were back at the big house, studying transcripts.

"It's interesting that they don't always use the same pieces of music, don't you think?" Froggy said. "I mean they always sign on with Beethoven, but then they have a selection of German composers between news and commentaries."

"Probably only reminding the world how superior German culture is," Pamela said.

"But I think we should identify and study each of the pieces chosen. Maybe the notes spell something out. Maybe it's the fourth movement of the third symphony or something, and those numbers signify dates?"

"I think you're chasing at straws," Pamela said. "If they want to send messages to German sympathisers or agents in Britain, they would have to be brilliant to work out things like that."

"Unless they have codebooks. Maybe Bach means one thing. Handel another."

"But we don't have their codebooks," Pamela said. "I wonder if MI5 knows more about this. We're shut out here, sworn to secrecy, and we have no idea what other ministries or departments know or don't know. I think we should ask Commander Travis about this."

"Maybe," Froggy said doubtfully.

When Pamela went back to her room that night, she opened a drawer to put away the items she had taken with her while camping out, and she paused, frowning. Someone had been through her things. She distinctly remembered leaving her one good pair of nylon stockings wrapped in a handkerchief so that there was no chance they would catch on something and get a run in them. And her diary—she was sure that had been under her spare nightdress.

Trixie arrived while Pamela was sitting on her bed, considering this. "Oh, you're back in the land of the living," she said. "Are you finished with night shifts?"

"For the moment, I think," Pamela said. "I say, Trixie, you didn't borrow my stockings, did you? I wouldn't be angry if you did, but it's just that they aren't where I put them."

"I jolly well did not," Trixie said. "You know me better than that, Pamma. If I want to borrow something of yours, I ask."

"Then someone has been snooping in my drawer," Pamma said.

"Mrs. Entwhistle, obviously," Trixie said. "I always thought she looked like the type who was a snoop."

"I don't know what she hoped to find, unless she gets a thrill from reading other people's diaries," Pamma said.

"Why, is your diary full of juicy details?" Trixie grinned.

"Absolutely not. It's about as boring as you can get. Yesterday we had cottage pie, and it was raining. That kind of thing. I never was the type to spill my innermost thoughts on paper."

"Neither was I," Trixie said. "Too many prying eyes in my house when I was growing up. With two younger sisters one had to be very careful."

"The same with me," Pamela said. "Well, I don't suppose it mattered that Mrs. Entwhistle looked through my things. I have nothing worth stealing. But it does feel a little creepy, doesn't it?"

"Maybe we could set a trap for her and catch her out," Trixie suggested. "You know, a letter in German, or a photo of Adolf Hitler with the message 'Meet me at midnight, *mein Liebling*.'"

Pamela laughed. "You are awful, Trixie."

"Well, she's a horrid cow. She steals our ration coupons and keeps the good food for herself. She deserves what she gets."

Next morning, Pamela and Froggy discussed whether it made sense to repeat their actual listening out at the wireless receiving station. Neither wanted to admit defeat. "We could take it in turns," Froggy said. "I could go out there for one day, and then you could. I don't see any reason to stay overnight. I think I could bicycle six miles, and you could get one of the RAF guards to run you over there and back."

"I suppose so," Pamela agreed. "Anything's worth a try at this stage, isn't it?"

After Froggy had gone, she paced around the table, staring down at the transcripts and their notes. Music. And now messages home from our boys in Germany. Names. Addresses. Should she try to check that these were real prisoners of war with real addresses? She went to ask Commander Travis how they could look into this.

"That would be a job for MI5," he said. "I'll get on the telephone to them and have them send someone over. Worth following up on, I agree."

Pamela went back to work, and that afternoon was informed that someone from MI5 was on his way up. Pamela smoothed back her hair and hastily applied some lipstick. There were rumours about the dashing chaps in the secret service. She knew that MI5 dealt with counterespionage, while MI6 sent out the spies abroad, but all the same, it must be dangerous dabbling in the grey world of spying. There was a tap on her door. In what she hoped was an efficient voice, she called, "Come in." The door opened, and the last person she expected to see came into the room.

She said, "Ben," at the same time as he said, "Pamma?"

Then they both laughed and said, "I had no idea," at the same time.

"You're really working for MI5?" she asked.

"I'm not allowed to tell you that, but since I'm here, I suppose you can deduce that the answer is yes," he said. "And you are not allowed to tell anybody. You do know that. Especially not anybody at home."

"Of course. And you're not to tell anybody I'm working here at Bletchley."

"We've only heard whispers and rumours about what goes on at Bletchley," he said. "Station X. That's how the rest of the world knows you. But it's something to do with codes, isn't it? Are you really a code breaker?"

She nodded. "Not a very good one, it would seem. We've been listening in on German propaganda broadcasts."

"The New British Broadcasting Station, you mean?"

"Yes. That's it. My boss seems to think there might be coded messages to fifth columnists within the broadcasts."

"Yes, we've considered that, too," Ben said.

"You haven't come across a codebook from a captured fifth columnist, have you?"

Ben smiled. "I don't think they make it as easy as that for us."

Pamela sighed. "Our problem is that we don't know where to start. If the coded messages are going to ordinary people—German sympathisers—then the codes would have to be quite simple. Nothing like the clever stuff the Germans use to send messages to their aircraft and ships."

"You've been working on those, have you?" he asked.

"A little. Not the decoding as much as translating. But there are some brilliantly clever chaps here. And I probably shouldn't be talking about this, even to you."

"Are you working on this alone?" Ben asked.

"No, there are two of us. But my colleague is off, listening in at the wireless station today. At first, they sent us transcripts, and then I wondered whether we were missing anything by not hearing the actual spoken words—possible inflections, clearing of the throat, or even the music they use between news and commentary."

Ben nodded. "Interesting. And what have you found so far?"

"These are the latest transcripts and our notes," she said. "They always end their broadcasts with messages purporting to be from servicemen in German prison camps. You know, all jolly stuff about how well they are being treated. So I wondered if they were real people and addresses and not somehow in code."

Ben peered over her shoulder at the papers on the table. He was horribly aware of her presence, of the faint fresh smell of her hair. "You want us to check that the names, serial numbers, and addresses are genuine?"

"That's right."

"Should be simple enough." He read down the page. "What a lot of rubbish they talk. I wonder if anyone believes it?"

"My boss says that people do. The news and commentaries play on their deepest fears—for the safety of their children and whether we are about to starve."

"And what's this music noted here?"

"That was another thought we had—that the piece of music was somehow significant. The chap I'm working with knows his music quite well. He's the one who identified the pieces we've mentioned. The only one that we could see might be important was the *Royal Fireworks* music."

"Golly, yes. Someone planning to blow up the king?"

"Exactly. Have your lot heard any rumours like that?"

"Plenty of them. Nothing definite, but . . . What words followed that particular piece?"

Pamela leafed through the transcripts. "Here," she said.

"'Our great German composer Handel wrote this for your English king, showing what a deep and abiding friendship there has been between our two countries and what a rich heritage we create when we are not on opposite sides.'" Ben paused. "Nothing obvious that one could read into that. No dates or places. Factual."

"I know," Pamela agreed. "We've been over it again and again, substituting letters, selecting words. Nothing."

"So apart from this, it's been mainly Beethoven and Bach?" Ben's finger was scanning down the pages.

"Apart from a couple of snippets of Wagner. Very loud and depressing." Pamela pointed them out. "My pal Froggy, who knows these things, says that they are from various operas, all part of the *Ring* cycle."

"What did you say?" Ben's voice was unexpectedly loud and sharp.

"The operas are all part of the *Ring* cycle."

"My God. That's it," Ben said. "Look, Pamma. I'm not sure how much I'm allowed to tell you, but we've been zeroing in on a secret group of fifth columnists, working actively with Germany. They are mainly aristocrats, and they call themselves the Ring."

"Crikey," Pamela said. "So this is their signature piece. They are saying 'Take note of what comes after this.'"

"It would seem so." Ben's finger was shaking as it ran down the page. "Sergeant Jim Winchester, serial number 248403. To Mrs. Joan

Winchester. 1 Milton Court, Sheffield. That must be it, Pamma. What's the betting this is a message for their operative in Winchester, or a meeting in Winchester, and those numbers are a date, or a telephone, or a street number."

Pamela's eyes were shining. "Oh yes. Brilliant."

"I should copy them all down and take them back with me. Some of the names and addresses will be genuine, to put us off the scent. But every one that follows the Wagner will contain information. Someone higher up than me will be able to figure out what and whom they might refer to. Have the Wagner passages become more frequent lately?"

"We've only been listening recently rather than reading transcripts, so they could have been going on for some time."

"And do you happen to know if the number 1461 has shown up anywhere?"

"Not that I can remember . . ." She frowned. "It could have been in the middle of a longer serial number."

"Don't worry. I can check," Ben said.

"Take a seat." She went across to a desk and brought out a pad and fountain pen. "I'll help you copy them."

They sat side by side in companionable silence.

"Are you going to Jeremy's party?" she asked at last.

"Yes, I said I'd go."

"Should be fun."

"I hope so. I'm bringing a girl."

"A girl?" She looked up abruptly.

Ben nodded. "I'm not sure that was wise, but Jeremy sort of invited her himself, and she was so keen that I couldn't back out."

"Is she nice?"

"I hardly know her. She may turn out to be a little too . . . enthusiastic . . . for me."

Pamela laughed. "Meaning that she's too keen on the physical contact?"

Ben blushed. "I actually meant that she may gush. She's terribly impressed that some of the guests come from titled families. And she was obviously impressed by Jeremy."

"Well, who wouldn't be?" Pamela laughed. Then she grew quiet again. "Do you find him changed, Ben? Since he came back?"

"I've hardly spoken to him enough to know, but he seems, how shall I put it—harder, more seasoned. I wonder if the fun has gone."

Pamela nodded. "I suppose he's grown up a lot, gone from boy to man in the time he was away. And all the horrid things he went through in the prison camp, and then to escape. It's no wonder he's not as fun-loving as he once was."

They finished copying the names and addresses that followed the Wagner interludes. Ben stood up. "I should be getting back," he said. "I want to be home before it's dark. It's not easy getting around in London once the blackout takes effect."

"The very least I can do is treat you to an early dinner in the dining hall," Pamela replied. "The food isn't bad. In contrast to my landlady's cooking. Trixie and I think that she's the enemy's secret weapon, put here to poison Britain."

They laughed as they went down the stairs. Outside, the sun was shining on the lake. People were sitting on the grass, others strolling under the trees. From the meadow beyond came the shouts of a game being played. Ben shook his head in amazement. "This place is unreal," he said. "You certainly landed on your feet, being sent here, didn't you? It's like a country club."

"Actually, we all work so jolly hard that we make the most of time off," Pamela said. "Until recently, I was on a twelve-hour night shift. And most of us work in those huts that are draughty and freezing in winter. And the pressure is enormous. Knowing that if you don't break a code, men on a ship are going to die. People crack all the time and get sent away for rest cures."

"That wasn't why you came home a couple of weeks ago, was it?" He looked at her with concern.

Pamela didn't want to admit to him that she had fainted. "I had some leave owing to me, and when I heard that Jeremy had come back safely . . ."

"Of course." Ben cleared his throat.

"Hey, Pamma, wait for me," a voice shouted behind them, and Trixie came running across the gravel forecourt. "Are you going to the dining room?"

"Yes, we were."

"Me too. I've decided I can't face another of Mrs. Entwhistle's suet puddings." She looked up at Ben. "Hello. Are you a new arrival?"

"No, he's from another department in London," Pamela said quickly. "He just came to drop off some papers, and we bumped into each other. We're old friends from home."

"How jolly," Trixie said. She held out her hand to Ben. "Hello. I'm Trixie. Pamela's roommate."

"I'm Ben. Good to meet you."

She squeezed his hand, an inquisitive smile on her face.

"Do you work at another hush-hush establishment?" she asked.

Ben chuckled. "I couldn't tell you if I did, could I?"

"It's just that they don't let just anybody come here, for any reason. So someone must have had a jolly good reason for sending you here." Trixie turned to Pamela. "I shall worm it out of you when we get home," she said. "Or I shall make a date with Ben and worm it out of him. You're not going to Jeremy Prescott's party, by any chance, are you?"

"As a matter of fact I am," Ben said.

"And he's taking a girl, Trixie. So hands off."

"Spoilsport." Trixie gave a mock pout. "I might turn on the full force of my feminine charms and lure him away from her." She gave Ben a flirtatious smile. "Come on, before there's a line at the cafeteria. I hear there might be cauliflower cheese tonight." She took Ben's hand again and dragged him forward.

On the train back to London, Ben sat staring at the names and addresses he had copied out. Some of the names were definitely also places. Some could be places. Mrs. North at 4 Hampton Street could well mean Northampton. Max Knight should be able to find out if they coincided with known meetings of the Ring. But did any of this have relevance to the photograph? If it was so important that a man's life had been risked to deliver it, then surely the message could not have been for general consumption but for one person's ears only. And they were no closer to finding out who that one person was. He tried to quell the sense of urgency he felt. The *Royal Fireworks* music and the date 1461 when battles were fought to depose a king made him believe that a plot to kill the royal family might well be imminent. But he reminded himself that he was on the lowest rung. If he was not given the full information, how could he be expected to interpret it properly? Still, he knew that the king and queen often walked through bombed areas of London, showing sympathy and support. How easy for a lone gunman, waiting for them in the shadows. He shivered and stared out the train window.

His thoughts turned to Mavis. If she could only find the site in the snapshot, then all would be explained. He tried to picture it now—the hill with the pine trees—but couldn't imagine any relevance, unless there was a stately home on the hill behind those trees where an aristocrat lived who was an important part of the Ring. Or that this might be a place the royal family had planned to visit.

Then he found himself thinking not of his assignment, but of Mavis herself. She was an attractive girl. Vivacious. Fun. But did he really fancy her? Was it just that she was nothing like Pamela, and he needed to take his mind off the girl he couldn't have? His thoughts drifted to her now—how soft and serene and elegant she always looked. How her eyes sparkled when she smiled. How her hair smelled somehow like fresh gardens.

Stop it! he commanded himself. *Think of something else.* Pamela's friend, Trixie. She had seemed interested in him, which he found amazing, because clearly she was the kind of debby girl who would go more for the Jeremy Prescotts of this world. The party might prove interesting after all.

CHAPTER THIRTY-THREE

Mayfair
Jeremy's flat

"You're looking remarkably couth tonight," Guy Harcourt said as he stopped by Ben's room. "Don't tell me you're going somewhere civilised?"

"A party in Mayfair, actually," Ben said.

"Good God. Are there still such things?"

"It's being given by a friend who has taken over his father's flat," Ben said.

"Anyone I know?"

"Jeremy Prescott. I think you do know him. He was up at Oxford at the same time as us."

Guy nodded. "Of course, I know him. We used to cruise around together on the deb circuit and then Oxford, of course, although he was a Balliol man, wasn't he? Do you think he'd mind if I tag along? I am actually in the slough of despond and in desperate need of cheering up."

"I don't see why not," Ben said. "He seemed to be asking all and sundry."

"Wizard! I'll go and change."

"I'd better give you the address," Ben said. "I have to pick up a girl at the station."

"You're bringing a date, you sly dog?"

"You don't know everything about me," Ben said with a grin. "However, I'm not sure how much of a date she is . . ."

"But she's a warm body. That's all that counts in wartime," Guy said. "God, I'm feeling positively sex-starved, aren't you? And all this having to keep silent about what we're doing. It really cramps one's style. The girls who would be impressed by my chasing German spies now think that I'm a physical wreck who is a filing clerk."

Ben nodded agreement. "It definitely is trying. But cheer up. You can drown your troubles in Sir William Prescott's good wine."

He left Guy putting on evening clothes and made his way to the station. Mavis was waiting for him. She smiled when she saw him, but there was a flicker of nervousness, too.

"Cripes, I didn't realise it was to be a formal affair," she said. "I'm dressed for an ordinary party."

"I'm sure you look just fine," Ben said. "And I'm also sure there will be some people there not wearing formal dress. I put this on just in case and because I don't have a decent-looking suit anymore. Mine was made before the war, and I've filled out since then."

"I think you look just right," she said and slipped her hand through his arm. She was wearing a little too much perfume, and her dress was a little too frilly, but her eyes sparkled and he liked the feel of her closeness.

"You didn't have any problem getting away, then?" he asked.

She made a face. "My mother wasn't at all keen on my going up to London alone, but I told her I was going with a group of friends from work, and we were going dancing."

"What time do you have to be back?" Ben asked.

"I told her I might spend the night at Cynthia's house," she said, giving him a knowing look. "I'm not sure that she believed me, but

Cynthia's family doesn't have a telephone, and I know my mum is not about to walk two miles to check on us."

They caught the bus down to Marble Arch. Ben wondered if he should have splurged for a taxi but reasoned that there were precious few to be found these days, and all sorts of people took public transportation. From Marble Arch they walked down Park Lane. It was almost nine o'clock at night but not dark yet, and people were still out and about, enjoying the fine weather. Several men in uniform were going into Grosvenor House, and Ben heard the faint strains of a dance band. So there were elegant evenings still for those who could afford it. An ARP warden, one of the volunteers who handled air-raid precautions, was standing watch on the corner of Curzon Street, ready to pounce on blackout violators.

"Off somewhere nice, then?" he asked as they passed him.

"We're going to a party," Mavis said.

"Make sure you keep the noise down, and don't let any lights show," he said. "Your lot in this area think you can disregard all the rules just because you have money."

"Pleasant sort of chap," Ben whispered as they walked away. Mavis laughed, and slipped her hand into his. Her hand felt warm and comforting. He looked at her, and they exchanged a smile.

Jeremy's flat was not in a large block, but occupied an entire floor of an older Georgian house. A small lift had been installed beside the staircase, and they rode this to the third floor. Ben was conscious of Mavis's presence and suspected that she was deliberately pressing herself against him. As the lift doors opened, the wailing of Benny Goodman's clarinet came to greet them. The front door to the flat was half-open, and music and cigarette smoke wafted out to them as they entered a foyer. Beyond it was a large and well-appointed drawing room. The blackout curtains hadn't yet been drawn, and the room was still lit by the last of the twilight. It was hard to make out the colours of the upholstery or to identify the Old Masters on the white walls tinged with a rosy hue. There were a dozen or more people inside. Two couples were dancing, but Ben didn't recognize either pair. Jeremy was playing bartender. He looked up and waved a cocktail glass as he saw them.

"Come on in!" he called. "I'm just about to open a twenty-year-old Châteauneuf-du-Pape."

"Won't your father kill you when he finds out?" Ben asked as they approached the bar.

"Doing him a favour, old man. What if we got a direct hit and all that lovely wine flowed into the gutter? At least we'll be enjoying it. And knowing my father, he'll find out where to acquire more once the war is over."

"Only it may be hock and Mosel," someone standing near joked.

"Oh gosh, you don't really believe the Germans will invade, do you?" Mavis turned frightened eyes on them.

"It's a possibility we have to face," the young man who had made the joke replied. "They had little trouble invading every other country in Europe. There are only twenty miles of Channel separating us."

"Let's not talk about gloomy things tonight," Jeremy said. "I'm home. I'm in a cosy flat with my friends around me, and we're damned well going to enjoy ourselves. Wine or cocktails? Help yourselves." Then he looked up as Guy came into the room. "Good God, it's Harcourt. How did he get here?"

"I invited him," Ben said. "He shares digs with me. I hope that was all right?"

"Of course," Jeremy said. "The more, the merrier." But Ben could tell that he wasn't pleased. Guy came over to shake hands. "Long time no see, Prescott," he said.

"Absolutely. What are you doing with yourself, Harcourt?"

"Pen pushing, I'm afraid. I failed the medical. I know I look like a strapping specimen, but apparently I have a weak heart."

"That's too bad," Jeremy said. "Well, drink up. They say red wine is fortifying, don't they? Now I must take a glass of wine to my favourite woman."

Ben had been surreptitiously scanning the room, looking for Pamela. Then he saw her standing in the doorway, and looking a little shy, which was unusual for her. Then he noticed she wasn't alone. Trixie came in with her, dressed in a black sheath dress with an emerald green opera cape over it.

"Hello, Ben," she said, deliberately pushing past Pamela to give him a kiss on the cheek.

"I must say you look stunning," he replied.

"Why, thank you for the compliment, kind sir," she replied. "Now where is our host?"

"Pouring drinks," Pamela replied. Then Ben noticed that Dido stood behind her, wearing more makeup than her father would have approved of and a slinky red Chinese-style dress, which made her look older than her eighteen years. Her face broke into a big smile when she saw Ben.

"Hello, Ben," she called. "I didn't know you were going to be here. How super. Won't it be fun?"

"However did you get your father to agree to this?" Ben asked.

"Pamela swore to watch me like a hawk and put me on the milk train home in the morning. But as you can imagine I had to beg, plead, whine, and pout before he said yes. I wish I had known that you'd be coming because he would have been happier knowing that you'd keep an eye on me. He thinks you are a wonderfully steadying influence."

"Gosh, what a responsibility," Ben said. Then he remembered Mavis standing at his side. "Dido, this is Mavis. Mavis, this is"—he hesitated and might have been about to say "Lady Diana Sutton," but Dido cut him off.

"Hello, I'm Dido," she said. "Golly, we didn't know Ben had a girlfriend. You are so secretive and naughty, Benjamin."

"We only met recently." Ben gave an embarrassed smile.

"Do you work together?" Dido asked.

"No, not usually. We met when I had to deliver some papers to the place where Mavis works."

Dido turned to Mavis. "They wouldn't have a job for me where you work, would they? I am desperate to do something useful."

"It's in Buckinghamshire, Dido," Ben said. "You know your father wouldn't let you live away from home."

"Pamela does. Mavis does," Dido said.

Mavis chuckled. "No, I don't. I live with my mother, worse luck. I had to tell some enormous fibs to come out with Ben tonight."

"Well done you," Dido said. "A girl after my own heart."

Jeremy handed Pamela and Dido glasses of wine. Then he saw Trixie. "Hello, another familiar face from the past," he said.

"I'm flattered that you remember me," Trixie replied.

"How could I forget? You were a brilliant dancer. I say, your season was a lot of fun, wasn't it? And as it happens, the last for a while."

"Don't remind me," Dido said. "Have pity on poor girls like me who will never come out now."

"You look as if you're doing quite well without coming out, young Dido," Jeremy said. "Drink up. There's plenty more. And food through in the dining room. Sorry that the eats won't be up to the same standard as the drinks," he added. "I had cook make a mousse from a couple of tins of salmon, and we smoked a trout from the lake, and I've some early strawberries from the garden, so we'll have to make do with those."

"Make do with those," Mavis whispered to Ben. "Where did he manage to get his hands on tins of salmon?"

"Better not to ask," Ben whispered back. She gave him a conspiratorial smile.

"Come and dance with me," she said. "I like this song."

"I have to warn you, I'm a mediocre dancer," Ben replied.

"No, you're not. You're a good dancer; don't be so modest," Pamela said. As Ben led Mavis toward the parquet floor where others were dancing, Pamela muttered to him, "She's nice. I fully approve."

It was a slow foxtrot. Mavis demonstrated that she was quite willing to rest her cheek against his. But it wasn't even quite dark outside, and Ben felt it was a little early in the evening for such things.

"So are those the two girls from the titled family?" she asked him. Ben nodded.

"They seem awfully nice. Not snooty at all."

"They are nice. I've known them all my life. We grew up together."

"And what about the sexy girl in black? She seemed rather keen on you."

"I expect she flirts with anything in trousers," Ben said. "She works with Pamela at—at another government department out in the country."

"I can see I have stiff competition for you," Mavis said. She looked around. "You have such glamorous friends. Your friend Jeremy is so handsome. He and Pamela make a lovely couple, don't they?"

Ben glanced up to see that Jeremy was now dancing with Pamela. He had no such reserve as Ben. His arms were wrapped tightly around her, and they moved as one across the floor. Her head was on his shoulder. Her eyes were closed. She looked perfectly content. Ben tightened his grip on Mavis, and she responded, moving closer to him.

At around eleven o'clock, the air-raid sirens went off.

"Should we go down to a basement or an air-raid shelter or something?" one of the girls asked nervously.

"You don't think they dare to bomb Mayfair, do you?" a man replied, making everyone laugh.

"I know," Jeremy shouted. "Let's go up onto the roof! We'll have a great view from there. Wait while I open the champagne first. It's Veuve Clicquot, the old man's favourite."

There was a loud pop. Champagne welled over the top of the bottle, and glasses were held out to be filled.

"Come on, this way!" Jeremy called, and as if he were the Pied Piper, they followed him through to the kitchen. "It's a bit tricky, but we'll manage," he shouted back over the drone of approaching aircraft. "I used to do it all the time." He pushed up the window, climbed out onto a narrow parapet. Others followed. Ben went first, then helped Mavis, who proved to be agile and fearless. Along the parapet they went and then up a short ladder to a flat roof above. Once there, they laughed at their own bravado and clinked champagne glasses. Jeremy went down and reappeared with the gramophone, and "In the Mood" blasted out. Some revellers started dancing.

Around them, London lay in darkness, but above, searchlights strafed the sky, making barrage balloons suddenly sparkle as they were caught in the beam. Big Ben was highlighted, and then disappeared again. And then the shape of approaching aircraft, flying in formation. To the south came the staccato sound of ack-ack guns, punctuated with the deeper boom as a bomb was dropped. The bombs must have been incendiaries because fires had now broken out across the river.

A girl jumped up on the parapet that ran around the rim of the roof.

"We're not afraid of you, Mr. Hitler! Do your worst!" she shouted, waving her champagne glass at the sky. A bomb fell nearer now, then another, shattering the calm of the night with deep booms that could almost be felt rather than heard. Then they heard explosions close by, and fire rose beyond the blackness of trees.

"What is that big building?" the girl on the parapet said.

"They've hit the palace!" someone shouted. "Oh God, they've hit the palace."

Ben felt his heart jerk. Was this the promised attack, the one they had been warned of? The *Royal Fireworks* music? The deposing of a king? *The palace is huge,* he told himself. *The royal family would be safely in the basement. They might have damaged a few rooms, but they couldn't make the whole place burn down . . .*

The first wave of aircraft was now overhead. Responding gunfire sent bright traces into the night, coming from close by in Hyde Park. Another bomb, closer now.

"That was around St. James's," one of the men said. "Getting too close for comfort."

"Don't be such a ninny," a girl behind Ben replied. It sounded like Trixie. "We're not going down. We're not going to show them that we're scared. We need Jeremy to bring us some more champagne. Where is he?"

Ben looked around and didn't see him. Then Pamela tugged at his sleeve. "Where is Dido? I can't see her," she whispered.

"Perhaps she was afraid and went back down," he said.

Pamela shook her head. "When have you ever known Dido to be afraid?"

"I'll come and help you look for her," Ben said. "Don't worry. She's probably only gone to the loo." He turned to Mavis. "Be right back."

Then he helped Pamela down the ladder and along the parapet. Not that she needed help. She walked with that same confidence he remembered from their tree-climbing days. He was just assisting her to climb in through the window when there was a whistling sound, a flash, a boom, and a blast that almost knocked him over. A building across the street burst into flames. Glass and debris came flying at them. He shoved Pamela inside, shielding her.

"Were we hit?" she asked, her voice shaking.

"No. Across the street."

They could hear shouting from the roof and a man's voice saying, "Get down from here, now. This is madness."

As they emerged from the kitchen, a door at the end of the hall opened and Dido came flying out. She was wearing only her slip and her hair was in disarray. "Have we been bombed?" she asked. "The windows just blew in. Oh my God. There is glass everywhere."

"It's all right. It's across the street." Jeremy came to join her. He was holding a towel around his waist.

Pamela looked at them, then said in a clipped voice, "Dido, get dressed now. I'm taking you home." She looked at Ben. "Do you think there will be a train at this time of night?"

"You might catch the last train if you hurry," he said. "If you miss it, you can come back to my place. I'll go and find a taxi."

Other people were now climbing in through the kitchen window, laughing a little too loudly, as those who have escaped danger often do.

"More champagne," a male voice commanded. "Bartender! Give us your best."

Jeremy had also gone back into the dark room, but emerged again, having hastily put on a shirt and trousers but no jacket and tie. "Of course. Drinks all around," he said with forced gaiety. As he passed Pamela, he touched her sleeve. "Pamma, I can explain . . ."

She shook him loose. "Don't touch me!" she said coldly. "Can we go now, please, Ben?"

Then she remembered. "I must just tell Trixie that I have to go, and I'll see her tomorrow. Someone will take her to the station."

At that moment, Ben remembered Mavis. He pushed through the stream of guests to her. "Look, something has come up and I have to take somebody home now," he said. "I'm frightfully sorry. Can I drop you at the station, or would you rather stay on?"

She looked confused. "I don't know. Is the party over? There's no train at this time of night."

"You could come back to my place, but . . ."

Her gaze went to Pamela standing rock still behind him. "I get the picture. I expect I'll be all right. I'm a big girl."

"No, it's not like that," he said. "I promise you. And I'm really sorry, it's just that . . ." He couldn't finish the sentence.

312

Guy appeared at his side. "A spot of bother?" he asked.

"Actually, yes. Could you look after Mavis and make sure she gets to the station safely?"

"Of course," Guy said. "But what are you doing?"

"Pamela and Diana Sutton need to leave now. Diana's not feeling well. I'll tell you later."

"All right, old chap. Don't worry about it. I'll be a perfect Boy Scout." Guy gave him a grin.

Dido emerged from the bedroom fully clothed. Her lipstick was smudged, and her hair still looked unkempt.

"Into the lift, now!" Pamela commanded.

Dido looked at her sister defiantly. "You wouldn't give him what he wanted, so I did," she said, then stalked past Pamela with her head held high.

Ben heard Jeremy shouting from inside the room, "Nobody needs to leave. A couple of broken windows are not going to spoil our party. Besides, we don't want to get in the way of fire engines and ARP workers. So let's keep going and have eggs and bacon at dawn as I promised. I have real bacon, people. Think of that!"

The lift doors closed, and they went down in silence.

CHAPTER THIRTY-FOUR

London

Ben found a taxi outside the Dorchester, and they sped to Victoria Station. Beyond the darkness of the parks, fires were burning.

"They got Buckingham Palace again, the buggers," the cabby said. "Blimey, I hope we pay them back. Make them suffer for this. I wouldn't spare a single man, woman, or child if I were Mr. Churchill."

"Is the damage bad?" Ben asked.

"I ain't seen it myself," the cabby replied. "They've got the road blocked off, ain't they? But you could certainly see the flames."

They passed Hyde Park Corner and headed down Grosvenor Place. Dido stared out the window, not saying a word.

"Will you both go back to Kent now?" Ben asked.

"I have to be at work in the morning," Pamela said. "I think there are trains on the main line all night. Besides I couldn't trust myself not to hurl her out of the train."

"So how will someone know to come and meet her at the station?" Ben asked.

"I'll telephone from Victoria. I'll tell them there was a bomb, and we had to leave in a hurry. Nothing more needs to be said."

"You don't need to talk about me in the third person," Dido said. "I'm a person. I have feelings too, you know."

"You don't deserve feelings," Pamela said. "You have no idea what feelings are. You always wanted what was mine, all the while we were growing up. And you took it, too."

They reached the station and ran toward the platforms.

"Eleven fifty-five. We should have time to get it," Ben said.

"There won't be a local at this time of night," Pamela said, gasping a little as they ran. "I'll tell Pah to come and pick you up in Sevenoaks."

"All right." Dido suddenly sounded very young and insecure.

"Do you want me to take her home?" Ben asked. "I'm on fairly flexible hours at the moment, so it would be all right."

Pamela gave him a grateful look. "Would you really? That would be so kind. I don't like the thought of her alone on a train in the blackout."

"You could both come back to my place if it would be easier."

"It really wouldn't," Pamela said. "I'm afraid I need to be alone, and I can't be civilised much longer. And I want Dido far away."

"Stop talking about me as if I was a piece of meat," Dido said. "Look, I'm sorry. It didn't mean anything. We were drinking, and we were excited by the bombs, and . . . and it just happened. And do you know what? It was jolly nice, and you're stupid to keep pushing him away."

"That's enough, Dido," Pamela snapped. She almost pushed her sister into the train.

"Tell Mummy I'll see her on Friday as arranged," she said.

"What's happening on Friday?"

"Mummy's having a little garden party this weekend, and she is in a panic because there's no proper food and not enough servants, so I said I'd come down and help." Pamela looked at Ben appealingly. "If you're not working, you wouldn't like to come down, too, would you? I was planning on asking Jeremy to come and help serve drinks and things, but now . . ."

"Of course, I'll come," Ben said.

316

"Trixie said she'd come as well. She said she'd dress as a maid and serve things." Pamela smiled, the lines of worry vanishing from her face for a moment. "We both managed to wangle Friday afternoon and Saturday off. So we'll hope to catch a train about four if you want to join us."

"I'll be there." He smiled at her as he climbed on board after Dido.

A whistle sounded. Pamela reached up to him and covered his hand with hers. "I'm so glad you're here, Ben. I can always count on you."

The train pulled out of the station. Ben looked back and saw her small, slim figure standing there, watching them.

The explanation of a bomb being dropped on the next-door building was readily accepted. Ben stopped at his father's house, where he spent the night, then he caught an early train back to London.

Guy opened his door as Ben came up the stairs. "So where did you get to?" he asked with a suggestive smile. "Was it two for the price of one? I can see why you chose them over Miss Mavis. A lovely girl but a bit too gushing for my taste. I deposited her at the station at six, as requested."

"Thank you so much. She must be furious with me."

"Not too furious, I think. I gave her a bit of a kiss and a cuddle in the taxi, so I think she had a good time and certainly plenty of tales to tell her workmates. How the toffs live and all that." He stared at Ben. "You look washed up. You'd better come in, and I'll make you coffee." Ben needed no second invitation.

"Thank God that coffee isn't rationed," Guy said. "My one vice these days."

"If you can find it," Ben added. He sank onto Guy's bed. "What a night," he said.

"So what was going on, really?" Guy asked as he filled a kettle.

"Pamela Sutton found her little sister in bed with Jeremy Prescott," Ben said. "The kid is only eighteen or nineteen."

"Eighteen isn't what it was before the war," Guy replied. "People grow up quickly these days. They have to. And many people's philosophy is let's grab it while we can because we might not be here tomorrow. And it's true, isn't it? If that bomb had fallen a few yards to the right, we'd all be toast by now."

Ben shivered. "You're right."

"So Diana was sent home in disgrace?"

"I took her home, actually. Pamela had to get back to work, and she was too upset."

"So she was dating Prescott, was she?"

"Oh yes. Ever since they were children."

"That's how the RAF behave: I live with danger, so I take what I want."

"I rather think he's always behaved that way," Ben said.

The kettle boiled, and Guy poured coffee. Then he said slowly, "There's something you should probably know. Lady Margot Sutton . . ."

"Yes, I heard. She was taken by the Gestapo in Paris. A rescue was being planned."

"And was carried out successfully," Guy said.

Ben's eyebrows went up. "Really? She's home? That's wonderful."

"Her family doesn't know she's home yet. I'm not sure when they'll be told. There is some debriefing to be carried out. But that's not what I wanted to tell you. I gather that Captain King has mentioned the secret society called the Ring to you."

"He has."

"So you know who they are and what they plan?"

Ben nodded. "Aristocrats who want to aid Germany."

"It seems that Margot Sutton showed up at a meeting the other evening."

"A meeting of the Ring?"

"That's right."

"Did Captain King, as you refer to him, know she was going to be there?"

"You know him, keeps his cards really close to his chest, but I think this took him by surprise."

"So Margot Sutton will be watched?"

"Oh yes, definitely. And when she is allowed home, I rather think that the task will fall to you."

"Crikey," Ben said.

As soon as Ben went to his own room, he wrote a note to Mavis, explaining that one of the sisters had drunk too much and become ill, necessitating that she be rushed to Victoria Station to catch the last train. He hoped she would forgive him and that Guy looked after her well. And he hoped their next date would be less dramatic. Then he took it to the postbox on the corner. With any luck it would arrive by the last post that evening or, at the latest, by tomorrow morning. He didn't want her to think that he had ditched her in favour of a more sophisticated girl.

Meanwhile, Pamela woke alone in the room she shared with Trixie. She felt hollow and drained, as if she were recovering from a bout of stomach flu. She wondered now if Dido and Jeremy had been having sex during those afternoon visits at his house. Hardly probable with his mother and the servants in the house, but one could never tell with Jeremy. He loved to live dangerously. She'd always known that.

Pamela stood up, stretched, then went over to the window to pull back the blackout curtain. It was a grey, gloomy day, matching her mood. *It was over,* she thought. How could she ever feel safe with a man who had betrayed her with her own sister? If they had married, would she picture the worst every time he was late getting home? Dido was a stupid and frustrated little girl, she saw that now. Dying for the things that had been denied her—the balls and flirtations of a season and now an active means of employment. No wonder she let Jeremy seduce her. *Had they actually completed their lovemaking before the bomb hit?* she wondered. Had Dido been a virgin before? If so, had it hurt? Her own insecurities came flooding over her while an express train rushed past her window with a wild shriek.

She had just finished washing and brushing her teeth when Trixie came home.

"God, what a night." Trixie flung herself down on her bed. "I drank far too much. We all did. My dear, I was so tired, I dozed off on the train. Luckily, it tooted a whistle or I might have woken up and found myself in Crewe." She sat up and studied Pamela. "Are you all right?" she asked.

"I think so. I'll survive."

Trixie came over and sat beside her. "Was it what I think it was? Jeremy in bed with your sister?"

Pamela nodded.

"I'm sorry. He would never have been right for you, you know. He made a pass at me last night after you'd gone. And when I said that he was NSIT—not safe in taxis—I meant it. Back during that deb season, he wouldn't take no for an answer, you know. And if the driver hadn't turned around and asked 'Are you all right, miss?' I'm sure he would have raped me. So you're probably better off without him." She stopped, looked at Pamela's face, then said, "What a stupid thing to say. You love him, don't you?"

"I've always loved him," Pamela said. "And I think I've always known what he was like. It was part of the attraction that he was a daredevil and afraid of nothing. I'll get over it, I suppose. It will take a while, but . . ."

Trixie nodded. "There are plenty more fish in the sea. I got friendly with a rather delicious RAF chap last night. And we'll have fun this Saturday at your mother's garden party, won't we?"

Pamela sank down beside Trixie. "Gosh, Trixie, I don't even want to go home now. How can I face Dido? How can I stand being in the same house with her?"

"It's a big house, and there will be lots of people. Why don't we both dress up as maids and hand around the eats? Wouldn't that be a lark?"

"I don't feel like larks at the moment. In fact, I think I'll send a telegram to my mother saying that I can't get time off after all."

"Oh, don't do that," Trixie said. "I can't go down there on my own, and I'm really looking forward to it. How long since we've enjoyed life as it used to be—tea on the lawn, flowery dresses and hats. It all seems like a lovely dream now, doesn't it?"

"Yes," Pamela said. "Yes, it does." She sighed. "Oh well, I suppose I must go. Livvy's not much help at organising things, and my mother will be in a tizzy."

"Jolly good," Trixie said. She stood up again. "Now, I'd better get dressed and stagger to work. It's lucky I'm not breaking codes, or I'd say that enemy aircraft were sighted in Bombay instead of Birmingham."

Pamela tried to smile as Trixie went to the bathroom.

CHAPTER THIRTY-FIVE

To Farleigh

Ben wasn't quite sure what he should be doing that day. He had delivered Pamela's radio messages to Dolphin Square with the suggestion that they might be matched to known meetings of Ring members. He had been to chivvy up Mavis to find the location on the photograph. So what now? Guy had hinted that he'd be sent to shadow Margot Sutton, but those instructions would have to come from Maxwell Knight. Ben felt uneasy and superfluous, but he also didn't feel like going to Dolphin Square and saying "Please, sir, what should I do now?" like one of the fourth formers he'd been teaching until he was called up. Initiative. That was what was required by MI5. He had wanted to be given challenges, to be noticed, and now he was at the heart of a major plot.

He turned on the radio and was glad to find that the royal family had been unharmed in last night's bombing. He twiddled the dial between frequencies, hoping to pick up the German channel but gave up after a while. Guy was off on a mission somewhere. Ben wondered what he did and how long he'd been working secretly for Knight. Then he paused, thinking. Guy seemed to know all about the Ring. He knew that Margot Sutton had been rescued. That meant he was part of an inner circle. Or . . . Ben paused. Guy fitted the profile of someone who would be part of the Ring. Aristocratic family. The sort, at Oxford, who took risks, liked his comforts. Had he told Ben about Margot Sutton to throw any suspicion from himself? Ben wondered how he could find out. But then Maxwell Knight trusted him, and Ben was sure that Knight was a superb judge of character. Or . . . perhaps Knight knew that he was a double agent and was using him. Ben would have liked to ask Knight but realised he had absolutely no proof that Guy wasn't exactly what he seemed. And he remembered what Guy had said about the so-called Captain King. He answers to nobody but Churchill. A man who could be dangerous and powerful. And it crossed his mind that Maxwell Knight himself might be just the sort of person to run a secret organisation like the Ring. Again, he found himself asking if he had been put on the job with the expectation that they were keeping Whitehall happy, but that he would get it wrong.

He wondered if he should go and see Mavis, but that seemed rather pathetic on a personal level and rather annoying on a professional one. He wondered if the photograph even mattered any longer. If the parachutist had come to deliver an important message, then surely the Germans had already sent the message by another means. He went to the British library and read up more on those battles, but found nothing that he didn't already know. A king had been deposed by a stronger rival. Many men had been killed. But it had eventually brought peace. He could see parallels, but couldn't work out what they might mean. He returned home and cheered up when he remembered he had promised to go down to Kent with Pamela the next day.

Margot Sutton stared out the window of the Daimler as she was driven out of London. City gave way to suburb and then to green and rolling countryside. It felt too good to be true that she was actually back in

England, that she was going home to her family, and the ordeal was over. She tried to feel happy and excited, but instead all she could feel was hollow and empty inside, as if part of her had died when they had taken her to that cell at Gestapo headquarters. The past days had been like living a nightmare, and she had steeled herself to accept that it would end in her death or at the very least in being sent to a German prison camp. Her fingernail had already healed. She bore no visible scars of her ordeal. The scar in her heart would take longer to go away. Gaston had denied ever loving her. He had shown complete disdain for her and for the pain being inflicted on her.

She watched green hedgerows flash past. *I was a complete fool,* she thought. *I gave up everything, risked everything, for a man who didn't even love me.*

Memories swirled back into her consciousness, Gaston strolling with her through the Bois de Boulogne, sitting opposite her at a little café, his eyes glowing with desire as he looked into hers. He had loved her, of this she was suddenly sure. Then she toyed with what Gigi Armande had said: that Gaston had shown disdain for her only to protect her. At the time she hadn't believed it. But now she realised it might have been true. His words to the German had been his way of saving her. By giving the impression that she meant nothing to him he had spared her from further torture. If Gaston was perceived to be completely indifferent to her suffering, then there would be little point in continuing it.

"He saved me," she whispered to herself. "He did love me. He loved me enough to die for me."

And she also came to terms with the realisation that nothing she had done could have saved him. He would never have betrayed his fellow Resistance members, and the Germans would never have released him. "True to the end," she whispered and felt a small glow of consolation inside the blackness of her grief.

And now she was free to resume her former life. Free. Not quite free, she knew that. But she would tackle the next hurdle when she came to it. For now, she was going to try to enjoy the Kentish countryside and her family. They drove through Sevenoaks, then their surroundings became familiar. She had ridden over these fields with the hunt when she was a girl. *It's strange,* she thought, *but I feel like an old woman, as if my life has already happened.* And she wondered if she would ever feel normal again. And then, of course, the worries crept back into her head. Would she dare to go through with it? And could she be brave enough to make Gaston proud of her?

Then they were driving through Elmsleigh. There was the village green with the cricket scoreboard still showing the numbers of the last game. The church beyond. Miss Hamilton walking her dogs. Nothing had changed at all. *Only me,* Margot thought.

Phoebe was in the schoolroom, reciting the order of English kings and queens to her governess. She had got as far as Richard III and was stuck. She paced around the room. "Richard III," she said again, and then . . .

"Battle of Bosworth," Miss Gumble reminded her. "What happened after that?"

"And then . . ." Phoebe looked out the window and gave a shriek of delight. "It's Margot!" she shouted. "Margot's home."

She rushed down the hall, down the two flights of stairs, shouting the good news.

Lord Westerham was in the morning room, reading the newspaper. He put it down and glared at his daughter. "What have I told you about that screaming and shouting? Doesn't your governess tell you that a lady never raises her voice?"

"But Pah," Phoebe said, her face still alight with joy, "it's Margot. She's home."

Around midday on Friday, Ben was getting ready to go to Victoria when Guy tapped on his door. "Listen, old chap. I have it on good authority that Margot Sutton is being driven home to Kent. I wondered if you could find a good excuse to be down there."

"As a matter of fact, I'm heading there right now," Ben said. "Pamela Sutton asked me to help with a garden party her mother is giving tomorrow."

A smile crossed Guy's face. "A garden party? Are there still such things? Remarkable. I might hop on a train and join you. Strawberries and cream on the lawn? So definitely prewar. What's it in aid of? Fundraising for our troops?"

Ben shrugged. "I've no idea. All I know is that Lady Westerham was in a panic about holding a garden party when she didn't have the staff or the supplies, and Pamela agreed to go and help."

"So you'll put on tails and pretend to be the butler, will you?" Guy chuckled.

"Actually, they still have their butler. He's too old to be called up. But no footmen and only a couple of maids."

"How the upper classes are made to suffer," Guy said with heavy sarcasm. "Mummy wrote that she had to clean her own lavatory the other day. Imagine."

Ben smiled. He realised what a shock wartime living must be for so many of Guy's class.

He was about to leave when he heard footsteps coming up the stairs and was startled to see a dispatch rider heading toward him. The man stopped and saluted. "Mr. Cresswell? I was told to deliver this to you immediately. It comes from Medmenham."

"Thank you," Ben stammered. The man saluted and stomped back down the stairs. Ben went into his room, closed the door, and opened the envelope. "I think I've located the place on your photograph," Mavis had written. "It's marked on the ordnance survey map. Actually in Somerset, not Devon or Cornwall as you had thought."

Ben's heart was thumping. He had to tell someone before he met Pamela at the station. He grabbed his overnight bag, then took the Underground and walked as fast as he could to Dolphin Square. He rang the doorbell down below, but there was no answer. He rode up in the elevator and tapped on the door. Again no answer. An elderly man was coming down the hall toward him. "No use knocking," he said. "They went away. I saw them with suitcases earlier this morning."

"Damn," Ben muttered to himself. He took the lift back down and stood in bright sunshine, trying to think what to do next. There was nobody he could tell about the photograph. Guy had gone out, and Ben had no idea when he'd return. Besides, he had an uneasy feeling about Guy. He'd have to go to Somerset himself. But Pamela was waiting for him at the station.

He sighed and headed to Victoria.

Pamela and Trixie were waiting under the destination board. Pamela waved when she spotted him. "You made it. How lovely."

"Hello, Ben," Trixie said. "I'm so pleased to see you're coming, too. I'm all set to be a maid. I wanted to rent one of those frilly French maid's outfits in a costume shop, but Pamma wouldn't let me."

"As if my family ever had a frilly French maid," Pamma said, giving Ben an exasperated look. "Even Mah's never had a French lady's maid. Hers is middle-aged and stodgy and called Philpott."

"Then your family needs livening up," Trixie said. "Mummy always had French maids, and Daddy always chased them. It kept their marriage happy."

Pamela pretended to be studying the departure board. "So there is a train in half an hour on platform eleven. That's good. Plenty of time to buy our tickets and get over there."

"Look, Pamma." Ben cleared his throat. "I'm not sure what to do. I have to go down to Somerset right away. Something I absolutely have to check on. So I should really head to Paddington and take the first train down there. But I did promise I'd come with you to help your mah. So I hope you understand if I back out on you."

"Of course," Pamma said. "It doesn't matter, I'm sure. You have to do your job."

"What's so important in Somerset?" Trixie asked. "Nothing ever happens there except for making cider and cheese." She laughed, but then she studied Ben's face. "You really are involved in secrets and intrigue, aren't you? I thought you had to be when I saw you at Bletchley. I know, let me come down to Somerset with you. I'm a Bletchley girl. I've signed the Official Secrets Act. I won't say a word, and I'm dying for excitement."

"It's not going to be exciting," Ben said. "I just have to check on a map reference."

"And you are certainly not going with Ben," Pamela said, giving Trixie a cold look. "If anyone goes with him, it will be me."

"You both have to help Lady Westerham," Ben said.

"But how are you going to get around when you're there?" Pamela asked.

"Train. Bus. My feet."

"They have buses once a week in places like Somerset."

"I'll manage."

"I have a good idea," Pamela said. "Come down to Kent with us, and we'll ask to borrow Pah's Rolls. I'll drive you."

"But what about your mother?"

"If we went straight away this afternoon, we could be back in good time before the party. Do you think it will take long, what you have to do there?"

"I've no idea," Ben said. "Frankly I'm not sure what I'm looking for."

"That sounds like a lark," Trixie said. "I still think that Pamma should stay with her mama and you should take me with you, Ben."

"I don't think I should take anybody with me," Ben said uneasily.

"Yes, you will," Pamela said. "You'll need someone to map-read while you drive. Or better still, I'll drive and you read the map. That will make it go so much faster."

"I suppose so," he agreed.

"So you want me to stay and slave away in your place," Trixie said with a mock pout.

Pamela gave Trixie a grateful glance. "Would you really?"

"I suppose so, if I have to. Slaving at garden parties for Britain. I may get a medal."

Pamela laughed. "You are a brick."

"That's me. Trixie the brick," she said. "Come on, we have to buy those tickets and there is a long line."

Ben pulled Pamela aside. "Do you think your father would let us have the Rolls?" Ben asked, still torn between catching the next train from Paddington and having Pamela beside him in a motorcar.

"If not, we'll ask the Prescotts. They have extra motorcars," Pamela said breezily. "And plenty of petrol, by the look of it."

"Do you think they'd really lend me a car?" Ben asked.

"They'd lend me one," Pamela said calmly. "They still think—"

"So it really is over between you and Jeremy?"

"How could it possibly not be?" she said. "But never mind that now. We have a job to do."

"It's really good of you, Pamela," he said.

"Not at all. It will be an adventure, and I need something to cheer me up."

When they arrived home, they were greeted by an ecstatic Phoebe, announcing once again that Margot had returned. This necessitated hugs and tears and ended up in having tea with the family.

"Just like old times," as Lady Westerham put it. "My greatest prayer has been answered, and my girls are all with us again."

Margot looked drawn and pale and gave a sad sort of smile. Ben debated whether he should stay, now that Margot was here, or go chasing the photograph. The latter won. Margot announced that she was really tired and would they excuse her if she went up to her room.

As Ben had feared, Lord Westerham did object to their taking the Rolls.

"I'm not allowing you two off on some joyride, using up the last of my petrol ration," he bellowed.

"But Pah, it's important," Pamela said. "Something that Ben has to do for his job, and I said I'd go along to help him."

"If it's important for his job, then the government can supply him with a vehicle. They get petrol. I don't," he snapped.

"I'm awfully sorry," Pamela whispered. "I didn't think he'd be such an old meanie. It's too bad that we can't tell him why we need the car. He doesn't realise it's a matter of national security. But he's right. Couldn't your boss requisition a vehicle for you?"

"It seems he's away for the weekend," Ben said. "And I just don't feel that this can wait."

"What is this all about?" Pamela asked in a low voice.

Ben thought there was no point in keeping quiet, now that she knew he was MI5. "That parachutist who fell into your field," he said, drawing her aside where they couldn't be overheard. "He had nothing on him at all. No identification. Only a photograph with numbers on it. And someone has finally found the location where it was taken. So I have to go there right away."

"We can't tell the Prescotts that," Pamela said. She looked out the window. "I say, there are loads of army vehicles sitting idle outside our house. Do you think we dare borrow one?"

"And be shot as we leave with it?" Ben had to laugh. Then he thought and said, "But I could ask Colonel Pritchard. He seemed like a decent sort of chap. He knows all about the parachutist. And I could tell him who I'm working for."

"Then do it," Pamela said. "I'll go and change into something more suitable for driving, and I'll pack my toothbrush, just in case we're stuck for the night." She grinned at him. "I never thought I'd smile again, but this is going to be fun."

CHAPTER THIRTY-SIX

To Somerset

Colonel Pritchard listened with interest but was hesitant. "I can't give you my staff car. Apart from that I've only lorries, tanks, and armoured cars here. You'd certainly be conspicuous driving around in one of those, and I doubt you even have the correct licence." He paused, then said, "I tell you what—have you ridden a motorbike?"

"A couple of times, when I was up at Oxford," Ben said.

"Then you can take my dispatcher's motorbike and sidecar. It doesn't use much petrol, either."

So half an hour later, they set off with Pamela in the sidecar and Ben sitting, rather uneasily, on the motorbike. Pamela had changed into slacks and an open-necked shirt. Her hair was tied back under a scarf. Ben had to concentrate fully on driving the unfamiliar machine and was hardly conscious that he had a passenger and the passenger was Pamma. It wasn't a powerful machine, and Ben soon settled down. Driving would have been pleasant on roads that were almost deserted, thanks to petrol rationing, except that all signposts had been removed and they took a couple of wrong turns before they reached the main road to the southwest. Then they breezed along at a good rate, encountering only the occasional army lorry or delivery van.

It was close to nine in the evening by the time they had passed through Wiltshire and driven into Somerset. Darkness threatened to come upon them suddenly. The setting sun had been swallowed into an ominous bank of clouds. A chill wind had sprung up.

Ben turned to Pamela with a worried look on his face. "Golly, we didn't think about rain, did we? I now see that a motorbike has distinct limitations."

"Then let's hurry up and get the job done," Pamela said. "How close do you think we are?"

Ben studied the map. "Quite close. That last village must have been Hinton St George. That means the hill should be ahead on our left soon. We've seen plenty of hills, but this one has a distinctive shape." He held up the copy of the photograph for her to study. "And see the church tower and those three big pines. They should be easy enough to identify."

Pamela nodded. "Then lead on, Macduff."

The lane took them through the Somerset Levels, where cows grazed in fields separated by water channels. It seemed to Ben that they had left the hilly part of the region behind, and he wondered if his map-reading skills had led him astray. Then they passed through a village of thatched cottages and Pamela pointed. "Look. That's it!"

As they came closer, they could see the church, rising above those pine trees. They looked at each other and smiled. It took them a while to find a road that led them to the top of the hill, but in the dying light of day, they drove up to the church, and Ben stopped the bike. Rooks were cawing loudly from the trees in the churchyard where old gravestones lay at drunken angles. The wind from the west hit them in the face as they walked forward. The church was called All Saints. Ben looked around and saw a small house behind the churchyard. Apart from that, there were no dwellings in sight. The place had a gloomy and forsaken feel to it.

"Now what?" Pamela asked.

Now what, indeed? They had passed a couple of small cottages as the road wound up the hill, but there was no sign of a village or the substantial manor house Ben had hoped for.

"I suppose we should visit the vicarage before we go down," Ben said.

"Are you expecting to find a hotbed of Nazi sympathisers there?" Pamela asked, half-joking. "Are you armed, just in case?" She saw the look on his face and burst out laughing. "I think we've been had," she said. "I think there was a hidden message in the photograph, and the actual place was irrelevant."

"I'm afraid I have to agree," Ben said. But he found a mossy path through the churchyard and knocked on the vicarage door. It was opened by an elderly cleric with wispy white hair and an angelic face. Ben said that they were driving around the West Country and interested in old churches, particularly remote old churches. They were invited in and served elderberry wine, made by a parishioner, the vicar told them.

"But where is your parish?" Pamela asked. "We didn't see any houses."

"Ah, well," the vicar said. "There is indeed a history to this church. It was once part of a monastery, taken over at the time of Henry VIII and handed to a local lord who turned the monastery into his manor. Then during the civil war, it was razed to the ground by Oliver Cromwell. But the church survived and has served the neighbouring farms and villages ever since."

"So the manor house is no more?"

"Part of the ruined walls still stand, but that's about it."

"So does anyone else live around here these days?" Pamela asked.

"Nobody for a good half mile," the vicar said.

"It must be lonely for you."

He nodded. "My wife died three years ago. A woman comes in to clean once a week. I do my rounds on my bicycle, but yes, it is pretty remote. Luckily, I have my books and the wireless." He stood up. "It will be dark soon, but would you like to see the church?"

"Thank you." Ben and Pamela rose to follow him. He took a torch from the hall table and shone their way between the gravestones. Inside the church, the last of the daylight came in through tall, perpendicular windows, giving an impression of a long nave with pillars on either side. The church smelled old and damp and was clearly in a state of disrepair.

The vicar walked them around, shining his torch on marble slabs marking tombs of dead knights. Then he said, "If you'd like to go up the tower, we've a wonderful view from the top. I won't come with you. The old legs can't take the stairs anymore, you understand. There is a light on the stair, but we shouldn't use it because of the blackout. Here, take my torch."

He showed them a door in the wall. Beyond it a stone spiral stair led up and up. The torch, covered in blackout fabric, picked out one step after another, but it was still eerie and horribly cold. At last they came to a little door, unlatched it, and stepped out onto the platform at the top of the tower. A ray of dying sun had pierced the clouds and painted the channels of water below pink. In the distance they could make out the open water of the Bristol Channel.

"This would be a good place to signal from," Ben said.

Pamela nodded. "But who would be doing the signalling?" she replied.

The wind now carried the first hints of rain. "We should get going," Ben said.

The vicar walked with them back to the motorbike and waved as they left. It was starting to rain hard now, a stinging wind-blown rain from the sea.

"So do you think we should come back again in daylight and find out who might be living nearby?" Pamela asked.

"I wonder what we'd achieve with that?" Ben said, looking around at the dark woods. "The vicar would have mentioned anyone strange or suspicious, wouldn't he? He said his parish was only neighbouring farms and cottages. Presumably country people who have farmed here for generations. We could examine the ruins of the old monastery in daylight, but again, wouldn't the vicar have noticed anything suspicious going on? Frankly, I'm not hopeful myself. I think you were right in what you said before. That it's a hidden message, not an actual place."

"I suppose." Pamela nodded. "So we'll go back to London, and you can report what you've found. And my mother will kill me if we don't get back for her party."

"We should stop for something to eat first," Ben said. "I don't know about you, but I'm starving."

"Good luck at this time of night." Pamela chuckled. "I bet they all go to bed by eight in the country, especially now that the blackout makes travel so hard. And I think you'll find it really difficult to drive home in the dark, Ben. Maybe it would be more sensible to find somewhere for the night and leave at first light tomorrow."

"Did you bring overnight clothes?"

She laughed. "A toothbrush. But I'll survive."

It had been raining as they wound their way down the hill, but the overhead canopy of trees protected them. As they came out onto the flatlands, the heavens opened into a downpour. "We can't go on in this, Ben," Pamela shouted over the drumming of the rain. Thunder grumbled in the distance.

"There was a pub in that first village," Ben shouted back. They crept along at a snail's pace, conscious of the water-filled ditches, now overflowing on either side of the road. Then the first houses appeared, and they could make out a pub sign. It was called the Fox and Hounds, and had a thatched roof and a nice Old World feel to it.

Ben parked the bike under an overhang in the courtyard, and they sprinted to the front door. When they came in, they were greeted by a low murmur of voices and saw several older men standing around the bar. A couple of dogs lay at their heels. The room had a beamed ceiling and an enormous fireplace. All eyes were on them as they approached the bar.

"Been for a swim, have you, then," the landlord asked in a strong Somerset accent. "My word, but you look like a couple of drowned rats." He chuckled.

"We were on a motorbike," Ben said. "Would you possibly have rooms for the night?"

"I've got just the one room," the landlord said. "I don't suppose you'll mind that, will you?"

Ben looked at Pamela. Before he could say anything, she gave a bright smile. "Of course not. That would be lovely."

"I'll see if the missus can send up an airing rack to dry your clothes," the landlord went on. "Should I bring up a couple of pints of beer or cider?"

Ben looked at Pamela, and she said, "Cider for me, please. And something to eat?"

The landlord frowned. "We don't serve food anymore, not since rationing. But the wife has baked pasties, and I dare say we can spare a couple."

He led them up a creaky staircase to the room. It had an enormous double bed, piled high with quilts. As soon as the landlord closed the door, Pamela looked at it and laughed. "Talk about the Princess and the Pea."

"And you, being of noble birth, will undoubtedly be too uncomfortable to sleep." Ben tried to sound lighthearted.

"On the contrary, after all that fresh air, I shall sleep perfectly," she said.

"We should take off our wet clothes," Ben said. "Do you want me to wait outside while you change?" His face was red with embarrassment.

"I'm not too badly soaked," Pamela said. "My legs were under the canopy of the sidecar. And my blouse was only wet around the collar. My jacket, however, is a disaster." She took it off and draped it over the back of a chair. "You, on the other hand . . ." She looked at him and laughed.

"Quite damp, I'd say." He laughed, too.

"Go on. Take them off. I won't look," she said.

Ben stripped to his underwear and wrapped himself in a towel that was hanging on the rack.

"You take the bed. I'll curl up in that chair," he said, not looking at her.

"You certainly won't. There is room for both of us," she said. "You need a good night's sleep as much as I do."

There was a tap at the door, and a landlady appeared with glasses of cider and two pasties.

"Give me the wet things, and I'll put them in the airing cupboard," she said, then gave them a bright smile and left.

The cider and pasties went down remarkably quickly, then Pamela climbed up into the bed, and Ben turned the light out before sliding in beside her. "Are you sure this is all right?" he asked.

Pamela put a hand on his arm. "Oh, Ben. You are so sweet. I feel perfectly safe with you. You're like the brother I never had."

"Good," Ben said. He didn't mean it.

They lay there in darkness, listening to the drumming of rain and the distant growl of thunder.

"I never felt safe with Jeremy," Pamela said suddenly. "I suppose that was part of the attraction—that he was not quite safe. Flirting with danger, you know. He wanted to make love to me, but I wouldn't let him." There was silence again, then she blurted out, "I was wondering. Do you think I might be frigid?"

"I hope you're not suggesting that I prove otherwise right now," Ben said, with an uneasy laugh.

She laughed, too. "Oh no, of course not. It's just that I've been wondering ever since. And feeling guilty. If I'd given Jeremy what he wanted, he'd never have seduced Dido."

"I don't think Dido needed much seducing," Ben said. "You, on the other hand, would want everything to be right before you committed yourself. That's the way you are."

"You understand me so well," she said. And she laid her head on his shoulder. He could hear his heart beating, horribly conscious of her nearness, the cool touch of her skin. *The brother she never had,* he muttered to himself. She fell asleep quickly, and he lay listening to her breathing.

They woke to a deafening chorus of birds and sounds of activity outside. A farmer was driving cows past the window. A tractor was heading for the field. They looked at each other and smiled. "A little rumpled but hardly the worse for wear," Pamela said.

"You look splendid," Ben said. "Would you go down and find my clothes, then we'll get some breakfast and be off, shall we?"

Down in the private bar, the landlady cooked them bacon, eggs, fried bread.

"That was wonderful," Pamela said. "After what we've been living on. My landlady is a horrible cook."

"You're out on a little holiday then, are you? Before your young man goes back into uniform?"

"That's right," Pamela said. "And we were interested in that hill over there. Does it have any sort of special history?"

"What, Church Hill, you mean?" The landlady asked.

"Is that its name?" Ben asked sharply.

"That's how it's always been known around here."

"What is it, Ben?" Pamela asked while the landlady cleared away their plates. "You've gone quite white."

"I was just looking at the calendar on the wall," he said. "It's the fourteenth of June. That makes the date 14, 6, 1941. Look at the numbers on the photograph. 1461. Today's date. I think I know what it must mean now. This was an order from Germany to kill Churchill today."

CHAPTER THIRTY-SEVEN

In Somerset

"We must let somebody know right away." Ben jumped up and headed for the door. "But who? My boss is away. Ten Downing Street. They'll know where Mr. Churchill is. They can take precautions." His heart was hammering, and he could hear himself babbling as he ran to catch up with the landlady. "Do you have a telephone?"

"There's a telephone box in the middle of the village outside the post office," she said.

"I'll collect our things. You go," Pamela called.

He ran down the street and stood in the telephone box, fumbling for coins. Did he have the right change? Surely the operator would connect him in a national emergency.

"Number, please," came the operator's voice.

"I need you to connect me with Ten Downing Street," Ben said, trying to sound calm. "This is an emergency."

"Are you being funny?" she asked.

"No, of course I am not being funny," he snapped. "I am with MI5 and I'm stuck in the depths of Somerset, and it is imperative that I speak with someone immediately." He was surprised at his own forcefulness.

"Very good, sir. I'll do what I can." The woman sounded shaken.

Ben waited impatiently, then a male voice came on the line. "Prime minister's residence. How can I help you?"

"Is the prime minister there?" Ben asked.

"No, sir. I believe he spent the night in the war rooms," the calm voice said.

"Then please listen carefully," Ben said. "My name is Benjamin Cresswell. I am an agent of MI5. My superiors will vouch for that, if necessary. But I have reason to believe there is a plot to assassinate the prime minister today."

"Sir, we get threats against the prime minister all the time," said the patient voice. "Can you substantiate this? And why has this information not gone through the proper channels?"

"Because my boss is away this weekend, and I can't reach him. I have been following a lead that started with a dead German, and I'm standing in the middle of the bloody Somerset countryside. And I thought you might like to know." Ben heard himself shouting.

"Can you give me details?"

"Obviously not over a public phone line where any number of people may be listening in," Ben said. "But I suggest he stays put in the war rooms today."

"The prime minister is scheduled to attend a ceremony at Biggin Hill Aerodrome," the voice said. "I'm sure he will not change his plans because of an unsubstantiated threat. And he will be at an aerodrome. Where could he be better protected?"

"I've done my part," Ben said as frustration boiled over. "I have warned you. If you choose to disregard my warning, upon your head be it."

"Look, I'll advise the prime minister's security detail to be armed and extra vigilant," the voice said. "But if you think the PM would ever stay home like a frightened rabbit because of a threat against his life, then you don't know Churchill."

Ben put the receiver down and walked back to Pamela.

"Have they told the prime minister? Will they take steps?" she asked him.

"I'm not sure." Ben sighed. "I don't know what else to do."

She touched his arm. "You've done your part. You were the one who worked out the plot against him."

"But all of that is no use if he gets shot anyway, is it? Bloody fools. So damned complacent. What else can I do? Telephone Biggin Hill, I suppose, and go there ourselves as quickly as possible. With any luck we'll get there before it's too late."

Phoebe awoke early, feeling excited and restless. It wasn't just the garden party and her mother's anxiety that all would go smoothly. Something else was going on. Why had Ben and Pamela left in a hurry on a motorbike right when Margot came home? She felt sorry for Pamela's friend, brought here and then abandoned while they went off without her. And then there was the telephone call she had overheard the night before. Someone in Pah's study making a phone call late at night. A woman's voice, but Phoebe couldn't hear what was being said through the thick wood of the door. Then Soames had come past, and she'd had to go up to bed. A morning ride, that's what she needed.

She put on her jodhpurs and riding boots, grabbed her crash cap, and went down to the stables. Old Jackson was already up and about. Phoebe paused and stared up at Miss Gumble's window. Was she already awake? Would she report that Phoebe had gone out riding without permission?

"Saddle up Snowball, please, Jackson," Phoebe said.

"Is the master all right with you taking her out alone?" he asked.

"I'll be good and not gallop and not jump over logs," she said. "But she hasn't been exercised enough lately, and she's getting fat."

"That's true enough," he agreed. "Do you want me to come with you?"

"No, you'll make me walk too slowly," she said.

He grinned. "Well, I don't suppose any harm will come to you. You're a grand little rider, I'll say that for you. A credit to your family."

Phoebe beamed and glanced up at Miss Gumble's window again.

"You don't need to worry about her," Jackson said. "She went out hours ago. Off on one of them bird-watching expeditions with her binoculars round her neck."

Phoebe mounted her pony, and they set off. Once out of sight of the house, she urged Snowball into a canter, enjoying the feel of the early-morning breeze in her face. She hoped she might meet Alfie in the fields, but there was no sign of him. She directed Snowball closer to the woods and the gamekeeper's lodge, but again saw nothing. She was on a bridle path through a stand of trees when she heard the sound of a motor vehicle driving up the track beyond a thick stand of rhododendron bushes. It didn't sound like a big army lorry, and she tried to get a glimpse of it, but the shrubbery was too thick. She heard the motor stop. Then she heard a voice.

"You got my message, then?"

It was low, hardly more than a whisper, but clearly a woman's.

"What's wrong?" This time a man's voice.

"I can't go through with it."

"You have to. It's all planned. You can't back out now."

"But I can't do it."

"You have to. Obviously, I can't do it now, so it's up to you. You agreed."

"Please don't ask me to do this."

"You know the consequences if you don't see it through."

Phoebe thought she heard a sob. The voice dropped to a mutter. Phoebe wanted to urge the horse forward but was scared that the chinking of the bit would give her away.

Then she heard clearly. "Here's the gun. Already loaded. Take it. Don't let us down."

Then a car door shut, and she heard the sound of an engine reversing. She looked for a way through the bushes, but the undergrowth was too thick to take a pony through. By the time she had found a way around, the track was deserted and only tyre marks indicated that the scene had just happened.

Phoebe's heart was racing. She had enjoyed her sleuthing and spycatching with Alfie, but that had been more of a game than anything. Now a loaded gun had been passed from one person to another. And that person was frightened. Who were they, and what were they doing meeting at Farleigh? She needed to tell somebody. If she went to Pah, he probably wouldn't believe her. Mah wouldn't be interested. She could have told Pamma, but she was away. And Miss Gumble was out bird-watching for the day. What did it say on that poster with the seven rules on it? *Report anything suspicious to the authorities.* That, likely, meant the village constable. She didn't think he was very bright, but he could at least pass the information along to the right people.

She had to find Alfie and tell him. He'd believe her. She rode back to the gamekeeper's lodge, dismounted, and tied Snowball's bridle to a tree branch. Mrs. Robbins looked uneasy and embarrassed as she opened the door.

"Oh, your ladyship, is something the matter? Mr. Robbins was having a bit of a lie-in this morning. He's still in his nightclothes, and we're not really ready to receive visitors."

"I'm sorry, but is Alfie awake? I'd like a word with him," Phoebe said.

"He's in the kitchen, having his breakfast. I'll go and get him for you," she said.

Phoebe waited, and soon Alfie appeared, wiping his mouth. "Smashing porridge she makes. She's a good cook all right." He grinned. "What's up? You look worried."

"I am worried," Phoebe said. "I don't quite know what to do. I was out riding, and I heard a car driving up that old track behind the rhododendrons, and then I heard voices. One was a woman and she was frightened, and the man said she had to do something and gave her a loaded gun."

"Blimey," Alfie said. "Who was it?"

"That's the problem. I was on Snowball, and the bushes are so thick there. By the time I found a way around, they'd both gone. So what do you think we should do?"

"Tell your dad, of course."

"I suppose so. But he'd think I misheard or was making it up. I was wondering whether we should go to Constable Jarvis."

"Him? He's as thick as a plank." Alfie looked scornful.

"But he is the authorities, isn't he? My father probably wouldn't believe me, and my mother wouldn't listen, and Pamma's away."

Alfie nodded. "All right. We'll go and see Constable Jarvis. But let me finish my breakfast first."

"Alfie, this is urgent," Phoebe said. "Get dressed. I'll take Snowball back to the stables and meet you down here in half an hour."

She urged Snowball into a reluctant canter all the way back, swung herself down, and handed over the pony to the groom.

"Is Miss Gumble back yet?" she asked.

"Ain't seen hide nor hair of her, your ladyship," the groom said.

"Oh." The thought had just come to Phoebe that Miss Gumble would be the right person to tell. She would take Phoebe seriously and know the right thing to do. But as she walked up the steps into the house, another horrifying thought struck her. Ben Cresswell had been suspicious about Miss Gumble, hadn't he? He'd asked about her telescope and her papers. And Ben was a level-headed sort of chap, and he and Pamela had gone off somewhere in a hurry. That meant something was going on. Phoebe revised her plan. Perhaps she should go down to the vicarage and see if he had come back. If not, she'd write a note for him. He and Pamma would have to be back before the garden party at the very least. If anyone knew what to do, it would be Ben.

No family member was in sight as she went into the dining room and grabbed a hasty slice of toast, spreading marmalade on it and gulping it down. She wanted to pour herself a cup of tea, but she knew that if Pah came in, she'd be in trouble for coming to breakfast in riding gear. She looked up when she heard footsteps, but it was only Pamma's friend Trixie who had come to help with the party. She looked pretty and elegant in a summery dress, and she smiled when she saw Phoebe.

"Hello, young lady," she said. "Going out riding? Lovely day for it. If I hadn't signed up for hard labour today, I'd come and join you."

"Actually, I just got back," Phoebe said. "I'm going down to the village with Alfie. Would you tell the others when you see them?"

"Of course," Trixie said. "Who is Alfie—your boyfriend?" She gave Phoebe a teasing smile.

Phoebe blushed. "Of course not. He's the gamekeeper's boy. But we are friends. And we've an important job to do. Something I overheard that needs to be reported."

"Good for you." Trixie nodded and smiled. "Only don't stay away too long, or your mother will not be pleased. It's all hands on deck today, as you very well know."

"Don't worry. I'll be back soon," Phoebe said and hurried out.

CHAPTER THIRTY-EIGHT

On the way back from Somerset

Ben pushed the underpowered bike to its limits as he rode back to Kent. He gripped the handlebars, staring straight ahead with a look of grim determination on his face. What if they chose to ignore him? How could he possibly make it to Biggin Hill before the prime minister arrived? And if he was there in time, what on earth could he do?

At least it promised to be a beautiful day, sparkling clear. *Lady Westerham would be happy for her garden party,* he thought. Of course, he had to get Pamma home for that. Another thing to worry about. Pamma would undoubtedly be chastised for not being there to help her mother prepare, but surely they'd all see that this was more important.

They passed Stonehenge, left Hampshire behind, then through the genteel gardens of Surrey, arriving at Biggin Hill around noon. The gate was closed, and a guard walked out to them as Ben removed his goggles.

"Sorry, the ceremony is already over," he said.

"Is the prime minister here?" Ben snapped out the words.

"Already left, mate," the guard said.

Ben heaved a sigh of relief.

"Is he going back to London?"

The guard grinned. "He don't tell me his plans, son. But I heard he wanted to pop in and see his house, seeing it's so close by."

Chartwell, of course. *A stone's throw away,* Ben thought. Should he go after the PM?

"What was this ceremony?" Pamela asked, climbing out of the side-car and stretching as she spoke.

"Remembering our chaps who went down at the Battle of Britain last year. And presenting a few gongs, that's all. Keeping up morale. There's one of our chaps just made it back to Blighty after escaping from a German prison camp. What a tale he had to tell. He was the only one who survived an attempted breakout. He was shot and played dead, but managed to get all the way across Germany and France. The prime minister made a big fuss of him."

"We know him," Pamela exclaimed. "He's a good friend. Is he still here?"

The guard looked around. "He was just saying good-bye to his family last time I saw," he said. "Oh, there he is, over there. Hold on, I'll get him for you. Oy, Gunner Davis. More friends to see you," he shouted.

A small, wiry man came toward them. He looked confused when he saw Ben and Pamma.

"Yes? Can I help you?" he asked.

"I'm sorry," Ben said. "Our mistake. We thought you'd be our friend. Flight Lieutenant Prescott. He also escaped from a German prison camp recently."

"Prescott?" The man shook his head. "He's back in England? Well, strike me pink. We all thought he was a goner."

"No, if it was the same prison camp, he survived the breakout by playing dead, just like you," Pamela said. "He was wounded, but he made his way back to England. He was awfully brave, as I'm sure you were."

The man scratched his head, pushing his cap sideways. "That's not right, miss. Lieutenant Prescott was in the same camp, but he wasn't part of the breakout. He was taken away in a German staff car a couple of weeks before. Gestapo, I'm pretty sure. In fact, when the Jerries were waiting for us in the woods as we came out of the tunnel, I thought to myself that they'd tortured Prescott and he'd spilled the beans. So he made it home, did he? I wonder how he managed that? We thought he was a goner."

Ben looked at Pamela. Neither of them could find anything to say.

"Thank you, Gunner Davis," Pamela said at last. "And congratulations on your medal. Well deserved."

Ben looked at her with admiration. No wonder people respected the upper classes. She'd just had a second devastating blow, but she remained calm, poised, gracious. Confused thoughts were buzzing around in his head. If Jeremy had been taken away from the camp by the Germans, how on earth had he made it home? Escaping from a prison camp was one thing. Escaping from the Gestapo was something else. And why had he lied about being part of the breakout? Swimming down the river? Ben glanced at Pamela. The only way he could have escaped from the Gestapo would have been if they'd let him go. Ben felt sick and cold inside. Jeremy had been his friend all his life. It was hard to believe that he'd turned traitor. There had to be a good explanation.

He collected himself. He had a job to do. "So the prime minister and all his entourage have left?"

The gate guard nodded. "That's right."

"And they are going to Chartwell?" Ben asked.

"That was the original plan, so I heard. But Mr. Churchill called it off because he didn't think it was right to open up the house just for him."

Gunner Davis was still standing nearby. "Just stopping by on their way to some garden party, I heard. Mrs. Churchill told Winston they shouldn't dawdle, or the Westerhams would be annoyed if they were late."

Pamela's face was ashen white as she climbed back into the sidecar.

"I can't believe it." She turned away from Ben. "I thought I knew him. But I didn't know him at all." Then she started to say, "You don't think that . . ." but she couldn't finish the sentence.

Phoebe and Alfie came out of the gate and headed toward the village.

"Who do you think they are going to shoot with that gun?" Alfie asked.

"Mr. Churchill, of course," Phoebe said. "He's coming here today for the garden party. We were right all along, Alfie. There must be a German spy in the neighbourhood. If only we could find out who it is."

"We can tell the grown-ups. Then it's up to them," Alfie said. "But the garden party should be pretty safe. They can put guards on the gate. It's pretty bloody impossible to climb that wall."

"Your language still hasn't improved," Phoebe said primly. Then she looked at him. "But I'm glad you're with me. I wouldn't like to have to do this alone."

They stepped into the hedge and heard the sound of an approaching vehicle. It was a small white delivery van; it slowed to a halt beside them.

"Where are you off to, young'uns?" Jeremy Prescott rolled down the window.

"Oh, hello, Jeremy," Phoebe said. "We're going into the village to report something serious."

"Serious? Not a lack of champagne for the party, surely?" He laughed. "My father already sent over six bottles."

"No, really serious," Alfie said. "Someone might be going to shoot the prime minister this afternoon."

"What? Is this some kind of joke?" Jeremy was still smiling.

"No. Not a joke. It's real," Phoebe said.

"How did you figure that one out?"

354

"Phoebe overheard this morning." Alfie moved closer to the van so that nobody could overhear. "A man told a woman she had to do it, and he gave her a loaded gun and she was very upset."

"Good God. Really?" Jeremy was no longer smiling. "You're right. This is serious stuff. We should go and tell the police right away." He got out and came around the van. "Jump in. I'll give you a lift."

He had opened the rear door. They scrambled into the back of the van. The door closed behind them.

"Hey, don't shut us in. It's dark in here," Alfie shouted, but the van was already driving off again.

When it hadn't slowed after a few minutes, Phoebe whispered to Alfie, "I don't think we're going to the police station, do you?"

"No. We'd better get out of here next time it slows down. Okay?"

"Yes, let's. I have a really bad feeling about this."

She slid across to the door and ran her hands over it. "There doesn't seem to be a way to open it from the inside," she whispered. "Let's bang and shout. Somebody will hear us."

"But he'll hear in the front seat. He might come around and kill us," Alfie said.

"Oh, don't be silly. This is Jeremy. I've known him all my life. He wouldn't ever . . ." She paused. "I don't think he'd kill us," she said in a small voice.

The van was being driven fast, throwing the children from side to side. At last it slowed and came to a halt. They felt it shake as the driver's door slammed.

"Now!" Alfie whispered to Phoebe. "Bang on the sides and shout. Ready, go."

"Help!" they shouted. "Let us out!" They banged with their fists on the sides of the van.

Then Alfie noticed something. "He's left the engine running," he said. "We'd better hope we're not in a garage, or we won't last five minutes."

"Don't say that!" Phoebe put her eye to the crack where the doors came together but could see nothing.

Alfie gave a sudden sob. "Oh God," he yelled. "Get me out of here!" He hammered on the door of the van.

"Calm down," Phoebe said primly. She put a hand on his back and felt him shaking.

"I hate being shut in like this," he said. "Ever since the door was blown in on the bomb shelter, and we couldn't get out and everyone was screaming, and I thought we were going to die. I've got to get out . . ."

Phoebe patted his shoulder. "It's going to be all right, Alfie. We'll find a way."

"How?"

Phoebe looked around, trying to think of something to make him feel better. "You're a Cockney," she said. "Don't people like you know how to pick locks?"

"Not all people in London are criminals, you know." He sounded miffed now, but at least he had stopped whimpering.

"Sorry, I didn't mean it like that. I just meant that you've had to do things we never have. Look, I've got bobby pins in my hair," she said. She took one out and handed it to him. "Give it a try."

She held her breath until he said, "It's no use. The lock seems to be on the other side."

"Golly," she sighed. "I can't think what else to do, can you?"

"Keep hoping, I suppose," he said.

"Oh, Pamela, there you are at last, you naughty girl," Lady Westerham greeted her daughter as the motorbike pulled up outside Farleigh. "You promised you'd be here to help me. Margot and your friend have been stellar. So helpful. And Dido, too."

"I'm sorry, Mah. It was a matter of great importance, or I'd never have gone," Pamela said. "A matter of national security."

"What on earth has national security to do with you?" Lady Westerham asked with disdain. "It's no business of yours. Leave such things to the professionals. And for God's sake, go and change before the guests arrive."

Ben was feeling a little better now that they were back at Farleigh. He had had a word with Colonel Pritchard, who did take him seriously but urged him not to worry. There were plenty of soldiers around. The gate could be guarded, the guests vetted before they came in. *But what if the enemy was already inside the gate,* Ben worried. He looked down at his rumpled trousers. He realised he was not dressed suitably for a garden party, but there was no time to go home and change. He would make sure he stayed out of sight, in the background, observing. As he walked around to the back lawn, he saw that chairs and tables had been placed under the large copper beech. A long table had been set up on the gravel beside the house. Champagne stood ready in buckets of ice. Plates of sandwiches and cakes were covered in white napkins. A large bowl of strawberries stood next to a jug of cream. Two maids were putting out teacups at one end while another carried out a tray of glasses.

Trixie and Margot came out through open French doors, carrying a large flower arrangement between them. Trixie spotted Ben. "Oh, you're back. Thank heavens. Lady Westerham was so annoyed. Are you all right?"

"Yes, thank you," he said. "I'm sorry we saddled you with all the work. Unavoidable. Caught in a rainstorm."

"Oh, we managed just fine," Margot said. "I've enjoyed every second. It's wonderful to be part of something like this. Normal life, the way it used to be. One never appreciates it until one doesn't have it. I mean, look at all this food and drink. We were starving in Paris. Living on turnip soup and foul bread."

"You must be so glad to be home," Ben said.

"I can't tell you how glad." Ben looked at her, but Margot didn't meet his gaze.

"But she had to leave her chap behind," Trixie said. "She was telling me all about it. So sad."

"He's probably dead by now," Margot said. "But he was very brave and wouldn't betray his friends. I admire him for that."

Ben looked at her critically. There were things she was not saying, he was sure of that.

"Now that you're here, I'm putting you in charge of pouring champagne," Trixie said. "I'm hopeless at opening champagne bottles."

"I'm not too hot myself," Ben said, "and I'm not suitably dressed for a party. We came straight back from the West Country."

"Did you find what you were looking for?" she asked. Ben was conscious of Margot standing beside him.

"Not really. False alarm," he said. "It was only an old monastery that had been burned by Cromwell's men."

"What was all this about, then? Some kind of scavenger hunt?" Margot asked.

"No, we were trying to identify a place in a photograph for my boss," Ben said. "I don't think it even matters now. So, where do you want to put me to work?"

"I think the maids will need help with that tea urn," Margot said. "It's jolly heavy. We're going up to change."

As he helped position an urn of tea, he looked around. The lawn on which the tables were set was surrounded by a rose arbour, tall topiaries, and shrubs. Plenty of cover for someone who wanted to hide. When the others had moved away, he set off on a tour, examining possible hiding places with an easy escape into the woods. Unlike the front of the house with its lake and lawns giving a view for miles, the rose arbour led to an enclosed rose garden, and then the kitchen gardens. And beyond them a thick stand of yew trees. Plenty of opportunity for a quick gunshot. He shuddered. Why on earth hadn't they held this on the front lawns? *Probably because they wanted to be away from the comings and goings of the West Kents,* he thought. Giving the impression of a serene country house, removed from thoughts of war, for once.

Pamela appeared at his side, looking serene and lovely in lemon-yellow chiffon and a large white hat trimmed with daisies. "So Trixie and Margot are upstairs changing right now. Trixie's been an absolute brick. You know I've always taken her for a bright young thing who'd be useless in a crisis, but she worked jolly hard this morning. And isn't it wonderful to have Margot home? It's a miracle, Ben. You don't know how I've longed for this moment." Her face, Ben noted, was strained, and her eyes darted around. "What next?" she asked.

"We wait. The colonel's men are at the gate. Nobody can get in. We should be all right."

She reached out and took his hand. "God, I hope so. I'm scared, Ben. If Mr. Churchill is killed, the whole country will crumble, won't it?"

"That's obviously what the Germans intend. We must make sure . . ." He stopped. How could he tell Pamela that he suspected her beloved sister?

Lord and Lady Westerham came out, she looking incredibly regal in purple flowery silk and a feathered purple hat.

"Well, I think we've done it," she said to her husband. "Now all we do is wait for the guests."

At that moment, the dogs rushed up, barking hysterically.

"Be quiet! Get down, you stupid beasts," Lord Westerham bellowed. He motioned to Soames who was hovering in the doorway. "Take them inside and shut them up. I don't know what has got into them. They are normally so well behaved."

One by one, the guests began to arrive: Colonel and Mrs. Huntley bringing Miss Hamilton from the village. Sir William and Lady Prescott.

The Musgroves. Colonel Pritchard from the West Kents. Ben noted that he was armed today.

"I've brought a few of my men to help out where needed, Lady Westerham," he said.

"How kind, but I think we have everything under control," Esme said.

Margot and Trixie came down together. Margot was wearing a light, tailored, form-fitting dress that was obviously the height of Parisian fashion. Ben examined her, deciding there was nowhere to hide a weapon. She didn't even carry a purse.

Pamela went over to Trixie. "Are you all right? You look rather washed out."

"I'm not feeling too wonderful, but I'll be fine," Trixie said. "A bit of a migraine. I might go and lie down as soon as the party starts. Nobody will miss me."

"I'll miss you. You've been a real brick," Pamela said.

Trixie smiled. "That's me. Trixie the brick."

"I should disappear, too," Ben said to Pamela. "I can't let the great man see me looking like a dishevelled farm labourer."

"I think you look just fine," Pamela said. And she gave him an entrancing smile.

Ben slipped into the shadows between the bushes. A figure was standing behind the rose arbour. A woman dressed in bright-red pyjamas. Ben crept up to her. It was Dido.

"What are you doing?" he asked.

She jumped guiltily when she heard him. "Oh, it's only you, Ben," she said. "If you must know, I'm sneaking a cigarette. Pah doesn't know that I smoke. But I felt that I needed something to calm my nerves before I face everyone."

Ben looked up. "I can hear voices," he said. "I think the PM has arrived. You'd better go and be visible."

Dido gave an exaggerated sigh. "I suppose, if I must, I must," she said.

As Ben watched Dido walk away in her sexy red pyjamas, he heard someone coming through the rose garden. He spun around to see Guy Harcourt coming toward him.

"What are you doing here?" Ben's voice was sharp.

"I did say I might come and crash the party, didn't I?" He grinned. "Actually, I came with the advance party to make sure all was well for the PM, old boy. Have you been keeping an eye on Lady Margot?"

"She's wearing such a skimpy dress that she couldn't have a weapon on her," Ben said. He examined Guy as he was speaking. Wasn't that a gun holster under Guy's jacket? Should he say something? It all seemed quite unreal. He decided to find the colonel and tell him to watch Guy.

"Ah, champagne. Jolly good," Guy said. "I thought this assignment might have its perks."

He left Ben and headed for the table where champagne was now being poured into flutes. Applause and cheers announced the arrival of Winston Churchill. Ben could see the great man coming around the house and walking toward the back lawn with Lord Westerham at his side. Clementine Churchill and Lady Esme walked together, chatting.

Then Ben heard a voice coming from the shrubbery behind him. "Are you there?" The words were hissed, and it was impossible to tell if it was a man or a woman. Ben crept in the direction of the voice. "I can't do it! I told you."

Ben came around a large flowering bush and saw Trixie standing on the other side. A gun was in her hand, but she was turned away from the prime minister and she was shaking. "Take it. I don't want it. I don't want any part of it." She held out the gun to someone standing in the deep shadow. Then to Ben's amazement, Jeremy stepped out and snatched the gun.

He said in a low voice, "You absolute weakling. You're not one of us. You'll regret this."

He moved into the open to get a clear shot at the approaching prime minister. Churchill was now in full view, some twenty-five yards away. As Ben heard Jeremy cock the gun, he stepped out in front of him.

"Get out of the bloody way. I don't want to shoot you, old man," Jeremy said. His eyes had a wild look to them.

"If you want to shoot Churchill, you'll have to shoot through me," Ben replied.

"Jeremy, no!" Ben heard Pamela scream as she rushed toward them. Jeremy glanced in her direction, taking his focus away from the prime minister for an instant. Ben took his chance and went for the gun, knocking it upward as it fired. He let out a cry as the force of the bullet threw him to the ground.

He was conscious of everything happening in slow motion, Pamela screaming, "How could you? You betrayed us all." She dropped to her knees beside Ben while Guy and the soldiers converged on them. They were looking down at him. Pamela was stroking his hair.

"Don't die," she whispered. "Please don't die."

"I'll be all right." Ben managed a brave smile. In truth, he didn't feel any pain, just strange and far away and warm with the feel of Pamela's hand on his forehead. "I think he just winged my shoulder." He tried to sit up. "I must go after him. Can't let him get away." Then he fainted.

CHAPTER THIRTY-NINE

In a van in Farleigh wood

Phoebe and Alfie lay sprawled, sleeping in the locked van. They had tried anything possible to attract attention, to kick their way out, but had given up in despair. The sides of the van were smooth metal. And nobody could hear them. The van rattled and hummed as the engine ticked over. Fumes began to seep up, making their eyes water.

"Someone will notice I'm missing and come looking for me soon," Phoebe said, trying to sound encouraging.

"But what if we're parked miles from anywhere? What if we're in the middle of a field or even in a garage?" Alfie said.

Phoebe put her ear to the side of the van. "I don't think we're in a building. I think I can hear birds."

"How much air do you think we have?" Alfie asked.

Phoebe looked at the tiny sliver of daylight where the doors closed. She didn't really think that it could help them much, but she knew it was her job to stay calm and positive. She was bred to be a leader. And leaders didn't show they were scared. "I think we'll be fine," she said. "And it's probably better that air can't get in, because then the fumes can't get in either."

"Cheerful thought," Alfie said, making her laugh in spite of everything.

At one point, their hopes were raised. They heard the sound of dogs, sniffing around the van and then barking.

"Those barks sound like our dogs. Good boys," Phoebe shouted. "Go for help." She turned to Alfie. "See. We can't be too far away. We might even be at Farleigh. They'll be here soon."

They hammered, kicked, and yelled again, but nobody came. After a while they lapsed into silence. "Alfie, you're not falling asleep, are you?" Phoebe asked.

"Bloody tired," he muttered. "Can't seem to stay awake."

Phoebe shook him. "You can't fall asleep. You absolutely can't. Do you hear me?"

Alfie just mumbled something unintelligible. Phoebe's own head was singing. "Must not sleep," she kept saying. But in the end, she, too, had passed out. They were roused by the van shaking and the slamming of a door. Phoebe couldn't remember where she was for a moment. Her head felt woozy, as if she had been drugged. When she tried to sit up, she was thrown back against the door as the van took off. It was clear it was being driven very fast.

Then something struck the back of the van with a loud crack.

"Golly, I think someone's shooting at us," Phoebe shouted, shaking Alfie. "Wake up, but stay down low."

Alfie mumbled again, still half-drugged. They pressed themselves to the floor, being flung from side to side as the van drove around bends. But there were no more gunshots. Alfie roused himself and tried to sit up.

"Look," Alfie said, awake now and wriggling toward the door. "The bullet made a hole in the door. That's good. We can breathe fresh air!"

"Not while we're being tossed around like this," Phoebe said. "Golly, I hope they don't shoot at us again. I feel sick, don't you?"

"I feel bleedin' terrible," he muttered.

"Don't swear," Phoebe said, secretly glad that he was awake and talking to her.

The drive seemed to go on forever.

"Do you think he's driving to the Channel to meet a German submarine?" Alfie asked.

"I don't know. We don't know if he's the German spy, do we?"

"What else would he be?" Alfie said. "He only locked us in the van when he knew you'd overheard about the gun."

Phoebe nodded. "Yes. He must be. I find it so hard to believe. He's Jeremy. I've known him all my life. He's one of us. How could he possibly behave this way?"

"The Germans must have forced him to work for them when he was in the prison camp."

"No true Englishman could be forced to work for Germans," Phoebe said hotly. "They'd rather die first."

"Let's hope he doesn't want to die now and is planning to drive us off a cliff," Alfie said.

"Why do you always have to be so cheerful?" Phoebe snapped.

Then there was a crash as they hit something; the van rocked but didn't slow. Then it screeched to a halt. A door slammed. Suddenly their door was wrenched open. Bright daylight flooded in, and fresh air. They sat up, gulping and blinking.

"You're still alive," Jeremy said, sounding more surprised and relieved than angry. He reached in and grabbed Phoebe by her hair, dragging her out of the van. "Come on. You're coming with me."

She screamed, blinking in the bright light, her legs wobbly and not wanting to support her as he set her on her feet. Alfie grabbed at her blouse, but Jeremy sent him sprawling, then dragged her forward. "Come on. Move. Faster."

She looked around her as she was propelled forward. They were on the tarmac of an aerodrome.

"Help!" she screamed. Jeremy put a hand over her mouth as he forced her along.

Alfie scrambled to his feet. His head still swum around, and he staggered after Phoebe like a drunken man. Jeremy and Phoebe were heading for one of the Spitfires lined up beside the runway. With a supreme effort he ran at them, flinging himself at Jeremy and trying to rugby tackle his legs. "Let her go," he shouted.

Jeremy turned and launched a vicious backhanded punch at him, sending him flying backward, and hitting the ground hard.

"Don't you hurt Alfie, you horrid man," Phoebe screamed as his hand had slipped from her mouth. She grabbed that hand and sank her teeth into the soft flesh of his palm. Jeremy let out a roar of pain and instinctively snatched his hand away. Phoebe reached out for Alfie. "Quick, run."

Jeremy drew a pistol, raised it, then said, "What the hell. Go on, you little brats. Go. No one can stop me now, anyway."

As the children ran toward a line of huts, they met an armoured car driving toward them. It screeched to a halt and airmen leaped out. "Two children," one of them shouted. "What the devil are you doing here?"

"You must stop him," Phoebe gasped, out of breath after their ordeal. "Jeremy Prescott. He kidnapped us. He's a German spy."

"Is that right?" the first airman was grinning. "Is this some kind of dare?"

"No. Of course not." Phoebe glared at him. "I'm Lady Phoebe Sutton, Lord Westerham's daughter, and we were kidnapped by Jeremy Prescott, and we think he was planning to shoot Winston Churchill. You can telephone Farleigh if you don't believe me, but first you should try to stop Jeremy Prescott before he does something awful. He just ran toward those aeroplanes."

Men's shouts made them look up. A Spitfire was taxiing toward the runway.

"He's stolen a plane." An airman came running toward them. "He shot one of our blokes and took a Spitfire."

The plane's engine had become a roar. It raced down the runway and up into the sky.

"Now do you believe me?" Phoebe asked, triumphantly.

"You were very brave children," the camp commander said when they had repeated their story for the sixth or seventh time and were seated in his office drinking cups of tea. "It's all over now. It's all right if you go ahead and cry, little lady."

Phoebe frowned at him and stuck out her chin. "My father would not like me to cry in public. We're supposed to set an example." She stood up. "Do you think someone could telephone my parents and drive us home, please?"

It was when she arrived home that the tears finally came. Phoebe discovered that they hadn't even missed her.

"We thought you were staying out of the way in the schoolroom because you didn't want to get involved with the preparations this morning," Lady Esme said. "And because you don't like being polite to strangers at parties."

"But didn't the dogs come to get you?" Phoebe said, the distress in her voice rising at her mother's calmness. "I was sure they would."

Lady Westerham stared at her in horror. "The dogs did come," she said. "They were barking and making an awful commotion right before the Churchills arrived. I had Soames take them inside and shut them up." Then she suddenly did a most uncharacteristic thing and wrapped

Phoebe into her arms. "Oh, my poor little girl," she said. "You might have died."

"I nearly did," Phoebe said. "If Alfie hadn't been jolly brave and tackled Jeremy, he might have flown with me to Germany. Or he might have killed me." And then, without warning, she burst into tears.

When she had been calmed and sat beside her mother on the sofa, her father asked, "My dear child, why on earth didn't you come to us if you thought that someone was planning to shoot the prime minister?"

"I wasn't sure you'd believe me," Phoebe said. "Besides, we're supposed to report anything suspicious to authorities. It says so."

"To the authorities?" Lord Westerham blustered. "That bloody idiot in the village wouldn't know a spy if one leapt out and bit him."

"Don't swear in front of the children, Roddy," Lady Westerham said.

"The child's bloody well been kidnapped by a rotten traitor and might have died, and you're worried about her hearing a swear word?" he demanded. "What we should be doing is sending her off to a good boarding school where she has less time on her hands."

Phoebe glanced at Dido and grinned.

"How come she gets rewarded for taking stupid risks?" Dido said. "How about sending me off to finishing school? Or at the very least let me go and drive a lorry."

"Over my dead body," Lord Westerham said. "Which it probably would be if anyone put you behind the wheel."

Alfie had been sitting, silent and uncomfortable, in the morning room, wishing he could go home. It was strange, but he now thought of the gamekeeper's lodge as home and found himself wondering if he'd ever want to go back to his mother in London, even if the war ended.

He stood up. "I should be getting back. Mrs. Robbins will be worried about me."

"Of course." Lady Westerham looked at him kindly. "Off you go, then. You're a brave young man. Thank you. Well done."

At the doorway, Alfie paused and looked back. "I found out about Baxter's yard. Do you know what he's building in there? Coffins. Lots and lots of coffins."

"In readiness for the invasion," Lord Westerham said. "Which now might be a little further off, thanks to what didn't happen today."

Lady Westerham looked around as if just noticing that one of her brood was missing.

"Is Pamma still with Ben?" Lady Westerham asked.

"Yes, she's still at the hospital," Margot said. "He was awfully brave. I do hope he'll be all right."

"I expect he'll be glad he was able to do something for his country at last," Lord Westerham remarked.

Pamela sat beside Ben's bed in the hospital. His shoulder was bandaged. His face looked white, but he was propped up and wide awake.

"I can't believe it of Trixie," Pamela said. "It seems she was working for the Germans all along. She was stealing information at Bletchley."

"Why would she do that, I wonder?" Ben said.

"The thrill of it, I suppose. No doubt she'll tell us in time. It does seem that her father has always been pro-German, pro-Nazi. But Jeremy—what could have made him turn on us that way? Do you think they brainwashed or tortured him in Germany?"

"I wonder if it wasn't a twisted sense of patriotism. I gather that some people think that by ending the war now, it is sparing Britain from the destruction of our most precious monuments, even if it does mean being under Germany's domination."

Pamela shuddered. "I don't think we'll ever know now," she said. "I wonder if he's flown to Germany in that plane. I suppose so."

They looked up as footsteps tapped across the tiled floor. A curtain was pulled back and Guy Harcourt stood there.

"Oh, sorry. I'm not interrupting a tryst, am I?" he asked with a mischievous smile on his face.

"Of course not. Come in, Guy," Pamela said.

Guy stood at the foot of the bed. "How are you feeling, old chap?"

"As if a mule kicked my shoulder, but otherwise okay. I'm told I was lucky, and the bullet went through nothing but muscle and out the other side."

"Damned lucky. Actually, I came with some news. Prescott's plane was shot down over the Channel."

"Our Spitfires chased him and caught him?" Ben asked.

Guy gave a wry smile. "No, quite the opposite. He was shot down by Messerschmitts. Ironic, isn't it?"

Ben reached out and took Pamma's hand. "I'm sorry," he said.

"Poor Jeremy," Pamela sighed. "What a horrible end."

"It's how he'd have wanted to go—blazing out like a firework." Ben stared past her, out the hospital window. In spite of everything, Jeremy had meant something to him, too, been an important part of his life, whether he liked it or not.

They remained silent while hospital noises went on in the background—the clatter of a trolley, the crisp voice of a nurse giving a command.

"I wonder why nobody picked up on that blighter Prescott before?" Guy said. "I suppose the enemy relied on the fact that they assumed nobody had survived that breakout to tell the truth about him."

"So the man who fell into our field had been sent to deliver a message to him, do you think?" Pamela asked.

"Undoubtedly." Ben glanced up at Guy and nodded. "That he carried nothing on him but the snapshot was a clear indication that he hadn't far to go. He didn't need money or a ration card or tools. Presumably, Jeremy had already arranged a place to hide him."

"And the snapshot was the go-ahead for the date to kill Churchill, once their agents knew he'd be visiting a nearby aerodrome," Pamela said, putting the pieces together.

"How did they know about the garden party at Farleigh?" Guy asked. "Shooting the PM at an aerodrome was surely a risky business."

"It wasn't supposed to be Farleigh when it was planned," Ben said. "It was going to be at Chartwell, but the PM nixed those plans, so the Westerhams offered instead."

"The message must have eventually been delivered by other means," Pamela went on. "One of those radio messages that we were trying to decode, maybe."

"He actually saw the photograph," Ben said. "He came to Aerial Reconnaissance while I was there, and the photograph was lying, blown up, on the table."

"When was this?" Guy asked.

"A few days ago."

"Oh, I think he must have had the whole thing planned earlier than that," Pamela said. "The way Trixie offered to come down to help at the party. It was all planned out some time ago."

Guy nodded. "I agree. We actually think it was part of a bigger plan, put into orchestration the moment he came back to England—a plan to facilitate the invasion, return the Duke of Windsor, and assassinate the royal family. With Jeremy at the helm."

Pamela shuddered. "Don't, please. I can't bear to think about it." She stood up. "I probably should be going. The family will worry about what has happened to me. Maybe Pah will let Margot drive over to pick me up."

"I could give you a ride home," Guy said.

"That's very kind of you." She gave him that radiant smile that had so entranced Ben. "I'll just pop into the ladies' room, then. I'm sure you two have things to talk about that you can't say in front of me."

"Sharp girl," Guy said as Pamela left the room. "And a looker, too. I must say she's taking this remarkably calm, considering she was his girlfriend."

"I think that party opened her eyes to his real nature," Ben said.

"So now you step in and fill the vacuum." Guy grinned.

"I'm not sure about that. She sees me as a brother."

"Oh, I don't think the look she just gave you was at all sisterly," Guy said. "Neither was the way she flung herself at you when you were shot."

Ben lay there, staring at the ceiling, feeling warm inside. There was hope. He'd bide his time, but there really was hope.

Then he remembered the unanswered question. "About Margot. Do you think she is working for the Germans?"

Guy moved closer to him. "I shouldn't be telling you this, but she's working as a double agent at the moment. Sending info back to the Germans, infiltrating meetings of the Ring but keeping us apprised of what is going on. She had to pretend to go along with their plans, of course. Oh, and she's asked to join special ops. She'll be going up to Scotland to train."

"Crikey," Ben said. "I'm so glad she wasn't part of this."

"Well, it could have been much worse. The Germans were trying to get her to kill the king at a garden party, scheduled for this weekend. The king and Churchill gone in one fell swoop. But Buckingham Palace was bombed, so the event was cancelled. And, of course, she had no intention of carrying out the assignment, but because she warned us about it, we'll be keeping an eye open for a future attempt. She's a brave girl. True blue."

Pamela returned. "Shall we?" she asked. She came over to Ben, leaned down, stroked back his hair, and kissed his forehead. "I'll be back in the morning," she whispered. And Guy was right. The gaze that she gave him was not sisterly.

CHAPTER FORTY

At the village church

On Midsummer Day, the Reverend Cresswell held a special memorial service at the church in honour of Seaman Robbins. The whole village attended, as well as Lord Westerham's family and the staff at Farleigh. Mr. and Mrs. Robbins sat together in the front pew, holding hands, looking down at their hymnbooks as the choir and congregation sang "O God, Our Help in Ages Past." Alfie sat beside them, feeling sad and proud at the same time.

In the pew to one side, reserved for the Farleigh family servants, Miss Gumble was deep in thought. If Phoebe was to be sent away to school—and she had already recommended a couple of first-class girls' schools that would make the most of Phoebe's good brain—then she would no longer be needed here. She had a good brain herself, and she might be able to be of use to her country. She wondered whom she could speak to about it.

Ben had been released from hospital and was recuperating at home, being spoiled by Mrs. Finch. While he was still in hospital, he had received a visit from Maxwell Knight himself and been praised for his good work.

"I want to keep you on my books," Knight had said, "even if you are an Oxford man."

Pamela had come down from Bletchley for the occasion. She hadn't seen Trixie since her arrest and still found it hard to come to terms with what had happened. Had Trixie been recruited even before the war and gone to Bletchley originally as a spy, or had she been turned or threatened while she was there? Pamela realised she might never know. And as for Jeremy . . . it was too painful still to think about him. She supposed the wound would heal eventually. Instinctively, she glanced across at Ben to see that he was looking at her, and she smiled.

HISTORICAL NOTE

This is a work of fiction but is closely rooted in the truth.

There were several pro-German societies and organisations working in England at the start of World War II. One of the most dangerous was a group called the Link. It was composed mainly of aristocrats, and they believed that it would be in Britain's best interest to make peace with Germany before all the national treasures were destroyed. Whether they would have actively aided an invasion, nobody knows.

Maxwell Knight really did run a secret branch of MI5 from his flat in Dolphin Square, under the name of Miss Copplestone. Joan Miller really was his secretary, and a terrific spy herself. And he really did keep animals in his office.

Bletchley Park was exactly as I have described it. You can visit it today and see the spartan conditions under which such brilliant work was done.

You may notice similarities between fashion designer Gigi Armande and Coco Chanel, who was able to live in the Ritz and survive the war, thanks to her being the mistress of a high-ranking German officer.

Lord Westerham and Farleigh exist only in my imagination, but the location is in a real part of Kent, close to where I grew up and went to school. And I have drawn on two real stately homes in the neighbourhood—Penshurst Place and Knole, both worth a visit. Winston Churchill's beloved Chartwell is also nearby.

ABOUT THE AUTHOR

Photo © 2016 John Quin-Harkin

Rhys Bowen is the *New York Times* bestselling author of more than thirty mystery novels. Her work includes the Molly Murphy mysteries, set in 1900s New York City, and the lighter Royal Spyness novels, featuring a minor royal in 1930s England. She also wrote the Constable Evans mysteries, about a police constable in contemporary Wales.

Bowen's work has won fourteen honours to date, including multiple Agatha, Anthony, and Macavity awards. Her books have been translated into many languages, and she has fans around the world, including twelve thousand Facebook followers. A transplanted Brit, Bowen divides her time between California and Arizona.